TIANANMEN SQUARE

Lai Wen

Spiegel and Grau

S&G

Spiegel & Grau, New York
www.spiegelandgrau.com

Interior design by Tetragon, London

Library of Congress Cataloging-in-Publication Data Available Upon Request

ISBN 978-1954118393 (paperback)
ISBN 978-1954118409 (eBook)
Published in the United States of America

First Edition
10 9 8 7 6 5 4 3 2 1

For all the children of the revolution

A flame burns brightest in the moment before it perishes.

PART

I

ONE

MY EARLIEST MEMORY IS OF MY GRANDMOTHER. I remember the smell of her. Somewhere between the scent of jasmine and the more earthy odor of the leather oil she used, working up the material to fashion slippers for neighbors on our landing. Her breath was the same: warm and sweet against the side of my face, but with the slightest tang of sourness. Most of all I remember her hands. The fingers gnarled but clever, still able to move deftly across the leather of the shoes she was tailoring, or quick to scatter rice in a boiling pot without being scalded by the billowing steam.

I remember too – perhaps I was no more than two or three – being fascinated by the bulging purple and green veins that ran like vines across the back of those mottled, burnished hands. They seemed so different from my own. Sometimes my grandmother would take my small hand – much lighter and smoother – and cup it in hers, and that would fascinate me. But more than anything I would feel the warmth that emanated from her leathery skin, I would feel that warmth on my own hand. And I would feel safe, protected.

The lines that creased her forehead, the jowls that hung from her cheeks – these details never repulsed me in the way old age can sometimes frighten children. Rather, my grandmother's face, her body, her *being*, were like an ancient map, both familiar and strange, to be read over and over by my eyes, and my fingers too. For I would often reach out for her face, running my tiny fingers across her thin gray eyebrows, playing with the thicker hairs that sprouted from her chin and which, for some reason, always delighted me. Sometimes I would pull on them and my grandmother would sneeze involuntarily. This would delight me all the more, and I would be reduced to the joyful and unending giggles of a toddler. My grandmother would watch me convulse – herself solemn and composed – only the slight curl of her lips and the twinkle in those gray-blue eyes betraying the beginnings of a smile.

My parents were a different proposition. They were devoted to me, in the way that a Chinese family in the 1970s was devoted to a daughter: a devotion tinged with a certain reluctance (my brother had not yet entered the world at that point). But more than that, we were, perhaps, incompatible. My father was a kind man – and a moral one. But throughout my childhood he remained a distant presence even though I would encounter him every day: in the morning when I was awoken for breakfast, in the evening when he returned from work.

Sometimes, I'd be wandering through the hallway of our small but noisy apartment, lost in my thoughts, having conversations with imaginary friends and doing battle with imaginary foes, when suddenly I'd be pulled back into reality, having run up against him. My father. He was, I realize now, rather small for a man, both lean and compact, but as a small child you inhabit a land of giants. And fathers are the tallest giants of all. My father was so large in my eyes perhaps because of the size of his severity; he would blink down at me, having encountered me in the hallway, and he would frown as though he had come across some midget-stranger rather than an emanation of his own flesh and blood.

My father would peer and squint at me, as though he was not quite sure what I was; then, as the silence between us unfolded, he would manage a brief, mumbled question: 'Have you ... have you ... done your homework?;' 'Have you finished your chores?' As a five-year-old I had no homework to speak of, but I would nod my head furiously, for it was in my mind that if I didn't acquiesce I might well be expelled from the apartment that same night. Nothing my parents ever told me, by the way, had in the least bit implied I might be ejected from the family home for failing to complete the nonexistent homework my father was so concerned I finish. But somehow I'd got it into my head that such a thing could happen. It was one of the many fears I had.

Looking back, I think my father was as terrified of encountering me as I was of him. So he said the first thing that came into his head. He was an academic, a cartographer in fact – he worked with maps and geology. A rather nondescript occupation, perfectly suited to the precise and harmless man that he was. And yet, he and people like him had been subject to persecution during Mao's Cultural Revolution. A good number of teachers, technicians and intellectuals lost their lives as a result of being branded 'bourgeois degenerates,' and I suppose the fear and uncertainty he inherited from that period never left him. It crossed into every element of his life. Even his relationship with his daughter.

I grew up in the aftermath of Maoism – after the death of the Great Helmsman – so that fear wasn't real to me, at least not until the events that took place some fifteen years later. But my father was never able to step out from that fear, from its shadow.

Perhaps my father alleviated that fear by allowing himself to grow faint, to retreat into the vague and abstract world of the graphs and charts that populated his study. A place where he would not be bothered by the hectic messiness of family life: the dirty diapers and detritus of toys strewn across the carpet; the bawling loudness of a toddler's tantrums; the slickness of small upturned faces, both expectant and outraged, lathered with snot and tears.

My mother handled her fears in a different way. She was hands-on, seeking to police every aspect and inflection of her family's life. She'd make sure we were all gathered around the table at precisely six, that the napkins we used were open on our laps. During the meal itself, we would be informed of the goings-on of our neighbors who lived on our landing: of the achievements they had laid claim to, and the scandals that took place behind closed doors. Most of all, the scandals. My mother was possessed of a shrill energy; like a tsunami, it could batter and overwhelm any structure that stood in its way. Local gossip was something she used to set herself in motion, to make sure we were all fed and watered, that our clothes were clean and our respective paths in life were cleared. It wasn't until much later that I realized this, however. At the time she just seemed oppressive and annoying.

At the tail end of the Cultural Revolution, my father had been demoted but had managed to survive. He had been incarcerated for a short period but returned to full employment. He was, I suppose, one of the lucky ones. To this day I don't know what indignities, or worse, he suffered. It was something he would never have considered disclosing to his family, especially a family of women. My mother, however, was convinced that the source of his woes – the source of all our woes – was simply a random error on the part of an otherwise flawless bureaucratic machine. For her, the government was hard at times but fair, and its authority and power had always worked in the best interests of the people themselves. As a child I shared my mother's belief that the Chinese government was best; that it was ahead, in every respect, of the Western imperialist powers that sought to bring it down. Every radio broadcast suggested that we, the Chinese people, were the flag bearers of humanity as it entered a more humane and free classless society. Such things we imbibed from an early age in the same way the children of America stood to attention each morning at school in order to pledge allegiance to their flag.

But again, looking back, I wonder how much my mother's credulous and enthusiastic devotion to the powers that be had further reduced my exhausted father, someone who had been battered by life and by the state he sought to serve. The relentless enthusiasm for the status quo on my mother's part surely must have grated. Perhaps, on occasion, he even bridled with anger. A rare flash of the type of emotion he had spent a lifetime learning to suppress. But he was never harsh to her.

On our corridor, husbands would occasionally beat their wives. Sometimes you could hear their arguments; you could even make out the sudden deadening silence before a hand met the side of a woman's face, and then the high-pitched yelp that followed. But even the battered women on our corridor retained a sense of decorum, a sense that there were certain things respectable people did not talk about, things that should not be acknowledged before neighbors.

On these occasions, the whole floor entered into the same strange and surreal charade; that everything was fine, that sometimes the corners of doors simply leapt out, like monsters in an ancient Chinese scroll, surprising a woman, striking her as she busied herself with the mundane details of everyday life. The sides of cupboards, the edges of beds – these things could be equally dangerous, equally provoking. The men they shared their lives with, however, were beyond reproach.

A child understands and absorbs such things as she goes along without ever framing them in terms of a conscious set of ideas. I understood that, on occasion, wives would be beaten, and I knew this was no good thing. I knew that the adults around me frowned on such behavior but did not speak of it. And yet, it happened. And even as a young girl, I remember feeling that perhaps the stark brightness of my mother might in some way be dimmed – that her compulsion to regulate every detail of our lives with her shrill sense of etiquette and respectability might in some way be offset – if, just once, my father struck her across the face. If, just once, he interrupted the never-ending flow of salacious gossip and hectoring demands.

He never did, thank god. But what remained was in some ways worse: a gray shell of a man who seemed old to me even though he couldn't have been more than in his early thirties. A man who'd had the stuffing beaten out of him. Or perhaps he had simply learned to drift away. To absent himself from the world around him. To feel only truly at home in his solitary study, musing over the graphs and reports. To this day, I don't know what happened to him during that period of time before Mao's death. He was detained. But was he physically hurt? Was he tortured? All I know is that he was reduced somehow, as a person. And, after all these years, and despite his absence, I still feel great pity for him.

But if my father remained a passive presence before the overwhelming furor of my mother, my grandmother was someone else again. Different from the daughter she had given birth to. It seemed to me that if my mother gravitated toward respectability, my grandmother was a natural rebel.

She had been born in 1921. Her birth coincided with a period of modernization in China, after the last dynasty had ended, but my grandmother had lived in the countryside where the past still exerted its strange and spectral grip. Her parents had stuck to the ways they themselves had inherited – they'd had their daughter's tiny toes broken and bent inwards in the process of 'foot binding' – but my grandmother had rebelled, screaming night after night, resisting the ordeal, until eventually her mother and father lost their resolve. When my grandmother eventually sneaked those bandages off her feet altogether, her parents pretended not to notice.

But now my grandmother was in possession of freakish feet. They were larger than the ideal of bound feet, yet they were smaller than feet that had developed normally. So my grandmother found it almost impossible to get nicely fitting shoes. And that's why, eventually, she took to making her own. She was unaware of it at the time, but there was a whole generation of girls who had resisted the practice of foot binding with exactly the same courage and determination she herself had shown. A whole generation of girls whose feet were too big to be bound, but too small to be considered normal.

In the years that followed, my grandmother would become adept at making shoes for those women who were described as having

'liberation feet' – feet, just like hers, which had resisted the consequences of the binding. My grandmother's ability in what is
considered the most traditional of things for a female – the ability
to maneuver a needle and a thread in order to weave and create
clothing – was at the same time bound to an act of feminine rebellion. Her life was cluttered with lots of smaller acts of rebellion
that were often expressed in more uncouth and unladylike ways. A
splutter of hawking laughter, a salacious wink, or even an almighty …

'BUUUUURRRRPPPP!!!'

I am in the process of maneuvering a lump of egg-fried rice
toward my mouth, my chopsticks raised in the air, but the sound
of my grandmother's belch is so loud, so violent, that for a few
moments all five of us are frozen in place around the table. My
father has a look on his face that I have never seen before, his mouth
slightly open, somewhere between puzzlement and consternation.
My mother – who had been babbling furiously about a neighbor's
daughter known to go around in sandals without socks (a sure sign
of deviant youth in my mother's book) – is so flummoxed by my
grandmother's belch that she is left momentarily lost for words, her
eyes blinking rapidly, trying to assimilate the ramifications of such
a sudden and obscene intervention.

My brother Qiao – who was then not yet two years old – also
stopped the sticky sound of his enthusiastic munching to allow a
little of the food to go dribbling from the corner of his mouth. His
face lit up with the grin of a baby who sensed that something in his
world had suddenly changed – and though he was not quite sure
what that change might have been, he was nevertheless delighted by
it. And last, but by no means least, was the figure of my grandmother,
whose large squat body and generous face had relaxed, her wrinkles

creasing in the beginnings of a smile, reclining in her chair like a great toad. She watched my mother with a gleam in her eye.

My mother's face went red. Inasmuch as she was controlled when it came to regulating timetables, the clothes her children wore and the kind of words her family used – when it came to regulating the emotions on her own face, she was often lost at sea, subject to sudden and intensely personal squalls of emotion. She blinked at my grandmother, trying to calm her rising indignation. Eventually she managed a few shocked syllables:

'You did that on purpose, Muqin, I know you did!'

My grandmother looked back, sphynx-like and unflinching, but perhaps touched with a hint of dark amusement.

'My dear, my sweet, when you get to my age, you come to realize that the body is much like a car. It erodes over time, and sometimes its emissions really can't be helped!'

My grandmother fluttered her eyelashes ever so slightly, her face assuming an expression of wounded dignity.

'Oh, save it,' she snapped. 'Your "emissions" almost always happen just when I am in the process of making some kind of point, just when I am trying to—'

'Buuuuurrrrppppp.'

Again, everyone was frozen in a kind of temporary paralysis. Except for my brother, who had unleashed the belch and was now grinning wickedly, still dribbling from the corner of his toddler's smile, happy as Larry that he had been able to get in on the fun.

My mother looked at my little brother with genuine horror before turning to my grandmother, the redness in her face blanched in an instant to a shocked, curdled white.

'You see, this is what you do! You are … corrupting my child!'

For the first time my grandmother's face lost all trace of amusement.

'Oh, don't be so dramatic. He's not yet two years old. Monkey see, monkey do!'

'Monkey ... *monkey?*' my mother spluttered. 'How ... how dare you! And I do not consider the moral development of my children ... something to be mocked!'

She had raised herself out of her seat by that point, was looming over us, gesticulating toward an audience we could not see.

All at once she focused on my father, hard.

'And you! *You!* Why don't you ever do anything to defend me?'

My father was suddenly shocked into the room. Whatever thoughts he had been mulling over that had shielded him from such tempestuous family strife were vanquished under my mother's intense and accusatory stare. The poor man tried to pull himself together, tried to marshal some kind of response – I could see him doing it – but even before he was able to utter the words, my mother gave a sudden helpless gulp and flounced from the room.

My grandmother's sardonic eyes turned on my befuddled father.

'She seems a little tense today. Is it perhaps time you attended to your husbandly duties with a little more frequency?'

If my father's anxiety had been provoked by my mother's sudden assault on him, it was nothing to the horror that crossed his face when my grandmother addressed him with this particular recommendation.

With as much dignity as he could muster, he stood up from the table and followed my mother from the room.

My brother was seated in his high chair and for the first time a shadow crossed the smoothness of his chubby face and those full, dark eyes widened in a moment of unfathomable grief, for he under-stood that things had changed, though he knew not how or why. He knew that only moments ago there had been people around him and now they were there no longer – and perhaps he felt the type of terrifying loneliness that arrives so suddenly and with such abandon and is particular to the youngest of children. Moments later his face was slick with warm tears.

My brother would often irritate me. He could be so loud and demanding. His presence was such that it seemed to suck all the conversation from the room, to draw everyone's focus into his orbit by the sheer gravitational pull of his need. But my irritation some-times blinded me to just how helpless he was. In that moment, I felt his vulnerability as if it were my own, his loneliness and his bemuse-ment as though they belonged to me. For a few moments it was as if I were in his head, blinking out at those who shared his world, somewhere between bafflement and fear. I got up and uncoupled him from his high chair as gently as I could. He was really screaming now, abandoning himself entirely to the welter of feeling that had swelled so suddenly within. I tried to 'coo' in his ear, the way I had seen my mother do. I held him up and nuzzled my lips against the softness of his belly – the way I sometimes would in order to get him to shiver and giggle – but the violence of his emotion rolled over my every attempt.

My grandmother gesticulated from her chair. Wordlessly, I handed her Qiao. He was still crying, but when she moved him to her mas-sive bosom she was able to enfold him with her size, her stillness and her warmth. Although his pudgy body was still heaving with sobs, at once it began to slacken, and he turned into her, nuzzling against her bulky softness, as she began to rock him up and down – a tiny vessel cocooned by the rhythm of the waves. Instinctively, automatically, he put his thumb in his mouth. Moments later, I could hear the soft gentle sounds of his snoring – his large closed eyes like smooth marbles, the tiny nub of his nose peeking out. Just like that, he was insensible.

All at once, my feelings were colored with a less virtuous motivation. My mother would rarely let me play with the neighborhood children, but my grandmother was not so strict about such things, so when my mother wasn't around, my grandmother became an excellent means to such an end.

'Po Po! May I go and play outside for a little bit?'

My grandmother didn't look up but she gave a small nod of her great turtle's head. She continued to rock my brother in her arms. I felt a shiver of illicit delight as I quietly opened the front door and slipped out onto the landing. I was hit by a wave of heat. It was summer then and the possibility of air-conditioning in most places was still years away. People left their balcony windows open and often the doors to their apartments too – so that there was a constant flow of air that might ameliorate the sticky heat of cramped conditions, especially during the early evening when stoves boiled and frying pans sizzled. There was a strange communality to life on our floor: the open doors and thin walls meant that the private lives of others were always within touching distance, and while this generated a certain camaraderie, it was also a source of gossip and competitiveness.

My mother was not one to scrimp on either. One of our close neighbors who I always called Aunty Zhao, even though she was not my real aunty, had come from the rural areas and had a thick accent that I sometimes struggled to understand. But she'd married a Beijinger – more than that, a factory manager – so she received the type of perks that weren't available to our own family. For instance, Aunty Zhao was the first one on our landing to own a freezer. I can still recall the day the men came to deliver it. It was almost twice as tall as they were, and they struggled with it up the stairwell and into the corridor, while the residents gathered to watch the spectacle in awe.

I remember the expression on my mother's face as she looked out through the crack of our door; the way her lips were curled down, pinched in resentment, the dull anger at work in her eyes. Aunty Zhao was one of our closest friends; I had known her for as long as I could remember, and I knew my mother liked her. My mother's reaction caused my throat to tighten. I felt the type of unease I did when I was in class and being made to decipher a letter or symbol whose meaning was just outside the borders of my comprehension. I saw my mother's face sour and twist only for a moment before she closed the door and began to busy herself with housework. But it was something I never forgot.

Now, as I am assailed by the odors of fried chicken, fish, satay sauce and sea cucumber, along with the starch scent of drying fabrics and the mustier tang of body heat, I catch a glimpse into Aunty Zhao's apartment. I see figures in the kitchen sitting at the table, the wide freezer door flung open, encasing them in its cool blue light, but I don't stop. Instead I move faster – children are not supposed to run in the corridors – but I have this sense of bursting excitement as I get to the stairwell, clattering down the stairs, before pushing open the door and exiting into the street. The heat outside is strong and oppressive even at this time; I can feel it squeaking in the small of my back, its vapors forming beads of liquid along the nape of my neck, but now I am outside, and it is as though I can breathe again.

TWO

I LOOK FOR THEM. I SEE THEM ALMOST STRAIGHTAWAY. They are gathered in an abandoned lot just off the main street and, as the sun goes down, the long slats of evening light catch the dust that has been thrown up from the powdery ground, forming streaks of glittering gold in the air above. Through this gold-flecked haze I can see into the distance. I can see the shape and outline of the buildings in the city center, and, on the edge of the horizon, looking toward the Forbidden City, I glimpse the forms of the great monuments that guard the entrance to Tiananmen Square. It seems to me as far away as some distant and mythic land, and its image – diaphanous and faint – shimmers momentarily, before it is lost to a plume of rolling cloud. My thoughts are back in the moment, in the neighborhood and I force myself to concentrate as I approach this group of children, allowing my walk to become slack, my face to become expressionless. I saunter up to them with a well-practiced nonchalance.

'All right, what are you up to?'

It is clear what they are up to, as Zhen, a small boy with delicate features and big eyes, is running his tongue along a border of crisp paper. The others are watching him like hawks, for his quick hands always manage to fabricate the most beautiful and effective paper planes and they want to discover his secret. I know what they are up to, but nevertheless I have to ask the question because it's something you have to say.

Jian's eyes don't leave the paper Zhen is folding, but he responds with a good-humored mumble as though they have hit upon a unique strategy to pass the time.

'We are making paper airplanes today!'

I nod, go to say something else, then fall silent. I play with my hands. I catch Al Lam watching me. When I meet her eye, she glances away, embarrassed. Even though we are in the same group, we rarely talk to one another. I think it's something to do with the fact that we are the only two girls. We know we are different from the others and if we were to hang out together perhaps that difference would be emphasized. Or something. Either way, we tend to regard one another warily.

Zhen has finished his paper plane. With a quick flick of his wrist, he sends it curling up into the air. We watch it, our faces craned upward against the full evening light, until the plane is no more than a dark outline. All at once it peaks, and – almost as though it were alive – jerks downward, plunging to the ground in a giddy swoop some yards from where we are. Automatically, we all burst into a run.

Jian picks up the flattened plane gently.

'Pretty good,' he says, examining the plane in his hands, his broad clean features lit in a pleasant open smile.

I don't think our group had a leader exactly, but Jian was the closest to it. He was nice-looking with thick black hair that spiked upward; he had a smooth but strong voice, he was good at sports and could run faster than all us others. Also, he was the tallest. When you are a kid, being tall counts for a lot.

'Let's play a different game!'

Gen looks at us with a strange smile. He is much smaller than Jian, he is not much taller than me. But everyone in our group has something. Jian is the strong one. Al Lam is the sensible one. Zhen is the one who is great at making paper airplanes. Gen … is the clever one. It occurs to me that perhaps I am the only one of our group not to be defined by any single quality. Maybe that's why people don't notice me all that much. The teachers don't seem to see me at school, and since Qiao was born, my mother and father don't pay me the same type of attention they once did (unless it's my mother telling me that I have yet again ruined my dress by rolling around in the mud – something that is very 'unladylike,' apparently). My grandmother sees me, of course. Her gaze seems to register every secret nestling inside your body, inside your mind. But that's not quite the same thing. Nevertheless, I know when I leave the house and come to play with my friends – even though there is nothing special about me – they accept me into their ranks without a whisper. It is as though we are all separate parts of a jigsaw puzzle that were always meant to be brought together.

But Gen is different again. Even though he is small, everyone listens when he speaks. He is confident somehow – not loud, but rather he says stuff that none of us others knows. That's what makes him clever. There is something about him that seems more adult, maybe even more adult than Jian even though Jian is the oldest and tallest of all of us. Also, Gen never gets into the type of arguments the rest of us have.

One time Fan – who is fat and smelly – accused me of picking my bum! He only said that because everyone knows he picks his own bum – and he was giggling and dribbling while he said it, as though it was the funniest thing in the world. I felt my face go red; it was the strangest thing, because I would never, ever pick my bum. And yet he had shouted it with such glee, and even though I would never do what he had said, I felt my cheeks burn and I felt my eyes water with tears. But not because I was sad. Because I was angry. And yet, to everyone else it must have looked like I felt bad about what he had said because it was true.

So I exploded.

'You stupid bloody retard!'

I punched Fan as hard as I could on the arm. At once his own eyes began to water, and then he began to scream. We watched as he ran home, as fast as his pudgy legs would carry him.

'That wasn't nice,' said Jian, looking at me with an expression of disappointment.

He spoke softly, his gaze was mild, and yet it was as though he had slapped me across the face as hard as he could. I was suddenly indignant, panicked.

'He lied. Wang Fan lied. He said I scratched my butt, but I didn't do it.'

I looked around in appeal. I looked to Gen, because he was known to be intelligent, rational. I was certain he would hear the voice of reason.

'I didn't do it, Gen!'

He looked down at his feet for a few moments and then raised his head, his brown shimmering eyes meeting my own.

'Yeah, I know, but that's not the point.'

'So what is? *What is the point?*'

I almost shouted that question at them, but they had gone back to what they were doing. Nobody told me to leave but I knew I had to. The next day I came back. Wang Fan was there, dribbling and laughing as they played. I rejoined them and it was as though nothing had happened. But from that moment on I got what Gen had said: 'Yeah, I know, but that's not the point.' In school they all called Wang Fan a 'retard.' Because when he ate his lunch, he would dribble much of his food over his shirt, and sometimes he would burst out in giggles for no reason anyone could fathom. But that was the point. Just as the group accepted me, even though I had nothing much to offer, so they accepted Wang Fan, because he was there, and he was ready to play. For us kids, at that moment, at that particular time, the best thing in the world was to play together even if you were a little goofy or different, or you had cross-eyes, or a funny belly. That was the point.

'Let's play a different game!' announced Gen.

When he said that, everyone took notice. Gen and I went to the same school but we were in different classes. Nevertheless, I'd seen him take to the stage in assembly to receive an award for his high scores in calligraphy. We also knew that his father was someone important, but how we knew this was unknown because Gen rarely talked about his parents.

'What game?' Jian asked seriously.

'Cat Catching Mice!' responded Gen at once.

Jian nodded his approval.

'Okay,' Jian said. 'Let's begin.'

He looked at me.

'Mouse!' he exclaimed.

I giggled involuntarily; everyone was looking at me, but I was especially happy that Jian had chosen me.

Then my blood cooled.

'Wang Fan – cat!'

At once the whole group began to chant:

'What time is it?'

'Just struck nine.'

'Is the cat at home?'

'He's about to dine.'

The aim of the game was for the cat to run after the mouse once the chanting had stopped, but unfortunately Wang Fan had not fully grasped this and he launched himself onto me before the chanting was finished. I felt myself falling to the ground, almost in slow motion, and then time seemed to speed up, and I was lying on the dusty floor, baffled, an array of sounds collapsing inwards, and the rustling noise of Wang Fan's enthusiastic breaths hot against my ear. I felt a warm spool of slobber touch my cheek.

I looked up at his big pudgy face giggling over me, and I had a sudden electric feeling of rage; I wanted to stick my nails into his eyes, I wanted to rip those moist quivering lips from his mouth. He was a kid, he was probably the most kid-like of all of us, and yet his body on top of me felt like something different; I could feel the heat that emanated from the flabby layers of skin surrounding his face and belly. I was aware of the sour scent that arrived from the creases on his body, his armpits, his flabby thighs.

He kept giggling, his whole body vibrating, but this time I didn't yell, I didn't call him a 'retard,' and I didn't spit at him (which was the worst thing one child could do to another). Instead I managed to swallow my disgust, concentrate, and with a lithe twist I was able to maneuver his flabby body to tilt it to one side, so that he toppled over and I was able to release myself.

I staggered to my feet. I looked at everyone else. And they were all laughing. I was shocked for a moment. I could still scent Wang Fan's odor in my nostrils. He was rolling about on the floor giggling as though it was the funniest joke in the world, as though he was being tickled by some invisible presence. I felt their gaze on me. And then I felt my own laughter. Forced. Strange. A sound that took place outside myself. Everyone else returned to the game. Except Gen. He remained watching me for a few moments longer, his expression quizzical, appraising.

The sun had slipped beneath the horizon. The floor was wreathed in shadow. At some point, we gradually began to disperse, to wander home in our separate directions. All at once it started to rain. But I lingered. And I felt Gen's gaze on me again. Curious, inquisitive.

'Do you wanna go see something?' he asked.

'Yeah.'

Darkness was coming and I knew I had to be inside before it arrived. That was the rule my parents had. Sometimes I would make an argument of it, but it was always half-hearted, because the truth was I didn't want to be in the streets when it got dark. But, in that moment, something held me in place, stopped me from returning home right away. Gen spoke softly, but there was an insouciance in his voice, and his eyes shone with amusement, as though he found me faintly ridiculous. If I had refused to go with him, it would have been like rejecting a challenge. As though I were afraid. And Gen would have smiled all the more. If I had just walked away, I would have felt those sardonic and amused eyes on my back.

Instead, I puffed up my chest and walked alongside him. The rain fell in soft gray lines and a murkiness arose from the streets, a misty vapor through which the outline of the buildings appeared shadowy and indistinct. The sound of the pattering rain seemed all there was as the shadows grew and the darkness took shape. I could feel the rain squeaking against the fabric of my shoes, stealing inside, making my socks soggy, and I could feel its droplets clinging to my eyebrows and hanging from the tip of my nose. I started to feel weary, as though the gray dampness had settled in my head.

'Where are we going? Is it much farther?'

'Not much farther,' said Gen, that same whisper of a smile playing faintly on his lips.

I felt a prickle of irritation. My legs were starting to hurt. I was about to tell Gen this was boring, that I had better things to do. But then he stopped.

'Here we are,' he said.

I followed the direction of his gaze. There was a large building many stories high. Its concrete walls were shadowy in the gloom, but there was a series of high arched windows running across each floor and from within came the faint glow of a pale orange light. The roof sloped upward in a hard metallic arc, so high above, riddled with piping and wires. Even from where we stood, we could hear the low hum generated by the building – its machinery turning over from deep within. In the darkness, it seemed both ordinary and monstrous, and yet I knew there was nothing to fear. I knew now where we were. The building had a great chimney that pushed out like a giant finger. I recognized that chimney because I could see it from my bedroom window at night. But gazing up at it now, the way its hard black outline seemed to jut so high into the dark vault of sky above, I felt so small, dizzy in my insignificance as it belched its ghostly steam into the black.

I looked at Gen. He was watching the building with a strange solemnity.

'Do you know … what this place is?' he asked, his voice so soft that I barely caught the question.

'Of course I know,' I said. 'It's the Beijing Children's Hospital.'

I had tried to make my voice contemptuous. But the sound died in the gloom, muffled by the night.

Gen turned slowly to face me.

'That's what everyone thinks.'

'What do you mean?'

His expression became grave.

'My father. He works for the government. So he knows things not many people know.'

'Like what?' I demanded fractiously.

'Like the fact that there are children in the building. But they are not there to get better. They will … never get better.'

His voice was almost a whisper.

'What does that mean?'

Despite myself, I was drawn in by the soft, austere sound of his voice. I felt the hairs on the back of my neck begin to prickle, the heat of the day evaporating before the first chilly tendrils of the night.

'It means that this place … it's not a hospital … it's a crematorium.'

'A crema … what?'

He smiled sadly.

'You really don't know anything, do you?'

'I know enough,' I said. I was ready to defend my honor.

'Okay, listen,' he said. 'A crematorium is not a place where they make children better. It's a place where they burn the bodies of all the children who have died!'

I looked at him, incredulous.

'You're a liar!' I spat. 'Why would they do that? Why would anyone do that?'

Gen's expression was blank. He spoke tonelessly, in a matter-of-fact voice, but in the way of one who has been burdened with all the secrets of the world.

'Because … that's what *they* do!'

'I don't believe you. You are making this up.'

He looked at me. He didn't disagree. He didn't say a word. He just watched me with that same strange solemnity. It looked odd on a kid's face; I remember thinking that, even back then. And the truth was I *did* believe him. I didn't want to. But I did. My heart was thrumming, a trippy electric fear pressing against the papery carapace of thin, fragile skin. But I still had the feeling he was trying to get the better of me. So I kicked back.

'If that's what they are doing, you try and prove it. But you can't, can you? Because you're just a big fat liar!'

Again my insult failed to provoke him, again he retained that infuriating calm.

'I can prove it,' he said softly.

Whatever response I had anticipated, it certainly wasn't that. I was shocked. And behind my shock was a creeping sense of fear.

'Go on then,' I managed weakly.

He craned his head upward, gazing into the darkness.

'The chimney, the smoke!'

'So what?'

His voice lowered again, imparting the most sinister of secrets.

'Each time they burn a dead kid, the chimney opens in order to let out the smoke. But the thing is …'

'Yeah …?' I asked, craning my head upward, a feeling of clammy dread rising within me.

'The thing is, the spirit never really dies. You know that, right?'

I did. My grandmother often talked of such things. I nodded my head.

'If you look into the smoke, as it goes upward you can see …'

'See?'

'You can see the spirit of the dead kid … or sometimes the dead baby … as it flies up into the night!'

My body was humming with adrenaline and fear. The dark seemed to draw in everywhere around me, clenching, smothering.

'No, you can't. That's not true. I don't believe you.'

'Well then. Why don't you … just look?'

I didn't want to but my head rose higher as if pulled by some invisible force. As I watched the ghostly strands of vapor curling into the vast dome of blackness above, those furls of silver seemed to thread together momentarily – smoke curling around the blackness of unseeing eyes, vapor outlining the gaping dark of a mouth frozen in its scream. I blinked rapidly as the tension in my body and the thrumming of my heart reached their zenith, and then I jerked away, tears of fear and shock hot in my eyes.

I felt Gen's hand on my shoulder. I pulled away from him and broke into a run.

The sound of my clattering footsteps was loud in the emptiness. I turned down one street then the next. Gasping, I came to a halt. My hair was lank from the rainwater and I'd run so hard that each breath I took caused a sharp pain to rip across my abdomen. For a few moments I struggled to breathe. Once again tears stung my eyes. But they were tears of humiliation now. I had allowed my imagination to get the better of me.

After my mother had screamed hysterically at me for what felt like several hours, I was sent to bed early. I sat in my room wearing a grim smile in the darkness. Gen had been able to frighten me by telling me a story fit for little children, and I'd swallowed it hook, line and sinker. I promised myself I'd get him back, I'd exact my revenge somehow, but behind those thoughts was a deeper and more elemental sense of unease. Lying in my bed, the familiar objects of my room seemed changed. They appeared as ethereal, alien shadows across a plain of dark – the outline of a teddy bear suddenly assumed sinister and sharper proportions, a pool of darkness seemed to spill out from the gap beneath my wardrobe in a black tide.

I lay in the dark, listening to the sound of my breathing, and the softer, deeper throb of my heart. I retained the traces of a memory from years before and it came to me as I lay there. The death of my grandfather. I couldn't have been much older than Qiao, my little brother, was now. Everything is a bit disjointed; images arrive in fragments rather than as a smooth unfolding set of events. Glimpses and impressions: the smell of candles burning, the sense of lots of people pressed together in a room, a vague outline of a stranger's face peering down at me. I know these are all snatches from the day of my grandfather's funeral. Years later I discovered both my parents wanted to mark his passing with a more secular celebration, but my grandmother would not have it.

My grandfather was laid out in an open coffin in the main room of our apartment in the way of a traditional funeral that would deliver him to the Ancestors. Neighbors flowed in to pay their respects as the evening faded into night. There was noise, chatter. It was probably quite cheery – the traditional ceremonies are often about joy as much as grief – but from the little I remember I don't recall it being that way.

I remember the sound of chanting. I remember being afraid. I recall clinging to my blanket, my natty little blanket, pressing its frayed edges into my mouth in my anxiety. Stepping into the room with all those bodies, gradually nudging my way through a forest of long legs toward that point – the point where the light from the candles was concentrated in a single glowing circle at the center of the room, illuminating the rich hue of the wood. The place where my grandfather was. I had a sense that he was there – that much I knew – so if I kept moving I knew I would see him, but at the same time I didn't want to. A dread had risen up inside me, only I couldn't stop moving, moving with all the inevitability of a dream, closer and closer until …

Until what? I remember the dread building until I found it hard to breathe. I remember being close enough to catch a glimpse of the profile of a head, its waxen, pallid skin, the shape of a nose – and yet now I think these are elements my mind might have added in retrospect, filling in the blanks. Had I actually seen him? Lying there in bed some years later, being pulled back into the strange haze of my earliest beginnings, I found I could no longer picture my grandfather's face, either living or dead. What I remembered was a number: he had departed the world aged seventy-three. That was older than I could possibly fathom, it was an age that went on and on, which climbed like a mountain into the misty heights of the clouds.

But Gen had talked about children. Children who had died. Children who were then burned to become smoke. He had even mentioned babies. Children who had reached no number at all. I began to turn the issue over in my mind, again and again. I couldn't stop. Why had they died? What had caused them to die? My heart began to race faster even though I was lying so still. Could it be happening to me? Could I die right then and there? I closed my eyes tightly, the darkness at once drawing in. Was this what my grandfather had felt?

I opened my eyes again. I looked across the room. Gen was a sly one, he had been making it all up, I told myself. And I was a fool for believing him. And yet, nothing could calm the disquiet inside me. I put my feet out of the bed. The floor of my room felt cold. I crept carefully toward the window and looked out. In the distance I could just about make out the thin trail of vapor snaking up from the chimney of the hospital building, ghostly and white, melting into the darkness above. I returned to my bed, pulling the covers up around me. At some point I fell asleep.

THREE

B UT IN THE MORNING, THE FEELING WAS STILL THERE. Like some burgeoning sickness. I went to breakfast and I found myself watching Qiao, who giggled while he ate. It wasn't as if there was anything for him to laugh about, and yet the haphazard business of eating was enough to raise a smile from him, especially considering he was the messiest eater of us all (my grandmother came a close second). He would stuff sweet-sticky rice into his mouth, his fingers shiny with honey dip, and he would smile delightedly, perhaps because we, all of us, seemed a tad ridiculous to him or maybe because the food tasted so sweet and warm. My mother batted at him with her hands, trying to avoid the debris that would inevitably slick his chops and cascade down his grubby top, but this made him laugh all the more, as though the whole performance was one put on exclusively for his entertainment.

'Mama … Qiao go "munch munch,"' he enunciated delightedly, as miniature boulders of food avalanched out of his mouth. He turned to me and grinned, flicking his chubby toddler's fingers in my direction, a display of happy triumph on his part.

I looked at his face – shining with mirth and newness – and whereas I usually felt irritation toward my brother because his bois-terousness was overwhelming, now I experienced a desperate and fearful sense of love for him. I looked at his face and his big open toddler's smile, and in his innocence he seemed both oblivious and vulnerable. What Gen had said about the dead children seemed ridiculous – something designed to rankle me – and yet I realized that I had in fact heard of children dying. A girl in the year below had been hit by a car. A boy in the year above had become ill. Their names eluded me, and the details of the illness, or the circumstances of the accident, were also invisible to me.

I'd heard about the events at the time, perhaps through second-hand conversations, or something said at a school assembly, but I'd never really taken in the specifics. Now, though, it was more real. I looked at my brother with his glistening dark eyes and his full cheeks bulging with food and felt my breath catch. All it would take was for some of that food to get lodged in his throat, or perhaps when our mother had helped him down from his high chair, his belly swollen, he might stumble, cracking his head smartly against the corner of a door. Or he could …

The infinite variety of ways in which my brother might suddenly be taken from this world ran across my mind, and all at once it seemed to me there was no way he would survive the day. I reached out to him instinctively; I squeezed his nose and he blinked and laughed, and I had to fight back tears. Nobody else noticed the sudden change in my behavior (before this day I was more likely to pinch my broth-er's cheeks to make him cry). But perhaps my grandmother realized something was different, for I felt the wrinkled darkness of her eyes upon me, curious, tinged with mysterious amusement.

But the situation for me was anything but funny. As my mother herded me out of the apartment that morning, as I felt the door close behind me, I was convinced I would never see my brother again. That something would happen to him while I was gone. I imagined his face no longer bright-eyed and shiny, but shut-eyed and gray, his body suspended within the strange orange glow inside that great building; then I imagined my brother being belched out from that tapering chimney, his dull death mask outlined in a smoke-filled scream. More than anything I wanted to tell my mother not to make me go to school – to let me stay at home – but the words wouldn't come. At that age there is such a gulf between your childhood certainties and the adult world your parents inhabit; even though I was certain my brother was in great danger (though I knew not from what), nevertheless I couldn't change the course of my routine, I couldn't give voice to my fears, for I knew I would never be able to make my mother or father understand what I felt.

So I sank into a wretched state. I sat at my desk in class with a feeling of dread broiling in my belly. Every minute passed as an inscrutable agony. At lunch I couldn't help but wander up to one of the other girls – Fulin – who always seemed amiable and sensible.

'Hey, Fulin!'

She seemed friendly but I would have to approach this with a great deal of caution and tact.

'Fulin?'

'Yeah?'

'Do you think that it is possible something really awful could happen at any moment, and that we could … die … at any point, and that when that happens they would take our bodies and burn them and our spirits … would end up coming out as smoke?'

She looked at me, blinking in much the same way my brother had done when I tweaked his nose.

'I can't chat right now. I have to … get started on my homework.'

The rest of the afternoon was equally excruciating. By the time I returned home, my thoughts had rolled over and over in my brain, and I was certain my brother was already gone. When I stepped into the living room and saw him being bounced on my grandmother's lap, for the second time that day I found it difficult to breathe. He looked up at me and gurgled cheekily, before returning to the intriguing topography of my grandmother's face, pressing his hands against her in the way I had once done myself. But my grandmother's eyes remained on me, curious and penetrating.

I went to my room. Qiao was okay, that was the important thing. Only then another thought arrived. A week before, I had been running with my friends after school and I had cut my knee clambering over a wooden gate. I didn't think about it too much at the time, even though I noticed a slight yellowing around the thin lip of red. The skin there tingled. It occurred to me that it had got infected – my mother was always talking about such things. Perhaps it was not Qiao who was the vulnerable one, but me.

And then, another thought came. Perhaps we were all vulnerable. Perhaps any of us could die at any time. But how could people live like this? With such an awareness? My eyes felt heavy but at the same time the tears wouldn't come.

I felt a great sadness. It was a feeling that seemed to separate me from my family, from the world. I watched my mother jostle with my little brother. I watched my father retreat into his study deep in thought. They all continued as usual. Had they never experienced such thoughts? Would we all end up in the place Gen had described?

Would we all end up as the dark smoke pushed out from some strange chimney?

I found myself wandering into my grandmother's room.

Her large turtle-like eyes fixed on me.

'Are you ready to let it go?'

'Let what go?'

'Let go of whatever it is you have been keeping inside you. It's like a volcano, you know. And eventually, all volcanoes must explode.'

Something in me seeped out in a rush of feeling. I felt tears forming in my eyes.

'There is this boy.'

'Ah yes, I thought you were a bit young for that. But if he is handsome and you really like him, and you are feeling these warm sensations in your belly every time you look at him, then perhaps ...'

'Eww, no! I don't like him at all. I hate him, in fact!'

'Well, love often begins with hate ...'

She smiled her great toad's smile.

'Po Po – be serious. He ... he told me something horrible.'

Her expression became gentle.

'What did he tell you?'

'He told me that there is a building where they burn ...'

Suddenly I was overcome by the rawness of my emotion. I felt my body heave in a single silent sob.

'Burn what?' my grandmother asked.

'Burn ... burn the bodies of ... dead children. And that their spirits come out in the smoke. But that's not true, is it, Po Po?'

'Where is this building?'

'The Beijing Children's Hospital.'

My grandmother sucked her bottom lip. She was concentrating. Generally speaking, that was what I loved about her. Most adults never take what children say seriously. They just respond with an uninterested and anodyne answer. But my grandmother really seemed to consider what I said. Only on this occasion, I wished she hadn't. Eventually she began to speak.

'I think what your friend said may be true.'

Something in me sank. It was one thing for such a story to arise in the world of children. But for an adult – and an ancient one at that – to give credence to what Gen had said made the hairs on the back of my neck prickle.

She smiled, a soft melancholy smile that caused the wrinkles on her forehead to become ravines, deeply etched into the skin. As I got older, I thought about aging more, as we all do. I came to think of old age as a fallibility akin to illness, something that left a person weak and in some way less than themselves. But I never used to think of my grandmother that way. Her hands with veins running across them like vines, the lines that crisscrossed her forehead, the full softness of her belly, the solidity of her arthritic shoulders, and those ancient, timeless eyes – to me these things spoke not of fallibility but of permanence. Of implacable strength, like an old gnarly tree that had been battered by wind and weather, but remained stubbornly set into the soil.

Indeed, while my father worked, my mother bustled and shopped, and my brother and I were at school each day, it was as though my grandmother had taken root in our apartment. And the awareness of her – her presence, the rich odor of leather oil that emanated from her – was something I sought to breathe in, for it brought me comfort. My grandmother could be wicked, and she had an acid tongue – my father had been lashed by it, and it was enough to turn my mother's face a crimson blush before sending her scurrying from the room. But although my grandmother sometimes slapped my wrists hard in a moment of pique, her attitude to me and Qiao was one of gentle amusement. Now, however, she looked serious; she thoughtfully stroked the hairs that protruded from her chin and began to speak.

'Do you remember much of your grandfather?'

I was suddenly anxious. I did not wish to displease my grandmother.

'I … I … remember the day his shouling began. I think so anyway. It was before Qiao was born. And they … I mean he … he was laid out in … our living room,' I finished lamely.

I could never tell whether my grandmother's expression would get light or dark. This time, though, no shadow passed across her face. Instead just a wan smile. And a confidential twinkle in her eyes.

'He was an old goat, that man.'

My mouth must have fallen open, because I had never heard my grandfather described that way. But my grandmother simply grinned wickedly.

'What you need to understand, Little One … is what times were like *before*. Do you think me and your grandfather saw each other one day and were struck by love and lived happily ever after? Like in one of your fairy tales? No, that's not what happened at all. My parents and his parents made a pact. We were promised to one another long before we ever met. The whole thing might have been forgotten though. I stayed in the village. Your grandfather came to Beijing. He was studying to be a railway engineer. Perhaps by that time he had found himself a girl, a more modern girl without broken feet.'

I was captivated.

'So what happened?'

'In 1937 the Japanese invaded. The Japanese army – they were hard, and fast, and they passed through the villages so quickly. So brutally. The villages bore the brunt of their soldiers. It was decided that a girl like me – I was just sixteen at the time – might not be worth much after the soldiers had come through!'

I was baffled.

'Why wouldn't you be worth much just because of horrid soldiers? You are worth a lot to me, Po Po. More than even two hundred Dragon Beards!' (Dragon Beard candy was the delicacy we kids prized above all others, though we never had the means to secure much of it.)

My grandmother looked at me, those dark eyes shining like a river at night. She spoke more softly.

'Times were different then.'

I realized I was being brushed off, that it was no kind of answer, and I went to press for more information, but she raised her hand.

'In one way, it was good the soldiers came. Because my parents sent me to Beijing, to your grandfather. And if they hadn't done that, well then – you wouldn't exist!'

She reached out and tweaked my nose with her fingers the way she sometimes did. It hurt a bit but it made me giggle anyhow. But I was still focused on the story.

'So Grandfather didn't even know you were coming?'

My grandmother chuckled ruefully.

'Nope. They stuck me on a mule, shoved some jewelry into my pockets, told me that once I got to his place, I was to put the gold into his hand and insist he make good on his parents' promise. That he make me his wife. In fact, he went quite white when I arrived.'

'Did he take the jewelry?'

My grandmother frowned.

'No, some bandits stopped us along the way. The rogues robbed us as the price of giving "safe passage." But, somehow, I got there. All the way to Beijing. And for a village girl, at that age, during that time – Beijing felt like the very ends of the earth.'

'But if you didn't have any jewelry …'

'Your grandfather was an old goat. But he was an honorable goat, in his strange, sullen way. He made it clear from the start that he didn't like me. And I wasn't too happy about being offered up to him like an item of livestock fresh from the market. But in the end he honored his commitment. He abandoned his studies. And we got married.'

'And lived happily ever after?'

My grandmother guffawed.

'Did anything about that story make you think that?'

I blushed. On the one hand it was exciting when an adult talked to you in this way about real things. But on the other, my grandmother often left me feeling out of my depth.

'No, there was no "happy ever after." But there was an "ever after." I was stubborn, mulish. Your grandfather was distant and aloof. He, no doubt, had his dreams about what his future would be. And I wasn't part of them. But he never mentioned that to me. We didn't like each other. But eventually we learned to get on. He'd sit in that chair exactly there. He'd rock back and forth. Smoke his pipe. Hardly say a word. When he got really old, I was the only one he'd let cut his hair. I'd be tutting the whole way through, telling him to be still. But … toward the end … I kinda liked doing it.'

I don't really think I ever saw my grandmother misty-eyed or emotional. That 'I kinda liked doing it' was about the strongest protestation of emotion I ever saw her give, and even then it was to the memory of a man she hadn't liked all that much. But there was something there. Even as a kid, I got that.

'But,' I asked timidly, 'what about the Beijing Children's Hospital? What about the dead children?'

My grandmother, removed from her reverie, seemed to see me again, in the present.

'I didn't like your grandfather all that much, and he wasn't always so sweet on me. But we got used to one another. And when he was gone … it was … different. Sometimes, in the years following his passing. When the window was open at night. I'd be sleeping. But even though it was hot and there was no wind, his rocking chair would be moving just a little bit …'

I looked at the chair. My face must have grimaced in horror, and if that wasn't enough, I lurched back automatically.

My grandmother chuckled. She reached out one leathery hand and placed it on my arm. I could feel the warmth of her, the blood rushing underneath her skin; it was as though something in her spirit transferred itself, calming my own clammy agitation.

'What I am saying to you, Little One, is that I didn't feel afraid. I would be in the midst of dreams – I'd see faces of people who lived centuries ago, I'd see the reflections of my past selves looking out at me with silent words, and I would feel … confused and … alone. And then I'd wake up in this room. And I'd feel your grandfather there with me. Brooding in silence, the way the bad-tempered old goat always used to do. And I wouldn't be … so alone. I'd feel him still.'

She put a thick, withered hand to her heart. The gesture was brief, tentative. But it filled me with an emotion I was still too young to understand. For a moment all the child-questions that had been jostling in my mind were silenced.

She looked at me.

'I don't really know if what your friend told you was true. But you shouldn't be afraid of death. You are not going to die for a very long time. And Qiao is not going to die for a very long time. And neither will your mother and father. But when that time eventually comes, it won't be the end. You will still be here. Smoke stealing across the sky, maybe. Or in the movement of a chair, back and forth, by the bedside of someone you once knew!'

She spoke so calmly. Somehow it put me at ease. So much so that I forget the manner in which she had promised my little brother and me long life, and both our parents, but had not included herself. Like so much of life, the full import of someone's words is often only revealed many years later, by which time that person has already slipped into the past.

FOUR

THE SUMMER OF '78 WAS PERHAPS THE STRANGEST I had known. The Great Helmsman had been dead for a couple of years by then. The old-guard communist faction – the so-called Gang of Four – had collapsed only weeks after Mao's demise, leaving a power vacuum. Into this had stepped the modernizer Deng Xiaoping, someone who was prepared to disavow 'the worst excesses' of the Cultural Revolution and modernize the economy according to a more free-market paradigm. Deng would make explicit overtures to the USA too – a fact that baffled many who had been born after the 1949 revolution. For they had only ever known the USA as the most diabolical adversary: the belly of the beast, the heartland of global capitalism, consumerism and commerciality. A place where the authentic human spirit went to curl up and die before the almighty altar of the dollar.

But if those who had been enemies were becoming allies, those who had once been allies were now enemies. China had assisted the North Vietnamese in the war against the Americans, but now, as Vietnam moved against Cambodia, the Chinese military was preparing to turn its weapons on Vietnam. Troops were amassing on the border. Everything seemed to be whizzing around on an increasingly unstable and shuddering axis; the certainties of yesterday were uprooted and all that was once solid was melting away in the balmy sweetness of that strange summer air.

It seemed too as though the adults – those bastions of certainty and seriousness – were rudderless, drifting to a point unseen. The event on everyone's lips was the visit due to take place toward the end of the summer. Brzezinski, top security advisor to Jimmy Carter, the American president, was due to make a tour of several of the biggest Chinese cities while chairing meetings with Deng; the whisper on the streets was one of rapprochement. In our own city the soldiers had already busied themselves, clearing the homeless from those streets where the US delegation and its convoy of cars would pass.

For us kids, we didn't experience things in quite that way. Rather we felt them as currents that formed a backdrop to our lives, brushing up against us every now and then. At night, we heard the stifled voices of our parents debating in urgent whispers. Neighbors huddled in the hallways using words we weren't yet old enough to understand. But for me and my friends that summer represented something more than just the faint rumblings of the great upheavals that were taking place in the adult world. We could sense a static charge in the air, glimpse the hue of purple on the horizon just before the sky darkened into night, and we knew our own lives were going to change.

For that summer was more than just a season; it came to form the bridge between our childhood and the earliest blooming of adolescence. Some of us were already experiencing the onset of puberty. Fan, the most indelibly childlike of us all, had developed a downy outline of wispy hair across the top of his lip that we all touched in fascination, making him squeak and giggle. Jian's handsome face had acquired stronger and leaner definition, and when he spoke – as steadily as always – there was a gruffness to his voice now. Al Lam, much to her embarrassment, was being sent to an all-girls school in Hong Kong, a fact that mortified her. Her family was moving there in less than a month. She was the quietest of us, and at first she didn't say much about it. But one day, out of the blue, she suddenly spat on the ground, cursed her parents, calling them 'ben dan' – which translates as 'stupid eggs' and doesn't sound that bad, but when we Chinese bring eggs into the conversation it is because we want to cut to the quick ('stupid eggs,' 'bad eggs,' 'tortoise eggs'). We all blinked at her in shock. I was impressed. She looked back at us mutinously before she spoke in a lowered voice.

'They are just … chongyang meiwai.'

In some ways this shocked us even more than the swear words she had used. Al Lam had insulted her parents with that phrase, a phrase that meant they were lickspittles and traitors, entirely subservient to foreigners. It was something people said, but you never said it about someone in your own family. In those times, even children knew you had to be circumspect, because you never knew who might be listening.

All at once she burst into tears.

I think we understood in our way that her sudden display of anger covered up a sense of frustration and fear. That she was being dragged from her home by her parents and there was nothing she could do. We all huddled round; at once we made unbreakable oaths – we swore to one another that we would descend on Hong Kong, that we would travel by night and that we would find the school where Al Lam was being kept and break her out. We began to devise all the different ways: we could parachute down onto the roof, or we could dig tunnels underneath, but whatever happened Al Lam should know that we would all be together again, no matter what.

I don't think she believed it any more than we did. But the gravity of the conspiracy was fun. And the tears on her cheeks soon dried away before the warmth and spontaneity of childhood laughter.

I think we all felt for Al Lam because something similar was happening to each of us. Not to the same extent, perhaps. But after the summer had ended, we were all going on to separate high schools. None of us really knew what our futures held. We were being pulled apart into a new stage of life, and we – all of us – felt it, but at the same time we were still kids and that was something we wanted to hold on to, more than anything.

So we did the only thing we could. The only thing children in our situation might.

We played *Teng-Teng the Tomato*.

Teng-Teng the Tomato was the game carrying most risk but also offering most reward.

Even though our neighborhood was rather run-down, it was also within a stone's throw of Chaoyang Park Road. This salubrious street happened to house some of the mid-level bureaucrats and their families. It featured long gardens with well-tended trees, and houses with sleek dark windows that framed the plush glow of their spacious, rich interiors. But what made those houses particularly fascinating to us – besides offering a glimpse of the children who lived there with all their incredible toys – was the fact that several of them had intercoms. This was in a time that predated computer games, at least in China; indeed, where we lived very few people even had televisions.

So for us kids there was a wonder to the intercom; you could press a button, speak into it, and a strange disembodied voice would return to you through the static. To that wonder, however, was soon added a sense of mischief – how often in childhood these two elements go hand in hand! Once we worked out we could summon a distant voice from within the house, we also realized we could say whatever we liked. We soon understood that the static muffled our voices, so that to the people inside we sounded like adults. So we began to put on the knowing tones of adults, to speak in voices of serious inquiry.

And that's how you play Teng-Teng the Tomato.

'I want to go first, I want to go first,' said Fan, his lips shining with saliva, his excitement such that he was bouncing anxiously on one foot, looking like someone desperate for the toilet.

'You can have a go soon, Fan,' Jian said mildly, his handsome features arranged in a kind smile. 'But let Zhen go first, so you can hear how to do it better!'

Fan beamed, still bouncing with excitement. Just as Zhen was the deftest of us all with his hands and the airplane models he could create, he had something of a gift when it came to bending his voice into accents. He could speak Mandarin in a posh Wu dialect and it always had us in tears. He moved toward the speaker of the intercom like a prizefighter weighing up an opponent. Even Fan went dead quiet. Jian raised his hand, flicked three fingers, then two, then one – counting down, before he pressed the buzzer. We held our breaths.

'Good evening?' a crackly voice said.

'Mwah yes, gwood evening …' Zhen answered. He drawled out the words, elongated them, before allowing them to fade. The silence stretched.

'Good evening?' the voice eventually came back, this time with a slight tension. 'May I help you?'

'Mwah yes, I was of course hoping that you mighhhht mwaaaah be so kind. You see I am looking for … Teng-Teng …'

Zhen allowed the final two words to become indistinct.

'I'm sorry, you are looking for whom?'

'Teng-Teng,' he whispered, his lips pressed against the speaker.

'Did you say Deng-Deng?'

'No, I said … Teng-Teng!'

Utterly baffled, the voice came back again, searching, almost desperate.

'Teng-Teng?'

This was the moment, the culmination.

All at once Zhen shrieked into the intercom in a deranged high-pitched voice:

'TENG-TENG … THE TOMATTTOOOOOOOOOOO!'

The astonished spluttering on the other side was drowned out by the rapturous peals of our laughter. No matter how many times we performed this routine, we always laughed till our bones shook.

Only then we heard the sound of the door being opened, along with an enraged shout.

Although the street was a long one, and there were many houses with intercoms, we weren't all that strategic or systematic in our targeting. While we often used different voices, different accents, it was quite possible that we had assailed this particular house more than once, always culminating in that rather goofy screech of 'TENG-TENG ... THE TOMATTTOOOOOOOOOOO!'

Perhaps that explained the roar of outrage that followed so swiftly on the heels of the 'punchline,' for it sounded as though whoever we had got through to had been menaced by a similar routine in the not-so-distant past. We saw a large man dressed in only a vast pair of underpants and a billowing dressing gown charge out of the door, bellowing – his bare belly wobbling with a fury his brain was struggling to process. His rage was acute, words uttered with such white-hot indignation that he was unable to form coherent sentences.

'Bastards. Shit bastards! Fuck bastard twats. Tortoise egg shits!'

We were all rooted to the spot. I don't think any of us had seen an adult lose control like that and there was something strangely compelling about that bare wobbling belly. And yet, in the next moment, the realization that this was real came slamming home and we burst into a run. Fan was a little slower off the mark than usual; he stared at the man with a fascinated curiosity before he made his way after us, but he was some way behind. He fell over and scraped his knee. It didn't matter because the man, still shouting, had stopped by the metal fence of his garden; he was gripping it and bellowing. It was dark. There was no possibility he would come after us now.

But Fan had started sobbing anyway. I don't think he was all that frightened by the man. I don't even think he was much bothered by the throbbing of his knee. I think more than anything he was frightened by the prospect of being left behind.

Jian stopped and walked back. He reached down and helped Fan up. I noticed a long trail of snot hanging from one of Fan's nostrils. But Jian didn't seem to.

'Pathetic.'

Gen was standing beside me watching them with a look on his face that seemed both adult and cold. He had spoken under his breath, involuntarily almost, not for my benefit.

Jian was trying to coax Fan up from the ground. I couldn't hear what he was saying but I heard his voice, gentle and patient. Even though I had never much liked the look of Fan, I felt a twinge of annoyance.

'He fell over. He is clumsy. It is not his fault!' I hissed at Gen.

He broke out of his reverie, looked at me as though only now realizing I was there.

'I wasn't talking about Fan,' he said. 'I was talking about Jian.'

He turned away. His answer left me baffled, for in all the squabbles we had had in our little group, Jian had always seemed above them. He was handsome and good-natured; none of us ever really thought to criticize him. I was lost for words.

Fan was still sobbing gently.

We gathered around him instinctively. Al Lam looked at the patch of red that was visible on his knee in the gloomy darkness.

'Woah dude! That wound is so cool!'

Fan stopped sobbing and blinked out at her incredulously.

'Yeah, it's true!' She smiled back. 'You're gonna have the most amazing scar!'

The others joined in. Complimenting Fan's injury. All at once the pudgy boy began smiling again.

'Hey, why do you think that old guy went so berserk?' asked Zhen.

'Maybe, maybe he was on the toilet, maybe he was in the middle of a number two, and that's when he heard the buzzer, and he got up, only he hadn't quite … finished …' Jian said thoughtfully.

'Ewwwwwwwwww,' we responded in unison, scandalized that Jian – who was the most well spoken of us all – would contrive such a disgusting scenario. To his credit, he threw his hands up.

'What?' he proclaimed helplessly.

Unfortunately that unleashed a torrent of scenarios. Perhaps when we had buzzed, the old guy had been busy snogging his tooth-less eighty-year-old wife, or perhaps he had been busy scraping away the warts from between his cheesy toes, or perhaps he had been in his basement torturing children like us who hadn't managed to get away. Each scenario, each more fantastical than the last, produced a deluge of laughter; the man – his belly wobbling, his inchoate fury – had turned into some kind of ridiculous fairy-tale monster we had managed to overcome together. We basked in the warmth of our collective triumph.

'We should … we should get him again!!! We should get him this month, and next month and the month after!' said Zhen, bursting with enthusiasm.

We all agreed so heartily that we almost didn't hear what Al Lam said. She spoke softly, but the words found us anyway.

'I won't be here next month!'

All at once, the elation and the excitement seemed to drain away. All at once we were awkward with one another, no one knew what to say. Al Lam blushed, mortified.

I suddenly spoke up.

'We should do something else. Something more. Before Al Lam leaves!'

She looked at me, surprised. I held her gaze. Everyone else was looking at me too and whereas usually I would have hated that, now I felt a sense of conviction.

'Before Al Lam leaves, Brzezinski is coming, right?'

'Yes, but so what?' asked Jian softly.

'Don't you see?' I said urgently. 'Haven't your parents been talking about it too? They say that everyone must stay inside. That nobody can be out in the evening when the cars come past. That the government won't allow it. But we should … we should …'

Their attention was completely focused on me. And I could feel a collective excitement. My words became smaller, an imperative whisper.

'We should go. One last time. One last time before Al Lam goes. See the convoy …'

My voice trailed away.

Their eyes were still trained on me. They looked anxious, but I could feel their excitement begin to build. You sense it more at that age; for a moment we were all one person.

'Yeah, let's do it,' exclaimed Zhen.

Even Gen looked at me as though he was impressed. I don't think Fan fully understood what was being proposed. Eventually we all turned to Jian. He always seemed to be the final arbiter of these things.

He looked thoughtful for a moment, but then he smiled.

'Yeah,' he said, 'let's do it!'

For a few moments no one said anything. It was as though a silent pact had been wrought, a line had been crossed, and we were – each of us – overwhelmed by the promise we had committed to. In the gloom of the darkening summer evening, something had changed. It was more than just a game; something had drawn us together in a serious and abiding alliance at the very point when our lives were about to diverge. Such was the solemnity of the moment, there were no giggles, no jokes … no words. Instead we began to make our way home. In silence. Gradually our numbers dwindled, and we nodded at one another as we each departed into the night.

Only Gen and I were left. I was so involved with what I had set in motion that I wasn't aware we were the only two remaining.

I felt his gaze on me.

His pallid features, the strange stillness of his unmoving eyes; his expression was quietly superior. Again it struck me how different he was from the rest of us. All the excitement and activity had dissipated now, leaving me feeling tired, irritated and bad-tempered. I wanted to stamp my feet on the ground the way my little brother did in the evening when he had been awake too long but nevertheless fought against going to bed. And in that moment, Gen seemed particularly annoying, particularly supercilious. If it had been my little brother, I could have just reached out and pinched his cheeks, sending him into a billowing fit of helpless tears. But I was not that brave with my own age group. And besides, there was something about Gen that unnerved me. His aloofness, the casualness of his contempt. He was the one in our group who didn't quite fit in, and yet there was this air of insouciance to him that unsettled me. He always seemed so quietly confident.

I felt myself bridle. We were almost at my street. I wanted to cut him down, to erase the faint smirk that always lingered on his lips. But I couldn't quite summon the words. Eventually I turned on him and managed, in a snarl:

'Why the hell did you tell me all that crap? All that stuff about those dead babies? Turning into smoke?'

Gen started. He seemed surprised by the sudden jolt of my anger. I felt a momentary satisfaction.

He looked at the ground and then he looked at me again, thoughtful.

'I guess I just wanted to see …'

'To see what?'

'To see if you would believe it. And well … you did.'

He gave a wan smile, and turned, walking in the direction of his own neighborhood. I opened my mouth and closed it again. Gen wasn't good-looking like Jian. He wasn't funny the way Al Lam could be in her quiet, thoughtful way. He wasn't good at doing voices or building paper planes like Zhen. And he wasn't kind-natured like Fan. In fact, there wasn't anything I liked about him at all. So I couldn't make sense of the fact that my heart was throbbing with indignation as I watched him walk away, why he always succeeded in eliciting such an emotional reaction from me.

It had started to rain lightly. The coldness of the rain from invisible clouds far up in the night formed a contrast to the balmy heat of the evening, and the feeling of tiredness that had settled upon me was pricked with the first tendrils of fever. I felt the sides of my temples begin to throb. We had all of us lost track of the time. When I returned home my mother fell upon me at once.

'Where have you been? It's already dark! You promised me you would never stay out late!'

I looked at her, my head buzzing with the surreality of the strange summer evening. The words came from me, but it was as though I was hearing them from elsewhere.

'I guess I just wanted to see …'

'See what?' my mother responded with barely contained fury.

'To see if you would believe it. And well ... you did.'

She gaped at me. Her mouth dropped open in astonishment and for a few seconds she was without words. Then she fell on me, slapping me across the head, pulling me farther down into the corridor, and despite myself I couldn't avoid the hysterical giggling that bubbled out even as my mother was beating me. I caught a glimpse of my father at the dinner table, my little brother in his high chair – their eyes remarkably similar, wide with apprehension – as my mother dragged me past. She pulled me into my room, flung me onto my bed and turned off the light before flouncing out and slamming the door behind her. I felt that same hysterical laughter bubble up within me.

I lay on my bed fully clothed. I kicked off my shoes. I looked over to the other side of the room where my brother's cot was. He was probably a little too old for it now. It was the first time that I had ever been put to bed before him. As a kid, being put to bed early was one of the biggest indignities you could suffer. Because you might not feel all that tired, and you were sure that the whole world and all the people in it were having the time of their lives, while you just wasted away in the shadows, cut off from everything and everyone.

And yet, that evening, I didn't feel the petulant fury of one who had been sent to bed early. Perhaps because I had been touched by the earliest onset of fever, perhaps because I could still feel the clammy dampness of the rain on my hair, I actually felt happy to be in my bed, to feel the warmth of the covers against me, the security of home. I could hear my family, my mother's high-pitched voice, my brother's delighted squeal, my grandmother's low, grumbling laugh suffused with its wry humor. I could see the light under the rim of my door.

59

And, despite my mother's anger toward me, I felt an abiding and warm sense of safety. Maybe it was because of what I had told the others, my friends; the plan I had devised for the evening of the convoy. Or maybe it was something deeper and more imperative still. The sense that everything was going to change in ways I couldn't even begin to fathom.

But for those moments, lying on my bed, my face still tingling from my mother's slaps, I felt a sense of well-being. The belief that my grandmother would always be there, her full body expanding gently in her chair, watching my mother gabble erratically; that my father, worn and exhausted, would have his face lit by a wry smile as he played with my brother in his high chair, and that my brother – ridiculous, excitable and overstimulated – would be eventually returned to my room, where he would croon my name from his cot before quickly succumbing to sleep. And I would follow the rhythm of his soft milky breaths in the gentle dark.

I held on to those few moments: the impression of my family intact, simply being themselves, just beyond my bedroom door. I heard the gentle burble of their noise, their life, and softly, in the blink of an eye, I was asleep.

FIVE

WHEN I WOKE THE NEXT DAY, THE SUNLIGHT WAS streaming in and the events of the previous night seemed far away and dreamlike. I turned my body in the bed, wrapping myself into the covers, enjoying the hazy warmth that lingers momentarily before you enter into full wakefulness. I lay on my back and stretched. I looked over to my brother's cot. It was empty. The apartment was quiet. I guessed it to be late Saturday morning. I must have overslept.

After brushing my teeth and getting dressed, I padded across the cold floor of the corridor. I thought my mother and father were out with my brother perhaps. The quiet was unusual. Even the people in the other apartments were quiet and the only thing I could hear was a bird, somewhere above in the sunlight, its cooing sweet, distant and melancholy. But despite the absence of human life I felt a sense of contentment bloom in my chest. The feeling of having a little time alone, of being unobserved, could be strangely precious to a person whose life was otherwise filled with the sounds of a squalling baby brother and bustling parents and neighbors who were always passing into your orbit.

Then I heard a sudden rustle. I froze mid-step, like a burglar caught in the act. The noise was coming from the kitchen. Beijing was a city infamous for its wildlife: we had hog badgers and raccoon dogs, we had chipmunks and even Siberian weasels. Oh god, what if it was a Siberian weasel? They were known for their viciousness, and although I'd never actually seen one, I had been reliably informed by Zhen that they were incredibly dangerous because he had a friend who had another friend whose eyes had been clawed out by one. I didn't want to go blind. Not just because of the pain, but because the thought of not being able to see forever and ever was just too horrifying to comprehend. How would I live? I wouldn't be able to do any of the fun things anymore. And imagine trying to go to the toilet …

My heart throbbing, I resolved to myself that if I was to go down, I would go down fighting. I quickly picked up one of my father's science magazines, rolled it into a tube so that it made – if I dare say so myself – a rather good sword. Then I stalked my way toward the kitchen with murder on my mind. As I got closer my resolve began to weaken. Nevertheless, I forced myself to keep going until, peeking round the side of the kitchen door, I came face to face with the source of the disturbance. My grandmother was in the kitchen, standing at the sink, emptying a carton of what looked like grain into a bag. She sensed my movement, and turned. For a few moments we stared at each other; me looking up, her looking down, both of us peering suspiciously at each other.

'What are you doing?' I eventually mumbled, making my voice as casual as possible.

She, also in an attempt to sound casual:

'Just preparing some ingredients for soup.'

'You are going to put all that grain in the soup?'

Her eyes narrowed.

'Yes. I put the grain in the soup. It is … an old Chinese recipe.'

I raised an eyebrow.

'An old Chinese recipe?'

She raised an eyebrow.

'Exactly as I say. An old Chinese recipe.'

Often when my grandmother wanted to justify something dubious, she would say, 'It's an old Chinese remedy,' or an 'old Chinese tradition,' or an 'old Chinese custom.' Mostly, this meant her being able to carry on doing exactly what it was she wanted to do in the first place. I may only have been young. But I was a quiet child, and watchful. I'd gotten wise to some of the more questionable practices of the adults in my family some time ago.

My grandmother and I gazed at one another for a few moments more. Perhaps it was my imagination, or were the corners of her mouth curling ever so slightly in the beginnings of a grin?

'Well, I'd better get back to my room. I've got a lot of homework to do this weekend.'

'Well, maybe that would be a good idea!'

My grandmother was poker-faced but there was a certain gleam in her eye.

I went back to my room. But it was not to do any homework. I made an elaborate show of slamming my door, only to open it again quietly and ever so slightly.

I waited. And I waited. In a child's timeframe, five minutes spent doing nothing whatsoever can seem like a lifetime. I must have been waiting behind my door for at least ten. Just as I was contemplating giving up, I sensed a movement. I peered through the crack. I caught a glimpse of my grandmother's sturdy figure moving swiftly down the corridor. She was carrying the bag of grain. She walked like one of those ruddy dwarfs from a fairy tale, her shoulders rolling, her head bowed, a determined, striding gait. But she didn't make any noise. When she got to the door of the apartment, she opened it carefully and quietly. She closed it gently behind her. I leapt into motion. I streaked to the door and paused for a few seconds before opening it carefully. I stuck my head out into the corridor to see my grandmother's retreating figure disappear down the stairwell. I crept after her.

I followed her out of the back of the building and across a barren patch of land where the grass had been baked into the dirt by the summer heat, where lizards scuttled from the brightness and into the shadows in darting streaks of movement, where ants swarmed furious through the eddies that had opened up between the walls of the building and the hard, hot ground. I watched my grandmother, a small stout figure shuffling through the open, empty space and the vast pooling brightness of the late morning, as she moved toward the array of dilapidated shacks and sheds that seemed to vegetate and decay on the other side. She reached one of those shacks and, with a quick furtive glance to either side, she ducked her head and slipped inside. I followed her. As I got closer I felt a different type of fear. Different from the panic that had gripped me when I thought about the Siberian weasel that was about to claw my eyes out. This feeling was smaller, but more unnerving somehow. I had the sense that I was about to see something I shouldn't. My grandmother's behavior had alerted me to something strange, something adult, outside my gamut of experience. Part of me felt I should pull back, but in the deepest corner of myself I knew it was too late for that.

I took the last few hesitant steps to the entrance of the shack, ducked my head and slipped inside. My eyes had to adjust to the gloom. The place smelled of grain and a stagnant warmth, the type of air you might get in a barn. Then I saw my grandmother hunched over in the shadows, leaning in toward something. I made out the faint outline of a small pen with a box in the middle. I took a step farther and my foot scuffed against the dry ground.

My grandmother spun around and yelled.

I screamed.

She blinked at me.

'Sweet Pangu, I thought you were a ghost. What in the name of the seven hells is wrong with you, sneaking up on people like that? You could have given me a heart attack!'

'What are you doing here?' I stuttered.

'What am I doing here, she asks! *What am I doing here?!*'

My grandmother moved toward me with menace. As a child well used to dodging the swipes of adults' hands, deflecting the rulers of teachers with a defensive arm, taking the sting out of my mother's slaps by covering up, I drew into myself. And then I heard it. A low but audible squeaking sound.

My grandmother stopped. I looked over to where she had been. Instinctively, I moved forward, peering into the shadow. I could make out a small shape bobbing along the ground.

'What is it?' I asked with wonder.

My grandmother looked at me, her lips pursed with irritation. Then she muttered something I couldn't quite make out.

'What?' I asked.

'It's a chicken,' she mumbled.

'A chicken?'

'Yes.'

'Like the ones you buy from the market, then make into soup?'

'Yes,' she said sullenly.

'But you … you didn't kill it?'

'No, obviously.'

I moved closer. I kneeled down. The little bird stopped its strutting, cocked its head and glanced at me before strutting on. Pecking at the grain my grandmother had scattered. The chick walked in a lopsided fashion, leaning awkwardly like a drunk. Every so often it tumbled to the ground, before pulling itself upright again and continuing in its lopsided trajectory. As my eyes grew accustomed to the meager light, I realized that one of its legs had been damaged, then wrapped in a delicate fabric.

'It was hurt?'

'Yes.'

'And you made it better, Po Po?'

'Yes.'

'Does it have a name?'

'Of course not, silly child. It is just a chicken. Who ever heard of a chicken with a name?'

'Who ever heard of a chicken with a bandage?'

My grandmother pawed me over the head.

'Owww, that hurt!'

'Good!'

'I think it should have a name.'

I edged my way closer. The chick looked up. I must have appeared as a giant, my massive face coming out of the gloom. So I tried to smile as nicely as I could, but only succeeded in grimacing. It's always difficult to smile properly unless something makes you smile and you don't think about it too hard. But the chick didn't seem to mind.

'I would call you Cinderella,' I whispered to the tiny bird confidentially. My grandmother sighed.

'Don't get too attached, Little One. It's just a bird.'

'Then why did you rescue her? Why did you make her better?'

I could feel my grandmother's eyes on me.

'This bird is small, even for a chick. And its leg got snapped.'

'So what does that mean?'

'It means that, even though it is weak, it has been fighting hard. To survive. And that means when it becomes a hen it will have learned to be strong, much stronger than the others. And it will lay the best eggs.'

I thought about it. My grandmother's logic was impeccable.

'Can I hold her?'

My grandmother nodded in the gloom.

I reached out slowly. The chick seemed to stiffen but did not bolt. It was as if she was hypnotized as I reached out, then gently wrapped her in my fingers. She was trembling violently as I raised her up in the cup of my hand, and she was so warm and soft and alive. I think I fell in love with her right there.

I began to stroke her feathers very gently. My grandmother leaned forward in apprehension.

'Be careful, not too hard …'

I looked at my grandmother, who was looking at the little bird with something like tenderness in her eyes.

.   .   .

Many years later, when I came to live in Canada, those early days felt strange and surreal, not least because people didn't treat politics in the same way. In Canada, they would go to vote every few years and some would have strong political opinions, others not so much. But politics more generally was something you could tune out – it never pressed on you in the same way. As an adult living in a foreign land, I found that disorienting, liberating and, at the same time, a loss somehow.

But the China of my childhood was very different. Even those people who didn't have strong political feelings nevertheless couldn't escape politics. In the week before the US security advisor Brzezinski was due to come to Beijing – where he was to spend two days – things started to happen in our neighborhood late at night. A curfew was declared. We Beijingers were told to remain behind closed doors after seven in the evening. There was an old police box that had been fitted outside our apartment block; it must have dated back to the time of the Kuomintang in the 1920s. It had always been a dusty relic but now for the first time a policeman had been assigned to it – a bearded man with red-rimmed, tired eyes, a walrus-like mustache and a big belly. His watery gaze seemed to look right through you as though he was looking back to another time. I had to admit that for a cop he wasn't particularly threatening.

A day later we heard the noise of drills and hammers. A small island had been added to the intersection where the end of our street met with a bigger road. Some of the neighborhood came out to watch the workmen lay down a patch of concrete on which another booth was erected. Two soldiers remained there, ever present, again not particularly threatening, more listless and bored. At one point a large horse-drawn cart was stopped, the soldiers shouting clipped, staccato commands. But once they had searched its contents, the cart was released and the horses were allowed to continue along their plodding path.

Nevertheless, an atmosphere of fear developed around the event. The silence that blanketed the streets during the curfew was interrupted by a sudden banging: soldiers went from door to door. They came to our apartment. Baby-faced but cruel, men not much more than children stood in our home, stony and solemn. My father ashen-faced, my mother babbling rapidly in tones of artificial cheeriness. My grandmother sat in her chair, full and stubborn, withering those young men with all the ferocity of her toad's grimace. We were told what our neighbors were told. That when Brzezinski's convoy rolled through the streets, it was imperative we stay indoors. In fact, we shouldn't even look out of our windows. The gesture might be misinterpreted. There was a possibility we might be fired upon.

As I say, in China, you may not be particularly interested in politics. But politics sure has an interest in you.

I observed all of this. I watched these incidents with a mixture of fear and excitement, but as the time drew closer the fear grew stronger and the excitement weaker. I had that feeling, the feeling one has in a dream, of being pulled inexorably toward some end point, a door at the end of a darkened corridor, for instance. And not being able to turn back. At first I thought my plan might evaporate the way so many of our childish fantasies do. But the others had talked about it in the days and weeks that followed. The whole hare-brained suggestion took on a life of its own, which I could never have anticipated. It became something that pulled the others together; they firmed it up in their own conversations, they refined the details of just how we were going to take to the streets and see the American convoy and maybe even pelt it with stones as it went by because we were heroic Chinese patriots.

The more they talked this way, the more I became discomforted, for I was a sensible child mostly, but not a brave one, and even Jian – who was so calm and level-headed – seemed to have been infected by the strange, savage euphoria that had possessed the others. Some days before the curfew came into force I still thought that there was hope. But on the eve of the curfew we gathered together one last time, the summer heat evaporating, the evening shadows outlining the severity in our faces. A meeting time was decided. We would slip out of our apartments, creep away from the bigger streets. The meeting place would be the dusty square where we always played. From there we would head toward the center, toward Chang'an Avenue where the convoy was destined to pass. Even at this point, I still thought perhaps someone might start laughing, and then the others too, laughing at the ridiculousness of it all. Only no one did. Instead we linked our fingers together: all of us, the two girls and the boys. We made a pinky swear.

And as every child knows, you can't break a pinky swear.

In the end it proved surprisingly easy to escape the apartment. I had felt sick the whole day. That strange, slick fear broiling in my stomach. By the time the evening arrived and the curfew had begun, everything in my apartment seemed oddly normal. My grandmother in her chair, working on her leather. My mother in the kitchen, steam from boiling pots billowing into the main room and making our faces glow. My brother giggling and burping, lost in his own private world. I slipped out, the sound of my heart threatening to unravel me, pounding in the quiet. I exited the main gate, edging forward, ducking down. In the cooling, darkening evening I could see the form of the policeman who had been posted in the booth – the indistinct shape of his body and slumped head – and I could hear the wheezing of his gentle snores.

I walked in the other direction. I thought that perhaps the others wouldn't make it, that they might have backed out, but as I got closer, I could make out five figures pressed up against a ragged, battered wall, huddling in the shadows. Every single one of them had come out. And in that moment I felt something change. The fear was still there, of course, but now a lump had formed in my throat. And I felt the first premonition of tears, warm and hot in my eyes. These were my friends. They were the only friends I had. And I experienced a surging sense of determination. Whatever was about to happen, whatever we were going to face, it was something we would face together.

I reached them. Night had fallen now. Each of them clutched my hands. There was a solemnity set into every expression; for a moment they were children as I was – but in the same instant, the shadows that pooled across their faces, shading their features, seemed to give a glimpse of the adults they would become: Jian, a lawyer defending some poverty-stricken vagrant accused of theft, Zhen the architect working on the creation of some fabulous skyscraper, Al Lam sitting on the board of directors of a world-famous orchestra. Of course, I couldn't possibly have seen this at the time. My knowledge of who those children would become has infiltrated my memory of who they once were. Nevertheless, standing there with my friends that evening, there was a strange coincidence of the past with the future. Which, perhaps, signifies nothing more than the present.

Even Fan took my hand gently. In my memory, this is the only time I recall when he wasn't dribbling or giggling or crying. I don't think he understood everything that was going on; I guess none of us did, but he even less. And I thought about how mean I'd been to him, and – in the confines of my own thoughts – how much he had disgusted me, and for the second time that evening I felt tears prick my eyes.

Perhaps the others were churning with the same type of emotions. I only know that we exchanged few words. Every other meeting we'd had over the years had involved laughing, bickering, shouting, sometimes crying – but that evening we exchanged barely a word. We simply moved together, darting across the main street, then into a smaller one. We kept moving. We walked past the area where we used to play Teng-Teng the Tomato. We walked past the large park where all of us had been pushed on swings as smaller children. The great trees that overshadowed the playground now seemed sinister and threatening. The temperature had dropped. But still we kept moving.

We walked and walked until we began to ache. Our route wasn't a straight one. Every so often, there would come a long orange beam of light churning through the dark, and we'd see the figures of soldiers hunched over a station in the middle of a street, so we would divert, slip down a back alley, then make our way ahead again.

Until we didn't really know where 'ahead' was. Gen had access to a map, he'd memorized the route, but the diversions we'd had to take had clearly baffled him, and he was muttering to himself every now and again. None of us wanted to speak. None of us wanted to express the hopelessness that was beginning to swell up inside. The apartments seemed even larger now, the streets darker and never-ending.

The only light was from the stars. It made us feel tiny; I had never before had such a sense of my own smallness. But we kept going. I think in each of us there was the same awareness: we had long since lost the possibility of finding our way back. None of us wanted to give life to despair, however. Until Fan, breathing hard, gave voice to it in the simplest way of all.

'I'm hungry. And I wanna wee too!' he blurted out.

Jian put a comforting hand on his shoulder.

'Not long now, mate,' he murmured.

Fan snuggled into himself, pushing his flabby chin into his chest, rubbing his eyes, in some way satiated, for he adored Jian above all, and was delighted when the older boy paid attention and was kind to him.

As for the rest of us, we felt the hollowness in Jian's words. And yet we kept on pushing ahead. My legs were hurting, not just aching; a pain was snarling through them. And my feet had gone numb. I had the urge to scream, to cry – a feeling I hadn't had since I was much younger, but at the same time that exhaustion was working its way through me, and I felt my panic dim and dull. I wished to God – my grandmother sometimes talked of Him even though Mao had prohibited Him – but I wished to God I had never come out. That I had stayed at home.

A moment later we stepped onto a street flooded with light under the dark sky. It was wide, with multiple lanes and traffic lights dotted throughout, and it was completely empty.

I knew this was Chang'an Avenue. The buildings were pale and ethereal, as though they had been crafted from moonbeam, and they rose so many stories high that we had to crane our necks to glimpse the tops. They loomed over us as giants, and beyond was a black sky dotted with a great constellation of stars: a billion pinpricks of silver, winking and glittering, from within an eternity of dark.

I felt something move inside me. Only moments before I had bitterly regretted this whole excursion and if I could have snapped my fingers and been back in my bed, I surely would have. But in that moment, tears welled in my eyes, for until then I had not been sure what we hoped to achieve by this strange and eerie pilgrimage through shadow and silence, and now I was filled by an absolute sense of purpose. We were meant to be here tonight. I turned to the others and I knew they were experiencing the same feeling, for they were all wearing the same timid and awestruck smile. We looked at each other, exhausted, frightened, but delighted. Nobody said a word.

For a while we moved down the great street, keeping close to the wall, cosseted by the dark. Oddly enough, it was Fan who became aware of it first. He stopped. He jerked his head to one side, and started turning his body in circles, a kind of lopsided spinning top.

He was giggling the whole time.

'Fan, we have to keep going,' Jian said, his voice soft and gentle but his eyes shining with urgency.

'Jian, Jian, listen, listen!' Fan trilled, as though he were singing a song. And then again:

'Jian, Jian, listen, listen!'

We paused. He was right. There was something. A distant rumble, but it was audible now.

Jian turned to us.

'This is it. I think they are actually coming. The convoy is coming!'

The sound grew louder. I don't know what we were thinking at that particular point, what we had planned to do. For a moment the awesomeness of the event was paralyzing.

'Duck down, hide,' barked Jian.

We tried to make ourselves small for when the convoy arrived. The rumble became louder until it resonated in the walls of our heads, but instead of a procession of sleek black limousines, what we saw was a fleet of police cars, their sirens screaming shrill blue light. They headed straight for us, a screech of brakes, and the violence of that serrating light shocked our eyes, blinding us; but somehow we managed to get to our feet and break into a run. We made for the nearest side street and I remember hearing the shouts and the clattering footfall of the men pursuing us. I was aware of my straining lungs tight in my body, the biting sharpness of agonized breaths. Our escape was chaotic and panicked, some of us went one way, others the next, and I was running with Gen a little up ahead, a flitting figure in the night. I pushed myself harder, a cold fear galvanizing my movements. There was someone behind me, I could hear the sound of his breaths, feel him almost on my back. My energy began to drain, and as I started to lose momentum, I felt a sense of helplessness that turned my legs to jelly.

My run stuttered, I found myself falling, only in the next instant I felt a rush of wind, and something seizing me, yanking me off my feet and into the air with such force that, from inside my body, I felt a dull popping sound as my arm was dislocated from my shoulder. The sudden violence of it, the way I was being handled, told me I'd been hurt and yet the pain didn't come all at once, perhaps because of the shock and adrenaline that had flooded my system. Somewhere up ahead I heard a high-pitched yelp and I knew Gen too had been grabbed. The man began to drag me back toward the main street and the cars, and that's when the pain came, and it was like nothing I had known.

I didn't so much cry as scream, not in protest, but because I couldn't do anything else. I hadn't realized it was possible to hurt that much. I was used to being manhandled – both my mother and grandmother pulled me and slapped me on occasion – but this was worse. I begged that man to stop, I pleaded with him, but he dragged me forward. I don't think I ever saw his face, but through the pain I felt the tepid warmth of his breath on my face – adult and sour, the odor of stale coffee and something meaty and putrid. Something on the turn. My head was spinning and I vomited a little, the effluent hot against my skin. He threw me into the back of a car.

Much of the rest is in fragments. I remember being curled up on the back seat. I don't remember wetting myself, but I recall the sensation of warm liquid between my legs. I remember gazing up through the darkness of the window and seeing those same buildings scrolling by, white and strange and high, and as distant as the moon. I remember biting my bottom lip, feeling that the intensity of the pain – of that burning heat inside my shoulder – was never going to end, and yet I wouldn't be able to tolerate one more second of it. The motion of the car, its wheels jerking across fissures and bumps, caused my body to vibrate, and with each vibration I moved, twisting myself in that back seat, and the agony came screaming through me. The pain and disorientation made me feel as though I might die.

I passed out, mercifully, for a period of time. What I remember next is being in a white room, on a hard and solid chair, and

I remember how I kept trying to find the ground with my feet, instinctively, but there was nothing there. I recall my exhaustion, and the gnawing agony in my shoulder. By this point, the tiredness was absolute. There was darkness, and then the dull bright of that white room, and this time Gen was there too. His gaze was vacant, but I knew he had been crying because the skin on his face was shiny. There were two men in the room. One of them had small black eyes, and that is all I can remember. In my mind's eye now they are but shadows. A voice:

'What were you doing there?'

Gen said nothing. I tried to raise my head but the effort was more than I could manage. Still the throbbing pain in my shoulder, and still that weight pulling me down, softening the shock of everything that was happening. The utter exhaustion. I managed in a wretched whimper:

'Please. We were just going out to play. We wanted to play Teng-Teng the Tomato. It was just a game. That was all it was …'

A voice from far away. It grew louder.

'It's never just a game. Nothing is just a game. Whose idea was it? Whose idea was it to inaugurate such counter-revolutionary action? To defy the spirit of the state that bestows its benevolent light on all loyal citizens. Who is behind this blatant act of anti-patriotic sabotage?'

The voice had risen, its words echoed in my head. I was aware that this adult, this figure in a uniform, was now shouting at me, I felt his hot spittle spatter my hair and forehead, but the words he used I didn't understand, and the tone of his voice terrified me into incomprehension.

'Who planned this?' he asked abruptly.

I finally managed to raise my head. I looked toward Gen, and he looked back at me. This question we both understood.

At that moment, Gen's face seemed quite blank, his eyes dark and dull – and yet I understood that he was seeing me, and I knew, instinctively, he had made his decision. Just like that. I knew, without any doubt, that he was going to say it was my fault, that I was the one who planned it. And although some part of me wanted to resist, the combination of exhaustion and fear and pain was such that for the first time in my child's life I felt a genuine sense of hopelessness. It didn't matter that Gen was about to blame me for everything, to reveal I was the one to have orchestrated the insane and fantastical plan we had followed. Nothing mattered anymore.

He looked at me with that same dull stare. And then turned to those men. His voice was toneless.

'She didn't have anything to do with it. It was my idea. I tricked her into it.'

I looked at him. His face seemed to move in and out of focus. Someone was pulling me up, dragging me out the door. I think I screamed, but Gen's face remained blank – that laconic, brutalized stare. I think I screamed as I was pulled from the room and he was left to whatever would happen next. I think I screamed. But I can't really say. Perhaps the scream occurred only in the confines of my head.

Time falls away again. Now I am waiting in that same building but in a different room. My parents enter. My mother is chatting animatedly with a different set of guards. One of them I can almost remember. He was pudgy and a little less threatening. But what I remember most was my father's expression. His face was completely white, drained of all color. He said nothing while my mother

78

gabbled away. At some point, they released me into the care of my parents, and my mother and father led me from the building. I recall asking my parents about Gen, and what was going to happen to him. I don't know if they responded or not. But what I remember most was the certainty that Gen would never leave that awful building. That I had abandoned him to those men, those tall figures, those strange uniforms. And the next time I saw Gen would be when I'd look out of my bedroom window. I'd see the smoke that billowed up from the incinerator at the Beijing Children's Hospital, only now that smoke would form in Gen's features.

SIX

PERHAPS THE STRANGEST THING OF ALL ABOUT THAT night, and the day that followed, was when I found sleep and woke the following morning – the pain in my shoulder rousing me once more. The biggest fear was not whether those men would come for me again, or whether Gen was alive or dead; in that moment, my fear was simply this: how angry would my parents be? I remembered my father's face in the police station, drained of all color; I had caught the tremble that had affected one of his wrists. I knew that spoke to something that, as a child, I couldn't fully understand and yet was fundamentally real. That was the most terrible thing, I think; the fact that my father had been forced to reveal an aspect of himself that he had hitherto kept hidden from the world, which no one should have glimpsed.

In the days and weeks that followed my father was even more taciturn than usual, and in his silences and his glazed-eyed stare, I would catch a sense of recrimination and regret; regret, I felt, that he had a daughter like me. But the day after we had been detained, it was the reaction of my mother I most feared. Getting hauled up before the authorities would not only terrify her but also offend her notion of social status, the fact that respectable people like her were not criminals and it was a humiliation to be treated in such a way. Naturally, I anticipated a furious reaction on my mother's part.

But the reality was different.

She came into my room the next day. As soon as my eyes had cleared of sleep, I flinched, maybe from the anticipation of a slap, maybe from the severity of the memory of the evening before. But instead her voice was soft. She beckoned me from the bed, her expression serious. I followed her as she led me to the bathroom.

Then she did something she hadn't done in years. She took off my clothes. She had already run the bath. I got in. The water was a little hot and it seemed to sigh as my body slipped into it. I don't think I have ever felt so fragile, and yet the touch of that water was blessed. I couldn't stop trembling. My mother took a sponge to my body, gently, gradually, and eventually it found the place between my shoulder and my arm. There was a deep dark welt there – an ugly shadow set into the smooth fabric of myself. I had never seen my own body changed in that way. I'd never experienced myself so transformed and distorted. The throbbing pain was still there, but I couldn't look away. I was hypnotized almost, by the fact of what had been done to me.

When my mother's fingers, gripping that sponge, found that place on my skin, I felt a single shudder run through her body. She touched the sponge to it once more, then gently laid it down. She looked at me briefly, and I saw that her eyes were filled with water. Then she turned away and left the bathroom.

In the days that followed, my family became themselves again. My mother was waspish and chatty, interrogating me, demanding

I fulfill my duties; my father would nod at me when I entered the room before rustling his paper; and my brother would pull a silly face before giggling mischievously.

But I was not the same. It was summer, so there was no school. But when my mother tried to send me on an errand, to collect something from the local shop, I would at once clench up, and if she pushed me, I would retreat into a corner, bowing my head, closing my eyes. At which point she would mutter something along the lines of 'silly, stubborn girl,' but she would leave me be, whereas before she would have dragged me out of the apartment and forced me to be on my way.

It was my grandmother who eventually came to me.

'I need you to do something for me, Little One.'

I looked up. The wrinkles crossed her face like ravines, but her eyes and the glimpse of her smile were unchanging.

'What?' I managed to whisper. I think I already knew she was going to ask me to leave the apartment.

'I want you to come with me, just a little way, outside. We won't be gone for long. We'll be back before you even know it.'

'I don't want to.'

'I know you don't. But the thing is this, Little One. I can't protect you from the world. From all the things that will happen, come what may. No one can. But while I am with you, nothing bad is going to happen. Because I won't let it. Do you understand?'

I looked into her face. She looked so old, yet somehow so strong. I wanted to cry, I wanted to throw myself into her arms. I wanted to run away from her, perhaps I even wanted her to go to hell.

But instead I felt the tears warm in my eyes. I looked away. I felt her hand on my shoulder. And I felt myself rise to my feet. She wasn't pulling me, but guiding me, perhaps. She led me to the door of our apartment, unclicked the lock, opened it. As I stepped through, the noise from the other people on our corridor made me flinch, but I felt my grandmother's hand. A couple of neighbors shouted playful greetings at me, but the sound seemed to blur in a malaise of abstract color before the thudding of my own heart. My throat was dry and I was struggling for breath. But my grandmother's hand was still on me, gentle but firm.

As I stepped out into that blinding light, the sun high in the sky, my eyes were burning. The old woman walked me to the place where I had followed her some time before, across the scraggy patch of land and into that small dilapidated shack. This time I was familiar with the setting, but I was still curious, still had that fascination children have before a living animal. I inched closer. I could feel my grandmother behind me, watching. I saw a movement from the pen she had fashioned, and as my eyes adjusted to the gloom, I saw the chick from before, much larger now, strutting back and forth effortlessly, her walk no longer impeded by the damaged leg, her feathers no longer the yellowy-white of youth, but now flushed with the dappled copper of burgeoning maturity.

I looked back at my grandmother with surprise.

'She got so big!'

'Yes. I told you before. Her leg got snapped at an early age. But that was what made her a fighter!'

I looked again at the bird. Her beady eyes glinted in the shadows. It was as though she was looking right into me, and that look wasn't exactly nice. In fact, the creature looked positively vicious.

'Hold out your hand.'

I held out my hand automatically. My grandmother deposited a scattering of grain into my open palm.

'Feed her!'

'I don't want to, she'll peck me.'

'Feed her.'

'I really don't want to!'

I felt myself on the point of panic. More than anyone else in the family, I listened to my grandmother. I don't know why exactly, it just always seemed to be that way. But at that moment I was ready to scream. I could feel my grandmother's eyes on me in the gloom. She spoke, almost coldly.

'You are right, Little One. She could well peck you. But if you are calm, and if you have courage, she won't. Do you know why?'

'Why?'

'Because although she can't speak like you and me, she can sense your mood. She can feel your feelings. So, if you can calm yourself, and be gentle toward her, she will feel that too.'

Tentatively, slowly, I extended my hand toward the bobbing bird. Having looked at me for a few moments, she drew closer. My hand was trembling. I felt a peck, and then a more gentle motion, as the chick began to eat from my hand. I felt her breast, her feathers, pushed up against my fingers as she fed. And the warmth of her, and the sense of her oblivion as she abandoned herself to the grain I was holding – it felt almost like trust. As though this creature had chosen to put its fragile and precious life in my hands alone. And all at once my face was warm with tears. I turned away from my grandmother so she couldn't see.

Her voice came to me nevertheless, soft but weathered.

'She hurt her leg, but she got better. Because she is strong inside, you see. She walks in a completely straight line now. And that's good.'

PART
II

SEVEN

THE REST OF THE SUMMER PASSED FAINTLY. ITS BALMY heat evaporated before the clear, cold light of autumn. I did not see my friends. I remained mostly in the house, though my mother would sometimes take me shopping with her, weighing my small frame down with heavy items as we left the market. On the way back, I must have appeared to the people on the street not so much a child but a collection of floating shopping bags. When we got home my arms were aching, but I didn't mind. The feeling of not being seen, of being camouflaged, was soothing.

As that strange, fateful summer reached its end, I was on the cusp of a new beginning. The day I'd go to a new school, to high school. I remember the day itself. The cool crispness of our early-morning start, the starched smartness of a school uniform acquired secondhand, re-seamed by my grandmother and then washed by my mother until it felt as good as new. I remember the cool autumn breeze against my outer layers, and on the inside, the warm, slushy anxiety at work in the pit of my belly. What would the other children be like? Would they be bigger than me? Would I make any friends?

Since the night I had been taken to the police station, there were moments where my body would feel heavy and I would struggle to breathe. My heart would race ahead of its own accord and a ribbon of dizziness would ripple across my brain. Objects would lose their coherence; the sky would become an indistinct haze of bright while everything below would collapse into streaks of dark shadow. I would have to stand still for a while before it passed, closing my eyes, listening to the thrum of my heart.

As we got to the school gates, I surveyed the school. It was a large building but of a simple design. It had three floors with many windows running across in neat rows. Its concrete was a smooth ocher that contrasted with the dark, cloudy windows. On the roof there were some large Chinese letters, skeletal figures that spelled out the word Ming – the name of the school. 'Ming' means 'brightness' but there wasn't much of that; even the ocher paint on the walls had faded. As I watched, a small army of children flowed across the courtyard and through the main entrance. My heart began to beat faster. The feeling of that weight on my chest. I looked up at my mother. I couldn't see her face, for it was wreathed in shadow and above her the sky had become a blinding expanse of light. I blinked. I mumbled.

'I don't feel well. Perhaps we could come back tomorrow instead.'

I could not see my mother's face, but even as I was uttering these words I knew they were futile. Her voice was hard as stone.

'You are going. You are not a little girl anymore. We paid a lot for that uniform of yours. We pay a lot for you.'

I turned away from her as the dizziness fizzed and sparked in my brain like an electric storm. The ground seemed to rear up in front of me, and I barely managed to keep my balance. I moved forward, joining the crowd of children flowing into the building. Inside was the smell of body heat and plimsolls, and the muffled, excited whispers of children pressed together, pushing through a long thin corridor until finally we spilled out into a large assembly hall.

We were made to sit while our names were read out, and we were directed to one or other of the six teachers who stood with arms folded, watching. My junior school had been small; two streets from our home, it was little more than a renovated apartment with a small backyard where fifteen or so children would play. Compared to this, it was tiny. We students looked at each other apprehensively, our eyes scanning the rows and rows of children, expectant, unsure. I sneaked fleeting, nervous glances, not wanting to expose myself, anxiety broiling in my belly.

And then I saw Gen. At first I couldn't quite believe it. My fear turned to excitement; in seeing someone I knew, I felt hope. As though the strangeness of the situation had been undone and now there was something familiar to hold on to: a solid rock in an otherwise sweeping, tumbling cascade of unknowns and intangibles. I smiled, I tilted my head, I raised one arm – I did everything I could to get his attention. And then, in that sea of children, his gaze found mine. I had thought I might never see him again and yet there he was.

He looked different in his uniform, taller and more severe, more adult – even though it was only a few months since we had last seen each other. But it wasn't simply that. In the moment I saw him, I was returned to that place; the sense of pain bleeding through my shoulder, the violence of my own screams echoing in my head. But the horror of the experience we had shared was tempered by my relief at seeing him again. So I smiled all the more. His eyes moved across me. I saw in them a flicker of recognition. And then he looked away.

Perhaps he had every right to ignore me. He'd taken the blame for my crime. He'd been interned and I hadn't seen him since I left that building. I hadn't seen any of my friends since that awful night.

But there is a loneliness that comes from being in the midst of people, especially when they are all strangers. You hope desperately for a nod of recognition, a smile of understanding. Everyone else knows each other, it seems, only you are all alone, and the awareness of that makes you flush and tremble. It's akin to being naked in a crowd perhaps – you feel your own vulnerability intensely. So when you see someone else – even if it is someone you don't particularly like – that recognition gives you a sense of security and relief, and you feel warmth toward the person in question. On seeing Gen I felt a great warmth, not simply because I could see that he was okay and unharmed, but because he was someone who tethered me to the familiarity of my past and my friends, and his appearance made the strangeness and isolation of this new reality that much easier to bear. But he had turned away.

That was such a shock to me. I felt utterly alone. They began to call out names. We formed lines. I moved through the process with a sense of disorientation. I felt angry at my mother – why had she insisted on sending me to this place? Those summer evenings of playing in the streets with my friends now seemed to represent the sweetest of freedoms, and a period of wonder from which I had been forever exiled. I thought about Al Lam. I knew she had hated the fact that her parents were going to take her away, but in that moment I envied her. It seemed to me that she had escaped.

I was led into a classroom and directed toward a desk. The teacher seemed impossibly old, though perhaps she wasn't much more than forty. Her tidy, dark hair was streaked with gray, her face was soft and a little plump, and she had dark, limpid eyes. Her name was Chu Hua, and her name, she explained, meant a type of flower: bright and colorful and, more important, one that grows well in the right conditions. That was her mission for us, she explained. She would help 'grow' us in the right conditions.

She was very smiley, so I liked her, and I'd always wanted to be taller than I was, because being tall was a major currency at that age. The taller you were, the more the other kids listened to you. So the idea of being 'grown' was a compelling one. I tried to prick up my ears and listen to what she had to say. As for Gen, I neither knew nor cared what class he had been put into. He could go to hell as far as I was concerned.

Chu Hua explained that there would be a time for listening and a time for questions. When the time for questions came, we should address her as 'miss' or, if we preferred, 'madam.' One smaller boy at the back of the class, who reminded me a little bit of Fan, asked in a small, querulous voice: 'Can we call you "plant grower," if we want?'

For the first time, 'madam's' soft doughy face darkened. Her lips tightened.

'No, that would not be a good idea.'

Her expression brightened once more.

'A people are a people. But they are also a legacy.'

I had always been intrigued by words. I would try and hold on to them, especially the ones I didn't know. I'd roll them around in my mouth, tasting them, like a sweet. 'Legacy' was one I didn't know. I murmured it under my breath.

'Yes?'

I suddenly realized the teacher was looking at me.

'Do you have something to say?'

I felt the red flush climb high in my cheeks, and the gazes of the other students burning into me. She hadn't spoken in a cruel way, exactly. And I desperately wanted to respond, to explain that I too wanted to grow like a flower, that I wasn't trying to be rude. But the words got caught in my throat as I felt myself blush.

Chu Hua turned away and her face lit up once again.

'Our legacy involves people just like you!'

She pointed at us, beaming.

'People with ordinary lives, just like you, are what makes our country so noble and free. Humble people but loyal people, the type of good people you will grow up to be. And do you know who was one of the best?'

We did not.

'A humble, loyal man named Lei Feng.'

We blinked.

'Let me ask you something more.'

Her features were animated, enthused.

'How many of you use a toothbrush?'

We glanced around at each other. A few of the braver ones at the front raised their hands. Gradually the rest of us followed.

'Well, Lei Feng was a great soldier who was once your age. And like you, he also used a toothbrush. And do you know what? He used that toothbrush until all the bristles fell away, but he kept rubbing his gums with that toothbrush for decades after because he would not allow himself to use a single voucher from the People's State to buy a new one. He did not want to cost the communist ideal!'

I was impressed by this. Lei Feng must have been very brave indeed, for I knew what it was like when the bristles on your toothbrush started to disintegrate: it got very painful very quickly. And while the idea of using only the wooden stump, rubbing it up against your teeth, seemed kind of odd, it also showed great determination. And, according to Chu Hua, this wasn't the only determined or brave thing this Lei Feng had done. Apparently he'd also refused to use spades and gloves in the fields, resorting to his own hands, so that his comrades could use the utilities he himself had declined. And he would do this in the frostiest winter conditions.

Unfortunately, Lei Feng had died in an accident.

The same small boy squeaked out from the back of the class:

'What kind of accident?'

Chu Hua gazed at him in a haughty fashion. And then, without responding, turned and beamed at the rest of us.

I wondered if the accident had involved some form of frostbite.

'Now,' Chu Hua declared, 'we are all to sing a song honoring Lei Feng's memory.'

There were many verses of that song. Many. The first ran:

> *Learn from Lei Feng's good example,*
> *Loyal to the revolution, loyal to the Party,*
> *All of China seeks to marvel,*
> *In his good stead, we hope, with faith and hearty!*

Each of us had to learn a verse, and then recite it. I was working with a cross-eyed and severe girl at the desk next to me. When our turn came round, she recited her lines perfectly, but I stumbled and misspoke. Again Chu Hua looked at me.

'When you are not supposed to speak, you mumble. When you are supposed to speak, you mumble. Can you do anything but mumble?'

A ripple of laughter ran across the class. For the second time I felt humiliated. I bowed my head. Then we did some maths, which was okay. In fact, it was a relief. I finished it quicker than some of the others as I had always been good at maths. In the interim, I jotted down the words of the verse I had misspoken. I went over them in my head. At the end of the lesson, as I had suspected, Chu Hua – or 'madam' – asked us to recite the verses about the peasant hero Lei Feng once more.

When it came to my turn, I recited my lines perfectly. Because they were automatic, dull even, I no longer worried about them. And that, in itself, felt good. I was no longer on the spot, no longer 'naked' among my peers. In committing a series of words to memory and reciting them automatically, I could become almost invisible. Nobody would look at me. Nobody would bother me. Nobody would see.

.　　　.　　　.

Those first few years of high school passed in much the same way. Chu Hua had a formal manner; she required us to memorize lines of verse or maths formulae, and when a student faltered or failed she combined her acid tongue with her sour voice to draw attention to their humiliation in front of the others. And yet, at the same time, she seemed genuinely concerned that we learn, and every now and then would award sweets if a student achieved a particular milestone. She was a bureaucrat – unquestioningly devoted to the state whether under Mao or the present incumbent – but there was a sense that the rules she imparted would see us right in the future, and this seemed important to her. Though I had no real evidence, no knowledge of her life outside the small crucible of our class, she struck me as being profoundly lonely. Perhaps it took one to know one. As time passed, the memories of my childhood friends – Jian, Zhen, Fan, Al Lam – gradually softened, fading into the mists of the past, and I no longer missed them with the same fierceness. I became comfortable in my isolation; it was like an old, mottled blanket I could slip over myself, a barrier between my being and the world. I would recite my lines in class automatically and when the teacher's attention moved on to the next student, I would drift off into a gentle world of my own imagining.

Of course, Gen was still there. He was not in my class, but I would see him every now and then in the corridor with other boys, but more often than not alone – in the courtyard at the back of the school, under an old blossom tree, a book propped in his hands. He was, perhaps, lonely too, but it never seemed to bother him. Even from a distance he had that same aloofness I remembered. Since that first day in the new school, we had not so much as acknowledged one another's presence. He had become someone I was only ever-so-slightly aware of. I would catch sight of him from a distance, and there was a faint flowering of memory, both bitter and sweet. The time spent with my friends that summer mingled with other images, other sensations. The sour odor of a man's sweat. The acrid scent of bleached floors. The feeling of a steel desk, glimpses of faces, hard and angry. I could not talk to Gen about what had happened that night. And yet it lay there between us, a darkness, never quite dispelled by the crowds of schoolchildren gathered in the courtyard, chattering and shouting boisterously in the afternoon sun. It would be several years before he and I would speak again, and that exchange would not take place in school.

Instead, it happened in Tiananmen Square.

When Chu Hua announced the school trip, she was smiling radiantly, her eyes so impossibly happy they were shining with tears. In the years she had been our teacher I had never seen her that way. She explained to us in a halting voice that it was her class, *our* class, who had been selected to make the trip. One of my classmates, Qiang Bolin, blurted out the question we had all been thinking: 'Where are we going?' Usually, if a student spoke without being asked, Chu Hua would fix them with a withering gaze; our teacher would look at you until it became painful and you would murmur repentance under your breath. But not this time. Chu Hua couldn't control her excitement as she squealed in delight:

'We are going to Tiananmen Square. We have been granted access to the mausoleum. You are all going to see ... *him*. You will all have the privilege of seeing ... the Chairman.'

We gasped. Alongside Confucius and the First Emperor, Mao Zedong had become one of the emblems of Chinese history and grandeur, even though Mao had only been dead for a handful of years while the others had had their reputations burnished by millennia. Even though many members of our families still bore the wounds of the Cultural Revolution. Of course, we children knew nothing of such things – or if we did, we intuited them vaguely, at the edge of our consciousness, like a dark and primordial memory one can no longer quite grasp. So we screamed and clapped on hearing the announcement, and rather than curtail our boisterousness, Chu Hua smiled all the more, tears of pride sparkling in her eyes.

When I got home, I was full of myself. I had managed to do well at school, not just because I kept my head down, but because I'd traveled some distance from those early days when I had played on street corners with my friends. Then, I had struggled to figure out the syllables and patterns of the Mandarin script; now I was much more at home with them. More than that, I found I liked disappearing into the books we were given. Each unlocked a world with its words, allowing the reality before me to evaporate, so I might slip into a more lulling and faraway existence.

I was as excited as the others. Like them, I knew Mao as a figure who could slay giants – I'd seen his image reflected back at me in a never-ending series of walls, posters, and flags. He was someone who had stridden across China in a single Long March, who had vanquished all our enemies. In the minds of us children, he was somewhere between hero and god: a fairy-tale figure who kept the monsters from the door. And now I had been chosen to see Mao Zedong himself. To stand only a few feet away from him. To gaze upon his face.

When I returned home that Friday, I was buzzing with excitement. I ran into my mother the moment I stepped through the door. Sensing I was happy about something, her face fell. But I couldn't hold back. I told her that I'd been selected to go on a trip to see the Chairman. I almost sang the words.

My mother flinched, as though she had touched something hot. At the same time, there was a real moment of indecision and struggle in her face. The honor that I and my classmates had been accorded was a real one. Not just to visit the mausoleum but to be allowed into the inner sanctum. To be in touching distance of the Chairman himself. As a young adolescent, I had my mother figured out in that respect. She was conflicted because, although she balked at the thought of praising me, at the same time she knew such an honor would also reflect well on her.

She stood there for a few moments; she was still a little taller than me in those days, so she was still able to look down on me. Torn as she was, she eventually snapped:

'You make sure you don't do anything to shame our family. Not in front of the ... the Chairman.'

I giggled involuntarily. I didn't mean to. It was the way my mother had spoken: sharp and declamatory, and then her voice had hesitated and softened. 'Not in front of the ... the Chairman.' Despite my own sense of reverence for Mao Zedong, he was nevertheless dead, and anything shameful I did was unlikely to be picked up on by him. Nevertheless, in my head I pictured the cadaver of the Great Helmsman suddenly punching his way through the barrier – like a zombie in one of those banned American films – before bursting out of the mausoleum, and rampaging through the city in order to find my mother and let her know exactly how shameful her daughter's behavior had been.

Unfortunately my mother was not privy to the humorous vision my mind had conjured up so instead she slapped me hard across the back of my head.

By the weekend before the class trip to Tiananmen Square, more and more of our neighbors had found out about the honor I had been gifted. My Aunty Zhao slipped into our apartment on Sunday evening, surprising us at the table. She was apologetic and yet she was looking at me with an expression of wonder, as though seeing me for the first time. She and my mother kissed cheeks in the way they always did, and Aunty Zhao apologized in a soft mumble for having interrupted our dinner, but her eyes never left my face. After a silence that began to grow uncomfortable, she darted toward me and slipped a single red rose onto my lap, a flower that had been carefully wrapped with cellophane.

'I know that they say you can't actually get that near. But, if you get the chance, my niece, please lay this flower as close to … as close to *him* as you can!'

For the first time I felt not so much proud as embarrassed. Nevertheless, I promised my aunty that I would. She nodded her head and shuffled out of the room.

We continued to eat. My mother's eyes narrowed and she glowered at me.

'You'd better be on your best behavior! You had better not disgrace Mao!'

My grandmother laid down her chopsticks. She looked at my mother.

'You haven't forgotten what happened at the end of the fifties, have you, daughter?'

My mother, sharp-eyed and cautious, looked at my grandmother.

My grandmother continued to munch a potato, turning it over in her mouth rhythmically and relentlessly like a tumble dryer. Her voice was placid, unassuming.

'I don't like to dwell on the past,' my mother remarked warily.

'But the famine, daughter. I am sure you remember that. The bodies in the streets. You remember them too, right?'

My mother's face was taut with an emotion I couldn't decipher.

'What's that got to do with anything? He was the leader of our country. He took us into the modern era. He gave us so much. You, you can't make an omelet … without, without breaking eggs!'

'And the cannibalism. In the countryside. Do you remember when that started happening, daughter?'

There was something terrible in my grandmother's toad-like face, something that belied the calmness of her voice.

My mother was ashen-faced. She arched toward my grandmother, extending a long brittle arm across the table, jabbing a finger.

'You, you won't talk about such … *vulgar things* in front of my children.'

In the same moment, my little brother Qiao, who was then almost six, raised his smiley face still slick with grease. He looked at our mother.

'What means … hanaballmism?'

My grandmother ruffled a sticky patch of my brother's cowlicked hair with affection, but her gaze never left my mother.

'You are right, daughter, I shouldn't be so … *vulgar*!'

The tautness in my mother's face seemed to relax. She turned to her food once again.

'But I tell you this much,' my grandmother continued with that same terrible calm. 'The bodies they left rotting on the dirty ground, they were vulgar enough. They caused quite a stench. I can still remember the smell of them. But I doubt it was anything compared with the smell that bag o' shit gives off in his clean and comfortable mausoleum.'

My grandmother looked at me, and all the sarcasm and sharpness in her expression were gone. Instead, there was a sadness that I couldn't quite fathom.

'Congratulations on your big day, granddaughter. I am proud of you. But if you get too close to *him*, don't forget to hold your nose!'

My mother shrieked at my father, who'd been watching the exchange from his world of subdued silence.

'Do you have nothing to say about this?'

She looked at the rest of us in anguish. As though we had betrayed her, everything she had done for us. And at that moment, I felt as though we had, somehow. She picked up the closest plate and dashed it to the ground. The sound it made ripped across the room and even my grandmother jumped in shock.

Not for the first time, my mother left the table in tears.

EIGHT

THE MORNING WAS CLEAR: A BLUE SKY, BOUNDLESS AND bright in the early light. We stood huddled in the crisp winter air, waiting to board an old bus, our hearts brimming with the type of excitement only youngsters can know, bodies in big coats jostling up against one another, suppressed giggles rippling through our numbers in waves.

All at once we were tumbling onto the decrepit vehicle and before I knew it I was pressed up against a window, the coach hissing as it pulled away from the school. There were two other coaches still parked up; we were in the first to depart, and as we pulled out onto the road, I felt a sense of exhilaration as though this was what it meant to be free.

It's strange, isn't it? The trips you take as a child – the ones that take you beyond the boundaries of your own neighborhood toward unknown horizons – seem to last forever. It feels as though you have traveled hundreds of miles. Only when you make the same journey as an adult do you understand it was not so far at all.

As I pressed my nose against the cold of the window, the excitable chatter of the other children seemed to blur and grow indistinct. Because of the morning's winter cold, I was wrapped in jumpers and a thick coat. Gradually, the heat of that rickety old coach and the warmth from all the passengers worked its way into me. The night before, sleep had taken a long time to arrive. My excitement, my anticipation of the day to come, had kept me awake. I'd woken early too – the coach was scheduled to leave some time before school would usually start. I felt tired. The chugging motion of the vehicle was rhythmic, lulling. My head grew heavy.

When I opened my eyes again the scenery had changed. The bus was moving faster now, on a bigger, wider road. We were driving by apartment blocks stacked many stories high. The multiple lanes of the road were heavy with traffic. It looked different in the light of day, yes, but I recognized it from that night, years before. We were passing through Chang'an Avenue. Before long we could see the rich red of Tiananmen Tower set against a pastel blue sky that seemed to go on forever. We were pressing our faces to the windows, and Chu Hua had to urge quiet. The bus came to a wheezing stop and we all lurched forward. There was a single yelp followed by laughter and then the voice of Chu Hua telling us once again to quiet down.

When we exited the vehicle, we saw soldiers in dull green uniforms, their guns slung over their shoulders. We walked to Tiananmen Square in silence. Only Chu Hua talked. She pointed out the various historical sites, her voice throaty with pride in the crisp cold air. Finally she showed us the Zhongnanhai compound where the most important party officials lived. She spoke of them with the same reverence the religious might use when entering a monastery. We came to the gate of the mausoleum, where a long queue had formed. Workers and peasants selected by their units for this honor were waiting politely alongside regiments of soldiers.

We waited for an hour or so, but again time stretched and elongated, so it felt like an eternity. We began to fidget and whisper in exasperation, so Chu Hua let us eat one of the sandwiches we had packed for the trip. Her gambit worked. Our building impatience was offset by the sound of our collective munching, when suddenly the queue surged forward. We hastily stuffed half-finished sandwiches back into bags in order to press ahead.

It was a little like being on a roller coaster. We'd had to wait for so long that I'd become listless, but when we began to move through the great doors of the building there was a rush of anticipation and excitement, bordering on fear. This was to be one of the most important experiences of my life. My mind began to race. When I laid eyes on the great man, how should I react? What would I feel? I decided then and there that I would feel something incredibly powerful. That his aura of nobility would by some magic transfer itself to me.

As we stepped into the first section, darkness fell, and for a moment we were all as shadows. I could feel the tripping of my heart. Then we crossed into a main chamber flooded with light, and I had to raise my hand to protect my squinting eyes. The long line of people was flowing around a large space; we walked along a strip of orange carpet that ran along the edges of the room. The walls were a soft ocher. At the far wall was a huge marble statue of the Great Helmsman seated on a chair, overlooking the ant-sized figures that were filtering through the chamber. His face was giant, formless and white.

In the middle of the chamber I glimpsed a glass coffin. We were separated from it by thick velvet ropes and some distance; and people were so densely gathered, it was difficult to see past them. I pushed and jostled as the long line continued its rotation of the room. I was afraid I might miss seeing ... *him* altogether. But I pressed underneath someone's arm and I finally had a clear view.

But I felt nothing.

All I saw was a rather portly old man, dressed in a gray suit, lying on his back. His face looked as though it had been laminated in the same orange hue as the rest of the room. For a few moments, I was certain I was looking at some kind of mannequin; I was sure that this was a fake, a construct shaped from wax that had been used to replace the real body of the deceased leader. For, despite the grandeur of this great orange room and that shiny orange face, he nevertheless looked like a small and unassuming elderly man. He looked ... *ordinary.*

I only had a short window of time to reflect on such impressions before the image of the Chairman was lost and the line filtered onwards, through the exit and into another room. This was a darker room, dimly lit, with a series of black-and-white photographs mounted on walls. Each photo featured men huddled together against a backdrop of mountains or swamplands. These were the faded images from 1934–5, the Long March undertaken by the Red Army, but I didn't take the time to examine them. I was standing with a group of students from my class; they were describing in excited tones the exhilaration they had felt at being in *his* presence. I tried to add my own voice to their enthusiasm. I made a casual remark – something along the lines of how seeing Mao in reality was so much better than seeing him on the posters – but it got lost in the general cacophony of adulation and nobody noticed. I felt bereft. I hadn't been touched by the experience the way the others had. There was something in me that was missing, incapable of feeling what I should have felt.

I wandered off a little way. I stood before one of those black-and-white pictures: a group of faded, exhausted figures trooping over a mountain pass, their rifles slung over their shoulders. They all looked old and tired, and their lives seemed so far away from my own as I stood in the pristine gloom of this modern building. I glanced back toward my school group. I could not make out their features in the soft shadow, but I could see the figure of Chu Hua, taller than the rest, gesturing with her arms, and I could sense the enthusiasm, their animation. I turned back to the faded picture. For a moment it was as though I was in a kind of limbo – an exile from time and place – and the feeling of loneliness was so exquisite that tears welled in my eyes.

I sensed someone standing beside me. I glanced up. Gen was next to me, his dark eyes shining softly, expressionless as he observed the photo. He had got considerably taller, his jaw had hardened and his face had acquired a sharper and more adult definition. He looked handsome, but in a cold, fastidious sort of way. He brought his hand to his neck, adjusting his tie reflexively, and yet there was nothing out of place in his neat, orderly appearance. He looked down at me, then cast a withering gaze back toward where our schoolmates had gathered.

'It's such a crock of shit,' he said softly. 'All this weeping and hand-wringing for some backward peasant who refused to take one step into the modern world.'

Although his voice had barely raised above a whisper, it sent a frisson of shock through me. With the exception of my grandmother, I'd never heard anyone speak poorly of Mao, and even she wouldn't have talked that way in a public place. But more than that, Gen had not spoken in an obscene way, the way my grandmother sometimes did. Instead his words were controlled and contemptuous, and he sounded deeply ... intellectual. I remember, despite myself, being impressed. He walked away without another word.

When I got home, the whole corridor was abuzz with activity. Various neighbors came shuffling into our apartment to quiz me in tentative tones laced with wonder. What was it like to lay eyes on him? Was it true that his gaze followed you around the room? Was it the case that his face had grown more youthful with the passing of time? My responses were feasted on, every word hungrily devoured. Even my mother seemed not to begrudge me my moment in the sun. I tried to meet their expectations with my answers.

But the more I talked, the more I tried to give life to the lie, the more degraded I felt. It was as though every word from my mouth became heavier, slower – the sounds petrifying until at last they were foreign objects, brittle and dead, bearing no relation to me. It was like birthing stone. As the minutes became hours, I grew ever more sluggish, ever more exhausted, until that sense of heaviness had seeped into my bones and it was a struggle to raise my head, to push out the next sentence. My mother's happy smile became taut and rigid, until at one point she gave the soft skin of my belly a hard pinch. 'Mrs. Liu just asked you a question, dear! Pay attention now!'

Mercifully, the neighbors began to slip back to their own residences. My mother peered at me through narrowed eyes as though

I had once again sought to undo her best endeavors – the consequence of some unfathomable sneakiness and malevolence on my part. But I was too tired to try to pacify her, to try to explain. In any event, I didn't have the words. I was about to head off to bed when I felt a gentle touch on my shoulder. A shiver of anxiety ran through me, for my first thought was that it was yet another neighbor hungry for details. But when I turned, I saw my father there, his mole-like eyes soft in the gloom. At that point he was still taller than me, yet already he seemed reduced. He was a little bent over, his shoulders hunched. He blinked rapidly – five times in succession – and then raised a hand to rub his eyes, the motion awkward, almost apologetic. If my mother was the sun, all heat and fire, perpetually ready to scold, then my father was the moon, a more melancholy presence that would peek out from behind a night-time shroud of cloud every now and again. He leaned into me, a small figure squinting in the dimness, and already in his frame, in his bearing, were the intimations of the old man he was never destined to become.

'Get your coat, daughter. I want you to take a walk with me,' he said quietly.

'Where are we going?'

'Get your coat.'

We slipped out into the night. The air was frosty, and our breath emerged in plumes of ghostly steam against the dark. We walked in silence. I found it difficult to talk to my father at the best of times, but on the few occasions we were alone together it was excruciating. We walked down a few streets. Eventually we crossed a road into a cemetery. I thought perhaps we might be visiting one of the graves there, but instead we continued on, exiting on the other side. Then we came to a quieter street. There was an empty bus stop illuminated in a melancholy glow. Beyond that, the outline of a large jagged wall. As we got closer, I could make out a scattering of figures gathered there. We got closer still. There must have been at least twenty people. They stood at various places along the wall, leaning in to peer at it. I had never seen anything so strange. I looked at my father questioningly.

'What are they doing? What are *we* doing?'

'It's called a "memory wall." And they are … remembering.'

'Remembering what?'

'You have heard about the Cultural Revolution at school, right?'

I nodded.

'Well, there are some things your teachers didn't tell you. But I think you are old enough to know. During that time, many people were disappeared.'

'Disappeared?'

'Yes. Taken. Often at night. Workers. Teachers. Engineers. Intellectuals. Some were put in prison. Some were …'

His voice trailed away.

'Why?' I asked in a husky syllable.

He unfurled a single small hand. The gesture was both poignant and helpless.

'I … I don't know. I think, sometimes, for men who are high up in government, power becomes an end in itself. They want to maintain that power, that control, at all costs. So they seek to control others. To regulate their lives. Sometimes even their thoughts.'

I frowned. I felt that what my father was trying to explain was terribly important. But it was elusive.

'And these people? This wall?'

'People put up letters on the wall. Accounts. Stories of what happened to them during the Cultural Revolution. Some were written from within the camps themselves, prisoners who would write clandestine notes to the families they had been separated from. Others are about those men and women who never returned home. Who they were in life. The things they liked to do. Some are poems written for those people. So they … are not forgotten.'

Even for a quiet man, his voice was softer than I had ever heard it. He placed a hand on my shoulder and gently moved me forward.

'Go see.'

I walked toward the others. Candles had been placed at the bottom of the wall and their soft light illuminated the patches of words and colors that had been pinned tenderly to stone. Some of the men and women stood farther back, taking quick glances at certain sections of the wall. I would later come to understand that people stood at a distance so they could make out what was written while others wouldn't be able to tell which bit of the wall they were reading from. For fear their activities might be seen by government spies.

I, of course, had no such thoughts or anxieties. By that point, I had come to love reading; words were the medium in which I moved most freely, feeling myself as light as air and as distant as the mountains. I slipped into the joy and sadness of those accounts of people who were no more; people who seemed to call out from the wall with silent voices. Accounts of suffering, but also of great love; stories woven into the fabric of stone; the names of those who had gone rendered as eternal as the stars. For some time I was just a presence in the darkness, when all at once I felt my father's hand on my shoulder, returning me to myself once more. In the arching, flickering glow of the candles, without saying a word, my father motioned me toward a single inscription. I peered at it, reading what had been written there.

I am not a writer, my words are awkward
Lonely rather than beautiful.
In the dark, everything is lost.
But it is there where I see my daughter's face

For a few moments I pondered the words. And then I realized. *I understood.* I must have been little more than a baby at the time he was gone. But he had written about me. I felt something fall away, and it almost stole my breath. I turned to my father. He was breathing so quietly but he couldn't look at me. I turned away because I did not want him to see the tears in my eyes. Very gently, and for a brief moment, he squeezed my hand. It is the only time I remember him ever doing that. We turned and walked back into the night.

NINE

I WENT BACK TO THE 'MEMORY WALL.' NOT WITH MY
father, however. What he had been trying to communicate
had been said that evening, and it was something we never spoke
of again. Instead I would visit the wall on my own. I wouldn't tell
anyone. Sometimes I would head there straight after school. I would
read the poems, including the one my father had left for me. I would
read the names of the people who had disappeared. Murmuring the
names of those people under my breath made me feel – wherever
they were – they might not be so lonely anymore. And that made
me feel less lonely too.

One day I arrived on a gray afternoon. And there was nothing left
but rubble. They had smashed it in the early hours. I had supposed
it would happen, sooner or later. I saw one or two people walking
on the other side of the road, but I felt certain I was the only person
to have come to see the monument. Now I was the sole mourner at
its wake. I did not feel sad exactly. Only a gentle, numbing feeling.
Hopelessness. The memory wall had been a delicately wrought structure, formed by the feelings and colors of the past, held together by

love and loss. It had been in some way … sacred, because it was more than simple bricks and mortar; it had, for a short and precious time, housed the ghosts of the past.

But what did any of that mean against the brute force of diggers and bulldozers? What did it mean when there was something stronger, something meaner, something harder that could come along and smash it to smithereens? It suddenly seemed to me this was life's inevitable corollary; that imagination would always be papered over by propaganda, that the poets and peacemakers would always be stamped out by those who had force on their side.

And yet. I'd memorized what my father had written about me; those words lived in me now. Perhaps the same was true for others.

I kneeled down and took a small piece of white rock and placed it in my pocket. From above, the grayness of the sky grew darker and it began to rain. Feeling the cold beads of water clinging to my hair and lacing my skin, I felt a shrill of warm melancholy. I stayed there for a few moments, as still as I could, a small human statue protruding from the rubble, but then the downpour became a deluge, and I bolted, running for cover. The sky above became a mass of churning vaporous gray, a great vortex bordered by slashes of vicious black cloud.

From within that mass of gray, lightning peeled and rippled, and the sound of thunder rumbled so loudly it shook the ground with its violence. Pulling my jacket up and over my head, I scooted down a side street, trying in vain to shield myself from the rain, but the street itself had become a moving river. My feet squelched and sank in the rivulets of water that were rushing down concrete gullies; the water was everywhere, squeaking in the skin at the small of my back, slithering across my toes. And when I tried to peer into the murky gloom ahead, my vision was blurred and fragmented by the rain.

Blinking furiously, I managed to make out the shape of a doorway – a shop. I stumbled toward it and pushed the door open, hearing a faint tinkle of a bell against the backdrop of slapping, pounding rain. Once again, a great yawn of thunder pealed across the heavens, shaking me to the bones. I slammed the door shut behind me with a gasp.

I wiped my face with a soaking sleeve and blinked. I was in a dark shadowy room of books. There were books everywhere. Books on old shelves. Books in piles on the floor. Books stacked in columns from the floor rising toward the ceiling, like thick, crooked plants shooting up from the ground. Rickety old stairs led down to the main section where someone sat at a desk, their figure illuminated by candlelight. I wanted to disappear behind a bookcase, to wait until the storm had spent its force, until my clothes and skin had been dried by the warm air that was rich and lazy with the dusky scent of old leather and paper. But the proprietor had already seen me. I had been raised to be obsequiously polite to adults, deferential to a fault, so I made my way toward him, still blinking the raindrops from my eyes.

'Hello, sir,' I said.

He looked up at me. His old puckered face was a rich burnished brown ravined with wrinkles, and two misty blue eyes gazed out, shimmering with amusement.

'Spot of rain out there, is there?' he asked, smiling.

In the same moment, the thunder crashed, and the bookstore itself seemed to tremble.

'Yes, sir, there is a drop or two!' I said, with as haughty a tone as I could, for even I realized when I was being mocked.

He smiled all the more, and then the lines on his forehead wrinkled in consternation, and he waved one straggly arm at me.

'Well, what are you waiting for?' he spluttered. 'Come in. Come sit down. I'll make us some tea.'

I took a seat at the old mahogany desk. The old man shuffled out of the room. When he came back, he brought two small cups of green tea. The china was cracked and worn, and the rims were a little dirty. But I didn't want to appear impolite, so I took a sip. Perhaps because of my damp and clammy skin, the tea tasted particularly sweet and reviving. In fact, it might have been the best cup I'd ever had.

The thunder rumbled again, though it sounded farther away this time. The old man's face wrinkled with delight.

'Are you frightened by thunder and lightning?' he asked.

'No, sir,' I said stiffly, feeling I was being mocked again.

'I only ask because some children are.'

'I am almost fourteen, sir.'

The old man smiled again, but this time with a hint of pathos.

'Forgive me. I am very old, as you can see. To me, most people look like children.'

I felt a little sorry for him then. So I ventured a confidence.

'I didn't think I was frightened of thunder and lightning. But just now ... outside ... I did get a bit scared.'

He nodded his head in grave understanding.

'You know what is interesting? Here in China people are taught from an early age to be afraid of thunder and lightning. But there are some places in the world where that is not the case. Did you know that?'

'I did not.'

'Yes,' he said, his tone becoming more animated. 'Do you know where Denmark is?'

'It is in Scandinavia, sir.'

'Yes, yes, that's quite right. A long time ago, the people who lived in those regions were called Vikings. They taught their children about thunder according to their religious beliefs. And they believed that thunder was the sound of one of their gods, Thor, fighting with evil giants in the skies. He would throw his invincible hammer and the sound it would make each time it struck an evil giant was the sound of thunder. So, at night, when the Viking children heard thunder, they would know not to be afraid. It was just Thor protecting their world from the evil giants who lived beyond it. Isn't that nice? Isn't that wonderful?'

The old man was clearly delighted with this information; he looked at me expectantly.

I nodded my head and smiled. It was a nice story.

His enthusiasm seemed to swell.

'I've got just the book for you. Just the book!'

He got up from his seat, his spindly body creaking and wheezing, and he stumbled away. I heard a rustling and rummaging and then a louder clatter. I couldn't help but smile. He returned, more disheveled and panting. He dropped the book neatly onto the desk, almost displacing his tea.

'There,' he said with satisfaction. '*Norse Myths*. As you will note, it is the '53 edition, a beautifully rendered work by Larsson with illustrations by Steig.'

It did indeed look like a beautiful book; the faint image of an otherworldly map, replete with castles made of cloud, scratched into the rich leather parchment. He pushed it toward me.

'Thank you, but I can't, sir.'

For the first time his eyes became timorous, almost fearful.

'You mean to say you don't like reading?'

'Oh no, not at all. I love reading. I love storybooks and poems and books about history too.'

'So what's the problem?'

'I ... I don't have ... money.'

His expression crinkled in a frown and he rubbed the stubble on his chin thoughtfully.

'Well ... well, how about this? You take the book home with you. And read it. And when you are done, you bring it back. What do you say?'

His eyes were shining with hope. For a second it seemed as though he were the child and I the adult.

I nodded. He clapped his hands in delight, the childlike gesture once again belying his years, and I couldn't help but smile shyly in return.

I shuffled out of the shop with my precious cargo clutched underneath my jacket. The storm had exhausted itself with its own ferocity, leaving in its wake only a mild drizzle, and from the streets arose a faint, diaphanous mist. The buildings appeared as dark shapes behind that gauze of gray and the few people who were fumbling their way through the beclouded air seemed as shadows, stencilled against the darkening gloom. The air was cool but fresh, and after the warmth of the bookshop and the hot tea, the tips of my fingers began to tingle.

I pressed the book against me. I was terribly excited and could not wait to get home to read it. Already I knew that I wouldn't tell my mother or father about the book. I wouldn't even tell my grandmother. It seemed to me that the old man and I had entered into a special pact. And it was nice to have some part of my life separate from my family. It was nice to have a secret. I thought about his ancient, withered face, but with eyes mild and youthful, and was filled with a sense of wonder. I think I understood why he had lent me the book. Because he knew I would come back to return it. And – in that little shop, nestled in that back alley – his days and his evenings were perhaps lonely. In that way, we weren't so different. I was surrounded by people at school, it was true, but I didn't have any real friends. Which meant I was lonely too.

I got to my building, climbed the stairs and entered the corridor. I was still wrapped in my thoughts of gods and thunder when I heard a muffled yelp. I turned. One of the doors on the corridor was ajar. I think, even at that point, I knew something was wrong. I knew whatever was going on behind that door was something I didn't want to see. Shouldn't see. But I was pulled toward it with dreamlike inevitability. I saw my arm stretch out in front of me, pushing the door open. I found myself stepping inside.

In the gloom I saw two people, our neighbors the Cuis. Dongmei and her husband Yunxu. They were a childless, younger couple who mostly kept to themselves. Dongmei was hunched up on the floor, her back pressed against a wall, helpless and terrified. Her mouth was bleeding. Yunxu was standing over her. A shopping bag had been split, its contents rolled out across the floor. My stomach lurched. Dongmei was trembling violently – I had never seen an adult so frightened. As though sensing my presence, Yunxu turned his head. When I had seen him in the corridor in the past, I had inclined my head slightly and said 'Hello, sir' as I did with all the adults on our block. He had returned my greeting, friendly enough but faraway, as though he were looking through me. That was not unusual, for adults rarely see children. But this time he saw me. There was something strange and desperate and ugly in his expression, and the corners of his lips turned downward in a feral leer. He blinked twice, and lurched his way toward me. I saw the shadows under his eyes. His gaze was bleary and bloodshot. He too was trembling. But not with fear. With rage. He leaned into me, deliberately. His breath stank of alcohol. He grinned but the grin was deformed and threatening.

'You like to listen in, don't you, you dirty little bitch!'

It was little more than a whisper, but there was in it something so obscene, something so hateful. He pulled his hand back. I felt he was going to hurt me, I was sure of it, but I remained rooted to the spot, paralyzed with shock. Then he brought his mouth close to my face, and gave a single rancid belch. The warm stench clung to my skin, and I felt myself gag.

He laughed.

I pulled away, my eyes hot with tears. I entered my own apartment. I kept my head down, passing my mother in the kitchen, slipping into my room without a word. I took out my book and laid it carefully on my desk. I could still taste the foul tang of Yunxu's breath. I felt a sob rise up within me. I lay on my bed and gazed up at the ceiling. There was a mobile in the corner of the room; fashioned from silver paper, it featured a gently rotating series of stars and moons. It was a relic from the days when my brother was a baby and had shared my room. Then the mobile had hung over his cot. Now it was turning in the gloom, the silver of its paper stars and moons catching the meager light, gleaming softly in the shadows. And I felt a yearning to be a small child again; to be cocooned in safety and warmth; vaguely aware that the world around you is one of magical stars and fairy-tale moons and that nothing in it is malevolent or sharp.

My mother called. I heard the sounds of my family settling down to dinner. My mother called again. I got up and went to join them. My mother had prepared a sweet and sour soup. It was piping hot and its steam sheened our faces. I felt the heat as a thick vapor, and warm water gathered in my eyes. My brother Qiao, now almost eight, was often so boisterous at the dinner table that my mother would have to shush him or my father would have to shoot him one of his 'very serious' looks. Even that wasn't always enough, because my brother's bawdy delight along with his gap-toothed grin could often steal a smile from the most severe of remonstrators. But that day he was quiet. I felt his gaze on me, regarding me with a gentle quietness, until finally he spoke a single question so softly it was almost a whisper.

'Why are you sad, sister?'

I looked at him and his image blurred, the steam rising from the soup, and tears filling my eyes. I tried to hold it in but instead I began to sob quietly, my family looking on in astonishment.

'What on earth has happened?' asked my mother.

I managed to pull myself together.

'It's nothing,' I mumbled.

My grandmother looked at me. She didn't really do consolation but when she spoke there was a softness in her voice that almost had me crying again.

'It's certainly something.'

Everyone was looking at me. I didn't want to – I didn't want to return to the incident, but I had to say something.

'Mr. Cui from number eight. He … he …'

My grandmother's face had hardened, her eyes were like stones.

'He what?'

'He told me … a bad word.'

'What was it?'

'I don't … want to say!'

I had started to cry again. But my grandmother's lips remained tight.

'I don't care what you want. I ask you again. What was it?'

I looked at her; for a moment she seemed like someone else, and her coldness frightened me. I looked at my mother, my father. Then I muttered the word 'bitch' under my breath.

My mother gasped. She threw up her hands. She stood up.

'I have always said … I have always known. They are trash, those people. She dresses in bin bags and every other week there's another bruise on her face. They fight and copulate like animals. These are the kind of people we have to live with, in this day and age!'

My mother sat back down, shaking her head. For a few moments nobody said a word. I felt exposed; something private and humiliating had been revealed and it made me feel weak and embarrassed. I wanted to finish eating as fast as possible and escape to the solitude of my room. My grandmother turned her head back down to her soup. I realized that she couldn't even look at me. I was certain I had shamed her, and that, more than anything, broke my heart. I watched her out of the corner of my eye. She took a couple of sips of the soup. Then she laid down her spoon, got up from the table and walked out the front door. My brother looked at me in bemusement. My mother shot my father a wary look. For a few moments, no one said anything.

Then there was an almighty crash, followed by screaming. My mother and father dashed out into the corridor. I followed them.

Other neighbors were filtering out of doorways, looking for the source of the commotion. I followed my parents down the corridor to the Cuis' residence. The door had been broken open. My grandmother had simply removed one shoe, used it as a battering ram, and smashed her way in. When I looked into the apartment, Mr. Cui was lying on his back and my grandmother was standing over him; a stout and robust old lady, she was raising that shoe, bringing its hard sole down onto the cowering man's head again and again, her face white with cold fury. Mr. Cui was trying to cover himself, but each blow sounded cleanly and smartly like a whip being cracked. In some other context, it might have been comical, except this was real violence; I caught the blood pouring down his shocked face as my grandmother continued to crack him. My mother was screaming. My father was shouting. Mrs. Cui was hunched up on the ground, crying hysterically. The other neighbors joined the commotion, until finally my grandmother was led away. She was frowning as she walked past me. She didn't look at me. Her face was expressionless, her eyes dull.

None of us returned to the table that evening to eat. The mayhem had driven my brother into a state, and my mother was with him, comforting him. My father had retired to his study, as he so often did. My grandmother had slipped into her room without a word, closing the door. I knew not to bother her then.

Even though I saw Mr. Cui a few times after that day, he never spoke to me again. In the corridor, on those occasions when we passed one another, he would bow his head and look away. After a while I forgot all about him. The Cuis moved away some years later, but I couldn't tell you exactly when or to where. That same night, however, I again found myself lying on my bed in the darkness, gazing up at the ceiling. The noise of the neighbors had quietened down. The corridor itself seemed to exhale in a quiet, night-time murmur. As sleep gradually settled on me, I thought of my grandmother. From somewhere far away came the distant sound of thunder. I thought about Thor, in the clouds, hurling his hammer and killing giants. And I felt safe.

TEN

I WAS ALWAYS AN OBEDIENT CHILD. I THINK IT WAS IN my nature. It was true that I had come up with a plan to break the rules when, on that night some years ago now, my friends and I had taken to the streets at a time of curfew. I had paid the price for that. I knew Gen had too. From that time onwards, I had lost any appetite for breaking the rules. I became adept at keeping myself to myself. My loneliness was not something that was hateful or upsetting to me – rather, paradoxically, it was comforting, a warm blanket of isolation that I could wrap around myself; something that protected me from the external world. Something that protected me from other people – and their violence.

And yet. It was the book I had borrowed from the old man. It was that book – Larsson's *Norse Myths* – that tempted me to break the rules for a second time in my life. I had come to love that book. I loved the way it looked – the glorious but faint images of clouds and mountains that graced its cover – and I loved how it felt as I ran my fingers across its brittle leather backbone. But beyond the antique delicacy of the design were the words themselves. In school and at home, I read whatever I could. I read some of the scientific journals my father collected; there were bits and pieces that were interesting, but most of them were beyond me. I'd also read a couple of my mother's novels – stories of paupers who became princes during the eighth-century Tang Dynasty. At school, we read accounts of peasants and workers whose sacrifices had helped protect the greatness of the Chinese state. I devoured those things, in the same way a starving man might eat the leaves from a bush, drawing every meager particle of nutrition from a dried and withered source. But I hadn't loved what I read. Not in the way I loved those myths.

It wasn't just the conflict and the characters, called into being by the type of colorful imagination for which the sky quite literally was the limit. There were also moments that made me smile. The image of the greatest of warrior gods, Thor, having to dress up as a woman under the pretense of marrying one of the most grotesque and terrible giants – as a means to retrieve the magical hammer that had been stolen from him – had me laughing out loud. And when the end of the gods' world finally came, when the father of the gods, Odin, was killed by the great wolf Fenrir, and when Thor, the giant-slayer, managed to kill the serpent that had wrapped its coils around the world, but was himself vanquished by the giant snake's final poisonous breaths, I cried. I cried, not only at the death of these immortal characters who had taken me on such a weird and wonderful journey, but also because the book had reached its end and I wondered, in that indelibly childlike way, if I would ever come across something as wonderful again.

Of course, I did what all young people do. I began once more. I opened the book at the start and read it again. I read that book over and over. And that was the reason why I wanted to break the rules and keep the book. It would have been easy. But at the same time, I didn't want to break the trust the old man had placed in me. The night before I returned the book, I clutched it to me under the covers, its cool leather merging with the warmth of my sheets and my body. Nevertheless, the following day, I brought it with me in my schoolbag, and, after my lessons, I made my way to the old man's shop.

It was a temperate evening, the icy clasp of winter beginning to unfurl before the first pinpricks of spring. I made my way down the same narrow street at dusk and pushed through the small door, hearing the bell tinkle in the muffled quiet. The old man was there again. I walked straight in, and sat down in front of him, at the same desk outlined with that glowing golden haze.

He looked up at me, blinking. He smiled a toothless grin, his eyes appearing aquamarine in the soft light, but they were strangely vacant, and as happy as he seemed to have a visitor, I had the impression he had no memory of who I was.

I took out the book. I pushed it toward him. My fingers flexed and hesitated the moment I slid it across the desk. Even then, it was as though the book somehow belonged to me, as though I was giving up something of myself. And yet, with that in mind, I felt incredibly noble. I could have kept the book – but I had chosen to do the right thing. I realized that I was a moral person, a very good person. And that felt good.

The old man patted the book with his hand.

'Very good, thank you very much. And see you again!'

He smiled out at me vacantly. As I realized I was being dismissed, my stomach lurched. I felt a moment of anger – didn't he understand that I had been true? That I had acted morally by returning his book, a book I loved, when I could just as easily have never come back?

I think even then I understood the fallacy in such logic. But it didn't stop me from feeling indignant. I muttered something, the type of platitude one delivers before leaving. And then I noticed his fingers. They were tapping rhythmically on another book. The book had on its cover a single eye. A human eye. I remember because it was wide and streaked with veins, and once I had seen it, it seemed to be focused on me. I'd never seen a book cover like it.

I paused momentarily.

'Sir, what's that book?'

'What book?'

I gestured at the book underneath his fingertips.

'That one there.'

'This one here?'

'Yes.'

All at once those strange and dreamy eyes seemed to clarify. It was as though he was looking at me for the first time.

'That's *1984*.'

'*1984*? Like the date? But that hasn't happened yet.'

'Indeed. And yet the book was written over thirty years ago.'

'But that doesn't make sense!'

The old man frowned. He took the book I had returned. He stroked the front cover. He spoke almost to himself.

'Larsson's *Norse Myths*. Oh how I loved these. So colorful, and very dramatic, don't you agree?'

I was almost boiling over in frustration.

'But sir, that *1984* book?'

He frowned, lines developing out of lines.

'That, my young friend, is not a book for you.'

'And why not?'

The words had sprung from my mouth before I had the chance to regulate them.

But he wasn't offended. His eyes shone with amusement before dulling into a more severe and fretful gaze.

'Because that book takes people to the type of world where they really don't want to be. It opens their eyes to things they really don't want to see. No, no, that book is definitely not one for someone like you, because ...'

In that moment he coughed softly, a dry cough, and then a little more. He put his hand to his throat.

'Forgive me, I am old, I must ...'

He coughed once more. Composed himself.

'Forgive me, I must fetch a glass of water.'

He pressed his hands on the desk, and raised his crooked body. He shuffled off toward the back room.

I watched him leave.

But as soon as his back was turned, I reached out for the book. For *1984*. I grabbed it, stuffed it into my jacket, and exited the store as quickly and quietly as I could.

Years later, I replay that scene. The old bookseller, who to me seemed so doddery, so confused. I imagine him walking away, his back turned. I imagine him hearing the slight rustle as I grabbed Orwell's novel, and made my thief's escape. And I imagine him smiling.

Three and a half years after that moment, I would glimpse my first erect penis.

I would touch it. Lying in bed, under the covers, my hand being guided downward by another – to another's body, the most intimate and private part of their body. And I would experience that same sensation, the same illicit spark of feeling I had when I secreted that book in my jacket and left the bookshop. A sudden charge of excitement combined with a feeling of disgust – not about the book or the penis – but about myself and the activity I was engaging in. The feeling I was doing something that I had quite clearly set in motion, and yet something that made me wonder about myself.

That was the type of guilt I brought to bear when I first opened Orwell's dystopian novel, closeted in my room, using the meager light I had. While the gods and monsters of Norse mythology were utterly compelling, they had also conveyed a certain type of innocence. The wisdom of Odin, the quiet, blinded god, perhaps resonated with the silence of my own father. Thor's hammer blows raining down somehow merged into the enduring power of my grandmother, who I knew would do anything to protect me. Even my brother – with his carefree and childish chatter – had a counterpart in the playful, petulant and sometimes ridiculous figure of Loki, god of mischief.

But *1984* was a different type of story entirely. It held my attention, I felt a grim sense of fascination. I had never before read anything that might be described as science fiction, let alone a book like this, with its dark and cynical power. I started off slowly – the grayness of the world in which Winston Smith lived was unpleasant – but as I read more, the novel began to assert itself and I was sucked into Winston Smith's strange and solitary existence. I read it in my room at night, under my bedclothes, using the weak light of a small flashlight. I read it voraciously as only a child can do; hungry to get to the end, and at the same time dreading finishing the book and being exiled back into my own reality. Its ending slammed into me like artillery. Before *1984*, most of the books I had read had happy endings. At school, the peasants or workers who suffered hardship in the stories we read were rewarded for their heroic sacrifices. Even in *Norse Myths*, the conclusion was, ultimately, a positive one in which a new world emerged to be populated once more.

But the ending of *1984*, which saw the soft-spoken and brave Winston Smith reduced to dull-eyed obedience to the regime that had persecuted him, was so shocking I found it hard to sleep. The desolation of the ending, the hopelessness of it, left a bitter taste; I turned it over and over in my thoughts. The book itself became an accusation. I was wracked with guilt because I had stolen it. And its pages represented a loss of innocence: the notion that even if you work hard and your behavior is moral – as was the case with Winston Smith – you don't necessarily meet with a happy ending. The horror of what had happened to the hero, the way in which he had been lobotomized, robbed of his identity, was an image I couldn't banish. I kept thinking about Winston and wishing this hadn't happened to him. I hid the book under my mattress, hoping that if I could no longer see it, I would be able to forget about it, and yet I felt that eye on its front cover burning into me with its accusatory gaze.

Eventually it was too much. I knew what I had to do. I tucked the book into my jacket and headed back to the bookshop. I went early in the morning, before school. It was cold and bright. I wasn't even sure if the shop would be open. But when I pushed on the door

I was greeted by that same moldering warmth, the same stagnant yet comforting smell of leather and paper. The old man raised his head when I came in, his eyes shining with expectation, and I knew he was happy to see me. I'd turned fourteen some months before, and yet, despite my newly found maturity, I at once burst into tears.

He beckoned me to his desk, and watched me quietly as I sobbed.

'Why are you so sad today?' he asked, as if that day of all days was no reason for someone to be sad.

I still didn't trust myself to speak. So I slid the book toward him across the desk. I nodded at it. Finally I managed mournfully:

'I stole it. I am … a thief.'

'Well,' he said gently, 'you brought it back too. That must mean that you are a … non-thief also.'

I thought about the way Orwell had played with words. And smiled through my tears.

'Besides,' he added, 'books are meant to be stolen.'

'What do you mean?' I asked. It seemed a very odd thing for a bookseller to say.

The old man looked at me.

'It is my belief that every one of us who ever reads a book steals a small piece of it. We take something from it, and what we take becomes part of ourselves. The only question, therefore, is – what did you take from it?'

His gaze was on me, gentle, curious and – so it seemed to me back then – very wise. I wanted to say something perceptive, something to convince him of my intelligence and maturity. But those mild eyes drew a different truth from me.

'I thought it was very compelling, sir. I read it, all of it, in two nights. But …'

'But?'

'I ... I hated the ending.'

I threw my hands up in a gesture of helplessness. And then I began to babble.

'It just seemed so hopeless and what happened to Winston was so unfair. I couldn't stop thinking about it. Do you ... do you think that there are actually places like that in the world? Like Oceania?'

The old man looked at me, a quiet pathos touching his eyes. He said nothing for a few moments, and then breathed a single word:

'Perhaps.'

'Perhaps.' Perhaps the old bookseller had wanted to fill my adolescent life with the wonder books can bring. Or perhaps he wanted me to make the connection between the society in which I lived and the world Orwell evoked. It was odd that my younger self failed to make the link, given that I had seen firsthand the way the Chinese state had deified in death its most prominent and authoritarian leader, and I too had experienced at a tender age something of the way the state authorities dealt with would-be dissenters.

But the truth was that I saw very little of my own reality in the pages of *1984* at that time. Even in the context of everything that had happened, I felt my life to be – for the most part – a free and untrammeled one. I had my family. I had my grandmother. I knew the area where I grew up like the back of my hand. I knew my neighbors and felt well liked by most of them. And I had books too. I did not feel repressed by the state. As with the memory wall, it seemed then that the most authoritarian elements of my society belonged to a past that I was too young to have known.

But when I pushed Orwell's book toward the old man, and when he reached out to take possession of it once more, I felt a stabbing sense of loss. And it was in that moment I understood. Why the travails of the quiet, unassuming main character had moved me so greatly. Why the ending – Winston's reduction to helpless conformity – had felt so unbearable.

He had reminded me of my own father.

ELEVEN

IN THE PERIOD THAT FOLLOWED, I VISITED THE OLD man's bookshop on many more occasions. He was the only person who seemed genuinely happy to see me. My mother nagged me constantly, my father seemed as remote as ever, my brother was a cute irritation, and my grandmother was an awesome rock, as strong and as weather-beaten as always. I felt each of these people loved me in their own way. But none of them seemed particularly interested in me. At least, not in the way that old man was. His eyes seemed to shine when I searched for the words to answer a question he had asked, or when I tentatively stammered out an appraisal of one of the books he'd been kind enough to lend me.

It was the first time I felt really listened to and he never seemed to want anything in return. He only ever asked me for one thing. It was on a day when we had been talking about a novel called *The Stranger* by a man named Albert Camus. The old man asked me what I thought about the book. I remained tentative and embarrassed, but I had spent enough time drinking hot tea with him that I felt brave enough to venture an honest opinion.

'I thought it was … strange. I don't think I really understood … him. In *1984*, Winston – he was repressed, that was why he found it difficult to speak out or to show his emotions. He had to hide them. Because otherwise he would have been punished. But the guy in this story. His mother died. But he didn't really say anything to honor her. It was like he didn't feel anything at all. But nobody was repressing him. Nobody told him to be like that. He just … was.'

The old man stroked his chin. His weathered face crinkled in a thoughtful smile.

'Perhaps that is the most powerful form of repression. When you can't say anything or you don't feel anymore. Not because there is some external power or rule preventing you. But because there is something in yourself that prevents you. That makes you both the prison and the prisoner.'

I thought about it. I didn't quite understand what the old man meant. But I didn't want to criticize him directly. It would have been rude.

'I don't think … I don't think I have ever met anyone like that, sir.'

His eyes grew vague and gentle again. And just like that, they were touched by a moment of sadness.

'You don't have to call me sir, you know.'

'What … what should I call you?'

'Well … er … if it's okay with you, I mean, perhaps you could call me … Second Uncle! If that is fine with you.'

Second Uncle is an honorific title for someone who isn't related to you by blood but might be thought of in a familial way nevertheless. Not for the first time, I glimpsed the old man's loneliness.

'That … that would be very nice.'

'Would you like to hold on to the book for a bit longer?'

'That would be very nice indeed ... Second Uncle!'

He smiled that guileless childlike smile as if I had given him the best gift in the world, then shuffled away in order to cement our newfound pact with a pot of hot tea. In the months that followed, 'Second Uncle' would lend me some more books with existential themes: *The Plague* by Camus and *Nausea* by Sartre. I read the first avidly but could make little sense of the second, even after discussing it with Second Uncle. He also loaned me *Moby Dick* by Melville, *The Old Man and the Sea* by Hemingway and *Treasure Island* by Robert Louis Stevenson. It struck me that Second Uncle had something of a passion for the water, though he was the last person I could ever imagine captaining a ship – what with his weak, squinting eyes and a body that may well have been lighter and weaker than my own.

Treasure Island was enjoyable, though under Second Uncle's guidance my literary tastes had grown more mature, and I couldn't help but feel (with some satisfaction) that the storyline was a little ridiculous and unrealistic. *Moby Dick*, on the other hand, was a more adult read. I had to push myself to finish the novel. The scenes with the whale itself were exciting enough, but the endless discussions of whales, whale oil, blubber and roping challenged my concentration and proved a remedy for sleeplessness.

Hemingway's *The Old Man and the Sea* was the one that really got to me. It was only a short book but I must have read it many times over. The writing was so beautiful it made everything else disappear. For a short time I *was* that old man, somewhere out there, a dot drifting across an infinite expanse of dark ocean with only the pale light of the stars to guide me. It was perhaps the most immersive novel I had ever read – not simply because it allowed me to smell the salt in the seawater or feel the rhythmic motion of the dark waves, but because it put me into the old man's head, allowing me to look out through his world-weary, yet wonderstruck eyes. It was that one book most serious readers come upon at some point. The one that allows you to escape the confines of your own individuality, to take the type of journey that your everyday existence would never permit.

It was this book I was reading after dinner, in the soft evening light, when my grandmother came to my room. She pushed open my door – she wasn't in the habit of knocking – and immediately I pressed the book behind a ridge in my blanket. The movement was reflexive, involuntary almost. I never kept my reading a secret, exactly, but it was something I felt self-conscious about in the context of my family life. I'm not sure why.

My grandmother noticed.

'You read a lot of things these days, Little One.'

I looked at her. She still called me 'Little One,' though by now I was a little taller than her. I looked at her, this robust, leather-skinned old woman who had always been a fixture in my life, someone whose presence had all the solidity and permanence of rock. Yet when she spoke about my books, her voice was quieter and in her eyes was something soft and uncertain. I had a brief glimpse of the girl she had been all those years ago.

'Why do you read so much?' she asked shyly.

A welter of feeling rose up in me. Books had become so important, and I wanted to convey that to my grandmother, because I wanted her to understand me. But that sudden rush of feeling trickled away into a few static words.

'Because … I like it … I guess.'

My grandmother frowned thoughtfully.

'When I was a girl some priests tried to teach us how to read and write. I never took to it, though. I didn't see the point. Why write something when you can just say it? Besides, nobody ever needed my hands to write. They needed my hands to cook, to clean, to pick vegetables and to lay seeds. But this world is a new world. It doesn't belong to people like me. It belongs to you, Little One. So I think it is a good thing that you read. You should read even more. Because that means you are smart and you will get a job where they pay you lots of money. You will become rich and not have to worry.'

I felt myself blush. I moved my hand to the Hemingway, I stroked the surface of the cover, an image of blue water that gradually faded into white sky. I looked at my grandmother.

'Why do we never go to the sea, Po Po?'

She regarded me with the same thoughtfulness.

'Why would you want to go there? Besides, the sea is thousands and thousands of miles away from Beijing.'

I was almost fifteen, so I knew that Beijing was not so far from the coast, but my grandmother had a tendency to exaggerate when it came to talking about distances.

'Also,' she added, her eyes narrowing, 'you can never trust the people who live close to the sea. They are not serious people. If you lend them money you will never see it again.'

She leaned into me conspiratorially before sharing an illicit and shocking secret.

'And did you know … some of them even have gills! Just like fish!'

I didn't know what to say to that. My grandmother gave a curt nod – the issue of the sea had been broached and dealt with, and the conversation was now concluded. She stood up. But before she left, she moved closer, that same uncertainty in her eyes. She reached over and gently brushed some hair from my forehead.

'You need a haircut,' she muttered. 'You look like Bozo the Clown.'

She stroked my face ever so briefly and walked away.

The next day my teacher, Chu Hua, asked me to see her after class. As the afternoon wound down my imagination did somersaults; I became more and more convinced that I was in serious trouble. My mouth dried up. I felt the thrum of my heart, and the dizziness of a developing panic attack. I managed to hold myself together, but when Chu Hua beckoned me to sit by her desk once everyone else had left, I couldn't stop myself from trembling. I was aware that my feelings were irrational, that I was a well-behaved student who worked hard and kept her head down. And yet, at the core of myself, there was a sense of illegitimacy, the sense that I had in some way transgressed or failed, and that it was only a matter of time before I would be found out. The dizziness began to flow across me in waves, for I was sure I was to be punished.

Chu Hua looked at me, serious and severe.

'I asked you to remain because I am to inform you that you have been selected for a new program, the Franklin-Confucian Young Learners Program.'

I blinked at her as I tried to process this.

'Whatever is the matter, dear?' Chu Hua said with a tone of mild irritation. 'This is, so I am told, an honor. It will mean you spending every Saturday afternoon with a teacher from the program. You will need the signature of one parent.'

'May I ask what it is for?'

Chu Hua brushed away my question impatiently.

'The government ... the new government ... has decided to initiate a more liberal set of education reforms.'

It was clear that my teacher felt that any such 'liberal' reforms were beneath our dignity.

'And ... why me, madam?' I asked softly.

'Because, some of your recent compositions have shown promise. I myself have found them a little wordy, a little flowery at times. Nevertheless, it is felt that you may be ... *university material.*'

The following Saturday I made my way to the school building in the early afternoon. It was spring. The sky was big and blue. The last shards of winter cold had melted before a warmer sun, and a breeze had picked up, teasing the new leaves in the trees, making their reds and greens flicker and dance. I walked without any hurry, enjoying the freshness of the afternoon and the sense that I had achieved something special. I thought about what my teacher had said – that I might be 'university material' – and I shrilled inside, for in that moment my future seemed as open and bright as the billowing blue of that great sky.

When I got to the building, the absence of people in the courtyard was strange. The front doors had been opened. I stepped inside, walking along the main corridor that was usually bustling with students, but was now so empty that my footsteps clacked and echoed. The positivity of my mood was replaced by nervousness. I knew that some other students had been selected for the course, and the thought of meeting new people was always painful. Would I not be better off back home, in my room under the warm covers, reading a favorite book?

I arrived at room 101, knocked and entered. Inside there were five other people, plus the teacher. My sense of anxiety was heightened by my sudden recognition of Gen, who was seated at a desk, watching me, unflustered and sardonic as ever, his lips curled in the beginnings of a mirthless smile. For a moment I was completely disoriented; I stood there blinking at him, before the man at the front coughed gently into his hands, regarding me with a quizzical expression.

'May we help you, miss?'

Shocked out of my reverie, I stuttered:

'No. I mean yes. I mean … I'm …'

I managed to garble out my details. The teacher looked young for a teacher; most of the others in our school were old maids like Chu Hua. This man could not have been much older than us. He had short dark hair and a pencil mustache, and when he looked at you his eyes smiled.

'Come in,' he beckoned warmly. 'Take a seat.'

His name was Liu Ping and one of the truly radical things about him was that he asked us to call him just Ping. Until then, we had always called our teachers 'sir' or 'madam.' Sometimes he'd saunter into a session with his shirtsleeves unbuttoned, and he would kick his legs out, leaning back in his chair. Sometimes he'd roll up his sleeves and go for a smoke in the spring sun outside. During our sessions with him, we felt impossibly adult. It was a strange limbo we had entered; the lessons that took place on those Saturday afternoons were more like discussions. It was neither childhood nor adulthood, neither school nor university, but the wistful and dreamy hinterland that lay between the two.

On that first day, Liu Ping looked at us, and told us we were going to play a game. In pairs, we were to come up with a 'hero.' It could be someone we knew or it could be someone famous we had never met. They could be living or dead. We would write their name on a piece of paper and then provide a rational account of why this person was important.

For this exercise, I was paired with a girl called Li Lei. She introduced herself by shaking my hand vigorously and repeating her name several times. It tripped off her lips – 'Li Lei, Li Lei, Li Lei' – almost as a mantra. She was impeccably turned out: her black-and-white school uniform creaseless and composed over her orderly and postured body, her hair combed into perfect submission. Only the manic shine of her dark eyes betrayed the nervous electricity that seemed to pulse just beneath the surface.

'I think we should go with Mao. They always want to hear about Mao. But then again, perhaps that is the trap. That is what they are counting on. So we should go with someone less well known. Perhaps we should go for the Tang Dynasty empress Wu Zetian, for that would show originality on our part, and the universities always want some element of originality. But perhaps that is too radical. Maybe we should go for Confucius. But perhaps he is too comfortable, too cozy. No, definitely not Confucius. We should go with Mao. No, not Mao. Too political. We should go with … Laozi. He ticks all the boxes. He was radical and traditional, centuries in the past, but still people talk about him today, famous but not clichéd. We should go with Laozi. We have to go with Laozi. Don't we???'

She began to blink with butterfly rapidity. Li Lei was regarding me with anguished expectation.

While she had been talking so rapidly, my mind had been moving much more languidly. Her words had barely scratched the surface; I'd heard them from far away, for I had become preoccupied by the question. Who was my hero? It probably should have been someone like Confucius, but when it came down to it the person who came into my mind was my grandmother. Which was ridiculous. A grand-mother couldn't be a hero. Especially not one like mine, who spent a good deal of time sewing shoes and picking her nose in a criminal fashion when she suspected no one else was watching.

So I looked back at Li Lei and nodded.

'I think Laozi would be great!'

Her face at once lit up and her eyes twitched momentarily before her whole body exhaled in relief.

'Yes, yes.'

She leaned into me, beaming her pleasure, before moving her mouth to my ear and whispering:

'We've made the best choice. Let's write it down. We are sure to win this one!'

Liu Ping looked up at us. He kicked his feet up onto his desk.

'Time's up, ladies and gents! Let's hear what you have!'

The first two boys held up their paper. They had gone with the Chairman – perhaps it was inevitable that one of the groups would. The reasons were also far from unusual: the Great Helmsman was a visionary, had come from nothing, carried the destiny of China in his loving bosom and so on. If Li Lei was right, and this was some kind of competition, I felt sure we would beat them.

When it came to our turn, Li Lei stood up and bowed shyly to the teacher and to our classmates. She had made bullet points, which she began to reel off. Laozi was important because he was the founder of Daoism, Daoism was important because it puts us back in contact with the nature we have neglected, nature is important because we are all ultimately natural beings … Her arguments were as neat and orderly as her appearance and I was impressed. I hadn't really thought much about Daoism before, but she wasted no words, and put our points across in a clear and logical fashion. I felt we might win after all.

Then it was the turn of Gen's group, another two boys. Gen gave a small tired sigh. He stood up reluctantly and without any sense of ceremony. He held his paper up for everyone to see. It had been marked with six single crosses. There were no letters.

Liu Ping gave a mild smile.

'I don't … get it. Would you care to explain?'

'Well,' Gen said quietly, 'rather than put a single specific name, we made our hero anonymous. To represent all those who have struggled or sacrificed yet never received any recognition. In other words, our unnamed hero represents the Chinese people.'

The young teacher looked at Gen thoughtfully, then smiled.

'What an excellent idea! What an intriguing concept!'

Gen nodded curtly and returned to his seat.

I looked at him with ambivalence. There was something arrogant about his fastidious, tidy appearance, his smoothness. And yet, I couldn't help but be drawn to the casual indifference he exuded, as though it was of no importance what anyone thought of him. I worried a lot about what people thought of me. Especially teachers. Li Lei, sitting next to me, and wearing the expression of someone who had just had a bucket of icy water dumped over her head, also clearly wanted to make a good impression.

But Gen had an aura of detachment that seemed so adult. He turned his gaze to me. I fought to hold it and then looked away, blushing, annoyed with myself, and I caught the flicker of his small sardonic smile. I scowled. Something inside me tightened, and I resolved not to look at him or speak to him again no matter how long we attended the same class.

At the end of the session, Liu Ping gave us homework. The task was to think of another person to write about, only this time we were to select someone for more negative and critical purposes. Someone who had had a detrimental effect rather than a positive one. We were to write up our research on this person for a presentation the following week. As soon as we had finished, I shoved my book into my bag, gave a brief nod to Li Lei (she still looked devastated) and took off.

As I was walking away from the school building, I felt someone catch up with me. Someone touched their hand to my shoulder. I turned. It was Gen. I felt that tightening in my stomach. I made my voice as formal and as cold as possible.

'Yes, may I help you?'

He flinched slightly. It was the first time I had seen a rip in his composure, albeit a paper-thin one. He mumbled:

'I thought … I thought perhaps you could come to my house and we could study together. For next week.'

It is a strange thing to find yourself with power over someone, a surprising thing. It was rare for me. There was something vulnerable and boyish in his face that made me regret my coldness.

'We could do that,' I said quietly.

He nodded his head, relieved, and I realized he'd made an effort in talking to me. We both shared a past, and yet we were, by that point, little more than strangers. I'd always found it difficult to talk to new people, but it hadn't occurred to me others had the same problem. He handed me a torn bit of paper with an address.

'Tuesday evening?' he said.

I nodded again.

TWELVE

WHEN I GOT BACK THAT SATURDAY EVENING, THE night was drawing in. But instead of slipping into my building, I lingered outside. I looked to the sky; the last streaks and fissures of sapphire blue on the far edge of the horizon were perishing before the enfolding darkness, and, above, the first stars were breaking out across the night-time vault in a rash of glittering silver. The dying evening was so beautiful in its scope and vastness.

I thought about Gen. Some of the other girls in my class talked about boys incessantly – especially those boys like Qiang Bolin who were good at sport. I could see that Qiang Bolin was handsome too, in a lantern-jawed and well-defined way, and, as those other girls said, he was 'hot.' But the way they would talk about those boys on the Ping-Pong and soccer teams – the way they would dissect their movements and compare their looks – made me feel brittle, cold and faraway. For I didn't know how to have those kinds of conversations. And yet, as hollow and empty and as beneath me as I sometimes told myself they were, they were also the types of conversation that, just for once, I would have liked to take part in.

Gen was about as far away from Qiang Bolin as you could get. Gen was tall and lanky – gawky almost. He walked with a slight stoop. Despite his fastidious tidiness, he didn't seem that at home in his own body. And yet there was something about him. A detachment, a sense of independence, which made it feel as though he was inwardly amused, as though life itself was funny and he didn't care if no one else got the joke. Was that sexy? I didn't know for sure, but when I thought about visiting his house on Tuesday evening, I felt a nervy anxiety that tingled in my belly. Something different, something exciting somehow.

What would I wear? What would I say? I was tying myself up in knots, and I felt angry for getting ahead of myself like this. Perhaps boys invited girls over to do homework all the time. It might not mean anything. And even if it did, did I actually like him? As in … *like* him? I was sure it was silly, that I was being as frivolous as some of those girls and their never-ending conversations about the boys' soccer team. And yet I couldn't avoid the goofy smile that spread across my face. The same fluttering anticipation in my belly. I had the urge to laugh out loud. And it wasn't just about the class today, or Gen's request. It was the sudden realization that life could change, that one's fate could pivot on a pin, as my grandmother was fond of saying. The future was rushing toward me and for a few moments the prospect seemed wonderful and dizzying.

I walked in the dark toward my apartment building. Then I caught a flicker of light. I saw my grandmother's small shed with the door ajar. I sauntered over, unwilling to return home just yet. As I reached the door, the smell of grain and bird shit hit me, a rich and musty aroma that could make you hold your nose but for me was familiar and calming, for I had known it as long as I could remember. I could see the figure of my grandmother inside, scattering the feed, and I could hear the excited cheeping of a gaggle of little birds as they bumped up against one another: fluffy chicks with great half-closed eyes, still dozy with sleep and warmth, awakened to feed.

I watched that stout, crooked woman leaning over the little birds – my grandmother's weathered, wrinkled skin peeling back from her rich, smiling eyes – and I realized that she had always been old to me, and the birds, little more than babies, were so very young. And it occurred to me that there would come a time when there would be no more birds to feed, when my grandmother was no longer in this place and when I would watch her no more. Whereas, before, the thought of the future was like a breeze that blew through me with its sense of exuberant possibility, now it became a shadow waiting on the edges of this small ramshackle shed, where the darkness of night met with the light cast from my grandmother's lantern.

I coughed gently.

My grandmother turned her turtle-wise face on me and her dark, rich eyes smiled all the more.

'Hello, Little One!' she said.

I made my voice as casual as possible.

'Which Little One do you mean? There are a few of them here!'

For a second she didn't understand, then I saw the awareness dawn on her face.

'Well, there is no point in me talking to the birds. They are just birds.'

She was aware of that, and so was I. But I knew she talked to them sometimes anyway.

She straightened up, releasing a satisfied wheeze, one hand pushing against a single stout hip.

'If you want to help, you can rake some of that hay over there. Check it for mice.'

I picked up the old rake. But my mind wasn't on the job.

'So,' I said, trying to make my voice as casual as possible, 'a boy has asked me to his house on Tuesday. We are going to do homework together.'

I caught the shift in my grandmother's posture, the way she momentarily stiffened. I wondered whether I should have told her. But I needed to tell someone.

My grandmother scattered some more seed, and turned to look at me. She studied my face shrewdly.

'And this boy, he is from a good family, yes?'

'Oh yes, his family ... is very good, I think.'

'And you like him, yes?'

'I think so. I think I do.'

She nodded and moved closer.

'We should talk to your father about this. That is the way these things are done.'

My heart leapt into my mouth.

'No, please, Po Po.'

The thought of having such a conversation with my father was inconceivable.

'Then you will have to speak to your mother.'

My mouth dropped open in horror. That was even worse.

'Please. It's just homework.'

My grandmother looked at me sternly.

'Will his parents be there?'

'Yes, it will be early evening. They will be there the whole time.'

My grandmother frowned. She sucked her lips. And, as if the decision had been made, she spat onto the ground.

'Okay,' she muttered.

My heart lifted. I had somehow managed to get away with it. I had escaped the humiliation of my mother's questions, probing and judgmental.

My grandmother looked me straight in the eye.

'If that little shit tries to put a baby in you, you tell him that you are on your monthly bleed. And if he still persists, you rake his eyes with your fingers, do you hear me?'

I blinked back at her in astonishment.

'Ewwwwwwwwwwwww. Po Po, ewwwwwwww! That's disgusting. He's not like that.'

'They are all like that,' my grandmother pronounced somberly.

But whatever qualms I had about Gen, however antagonistic our relationship had sometimes been, I never felt he was a danger to me. I knew I was safe around him.

My grandmother never told my mother and father about that first meeting with Gen. She kept my confidence. But as we sat down to dinner that night, I felt her old turtle eyes on me, searching my face, thoughtful and concerned.

.   .   .

Time is a strange thing. The three days that hung between the Saturday and my visit to Gen's house on the Tuesday evening seemed to stretch into centuries. And yet, when I stood outside his door, my trembling hand on the verge of knocking, it was as if that same period had flashed by in an instant. I felt the clasp of time in another way too. Some years before, Gen and I had been children. He had irritated me back then, and, one fateful night, he had also saved me. He had taken the blame for what happened when those men in uniform had brought us children to a place only adults should know.

Did he think back on that night? Did he ever feel the same tightening in his chest as I did? Did he recall the way we were as kids? Or was it simply a hazy, bygone world for him? Then, he had been to me a bluff annoyance, always able to pull my strings, someone I regarded with a sense of scorn and disregard. And yet here I was outside his door – and the feelings I had were so much more complicated, so much more contradictory. Who did I see now when I looked at him? And who did he see when he looked at me? The stubborn, defiant and dirty-cheeked little girl I once was? The shy and studious creature she morphed into? Or someone else entirely?

As I stood there, these thoughts swirling through my head, it came to me that I had never seen Gen's house. All my other friends – Jian, Zhen, Wang Fan and Al Lam – had lived in modest accommodation much like my own family. But Gen's place wasn't even an apartment. It was a house. And it was something else! It was already dark by the time I found it; with difficulty, I pushed open a gate that must have weighed more than I did. Then I followed a path up to the residence, its walls backlit by orange lights flickering in the gloom.

Eventually I arrived at the house itself. It was a single-story property, the main section like a large head with broad shoulders, the surrounding wings like an arm on either side – a whole person in repose, stretching out. When I knocked at the door, it was solid and expensive: a perfectly finished black surface overlaying rich oak hardness. My knuckles thrummed but my hand barely made a sound.

I was about to try again when the door opened. In my mind's eye I half expected a butler in a suit, a kind of awkward, stiff, comical creation, excessively formal, like the guy who worked for Bruce Wayne in the American *Batman* comic series, but instead I was confronted by a shiny-faced woman with dark, fluttering eyes. I knew straight away she was Gen's mother. She was young-looking. She had softer features than Gen, but the eyes were the same, and she had the same thin lips. It threw me off balance for a few moments, for they were different and yet the resemblance was uncanny; it is strange to see someone you know looking out from the features of someone you have never met.

But the physical resemblance was where it ended. Whereas Gen's face was always somber and serious, almost as though it had considered carefully in advance what expression to wear, this woman's face was lively, almost hypertensive; her eyes flickered and shone with a barely suppressed animation.

'So happy you have arrived. You must be Gen's friend. Welcome to our home. Please come in. May I take your jacket?'

She fluttered and flustered around me, a warm, gentle but incessant breeze, and before I knew it she had removed my outer layer of clothing and floated me through a shadowy hallway into a dining room illuminated with gentle light. I could smell duck pancakes and pork dumplings (if my nose wasn't deceiving me, and as a hungry teenager it rarely did). Gen's mother hustled me to a seat at the same moment Gen stepped into the room. It was a further shock to see him out of his school uniform. He was wearing a loose-sleeved blue shirt and a pair of dark trousers, and his thick black hair had been tossed to one side. He looked almost relaxed. I remember thinking it suited him.

He strode up to me, kissing me on both cheeks. The gesture was casual, and at the same time sophisticated, European, and I almost dropped the bag I was carrying. I recovered my bearings and took out the cookies my grandmother had baked. I presented them to Gen's mother. She tore open the paper and looked at them with an expression somewhere between shock and delight. She blinked back at me.

'Wonderful,' she said.

And then, in a fainter voice:

'Truly wonderful.'

She seemed in that moment almost disoriented, blinking out at us, and Gen took the cookies from her hands, gently, almost the way one might retrieve sweets from a confused toddler.

'Let me take these, Mother,' he murmured.

He looked at me.

'Thank you.'

We sat down and began to eat. Gen's mother talked rapidly. She was wholly focused on me, and it felt strange that an adult should lavish me with such attention. Of course, there was something in her manner and speech that was not quite adult at all. She talked to me of Gen, her son, and her face shone with pride as she spoke of his achievements. I could see the corners of his lips curl in a pained wince – he would mutter softly under his breath, 'Really, Mother, she doesn't need to know about that' or 'Really, Mother, I didn't win the competition, actually I came third ...' – but none of this was enough to dampen her enthusiasm.

For his part, Gen's voice was soft; he spoke to his mother with a gentleness that I couldn't have imagined, for there had always been, in my experience of him, a sharpness, even when he was a child.

Now his mother had made him awkward, watching him with that doe-eyed gaze of wonder, and yet his tone never hardened. Every now and then, his eyes would flicker toward mine, then move away with some embarrassment.

'Would you care for some yellow wine?' his mother asked.

'Mother, I don't think that is appropriate …' Gen began.

But I cut across him gently.

'I would be delighted. Thank you.'

The two women at the table, she and I, shared a complicit smile as she poured.

My own mother distrusted alcohol on principle; my father would have a sip at mealtimes now and then, though never excessively, as I think he always feared losing control.

My grandmother, however, had no such constraints; she had entered into an unholy pact with another of the rebel grandmothers on our corridor and between them they had cooked up some lethal baijiu over the years. That spirit would have been too strong for my tender taste buds, but my grandmother had been in the habit of slipping me a snifter of wine underneath the table ever since I was about seven years of age.

So a little yellow wine didn't bother me.

We clinked glasses, Gen's mother and I, and this elicited a wry grin on his part.

Then everything changed. Gen's father walked into the room.

Gen's father didn't look much like Gen. Gen was angular, tall and lanky. His father was short and compact. But their movements were similar. Considered, precise.

His father walked toward me, I made to stand up, but he waved me to stay seated. He bowed to me. I bowed back.

154

'Very pleased to meet you!'

His voice was clipped and husky; he seemed almost Japanese in terms of his rigid formality.

Gen's mother had changed. Whereas with her son, she was overwhelming in her positivity, with her husband she became much more measured and hesitant. It was clear that she too was in awe of him, but it was something closer to fear than wonder. She hovered around him, asking him if he wanted one thing or the next, and for the first time I saw a look of real irritation cross Gen's face. His father was polite, but curtly rejected her offers; defeated, his mother sat down.

For a few moments we ate in silence. I wanted to make conversation, to say something, but not only was I shy, the food was also so dammed good. Gen's mother must have been a good twenty years younger than his father, and she struck me, even back then, as being artless and perhaps a little childlike – but once they were gathered as a family a formality descended on the table as thick as fog. It was bizarre to me, because my own family meals were filled with chatter and recrimination and dirty jokes (my grandmother) and every sort of belching, snuffling, eating sounds you could imagine.

Eventually his father spoke.

'Honored guest, may I ask what your parents do?'

I was taken aback by the question. No one had ever called me 'honored' before.

'Well, my father. He was ... I mean he *is* a geographer and meteorologist. But I think he only works part-time now. And my mother, I think that maybe she just works to look after us.'

I gave an awkward giggle.

The seriousness of his expression was unchanged. He regarded me gravely.

'This is good. Your father is a scientist. We need men of science now, more than ever. The world is changing. I am also a scientist of sorts. But I don't try to predict the weather. I predict the economy. And in this situation, our nation is on the back foot. The Singapore economy has continued to accelerate. One suspects that the Taiwanese economy will be next. I have already invested in shares there. And I hope that our own economy might follow suit if our current administration were to be a little bolder.'

He bowed his head after he had made this pronouncement, not waiting for my response.

But in the event, it was Gen who spoke and not me. He spoke softly, but with an authority that belied his years.

'Perhaps there is more to life than coins and yuan, Father.'

A silence fell on the room, so thick you might drown in it. Gen's mother looked at him with horrified, muted eyes.

Gen, in turn, continued to pick at his duck pancake with the indifference he seemed to have been born with. And in that moment, I admired him a great deal.

His father spoke to him in the same clipped way.

'Perhaps there is. But it is coins and yuan that provide the basis for *your* life! For the food you are eating right now.'

For the first time I could see the lips of Gen's father tighten, something stronger than dispassion in his gaze, something that resembled anger.

Gen glanced up at his father. His eyes clouded over in a vague, gray non-emotion.

'Yes, Father. Of course, Father!'

He returned to his food. We all did, except for his mother. She looked as though she had been slapped. And I wondered how many times this conversation had played out.

Shortly afterward, we finished eating. Gen's father left the table, made his apologies softly, and bowed at me once more as he took his leave. I couldn't say I liked his father exactly, but I felt that he was an important man, and the fact that he took the time to apologize to me and bow to me as though I was someone important gave me a little thrill inside. His mother kept asking me how I found the food – she must have asked me some ten or eleven times, always with that same supercharged brightness that verged on hysteria. But her I liked a great deal.

I followed Gen into a different room.

'My parents won't bother us in here. My mother doesn't like this room, and my father doesn't leave his study after 7 p.m. We can concentrate on the project.'

I smiled awkwardly and scrunched up my fingers. Now that we were alone, words seemed harder to come by. And while the dining room had been bright, and the table sleek and modern, this room was cosseted by shadow, the furniture classical and expensive, but dusty-looking. Everything was softened by gloom. In the far corner was a smoldering fire. Gen went over to it and began to stoke it, beckoning me to one of the old chairs.

I laid my school satchel by the side of the chair and sat down. It groaned and wheezed as I sank into it, the noise somewhat ridiculous against the timeless sound of the crackling flames. Gen and I looked at each other, smiling involuntarily, and the sense of tension was broken. When he smiled spontaneously like that his face lit up. He was … pleasant-looking.

'Who's your figure?'

'My figure?' I asked, blinking.

'The person you are going to critique in your presentation.'

'Oh, I don't know. Maybe Chiang Kai-shek. You can't go wrong with Chiang Kai-shek. Everyone thinks he was a rotten egg!'

'Hmm.' Gen pursed his lips, thinking about my selection. 'That's true enough.'

He wasn't disapproving exactly, but I felt he was holding back from commenting further.

'Who are *you* going to choose?'

'I don't know. I'll come up with someone. There are enough bad people to choose from.'

I nodded sagely.

We slipped back into silence. We looked at each other.

'Well, if you want to use those encyclopedias, go ahead. They are … very comprehensive.'

I hadn't taken in the books. But there was a perfect set of hard-backed encyclopedias whose black leather was seamed with gold-embossed binding. They looked magnificent. I ran my finger along the spine of one and the tip was kissed by a thin layer of dust. I thought about the old man and his bookshop and how much he would have loved to get his hands on a set like this. I looked back at Gen.

'May I?'

'Sure.'

I looked up Chiang Kai-shek. He was listed in volume thirty-six of the forty. I took it out and returned to the chair. For a while, we were quiet, Gen scribbling a few notes, me skimming my finger across the page, the arch and delicate writing luminous in the soft light of the fire.

I breathed out in a sigh of wonder.

'Wow!'

Gen looked up at me.

'It's so interesting. Chiang Kai-shek and the Chairman. They were the most bitter enemies. But their lives parallel each other's. Chiang Kai-shek took power in Taiwan in 1949, the same year Mao came to power here. And they ruled for almost three decades. And they died within a year of each other. I've heard that twins sometimes do that too. That when one dies, the other dies soon after.'

I had let my enthusiasm carry me away; it was rare I had the chance to talk about the contents of books with anyone other than the old bookseller. And sometimes, when the old man was peering at me, resting his chin on one hand, I had the distinct impression he'd fallen asleep.

But Gen's expression was keen and also cold, that slight half-smile playing across his lips.

'I don't think you should read any great cosmological destiny into that. Chiang took power in Taiwan because he had fled Mao and the communists that same year. And as for the time of death, well, they were both old men. Old men die. That's what they do!'

He looked up at me, his eyes glinting amusement. All at once I felt about three inches tall.

'Yeah, well, who are you going to choose then?' I muttered mutinously.

Gen looked at me with a serious expression. Every hint of sarcasm was gone. He spoke softly, sincerely.

'I tell you who I'd like to choose, if I was brave enough to stand up and denounce him.'

'Who?'

He looked at me for a few moments longer. And almost whispered the words.

'My father.'

I thought about this.

'But why? Your father seems … okay.'

'You think,' muttered Gen.

'Well yeah. He was really polite to me at the table, he treated me like an honored guest. Whereas my lot – my mother, grandmother, father and brother – when we are having dinner, they treat me more like a … *dishonored pest*!'

I laughed a stilted laugh. I was trying for levity – the sudden turn in conversation had caught me off guard – and I winced at the poorness of my pun.

But Gen didn't seem to have heard.

'You know, he bought those encyclopedias some years back,' he said bitterly. 'They were very expensive, as you might imagine.'

I looked at him.

'That doesn't seem like such a terrible thing to do.'

'You don't understand. Because you don't understand him. He paid all that money, but he never uses them. He has never opened a single one. He bought them because he thinks that an educated, important man should own a set. Do you see?'

I waited for him to continue.

He bit his lip.

'That … for him … is the most important thing. Appearance is all-important. It doesn't matter if he reads the books, as long as the people who come to this house think he does. There is the appearance that he projects. And then there is the reality underneath. Whether it be encyclopedias or whether it be …'

He turned away. He was on the verge of saying more. Of opening up.

'Whether it be?' I whispered softly.

Gen turned to me. All the artifice was gone.

'Whether it be passing himself off as a good family man when actually he has a girlfriend in the city center he stays with while claiming to be away on business.'

I was shocked. I couldn't speak. But part of me – and I felt deeply ashamed – was thrilled. For this was the most personal revelation I could have imagined. And Gen had chosen me to share it with. At once, I injected a tone of serious responsibility into my voice.

'But can you really be sure? I mean, do you know for sure?'

He looked at me. Not angrily, but ruefully.

'I am not stupid. And I'm not a kid anymore. I know the signs.'

He seemed to me in that moment to be so impossibly worldly. The thought of my mother or father having an affair would never have occurred to me. Until that moment, it would have seemed like something that broke the laws of physics and nature.

'And your mom?' I asked softly.

'She knows. I know you probably think she is a bit superficial because she is so smiley all the time. And the truth is, she's not that smart. But she's a really lovely person. And because she wants to believe that other people are that way too, she overlooks it. She overlooks what … *he* … is. She pretends it isn't happening. She's the one I feel for. Because she doesn't deserve it.'

He turned away.

I felt something move in me. I reached out for him and placed my hand on his.

'I don't think you deserve it either.'

He turned to me almost in surprise. The darkness of his eyes shone with the beginnings of tears. It was as though he had never considered this, his own vulnerability.

He looked at me. Automatically and instinctively, he leaned forward and kissed me softly on the lips. Then he blinked again, as if awakening from a dream.

'Oh God, I … I am sorry. I didn't mean to …'

He began to move away, but I stopped him. I felt the kind of tenderness I used to feel with my little brother when he had a tantrum and I was furious with him, only then he would be sorry, and all at once I'd be overwhelmed by sweet anxiety. But now there was a more adult intensity present too. I cupped the side of his head and guided him, gently, back to me, our lips meeting again. Despite the awkwardness that had always marked our interactions, and our mutual wariness, it was perhaps the most natural, the most wonderful second kiss I could ever have hoped for.

THIRTEEN

W E WERE AT THE LOCAL PARK. MY GRANDMOTHER and I, and my baby brother. Of course, he was no longer a baby. The park was a large one. You entered it by joining an old stone path that ran parallel to a long waterway. Alongside the path was a strip of grass and a series of willow trees, their squat dusky trunks overwhelmed by a sprouting fountain of green plumes that reached out, overhanging the water. It was early spring, but there was still a winter tang in the air, and my grandmother's cheeks were rosy. She pulled her coat in as she walked forward, her stolid dwarf's march – rhythmic and unrelenting – defiant in all seasons. Up ahead my little brother skipped, jumped and bolted forward, his movements more erratic. As he ran he gibbered and communed with imaginary friends and make-believe foes, engrossed in a world of his own making. At one point I heard him cry out:

> *What time is it?*
> *Just struck nine.*
> *Is the cat at home?*
> *He's about to dine.*

The words floated into my consciousness in a gentle echo, my brother's singsong voice soft and faraway, and I remembered this was a song I'd once known, a game I had once played, although the details of it were soft and distant. I looked across the water of the river. It shone a thick deep green, except where the light hit it in the middle in a splash of shimmering white. We came to an old bridge across the water, with traditional bamboo arches. My brother scampered across the bridge to the other side, where the green strip widened into a grassy knoll. On the far side was a playground with swings and slides and everything else that tickles a kid's fancy.

My grandmother stopped suddenly.

'Hold on,' she said, waving one arm. Her breathing was ragged.

'Are you okay, Po Po?'

She waved her arm again, dismissing the question.

'Of course I am okay. It's just that the air is cold and damp. It doesn't always sit well on my lungs.'

I looked at her. I was a nervous teenager at the best of times, and the thought of my grandmother being frail or fallible sent anxiety straight through the core of me.

She caught the expression on my face. Her eyes narrowed in that wicked, shrewd way I was so familiar with, her lips curling in the ghost of a smile.

'Don't be writing me off yet, Little One. I may have got a little puffy. But don't forget, the biggest, most powerful factory produces a lot of smoke.'

She breathed out, her breath forming a plume of steam in the cold.

'Whereas in the smallest, littlest workshop, no true power is given off. So there is little smoke. And such a workshop can collapse given the slightest earthquake.'

She looked at me.

'What I am trying to say, Little One, is that I am like the really powerful factory and you and your dozy brother over there are like the small, weak workshops …'

'Yes, I understood that, Po Po. I got the gist of your comparison,' I said haughtily.

My grandmother smiled all the more wickedly.

'You got the "gist" of my comparison, did you? How fancy your language is! Is it as fancy as this boy you went to meet?'

I felt myself flush red. But my grandmother didn't press my embarrassment. Instead she took pity on me.

'You are a sensible girl. And as long as you are sensible, you don't need to be ashamed. I think you should enjoy life. Somewhere along the line, your silly parents forgot how to do that. And life … It flashes by faster than one of Emperor Huizong's best fireworks. It really does. And you realize that when you are coming to the end of it.'

I looked at her. Her face was ruddy in the cold, her eyes set straight ahead. I wanted to say something. I knew she had shared a confidence with me, I knew this moment meant something. If I had been a little older, perhaps I would have been quick-witted enough, skillful enough, to laugh gently and tell her that she was the one who would outlive us all. My mother had said something similar on occasion. But I doubt my grandmother would have bought it.

In the event, the moment was interrupted. My little brother came barrelling in, his head lowered in a bullish run, charging at my grandmother's waist and laughing like a fool.

My grandmother gasped at the impact and looked down at my brother's upturned face, flushed and happy, desperate for attention.

'And what are you about, you naughty little bastard!' she said, ruffling his hair with genuine affection.

'Po Po,' I said, scandalized. 'You can't speak to him like that! You can't use that word in front of him!'

'No, no, of course,' my grandmother said with severity, miming zipping her lips shut.

My brother was giggling uproariously, in that shocked way children do when they identify an adult who has broken the rules they themselves have set.

'You said "bastard," you said "bastard!"' he squealed delightedly.

My grandmother tickled him underneath the cheek.

'Maybe I did, maybe I didn't. But you can never tell. Now go play.'

She slapped him hard on his backside, and he giggled all the more before running off toward the swings and the slide.

She watched him go. There was such love, such affection in her eyes.

We followed him to the playground. There were other children there. As gregarious as my brother was with us, a shyness had recently crept into his behavior when he mixed with children his own age. I felt shy so much of the time and I hoped he wasn't becoming like me.

I left them there, my grandmother standing as solid as a rock on the perimeter of the playground, watching my brother with wry amusement. When I returned from the park toilets, the sun had slipped behind a cloud. I walked over to my grandmother, who was now sitting on a bench, gazing at the grass. I scanned the playground for my brother.

But he wasn't there.

At first the scene didn't make sense. I was sure I hadn't grasped the whole picture. That I'd missed him on first glance. And yet those instinctive pinpricks of dread had already touched me.

I looked again, trying to quell the building fear.

He wasn't there.

My grandmother was staring at her feet. Her eyes were glazed and there was a half-smile on her face, one corner of her mouth curved downward; her whole expression was lopsided, vacant somehow. I ran to her.

'Po Po!'

She didn't seem to hear me.

I put my hand on her shoulder and squeezed.

She blinked and looked up at me.

'Where is he?' I asked, trying to keep the panic out of my voice. She blinked again.

'Qiao, my little brother. Where is he!'

'I … I …'

For a moment she seemed frail, an old woman lost in memory, trying to find her way back to the present. Then her eyes narrowed as she looked at me, her awareness returned and her voice sharpened.

'Don't be stupid. I am sure your brother is fine. Maybe it's time you stopped being such a frightened little girl!'

I stepped back as though I had been slapped. My grandmother could be acerbic, and I had been on the wrong end of some of her more cutting retorts, but now she was trembling with an anger that shocked me. I looked at her in disbelief, winded by what she had said, but there was no time to process her words – my brother had vanished. Blinking in terror, I scanned the field again, and then, in desperation, I ran back toward the river, retracing our steps.

I was panting, the cold air sharpening lungs that were ill suited to bursts of motion, as I'd always been terrible at sport and rarely exercised. And yet I drove myself forward, moving as fast as I was able. I caught the outline of the river – the opaque green of the water's surface, still and pristine – but then I saw my brother's face underneath, his eyes open and lifeless, gazing out from that emerald stillness.

I blinked the vision away and told myself not to panic, but my heart thudded violently. And then I heard his voice, heard him singing softly under his breath.

> *What time is it?*
> *Just struck nine.*
> *Is the cat at home?*
> *He's about to dine.*

He was crouched under a willow tree, totally engrossed in his play. The tears were hot on my cheeks as I pulled him to me and pressed my mouth into his neck, and he kicked and protested and went, 'Eww!' in the way younger boys do.

Strange, I guess. My brother was capable of doing some truly disgusting stuff. He was fascinated by all manner of grotesque creatures: the dung beetles that waddled across the soil in the parks, the segmented worms he would turn up and poke in the grounds outside our building, the hornets that stuck themselves to our windows with a bleary, drunken buzz at the height of the summer's heat. Many of these creatures he would endeavor to capture and preserve; he was fascinated by the way they flapped, jerked and oozed, and he would unleash their cadavers upon us at the most inappropriate of times.

And yet it was a sudden display of affection from his older sister that truly grossed him out.

I didn't mind, however. I nuzzled his neck all the more, and laughed. I was so happy he was okay.

We made our way back to the playground and our grandmother.

She patted his head and grinned.

'You little bastard,' she said.

He laughed out loud.

She grinned and took his hand. But she didn't look at me.

We began to make our way back.

FOURTEEN

I T HAD BEEN A COUPLE OF WEEKS SINCE GEN AND I HAD
last seen each other. We had, as planned, given our presentations
at our session on Saturday with our teacher Liu Ping. I had considered giving my presentation on both Mao Zedong and Chiang
Kai-shek, the crux being that as much as they were enemies they
were also symbiotically linked by history; to use a much abused
Chinese phrase, they represented the Ying and the Yang. But then
I thought about what Gen had said, about how tenuous the connections I was trying to make between the two really were, and I
remembered the amused and ironic gleam in his eye. I was sure
he was right. My mind was liable to go off on fanciful and literary
tangents that had little to do with the factual details of historical
events. It was only since I had been attending Liu Ping's classes
that I had made the effort to read more history books, and I knew
I was on shaky ground.

So when I gave my presentation, I gave it on Chiang Kai-shek
alone. And I toned it down. I gave a brief but concise outline of the
major political events in his life. I was proud of myself for speaking

clearly in front of my peers, and I was graded high, third in the class in fact. But Gen's presentation was something else. As he had told me – that evening back at his house – he wasn't brave enough to do it about his own father. But Gen's selection was brave in a different way. All of us students were supposed to talk about a reviled figure, someone who warranted critique. And this Gen did. For he talked about a journalist and scholar named Chu Anping who had been anathema to the government and continued to be despised in all the state sources.

But while Gen spoke about this man seriously and soberly, it soon became clear he was not describing an enemy or a figure of hate. Chu Anping had been a dissident during the Mao era. And even though Gen made the standard comments about the futility of standing against the 'greatness' of Mao, such a 'critique' of Chu Anping only served to illuminate the bravery and creativity of his dissent. Paradoxically, it was Mao's regime that sounded dull, unthinking and cruel. We, the other students, were thrilled by Gen's presentation because it was illicit and radical and cleverly crafted. I felt proud inside, for not only was Gen a boy I had kissed, but I was also reminded of my father, and the memory wall he had taken me to some years before, for it seemed to me that in Gen's words, and in his quiet but determined confidence, he was reviving something that had been forgotten or suppressed. And despite the polemical nature of his disquisition, Gen was awarded first place. Our young teacher was, I suspect, sympathetic to the kind of gentle subversion Gen had carried out.

When I saw Gen after the class, I gushed, 'Your presentation was so good. Congratulations. You deserved first place.'

He looked at me almost sadly.

'Thank you. That's … kind. But the truth is I only conveyed the greatness of another. When you have never done anything in the world yourself, it's easy to allow the light of someone else to fall on you.'

He spoke softly, shyly almost, but his words struck me with their depth and profundity.

I looked up at him.

'Yes, that may be true. But you were the one to see that light. To recognize it. I think that's important too.'

He looked at me and winced.

'Do you know what I left out of my presentation?'

'No.'

'I didn't say what happened at the end. His end. You see, Chu Anping killed himself. He killed himself rather than follow the moral norms society imposed on him. And that's what men of conscience should do. I truly believe that. One has to be brave enough to turn one's back on one's own life when the circumstances demand. Only I am not certain I would have the courage to do that myself.'

He turned away.

In a move so bold it surprised me, I moved my arm, allowing my fingers to touch his.

He looked down at our touching hands, then looked at me and asked:

'Can you get away Wednesday evening? Meet me, let's see a film!'

And that was how I came to be waiting for Gen outside the red velvet doors of the Auditorium of the North District.

In the time of the last emperor, this venue had been a prestigious theater frequented by the most senior mandarins and the imperial elite. In the decades that followed, it had been reinvented by the Kuomintang and used as a device to promote the nationalist movement, before falling into the hands of Mao and the communists, when theater was rejected as something hopelessly decadent and bourgeois, at which point cinema screens were installed, using the latest technology to promote images of wholesome workers and peasants laboring joyfully in factories and sun-drenched fields. Under Deng, the censorship of much that was considered anti-government or anti-communist was still very much in effect, but because the premier had opened up China to international trade and set the stage for a more market-focused economy, certain Western products were now available for Chinese consumption, including some movies.

With its imperial balconies, its faded leather seats and decaying grandeur, the Auditorium of the North District had become a cinema that appealed to young bohemians in particular: those with some measure of wealth, but who considered themselves the more idiosyncratic and alternative face of China's youth. The cinema, therefore, tended to show movies that were avant-garde and European. They were not necessarily political in tone, although occasionally a more subversive film managed to evade the censors. But the film I was here to see with Gen was called *8½*. I knew almost nothing about it – only that it was an Italian film, and one Gen had been looking forward to. He could already talk about the traditions and the directors, almost casually, as though he had been born with the knowledge. The cinema was a familiar experience for him, but this was my first time and I was terribly excited.

It was a warm spring evening and it had just started to rain, a faint drizzle that moistened my hair as I stood outside the old auditorium. The crowds filtered past in the night. There were vendors selling snacks from makeshift stalls, taxis bumping up against one another and beeping, and a group of buskers playing Mandopop songs, their guitars accompanied by the beats and bursts of a loudspeaker that provided the sound of drums and violins. The music was both cheesy and serious, upbeat and melancholy, ridiculous and wonderful, all in the same moment. In the darkness above, I could see the faint whites of the stars veiled by the clouds of petrol and heat that the street was throwing up. The stillness of those stars resonated as the singers crooned out their longing, and for some reason I felt like I was about to cry. Not because of the music exactly, but because there I was, in the midst of the clashing color of all human life, under the darkness and the stars, and in the evening everything felt possible. I wished the feeling might last forever.

I felt a hand touch my shoulder. Gen was precise with his movements, but also gentle, and I realized he hadn't wanted to startle me. I looked up at him, his thick dark hair flecked by the warm rain, his broad face strong and youthful, his skin olive against the darkness. His eyes with that same irony, but the slightest hint of bashfulness now too.

I thought he looked very handsome and it seemed strange to me that I had taken so long to see it.

He leaned forward, we pecked each other on the cheeks, but we didn't pull away. I could feel my heart throbbing. Our lips came together and we kissed, gently at first but then a little more passionately, and with the warmth and intimacy of his mouth came another feeling. This is what it means to be an adult, I thought. I am out here, I am with a young man, and we are kissing in the street.

My mother would have killed me. But she seemed so far away.

Gen put his arm around me, and we entered the auditorium. He bought the tickets and when he went to get them clipped, he exchanged a few words with the man on the door, whom he obviously knew, two men of the world shooting the breeze.

We snuggled into our seats, and I could feel my hair tingle as it dried. The curtains peeled back and the screen came on, a blinding white that cohered into forms and images, and everyone in the audience clapped. It was … magical.

There were a couple of messages from the Chinese Communist Party that weren't so magical. While the government propaganda was being projected through the auditorium, Gen and I locked lips again. This time, he placed his hand on my leg, and allowed his fingers to move a little way under my skirt. I think if he had gone any further, I would have been shocked and mortified. But the feeling of his fingers gently stroking the skin there, illicit and intimate, sent a rush of desire through me – dizzying, and so very new. I found myself kissing him all the more passionately.

Then the picture dulled and dimmed before coming to life once more as the main feature began. I was prepared to be bedazzled, for everything else in the evening had felt so wonderful and new and, at first, the film was both those things. The weird beauty of what I was seeing was intriguing and exotic, but also overwhelming. There was a relentless barrage of bizarre images, and I found it difficult to connect them. I tried to concentrate, but I felt my attention slipping. I looked at Gen. His face was upturned, the light from the screen rippling across it. Again he seemed so good-looking to me; there was a nobility, an intelligence in his expression, and I gently cupped the back of his head, seeking out his lips.

He smiled, but his eyes never left the screen. It was a frigid smile, and for the briefest of seconds I was reminded of his father: the decorum and the coldness. He turned his face from me.

Perhaps that's the way life is; the best moments so easily elide into the worst. Nothing significant had happened, of course: he just wanted to watch the film, and I knew that. I knew that I was interrupting him, and that the fault was mine, yet that moment came as a body blow. I felt humiliated, bereft. I wanted to run out of the cinema then and there, and for the second time that evening there were tears in my eyes. But I understood I was being irrational. So I resisted the urge. I pressed myself deeper into the seat and focused on the cascade of images, trying to take everything I could from the experience.

It was so very different from the novels borrowed from the old man in the bookshop, which I devoured, reading under my bedcovers late into the night. There, the plots followed a coherent course – a fisherman failing to make any catches until he lands the fish of his life, only he is too far out from shore. This movie was like nothing I had ever experienced. The main character was a film director struggling to develop his next film. He gets more and more anxious before retreating to a luxurious resort to recover his confidence. This much I understood. But after that, he meets his wife and his girlfriend, and also a priest. Then he becomes some kind of lord presiding over a harem of exotic women who go mad and attack him. The scene shifts again and he is a movie director once more, attending a conference with lots of journalists at which point he shoots himself in the head. Then we discover the suicide never really took place.

None of it made sense. It left me with the confusing and uneasy aftertaste that a series of disconnected, strange images from a dream leaves in the moments just after one wakes. And yet, when the lights in the auditorium came on, and we began to make our way down the rows of seats toward the exit, I heard a couple behind us say:

'Have you ever seen anything like it?'

'No, it was most remarkable. I felt they peeled away everything on the surface and really got to the essence of human reality. I feel as though it has truly opened my mind.'

I caught their faces in the shadows, a woman in her late twenties perhaps, the man older still. Both were dressed impeccably; the man's glasses caught the meager light, and I could see the shape and outline of his tidy beard. It occurred to me they might be journalists or professors, or intellectuals of some stripe. Clearly they had under-stood what I hadn't, and I concentrated, trying to review the film in my mind, endeavoring to find a deeper meaning.

When we stepped out into the street, the buskers were still strumming their guitars and crooning out their longings and their pleasures, and into the warm meld of sounds arrived a harsh whisper:

'Street trash!'

I turned. Walking behind were the same couple from the cinema, the woman's face drawn in, her eyebrows knitted together, her nose elongated in its starkness – her whole face at once sharpened in its expression of malicious distaste. She had looked at the buskers and spat those words, not loud enough that they would hear, but I heard, and to me it felt like a small drop of poison being added to a ball of candy floss.

Gen guided us into a back alley where the sounds of music and the chatter of the crowds grew softer. He led me through a dark doorway, then up a staircase and into a smoky bar. It was quieter here. In one corner an old man was sitting at a piano, tapping the keys softly, playing a jazz melody, whimsical and dreamy. The people at the tables were older than us, in their twenties – sophisticates who carried themselves with the dapper casualness wealth inspires.

I looked at Gen. I took in his broad, clean features, his small dark eyes, the tidiness of his thick hair and the olive smoothness of his skin, and it occurred to me that he looked older than he was. Neither of us was seventeen yet, and yet Gen snapped his fingers, summoning a waiter. He ordered us two whiskeys with ice, which, he explained, was how they were supposed to be drunk. The drinks arrived promptly. As the spirit warmed and sizzled against my insides, my incredulity about the world Gen had introduced me to seemed to heighten and sparkle; the soft laughter of the denizens of this late-evening bar, the marigold candles that flickered in the warm dark, the pop of champagne bottles, the tinkle of the jazz music – all of it so wonderful and so impossibly adult.

Gen looked at me and allowed himself a slight smile. I noticed he sipped at his whisky, whereas I had already drunk almost half of mine. I felt a little dizzy and unladylike. I hadn't realized it was so much stronger than wine.

'So ... your thoughts?'

'Er ... on what?'

Now he really did smile, easily and fully. I think it was one of the few times I saw him do that.

'On the film, silly.'

He whispered the words.

I thought about it.

'Well, it was ... it was ... definitely memorable.'

'Wasn't it, though!'

'But kinda odd too, right?'

'How do you mean?'

The smile was still there, but it had faded a little. However, the whisky had made me talkative.

'Oh, I don't know. I guess it was difficult to follow at points. One moment the guy was in a traffic jam in a dark tunnel, then he was in the clouds, and then he was on a beach, and after he did that ... thing ... with his gun, and all the different women ... I guess ... I don't know ...'

The smile was tighter now.

'For someone who "doesn't know" you have firm opinions!'

He had spoken softly. There was no aggression in his voice. But, just as when he had turned his face from me in the cinema, I felt my heart sink.

'I mean, I think,' I stuttered, 'I think ... the film had several layers, and I imagine I didn't completely understand everything ...'

My voice trailed away.

Perhaps Gen picked up on my vulnerability, for he became kinder.

He reached out across the table and touched my hand with his fingers. At once I felt a whooshing feeling of relief, for the evening had been so perfect, and I hadn't wanted to spoil it. His face softened.

'I suppose I have to remember,' he said quietly, 'that even though we played together as children you and I come from very different places, and have very different perspectives. Maybe you could try watching the film again sometime. Because I think it would be worth your trying to engage with Fellini. I really do. If you let go of your preconceptions, and if you give him the chance ... I feel as though he would truly open your mind!'

I brought my other hand across and placed it on his.

'I definitely will watch the film again. I think I really need to give it a second try!'

He smiled bashfully.

'I'm sorry. I shouldn't be … the way I am. It's just that … I guess these films mean something to me. And now I find myself … wanting them to mean something to you too.'

He looked away and gazed out into the dark. In that same moment, all his assurance and adultness seemed to slip away, and I was looking at a vulnerable boy, just as I had when he'd confided in me about his father's infidelity. I wanted to comfort him, to make him know beyond a doubt that although there were sharp corners in the world that might hurt him, I never would; that he could trust me, that I understood him and would support him.

I squeezed his hand.

He looked up at me, bashful still, but with renewed intensity. He leaned forward and kissed me on the lips once more. We kissed for a while in that jazz bar and it felt like the most wonderful evening I had ever known.

FIFTEEN

IT WAS PERHAPS A LITTLE PAST CLOSING TIME, AND dusk was falling outside the murky windows of the store, but inside the warm flickering glow of candles lit the shelves stocked high with dusty old books. In the soft light, the old man looked at me, his eyes smiling over half-moon spectacles. But I was the one doing all the talking.

'And then, the guy in the film was transported into this traffic jam, and then he was in this desert and after that he shot himself, only then he was alive again …'

I quieted down, a bit embarrassed.

'It's just that … none of it seemed particularly real.'

The old man smiled all the more.

I glanced around before taking another sip of tea, its heat melting into me and raising me in a warm glow. It occurred to me how much I loved this old bookstore. And there was something easy and gentle in the manner of the old bookseller that made me realize he was one of the few individuals I knew whom I could really talk to about books or films, the interests that had come to matter to me.

And yet, as he looked out at me, I realized how little he ever spoke about himself.

'Do you … ever go to the cinema, Second Uncle?' I asked in a whisper.

His eyes widened ever so slightly but they did not dim in their luster. They twinkled with youthful curiosity despite his great age. His body began to shake as he nodded his head with enthusiasm, and a mischievous grin crept across his face. He coughed a little as he spoke, as though he had been waiting for years for someone to ask him just this question.

'Yes. In fact, I was one of the first people ever to see a moving film in China. It was in the 1920s and it was highly unusual in those days. Also, I was very young back then.'

He stopped speaking. For a few moments, he sat there, his lips slick with saliva, his expression dreamy and vague, staring into the middle distance. I realized he had lost his thread, and I was anxious to return him to it.

'And, and …' I prompted.

He blinked at me.

'Oh yes. I hated it. We all hated it. After, we never wanted to go again.'

I was puzzled.

'But … what was so bad?'

'Well,' he said, drawing in his lips thoughtfully, 'in those days none of us had ever seen a film before. We had seen photos, of course. But never a moving image. So we didn't know what to expect. And when the lights went out, and the screen came on, the first thing we saw was this great steam locomotive running toward us. Getting bigger and bigger. We all screamed and jumped out the way!'

Part of me felt secretly relieved. I may have missed some hidden meaning in the film Gen and I had seen, but I hadn't reacted in quite so naïve a way.

'So you never went back?'

'Oh yes, sure I did. When I was older I went to see films on the odd occasion. Especially those that were based on books I liked. But you know what I realized?'

'What?'

'When you read a book, it changes you, but you also change it!'

I thought about this.

'I don't understand.'

He coughed a little more throatily. He was keen to get the words out.

'The Hemingway. *The Old Man and the Sea*. What was the old man's name?'

I looked at him.

'Santiago!' I said without hesitation.

He leaned back, pleased and happy.

'Very good. And what does Santiago look like?'

'Look like?'

'Yes.'

'Well, he is just ... just an old man.'

'Yes, but what type of old man?'

I thought about it. I had read the novella many times over. I had watched Santiago on that great expanse of dark ocean under the stars. And I found I could see him still, in my mind's eye.

'Well, he has white hair, and he has tanned skin, because it has been exposed to the hot sun for many years. And it's wrinkled like leather for the same reason. And he has that long white beard that comes down to his chest.'

'Well, you are right about the skin part. Hemingway tells us that the old man has wrinkles and his skin has been burnished by the sun. But' – the old man's eyes danced playfully – 'Hemingway says nothing about a beard. White or otherwise!'

'Okay, so I got that part wrong.'

For the first time the old man became serious, grave almost. He spluttered, and coughed into his sleeve.

'No, no, you didn't get it wrong at all. You are quite right. That old man did have a beard. I've seen it too. Many times. It's just that there are parts of the story that are not told to us by the author. Hemingway doesn't tell us all the details about the man … so our minds have to fill in the rest!'

The old man looked at me earnestly.

'A book is a dialogue, you see. A conversation between author and reader. But those films, on the other hand … they always felt to me … more like a monologue.'

He looked around him, eyes shining. He gave a small gesture with one hand, to encompass the shelves around us, heavy with their contents, and then he spoke almost shyly.

'Books are better, I think.'

By the time I got back, it was later than I thought. Although the old man moved and talked slowly, time spent with him seemed to pass rather quickly. It was pitch-black by the time I left the shop. When I got home, my family were already at the table. The rule was that we gather on time for dinner and I had broken it.

But as I took my place, my mother smiled and slid a plate toward me.

I sat down, turned my eyes to the food, worked on maneuvering my chopsticks. For a few brief seconds I dared to hope there would be no comeback.

Then my mother's voice, almost casual, matter-of-fact.

'So why is it you are late this evening, daughter?'

I looked up at her. It was a mistake. Just making eye contact caused me to blush. Even though I knew I had done nothing wrong, my mother had that effect on me. I looked away, cursing myself inwardly.

'I … I went to the bookstore after school.'

Silence descended. We resumed eating. Again that faint, fleeting hope that the matter would end there.

'It's just that,' my mother said in her most equitable voice, 'you seem to be out more and more in the evenings. And I'm sure that can't only be about visiting one bookstore.'

My heart had upped its tempo.

Suddenly my mother slammed her cup onto the table, the impact causing everyone to jump. She fixed me with a cold, triumphant stare.

'Do you really think I don't know about your boyfriend?'

I gasped. The transition from soft-spoken curiosity to rage-filled accusation had been carried out so seamlessly, so expertly, I found myself stuttering.

'Who … who told you about that? How did you find out?'

I shot my grandmother a mournful glance, but she turned those old turtle eyes downwards. My mother smiled.

'You did. You told me just now.'

I glanced again at my grandmother, but she merely shook her head, regretting her granddaughter's stupidity.

I turned to face the cauldron of seething self-righteousness that was my mother. I tried to make my voice strong.

'His name is Gen. I have known him since I was small. We are in the same class at school. And he is a very good man!'

My mother threw up her hands. From the rage of betrayal, her mood had now graduated to the rueful regret of one who knows they are to be forever disappointed by the unworldliness and stupidity of those around them.

'He is a very good man, *she says*! A very good man! Because, of course, she knows a lot about very good men!'

This was another of my mother's gambits. It could be used about anything. If I had pronounced a carrot a very good carrot, she would have responded with the same astonished sarcasm: 'It is a very good carrot, *she says* … Because of course she knows so much about very good carrots!'

At this point my brother chose to chip in.

'My sister kisses the boysie boys, my sister kisses the boysie boys!'

I watched my grandmother smother a smile in her napkin and I shot her a dirty look.

Now, however, my mother had passed from disappointment to self-pity.

'I suppose it's too much to expect honesty from my family, from my own children.'

Then she focused her steely eyes on me.

'But you will not do this behind my back. You will invite this boy to dinner. You will invite him to our table this Thursday evening. So we can see for ourselves who has been encouraging such mischief!'

Something unraveled in me, a terror too deep to articulate.

'No! I mean, I am not sure it would be the best time, he is very busy and he is …'

The steel never left her eyes.

'You will invite him to dinner!'

·   ·   ·

In the event, we had my grandmother's spicy frog stew, and perhaps that was where the trouble began.

My grandmother had been cooking up that frog stew for as long as I could remember. It was a Hunan peasants' dish, centuries old – according to her at least – sizzling with white tendrils of amphibian meat, sweltering in a black bean and green pepper sauce. It was something my grandfather used to swear by. My grandmother would cook it up on special occasions and, having grown up with it myself, it seemed normal to me.

A bigger concern about Gen's visit was the apartment. I knew it was petty and shameful on my part, but having seen the grandeur of Gen's house, I couldn't help but look at our own apartment and its modest dimensions with a sense of embarrassment. And then there was the question of my family. I wasn't ashamed of them exactly. But when you are a teenager and you enter into relationships with other teenagers, much of it is about convincing them (and perhaps yourself) that you are a fully fledged adult. That you are experienced and worldly and independent. Allowing Gen to see me in the context of my family, and especially my shrill, overbearing mother, seemed like the quickest way to reduce myself to the kid that, in my heart, I knew I still was. A sister. A daughter. A child.

And yet, another part of me was thrilled. There was something about Gen that was both intellectual and adult. The way he spoke to older people, to teachers, to his own father. Even though I was dreading his visit, at the same time I felt a sense of anticipation. Showing Gen to my family, 'unveiling' him as my boyfriend, might make my family see me in a new light. As more than just a daughter, sister or child. As a person in my own right.

I had dreaded broaching the subject with Gen. I had no idea if he would want to visit my home, but in the end I need not have bothered with the tactful hints and circuitous preambles because he seemed pleased to be asked. He accepted at once. Not for the first time in our relationship, he surprised me. And it was all to the good.

And yet, in the hours before he was due to arrive, I was in a state of heightened tension. I tore through the rooms of our apartment, bumping up against each and every family member: beseeching my grandmother not to fart at the dinner table (to which she responded with a knowing grin and the rather enigmatic Confucian phrase: 'Hot wind from earth always finds way into heavens!'); begging my mother not to interrogate Gen about his family's 'lineage' or the occupations and social status of his parents. Finally, in abject panic, I cuffed my brother on the back of his head when he kept shrieking, 'My sister kisses the boysie boys, my sister kisses the boysie boys!' This was not a line I wanted him chanting when Gen eventually arrived in our midst.

I hit my little brother harder than I intended, and that was probably why he burst into tears and went scurrying into the arms of my mother. My mother is one of the least tactile people I have ever known, but when it comes to uniting with a family member against me she embraces the opportunity wholeheartedly, so she swept my little brother up in her arms, caressing his tear-stained cheeks while simpering in that supremely annoying way adults sometimes do to children: 'Oh it's okay, sweet pea. *Diddums*. Don't worry about your selfish sister. She doesn't mean to be so nasty. It's just that sometimes she forgets that we are her family and that we love her!'

In that moment of general commotion, we heard the sound of tapping on the door.

And I realized this was it.

I ran to the door. At the last moment, I tried to compose myself, to put my hair in order, to still my hurried breaths. I opened the door and attempted sophistication.

'Hi, Gen, welcome to our home!'

He smiled at me, kissed me on either cheek in that European way of his, and squinted his eyes curiously, but with good humor.

'You sound different today!'

'Oh, I don't think so,' I said breezily. 'Well, perhaps. Who knows?'

I attempted to smile as broadly as possible, but instead unleashed a kind of rictus grin.

'Please, come in.'

Faintly bemused, Gen entered. I ushered him to the kitchen table where dinner was just being served. He shook my father's hand firmly. He then nodded at each of my family members in turn, before stopping at my little brother, giving him a suspicious look. Qiao blinked back, regarding him with wide, hostile eyes. Gen said severely, 'You seem to have got something stuck in your ear. Let me relieve you of that!' Before my brother could register his astonishment, Gen shot out his hand, stroked the side of Qiao's face and in the process produced a single silver coin that he pressed into my dumbstruck brother's hand. Qiao giggled. Despite herself, my mother smiled too. Gen looked at her, and his own smile vanished. He said with great sincerity:

'You have a very wonderful home. Thank you kindly for inviting me into it.'

My mother was taken aback. She was not used to being treated with such elegant deference.

'Well, well, no, I mean … it's our pleasure, of course, please help yourself to some of these prawn toasts. They are fried well, I hope. We used duck fat rather than the vegetable crap … I mean, the vegetable oil, which of course is of a lower quality and which …'

My mother's voice trailed away. I could tell she was discombobulated but also pleased. Gen was dressed in simple clothes – a pair of dark trousers, a plaid shirt – but he looked well groomed, expensive almost, and this was something my mother tended to pick up on. My father's expression had softened, while my brother was gazing at the newcomer with something akin to wonder. I felt a sudden rush of pride, and great affection toward Gen who was making such efforts to put my family at their ease, so smoothly and with such casual aplomb. I noticed, without really registering it, that my grandmother's expression was unmoved almost to the point of blankness.

'Delicious!' Gen said, having bit into a prawn toast, before wincing with embarrassment as though his enthusiasm had carried him too far. But my mother was beaming. She got up from the table, went to the kitchen, popped a cork and came back with a bottle, pouring some of its contents into our glasses.

'This is called sake! I have been saving it for a special occasion. It's been imported from Japan, you know.'

She gave me a glass and dribbled a little liquid into my brother's cup, so he wouldn't feel left out, for he was capable of squalling when he felt neglected. In a matter of minutes it was as though Gen had drawn the attention and benevolence of the room to himself, yet at the same time he had spoken quietly and hadn't even said very much. I thrilled with pride.

My mother took a swig of the sake, her cheeks rosy, her mood buoyant.

'And so, Gen, pray tell. You seem like such a nice young man. I am sure you are from a good family. What does your father do? And what of your mother?'

Gen swallowed the rest of his prawn toast daintily.

I glowered at my mother.

'Gen's parents are very—' I started to say.

But Gen's voice cut across my own, smoothly cutting me off.

'Well, my father is …' Gen looked down demurely, 'that is to say, my father works for some lowly branch of the government, doing, I imagine, tedious governmental things.'

'Oh really?' breathed my mother.

'Yes. However, it is my mother who has the hardest job of all. You see, she has to look after my father and me. And to run our household. And I think there is nothing more important than that. My father came from wealth. But my mother, she came from poverty, from the working classes. She worked her fingers to the bone. And that is something I have always admired.'

My grandmother leaned forward, reaching out to Gen, a leering smile on her face. She leaned her squat body across the table, plates clattering in her wake, and for a minute I had the most surreal and terrifying thought: my grandmother is about to kiss my boyfriend.

Perhaps Gen had the same vision, for he seemed to recoil and go quite white, only it was too late: my grandmother was already bearing down on him, having put her hands over his, pinning him to the spot. He looked up at her, helpless as a fish on a line, his eyes wide with terrified incomprehension.

She started to massage the tops of his hands with her leathery fingers. She looked at him and winked salaciously.

'Your mother worked her fingers to the bone. And you admire her so much! And yet, the skin on your hands is as soft as a baby's bottom! Now, I wonder why that is?'

Gen looked at her, all his composure and confidence gone. He began to bluster:

'Well, I … I mean I have never … I mean because she …'

In the same moment both my mother and I lurched toward my grandmother.

'Po Po,' I all but shrieked, 'what in the name of hell are you doing?'

My grandmother looked suitably chastised, and reluctantly removed her fingers from Gen's hands.

'I just wanted to touch his hands, that's all. And they are … really smooth.'

She gave the crestfallen Gen another saucy wink.

He looked at her, his bottom lip wobbling. At which point my little brother interjected:

'My sister kisses the boysie boys, my sister kisses the boysie boys!'

Gen's look became almost vacant. My mother jumped up and began to bustle around him.

'Forgive us, Grandmother is not used to visitors. Indeed, she behaves strangely even with members of her own household. It is just the way she is.'

My mother shot a dangerous look at her mother.

I felt as though I had lost the ability to speak.

'Anyway,' my mother said in a light flurry, 'should we have the main course?'

The stew was served out to those around the table, including a rather shaken Gen. In that moment, I realized I was living my worst nightmare.

The conversation died down as everyone ate. I saw Gen, utterly shell-shocked, trying manfully to scoop the stew into his mouth. I saw the flush of color that passed across his face as he gamely tried to cope with the potency of the green pepper. For a few more minutes he struggled on.

Everyone was silent.

Perhaps it was the pressure of that silence or the heat from the pepper that made Gen finally say, in a wavering and helpless voice:

'This is ... quite delicious. But ... erm ... would you mind if I inquired exactly what the ingredients are?'

We all glanced at each other, except my grandmother, whose eyes were lit with a malevolent gleam.

She peeled her lips back in a hideous grin, white tendrils of amphibian meat crisscrossing her teeth and her bulging purple gums.

'Didn't Mommy ever cook this for you? It's good working-class fare. It's the flesh and innards of the fattest frogs I could find plopping about at market!'

If Gen's surprise at being seized by the wizened woman before him had widened his eyes, the frog-meat revelation turned those same eyes into saucers of incredulous horror. Instinctively he put his hand to his throat. And then he started to make rasping noises.

My grandmother's toad-like grin widened all the more.

Gen leapt up with such violence that his chair fell backwards, and then he ran out of the room. We heard one door slam, and then the next, before he found the toilet. We sat in silence as we listened to the sound of repeated retching. Some moments later we heard the front door open and close.

I looked at my grandmother. I was trembling with rage. I finally found my voice.

'Why would you do that?' I whispered. 'Why would you do that to me?'

For the first time my grandmother's expression showed something like pain.

I got up and left the room and ran out into the night.

SIXTEEN

I MADE MY WAY TO THE BUS STOP NOT FAR FROM THE place where, some years before, I had visited the memory wall with my father. The wall had long since been destroyed and my thoughts were not of my father but of Gen. I felt a sense of anguish, as though in those moments his embarrassment and shame were my own. I clenched my fists as I willed the bus to come, and finally it did. The journey seemed sluggish, as it always does when you are desperate to reach your destination. Rain trickled down the large dark windows at the front of the bus, and beyond them the lights from other vehicles were rendered in bleary oranges and reds, which seemed to smudge and dissolve in much the same way the colors of a painting might run. In the darkness, those lights were strange and spectral – detached from their source. I watched for a while as the rain pattered against the roof of the bus.

I had never felt so angry with my grandmother. She was a force of nature, she could be belligerent, and she had the sharpest tongue you could imagine. But I had always felt that, because I was so different from her, because I was in many ways shy and quiet and uncertain, she had taken me under her wing, that she was aware of my vulnerability, and that in her gaze I could feel a softness that she rarely showed to anyone else, except perhaps my little brother. But within minutes she had blown my adolescent world apart. I realized that, although I had regarded many of the girls at school with quiet contempt as they obsessed and fretted about boys, I too desperately wanted a boyfriend.

And while, once upon a time, Gen might not have been my first choice, now that I had got to know him again – had got to know his intellect, his aloofness and the odd moment of vulnerability when he seemed like a little boy again – I realized I wanted him with all my heart. It was gushing and sentimental and ridiculous and blushworthy – but it was important to me. I was devastated that my grandmother would choose to deliberately hurt and humiliate someone of such significance to me.

The bus doors wheezed aside. I had not brought anything to cover my head, but I hardly felt the rain, such was the pounding of my heart. I had not been invited to Gen's house, and fear formed a lump in my throat. But I had to do something. I knocked on his door. His mother answered, and when she saw me her face relaxed into an expression of bemused pity. She hustled me inside, murmuring gently the whole time. I tried to find the words. I nearly choked on a sob. Finally, I managed:

'Is he here?'

'Yes, he's here. He is in his room. He came back quickly. And he was wet, like you. But, don't worry. He is all dried off now. I am sure he will be happy to see you!'

She led me down a different corridor, away from the large rooms, the kitchen and the drawing room where I had been before.

I followed her down a narrow and dimly lit corridor, the old carpet soft and doughy against my steps, until finally we reached a door. With a smile she gestured to me to enter, before slipping back into the gloom. I knocked tentatively, then opened the door.

The room smelled of boy. I don't know how else to describe it. It was musty, verging on unpleasant, and I noticed a couple of discarded socks and T-shirts on the floor. And yet I felt a thrill of excitement: this was Gen's actual room, and there was something intimate and private about stepping into it. My heart thrummed. I had no idea how he was going to react.

He was sitting on his bed, reading a book. I didn't catch the title. As I came in, he looked up at me, and his face assumed an expression of gentle surprise.

'Oh hello,' he said, with a faint smile.

There was a wistfulness to his voice, as though I was someone he had not seen for a very long time. The irony and aloofness were gone, and what remained was the indelible image of a child, somewhat baffled, unsure of what to say but pleased, almost, by the attention. I sat down on the bed beside him.

'I'm so, so sorry. About what happened. My grandmother's behavior …' My voice was husky; it trailed away.

He wouldn't look at me. He was staring at his feet.

'Really, you shouldn't exaggerate,' he murmured with that same faint smile. 'It wasn't that bad. It was okay. I just didn't feel so well.'

At that moment he seemed vulnerable and I the strong one. A lump of emotion had formed in my throat.

I wanted to tell him I understood it was more than that: that he had been humiliated, and quite unfairly, not least since his own family had shown me such courtesy and care. I wanted to tell him that I was nothing like my grandmother, that her coarseness and vulgarity had no bearing on me. But how to get these things across when your emotions are swirling and your head is spinning?

Instead I moved instinctively. I reached out and turned his head as gently as I could. I pressed my lips to his. I kissed him passionately, because I yearned to show him that I needed and respected him – that he was safe with me, and loved, and that I would never again allow him to be hurt or humiliated. We were kissing, and now all there was was the feeling of him and the warm feeling rising up from my belly.

He felt it too. I heard him moan, a low whisper of a sound, breathed into my mouth, and we were guiding one another back onto the bed. Our lips were smeared with saliva. If you had told me that about kissing, even a few months before, I would have said it was disgusting, but the intimacy of it – the sheer physicality of our connection – felt like floating away in a wave of warm heat. All my inhibitions began to evaporate before the heat and beauty of the person who was holding me. His fingers were on my arms, on my belly; they made their way to my breasts, but hesitated, and I could feel his fear, his uncertainty; there was that childlike element again, and I wanted to tell him that everything was going to be okay.

Suddenly his hands shot downward. He pulled his trousers down somewhat along with his pants, and I glimpsed his penis, smooth, soft brown, strange and yet somehow perfect, swollen into life, and even though I had never seen a real one before, I felt a thrill of illicit delight. For I knew it was me – my words, my touch, my body – that had made him expose himself this way, which had brought him to the point of such excitement. He touched my hand; very gently he guided it toward his penis. There was nothing aggressive in his movements, only a helpless longing.

'Please,' he whispered. 'Please.'

I held it in my hand almost automatically. It felt natural. I began moving my hand up and down, because I intuited this was what he wanted me to do, and he was looking at me with such longing, and everything my grandmother had done had been undone, and it was just him and me, and in that moment he looked childlike and beautiful, and as tentative about any sexual contact as I might otherwise have been, in that moment I was the one in control. As I moved faster, and as I felt his breathing become lighter and more rapid, as I felt the heat of his long, smooth erection against my hand, and the sheer intimacy of it, I too felt an intense feeling of pleasure ripple across my belly and flare between my legs.

It was the most wonderful, strange and delicious feeling. I'd had premonitions of it before, of course, but never to this degree of obliterating intensity. It was a yearning I didn't quite know what to do with; a joy that was also momentarily painful, for there was no release. All at once I felt Gen shudder; I felt something warm spatter against the palm of my hand, and I heard him gasp as though he were struggling for air. In the same moment, he pulled the material of the sheets against my fingers and his thing, trying to wipe away what was there.

I giggled.

It happened involuntarily. As excited as I was, there was something about the absurdity of our feelings and our bodies, about this whole scene, which struck me as comic.

He turned away.

I realized I had made a mistake, I tried to reach for his mouth again, and was able to brush my lips against his, but even though he smiled, his smile was empty now, and it was as though all the life had been drained from him. He pulled up his trousers and his pants.

I had the feeling that I had done something very wrong. But I couldn't talk to him about what had just happened, the intimacy of it. Because that wasn't something I could even put into words. So instead I murmured:

'Are you okay?'

He had turned away from me on the bed. His voice was detached and cold. The same aloofness, the same sullenness, only now it seemed more pronounced than ever.

'Yes, I am perfectly fine. I am glad you came by. And I thank you for your visit. But we do have school tomorrow. So maybe we should ...'

He let the words trail off.

And it felt like being punched in the face.

A panic reared up in me. When my voice came, it was small and timorous, pleading almost. I hated myself for that.

'Is this ... is this because of what happened with my grandmother?'

He turned his head and looked at me for the first time. He made the effort to smile.

'I'm sorry. I didn't mean to be abrupt. It's just that I am a little tired. It's been a long day.'

I was lost for words. All I could manage was repetition.

'This is about my grandmother, right?'

His face settled into a more confident smile, firm and reassuring.

'No, it's nothing to do with that. It wasn't the perfect dinner, I'll grant you that. But I also know that your family and my family come from very different places. So I guess some type of friction is to be expected, don't you think?'

I nodded dumbly. I couldn't find anything else to say. But those words, that 'your family and my family come from very different places' – despite the amicable tone in which they were delivered – hurt me deeply. I couldn't deny that my grandmother had behaved appallingly to Gen. But what he said pained me nevertheless.

A few minutes later I was on the bus as it swished through the darkness, my thoughts swirling like rainwater.

Eventually I stepped out into the gloomy drizzle, which spattered my hair and left cold, clammy drops clinging to my skin. A feeling of sorrow had opened up inside me. Some part of me desperately wanted to cry, but a numbness had fallen on me too, and a cold hopelessness that sealed off my inner world from the outer one. I wanted to cry, I felt the need to, but the tears would not come. Instead I trudged on, feeling the rainwater on my face and yet not really feeling it at all, all sensation somehow abstract and distant.

I got home. I could hear my brother playing noisily and happily, engrossed in the world of his own imagination, bashing one toy against the next with jubilant, clumsy hands. I could hear my mother washing up in the kitchen, the hot water from the tap steaming and splashing, and although these sounds were familiar they were at the same time strange, as if coming from a great distance.

I knocked on my grandmother's door, then pushed it open. She was sitting in the old chair that had been so favored by my grandfather toward the end of his life, the place where he would sit while she cut his hair. She was rocking gently back and forth, working in the shadow, the soft light from a candle casting its smooth glow over those weathered stubby fingers, which nevertheless moved so dexterously across the material of the leather with needle and thread.

She was humming under her breath, the sound soft and croaky and oblivious, and a lump formed in my throat because in that moment she seemed vulnerable, so unlike the wild and furious figure that had physically imposed itself on Gen, humiliating and reducing him. In so doing, she had hurt me badly, and despite my numbness and incomprehension, I felt certain of one thing. It was her fault Gen was angry with me.

I stepped closer. She sensed the movement and raised her old turtle's face; a leathery smile creaked across her lips as though nothing had happened. I felt myself trembling, my anger severe and acute, clearing my head. I stepped closer still. Measured my words.

'You were cruel and unpleasant at dinner. And I don't understand why.'

She looked up at me as though she had been slapped. Blinking, baffled. I had never spoken to her in such a way. I felt my voice falter but the words came nevertheless.

'You were nasty to Gen. He was our guest. *My* guest. And you treated him so badly. I don't understand why you would do that … *to me.*'

My words trailed away and now I felt like I was about to cry. Her expression narrowed, the anger sharpening in those dark eyes.

'Ah yes, him.'

She turned back to her material, though her fingers had never really stopped moving.

'Him?' I whispered in exasperation. 'Is that all you have to say?'

Her head snapped up with violence.

'That boy is a worm, a creepy-crawly, and he is beneath you.'

Her voice lowered into a malicious whisper, harsh and grating.

'But then you always wanted to climb the greasy pole, to move up in the world, to leave your family behind, didn't you, Pin Yin? And his pole is no doubt greasier than most!'

She gave a salacious wink, but there was no humor in it, just the bleakest contempt. My tears were flowing as I backed away. The lewdness of what she said, the ugliness of it, made me reel. The memory of lying on Gen's bed came to me, of moving my hand up and down on him, the look of disdain in his eyes, then the sight of the frog's meat smeared across my grandmother's bulging purple gums; all these images whirled and swirled in my head as I staggered out of the room, blinking away my tears.

It wasn't until I got to my own room, closed the door, and fell on my bed, pulling the covers around me, that it came to me. As I lay there, my breathing slowing, the pace of my heart relaxing, I realized. In her sudden outburst of emotion, my grandmother had called me Pin Yin. That was my mother's name. Not mine.

SEVENTEEN

EVERYONE FORGETS. BUT SOMETIMES FORGETTING IS a choice. Sometimes we choose not to notice. Not to remember. After the argument with my grandmother, I was shocked and angry. With the petulance that only an adolescent can summon, I swore to myself that she was dead to me. That I would never speak to her again. And yet, the anger occluded something else. A deeper, less conscious sensibility. I was aware she had called me by my mother's name. How in those moments she seemed to be speaking to someone else, rehearsing bitter arguments from a different time. I was aware of how she had lost track of my brother in the park some weeks before. I was aware of a host of other little slips on her part.

Sometimes we feel the dark shadow of what is to come creeping closer, and yet from the bustle and light of the present – our routines, our sense of everyday normality – we convince ourselves that the darkness on the periphery is not really there. That little mistake – the confusion of names, the forgetting of something that occurred only a few hours before – we tell ourselves it is nothing, that such things happen all the time. They are not important in the scheme of things.

And we ignore that deeper, more elemental voice. The one that is telling us they are important.

That they are the most important thing of all.

It was early, and the morning sun was streaming into my room in long slats of voluptuous light. Entangled in my bedsheets, still lazy with the warm hum of sleep, I was reading one of the old bookseller's most recent recommendations, *Heart of Darkness* by Joseph Conrad. I was engrossed. Suddenly the weightless flow of my concentration was interrupted by a collision of voices; from outside my door I heard the reedy shrillness of my mother, and then the lower, richer rumble of my grandmother's voice. I slipped on my dressing gown, feeling the coldness of the floor against my feet, and wandered out into the hallway to see what was going on.

They were outside the bathroom. My mother, thin and sticklike, was standing over my grandmother, trembling with indignation and brandishing a toothbrush. My grandmother was watching her with pursed lips.

'Don't you realize how unhygienic that is? I don't want you using my toothbrush. I don't want to pick up all your germs. Mine is the red one. Yours is the blue one. I am going to have to bleach mine now because of you!'

My grandmother fixed my mother with a grim, level gaze.

'You know, I remember when you weren't more than three years old. I found you eating mud in the garden more than once. It occurred to me then that you weren't the smartest of kids. But it never did you any harm. Those feel like simpler days!'

'Eww,' my mother squealed with indignation. 'Eww. Why would you even tell me something like that? What's wrong with you?'

My grandmother shrugged her broad shoulders.

'It's just a toothbrush.'

My mother's face suddenly seized in a grimace of rage.

'You make my life a misery sometimes, old woman. Is it really that hard? To *remember* the difference between red and blue? Can't you even manage that? Is *that* really too much for you?'

This time my grandmother didn't say anything. My mother flounced away, a whirlwind of wounded self-righteousness, and my grandmother simply sat there, quiet and unmoving. I watched her from the gloom of the corridor. She seemed lonely.

I slipped back into my room.

It was Saturday, and I was due to attend my class with Liu Ping at one o'clock.

I was walking down Pingjiang Road – a wide street decorated with a series of ash trees, whose crisp thin leaves flickered and rippled as a wave of warm summer wind passed across them. I knew that they were ash trees, for my grandmother had taken me for walks along this street when I was little, and she knew so much about the different trees and would name them as we went. As a small child I had been particularly fascinated by trees. In the daytime I loved looking at them, but at night I feared them, for I believed their long crooked branches were arms that might snatch me up and pull me into their darkness, never to be seen again. This was a constant in Chinese fairy tales, young girls straying into forests or caves or swamps or castles. Never to be seen again.

But when my grandmother taught me about the trees, I began to shed that fear. The ash trees were particularly important to her; she said their leaves could be crushed and used for a variety of medicines. As a citizen of the modern world, I am skeptical about the herbal medicines my grandmother prepared. But at the same time, she was also the first person to show me that the external world was not something to be frightened of but something to be understood, and that there was a real power in that.

I stopped being frightened of many things because of her. And then I realized. When my mother had shouted at her, 'Is it really that hard? To remember the difference between red and blue?,' my grandmother had grown quiet and subdued and there was an expression on her face I didn't recognize. One I had never seen before. And in that moment I understood.

She had been afraid.

When I got to the school building the others were waiting outside the classroom. Liu Ping had not yet arrived with the keys. Gen was there. We nodded at one another politely. We had remained on polite but distant terms when we met for the class, even after we had become involved romantically. But that day, such curt formality cut especially deep. More than anything, I wanted to linger, to have him reassure me that we were okay. Instead it felt as though I was living in some kind of limbo, sickening and precarious.

The atmosphere among the others was buoyant, however. Today was the day when we were going to get our assignments back, papers we had been working on for months, and there was a sense of expectation in the air. Li Lei was going from one student to the next in a state of nervous excitement, her small dark eyes blinking, her words breathed out in a flurry of fluttering syllables. She approached me. She was only slight, but she drew in close enough that I could feel the hot softness of her breath on my face. She seemed to be in the grip of the type of ragged hysteria that comes from not having slept.

'I know I've done so badly. I've really failed this time. Liu Ping is certain to give me an F. Of that we can be sure. I knew it as soon as

I handed my paper in. If I get any higher than an F, that would be a miracle. But I know I have failed on this occasion.'

Her lips twitched into a hapless smile, before she was off again, to the next student, to explain much the same. I found myself watching her. I stole a quick glance at Gen. He was speaking with another boy, Bingwen, and in that moment I felt a yearning to be by his side, to be the one he was talking to. If the heavens had opened up and struck Bingwen with lightning, I would have felt some small relief. The force of my yearning left me feeling miserable and petty, and I turned back to look at Li Lei. I realized how much I envied her.

For her, the whole world was contained in the books she read and the papers she wrote, and the parameters of that world were delineated neatly and securely by the graduation in grades from A to F. Until some months ago, we had not been that dissimilar. Like her, I took great solace from my school record, from the high grades I achieved, and my world too had been largely defined by the contents of the books I read. I glanced at Gen and was overcome by another wave of that same miserable longing, and it occurred to me that, with everything that had happened, I hadn't even thought about my paper or its grade; in that moment, whether I did well or poorly was a matter of dull indifference.

Liu Ping came walking up to us, briskly, jangling a set of keys. He had a smile on his face and a set of papers wedged under his arm. Li Lei gazed at them with what I can only describe as hunger. Liu Ping opened the door and we followed him into the class.

He stood at the front smiling brightly.

'Well, I won't keep you in anticipation any longer. After all, that would be cruel.' He winked.

We laughed nervously.

He handed out the papers.

I was sitting next to Li Lei. I caught a glimpse of her paper. It was covered with corrections in red, and at the bottom I saw a single F scribbled with the same red pen.

She looked at the paper for a few moments. She drew in breath. And then she burst into tears. Liu Ping looked mortified. He hurried over to her at once. She was sobbing with abandon, great teary, snot-filled gasps of anguish, her shoulders rolling, her body heaving; it was as though some kind of barrier had broken, and the emotion had come through in a deluge. Eventually Liu Ping was able to calm her down such that he was able to coax her from the class. He stood outside talking to her for a few minutes. I couldn't hear what he said but I knew it was gentle. Every so often she nodded.

When they returned, she had her head bowed. She looked devastated. Everybody was staring at her. She kept her eyes on her desk. Then Liu Ping started speaking again and people looked away. At that point Li Lei looked at me, her eyes still glistening.

'He said I could go home,' she said softly. 'The teacher said I could go home if I wanted, but I thought I'd better come back. Just because ...'

Her voice trailed away. 'Just because ...' But I understood nevertheless. She had chosen to confront her humiliation, knowing that everyone had witnessed what had just happened. She had forced herself to return to the class and begin to build again.

Li Lei is so much braver than me, I thought.

Liu Ping looked at us. He looked at Li Lei in particular.

'You are in this class because every single one of you is a gifted student and every single one is a pride to China.'

Li Lei gave him a shy watery smile, and there was light in her eyes again.

'Part of what we are doing in this group is preparing you for the next stage. Your school hopes that you will go on to university and will eventually do great things for your country. The last assessment you will have in this class is the most important. You are to write a five-thousand-word essay. The essay should be completed by January 28 next year. Should you do well, the assessment will be added to your university application form, regardless of what subject you choose to apply for. In other words, it will stand you in good stead and open the door to some of the best institutes in Beijing. Needless to say, you must approach this assessment with the utmost seriousness and dedication.'

It was as though the air had been sucked out of the room. The eyes of all the students were on the teacher. I looked at Gen. Even he seemed stirred by the words of Liu Ping; the casual insouciance that was his trademark had for a few moments disappeared.

Liu Ping relaxed his shoulders and smiled.

'Don't look so frightened. It's not all that bad. The assignment is as follows. You need to write your words on the subject of what it means to be a human being. Now I know that sounds a bit grandiose. But it doesn't have to be. You can write about the things that make you who you are. Your hobbies, your interests. Or you can write about someone else. Someone you know. Someone who inspires you. Or you can be more general. What is it that is essential to a well-lived, productive life? I think the important point here is, however you go about it, that you invest your essay with belief. With passion. That's all. Class dismissed.'

Gen was the first one out. I watched him. The same quiver of painful, delicious anxiety ran though me whenever I laid eyes on him these days. I hurried after him, my heart beating. I followed him down one street and then the next, trying to pluck up the courage to speak to him while not seeming needy or desperate. Finally, I caught up with him, my heart pounding. I tried to make my words casual.

'Hey!'

He looked at me.

He smiled.

'Hey,' he said.

I felt myself light up.

'Hey,' I said again, somewhat stupidly.

He smiled once more, and then his eyes flitted away.

I watched him while he was unaware of my gaze. The thickness of his dark hair, the slight curve in his nose, but most of all the faraway expression in his eyes, as though he was not quite with the rest of us. As though he were elsewhere. I looked at him and remembered how I had … stroked his *thing*, and felt that warm spatter against my hand. And in that moment it was as though he and I were the only two people in the world. So how could I feel so distant from him now? Why did it seem as if we were little more than strangers?

Gen turned to me, his gaze hesitant but focused now.

'Hey, do you remember when we were kids? All those years ago?'

Our childhood was something we had never really talked about.

'Yes, of course.'

'And do you remember how we used to play in that abandoned parking lot? You and I, and Jian and Wang Fan and Al Lam, and Zhen?'

'Yes, I do!'

Gen seemed to relax.

'When it was getting to evening, and the sun was setting, we'd all go home, in different directions. Only sometimes, after we had said goodbye, I'd wait a bit and then come back to the lot when there was no one else there. After you had all gone.'

'Why?'

Gen frowned.

'I don't really know. I think I had picked up on the coldness in my own house around that time. How my parents were different from other parents. My father much older than my mother. The fact that they didn't really talk. I'd started to dread going back to that house, always so cold. And I imagined that you all had families who were very close, who spent a lot of time together, who laughed and played and enjoyed each other's company. Your family is like that. I noticed it when I visited.'

I didn't know what to say. I think it was the closest thing to a compliment Gen had ever given me.

'But my family never was. I really loved spending time with you guys. But when you had gone … sometimes I would linger, hang around, before heading back.'

He looked at me again and smiled faintly.

'Do you remember in that same lot there was that old gnarly tree? Fan got stuck up there once. And my god, did he holler! And we all laughed as Jian tried to coax him down!'

I nodded and grinned. I hadn't remembered that until Gen spoke of it, but now the memory came, full and vivid. I laughed.

'Yes, yes, of course!'

Gen's expression grew more temperate.

'Well,' he said, his eyes shining at the absurdity of the recollection, 'when you had all gone, I'd sometimes creep back and climb that tree!'

I looked at him and giggled. He was smiling too.

'Well, why on earth did you do that?'

'I'm not sure exactly. Maybe just because … just because it was beautiful. That lot was on the top of a sloping road, and when you climbed the tree, you could see across the city. And when the sun was setting, it looked amazing. All that red and orange in the sky. And in the distance, I could see the outline of the Forbidden City, I could see all the way into Tiananmen Square.'

He seemed far away again. Far away from me.

'But what made you think about that now?' I asked.

He turned to me again. Another smile. I would have paid the world's weight in gold for one of those smiles.

'When I was that age, I had never visited the Forbidden City, never walked in Tiananmen. But the fact is that I could still see it, from that old twisted tree, so far away, just before the night came. It was beautiful, yes, but it also frightened me.'

'Frightened you?'

'Yes. Seeing it in the distance. The outline of the imperial palace, that great square. Sitting in the tree I felt secure. And yet, beyond, in the far distance, was this whole world that I could see but didn't really know. I knew one day I would go there. But in the meantime, looking out that way, seeing that place underneath the sunset – it felt as though I was looking into my own future. A whole world where I would one day be!'

Gen flushed, his cheeks darkened, his eyes darted and turned away. I could see he was embarrassed. I spoke quickly but with great sincerity.

'I understand exactly what you mean. I mean, I really do. But ...'

He glanced at me nervously.

'But?'

'But I don't get why you are telling me this now.'

His shoulders relaxed again.

'I didn't make that clear, did I?'

I shook my head briefly.

He smiled, but this time the smile was thin and wan.

'It's just that today, when teacher ... when Liu Ping was making his speech about the latest assignment, and how we need to take it seriously and all of those things, because of university. Usually that stuff never bothers me. But today, I felt that way – the way I did when I was a kid. Perched on that tree. Looking out toward Tiananmen Square. Like it's really real. We are actually looking at the future. And from this point on, nothing will ever be the same again!'

I crept my hand into his, my fingers locking with his. He squeezed my hand in return.

'Do you want me to come back with you? Talk some more?'

His grip on my hand relaxed.

'I would like that. But I think I want to jot down a few thoughts on the project. And I don't think my mother is expecting a guest tonight. I hope you understand.'

'Of course, of course.'

I gave a silly, dopey grin. Prim and ridiculous, beaming like an idiot, while something inside me broke apart.

Gen gave one last smile. I watched him walk away.

I stood there for a few moments longer. Perhaps the project was an excuse; perhaps he simply didn't want to talk to me any longer. Or maybe he really was going home to start work on the assignment.

The essay was far from my mind, however. All I could think about was him. I took some comfort in the fact that he had gripped my hand, had opened up to me and told me about his deepest feelings. He had shared a memory from our childhood.

And yet I felt bereft. After all, I was the one watching his figure disappear in the distance. I watched it intently until I couldn't see it any longer. It was late autumn but still warm. I was sweating, I could feel it on the inside of my clothes, not just because of the balmy weather, but because of the effort I was making with Gen. I needed him to like me so badly.

Later, I realized I hadn't even looked at my own essay. The essay Liu Ping handed back to me. I took it out of my bag. He'd given me a B, which was good enough, I guess. I thought about what he had said – how the next one was to be based on the idea of what it is that makes us human. I didn't have the first clue about how to approach that. But I didn't want to go home yet either.

So I made my way to the bookstore. When I got there, I pushed open the old door, which scraped in the quiet, and I heard the gentle tingle of the bell before I was enveloped by the lazy odor of parchment. The old man looked up at me from where he was sitting at the center of the store, his pale eyes shining in the late afternoon light, the same expression of bemused pleasure he wore whenever he saw me. It was a great relief to step into this place, a place no one else knew about but me – a place where there was someone who always seemed glad to see me.

At once he stood up and shuffled off, and then I heard the kettle boiling and saw the delicate vapor of steam snaking its way from the back of the shop. Moments later, we were sitting together at the small desk, and I was inhaling the sweetness of the green tea he had poured into our cups. I felt a sleepy calm wash over me, a sense of warmth and safety, and I had the urge to curl up and go to sleep. I blinked, and felt his gaze on me, the blue of his eyes shining faintly, and it made me think of the sea. Then I thought about the project I had been assigned. I looked at the old man.

'Second Uncle. What does it mean to be a human being?'

I think I expected him to laugh, for even at that age I knew my question was naïve. How could such a thing be summed up in a sentence or two? But the old man looked at me seriously, as though my words were important. He stood up for the second time, his movements halting and creaking, and I saw in the soft light just how hunched his back was. He walked with a stoop, his crookedness an expression of the interminable weight of time. He was even older than my grandmother, I was sure of that; I think he was the oldest person I had ever known.

He went over to one of the shelves and withdrew a thick hardback book. He was panting in the way old people sometimes do, quiet rasps under the breath. His lips were slick with saliva and I could see the papery thinness of his skin, and the shape and outline of the bone underneath. With jerky movements, he managed to open the book to a particular page; then he flattened the paper with his hand tenderly before easing himself back into his seat. He pointed at the image, still breathing hard, unable to get the words out, before finally:

'This ... this is what it means ... I think.'

I leaned in, intrigued. Under the candlelight was a photo of a cave wall. On the rusty sepia of its rock, there was a profusion of handprints. They were lighter than the surrounding rock. They formed circles almost like bouquets of flowers.

I looked at the old man.

'I don't understand.'

He pointed again at the picture.

'These images were made by some of the first men. They are ... many thousands of years old. Our ancestors would take shelter in caves ... like this, and they would make these kinds of images.'

'They are ... *pretty*,' I said, a little nonplussed.

The old man flapped his hand hurriedly, still trying to recover his breath.

'What was it like for those first men? There were dangers everywhere. The animals waiting in the darkness as they huddled around the fire. Or the illnesses, the diseases they couldn't see and couldn't understand. Life was ... so short. It must have passed by just like that.'

The old man clicked his fingers. He was still smiling, but the smile was rueful now.

I thought about those people, all those years ago. I imagined the crackle of the fire. Eyes glowing in the darkness beyond.

He pushed the book toward me.

'So they made these images. On the walls of caves. Something that says, I am gone now, yes, but once I lived. Just like you.'

I looked at the images again. The hands reaching out across millennia. The faint echo of a plea. 'I am gone now, yes, but once I lived. Just like you.' I felt as though I could hear it in the resounding silence of the great cave. The whisper of what was. All at once, those handprints, faint and fragile, seemed so delicate, so beautiful, and I felt a sadness move in me, but also a joy. I thought about Gen, how he'd described looking out at the horizon when he was a child and seeing in the distance Tiananmen Square; our childhood and adolescence began to blur against the shadow of what was to come; the past and the future seemed to roll together in a way I couldn't quite fathom.

I looked at the old man.

'So being human means being remembered after you are gone?'

He looked at me and shrugged.

'Perhaps. And remembering others too.'

He gazed at me for a few moments, his eyes looking into mine. A helplessness there. And a hope.

I am gone now, yes, but once I lived. Just like you.

And I realized the plea wasn't just in those hands that had once touched that wall.

I wanted to tell him that I would always remember him. But instead I turned away and sipped my tea. For there are times when words won't come. Perhaps that too is part of being human.

EIGHTEEN

WHEN I LEFT THE BOOKSTORE, NIGHT WAS FALLING. The afternoon blue had deepened and a great shadow had crossed the sky. Behind the shroud of dark, I caught the ghostly outline of the moon, and I watched it for a few moments before it was swallowed in darkness. I allowed the thought to come to my mind for the first time, unadorned in all its terrible simplicity: there is something very wrong with my grandmother. She is deteriorating.

And I think she might be dying.

I made my way slowly back to the apartment, the first shards of cold slipping into the evening air. By the time I got home it was almost completely dark. I could no longer see the moon, but there was now a spattering of stars against the charcoal black. Set against their distant shimmer came the sounds of human life from my building: the chattering laughter; the sound of people moving, gathering for dinner; the warm, throaty noise of a baby crying. I climbed the stairs, crossed the landing and entered my own apartment.

I felt a wave of heat from the kitchen. My family were all gathered at the table and as usual there was a lively clatter, my father the only quiet one. I sat down. My mother acknowledged me with a curt 'You are late,' my brother giggled and my grandmother smiled her warm, weathered toad's smile before they got on with the meal. For a few moments I drank in the atmosphere. It was such a familiar scene to me, and I could almost convince myself that everything was okay. I watched my family but at the same time I felt the weight of that deeper realization, a darkness creeping through my mind. I watched them but I felt separate from them, as though they were the participants in a drama and I merely the observer.

After dinner was finished, my grandmother went to the living room to do her needlework while my brother played a board game on the carpet beneath her feet. I went to the kitchen. Through a cloud of steam, I could see the silhouette of my mother doing the washing-up. I walked over and stood next to her. We worked in silence; she handed me one plate after the other to dry, again a routine that was well worn and familiar, and yet again it felt as though I was on the outside looking in. My voice came, hollow and unlike myself.

'I want to talk to you about Grandmother.'

'What is there to talk about?' my mother said curtly.

I felt my resolve falter.

'I think she may be ... ill in some way.'

'Ill? What do you mean?'

'Ill ... in her head somehow.'

'Ill in her head somehow?'

'Yes, and I think you have seen it too. She forgets things.'

'I don't know what you are talking about. All those books of yours. They make you think too much!'

'She loses words. Sometimes she can't finish a sentence.'

I felt my voice rise. I felt helpless, terrified even. Giving voice to these thoughts made them all the more real.

'There have been other things too. A while ago she lost track of Qiao in the park. She let him wander off!'

My mother stopped washing up. She wouldn't look at me. She stared at the wall.

She spoke in a low, empty voice.

'You know nothing. It's called getting old. That's all it is.'

I think it was at that moment I realized she was as frightened as me.

.   .   .

As the nights grew longer, I spent more and more time in my room. At the small desk by my window I would work on the assignment in the meager light from a single candle. Outside, I could see silky shreds of fine dark cloud scrolling across the pale moon. Underneath, the city formed its shapes in deep shadow, touched every now and again by the glow of forlorn light – like a great ship rolling through the darkness.

There is something about working at night. The sense that everyone else is asleep, that the building itself is groaning under the weight of all the slumbering bodies and sleepers' snores. That you alone have entered into some kind of demi-world where human life has given way before the shadows and stars and the strange music of animals: the rustling of mice, the scraping of insects, the solitary yowling of a lonely fox. Working at that time produces a different quality of writing, in much the same way the flame of a candle looks different depending on whether you see it in the day or at night. In daylight it appears quite ordinary. But in the darkness that same candle becomes a solitary beacon whose slim silvery flame seems to resonate with sadness and melancholy, beckoning you close. So, it seemed to me, did my words attain a silvery edge, touched by the type of melancholy that is born to silence, where the only companion you have is the sound of your own breathing, the beating of your own heart.

It was on such a night that I was sitting at my desk – my thoughts roaming the darkness, time creeping into the early hours of the morning – when I heard a loud rustle and then a clatter. I sat bolt upright. For the sound hadn't come from the outside. And it had been too loud for mice.

Someone was in the apartment.

I crept out of my door and into the corridor. The door to my parents' room widened just a little, and in the gloom I caught the startled face of my mother peering out. She was holding a single candle.

There was another clatter.

It had come from the kitchen. We looked at one another. Warily we began to move farther down the corridor, the glow from the candle casting ghostly circles of light before us. In the night-time gloom our living space was transformed into an alien terrain, the shapes of household objects assuming strange and sinister proportions, leaning into us as we crept closer.

My mother touched her hand to the door of the kitchen and pressed it open gingerly. We moved inside.

In the darkness, the candlelight revealed a single shape, a shimmer of white. The phantom seemed to rotate on its axis, turning its withered face toward us before floating its form in our direction, its eyes skeletal pools of black, its mouth a puckered dark clasp. My mother let out a violent wheeze, staggering backwards, but

I remained fixed to the spot. I blinked and the image clarified. I saw my grandmother dressed in the shimmering white lattice of her ancient nightgown, her eyes impossibly wide. Cereal had spilled all over the floor, along with a smashed plate.

My mother blinked at her.

'What in the name of god are you doing, old woman?'

My heart was no longer pounding, but now there was a new fear – deeper, sadder. There was something trancelike about my grandmother's demeanor, as though she were sleepwalking. She looked at my mother and said in an impossibly small voice:

'I was looking for cookies.'

My mother looked at her, astonished.

'At this time of night!'

My grandmother said in the softest of tones:

'Please don't send me away, Chou Chou!'

My mother's face drained of all color.

My grandmother looked at me, and the biggest smile came over her face; she suddenly seemed so happy.

'Little One!' she whispered.

I looked at her, the thinness of the gown through which I could glimpse her withering flesh, her eyes wide and childlike, and finally the trails of blood that glistened along the floor, from where the skin of her twisted, leathery, broken feet had met with the fragments of smashed china. I blinked away my tears. I moved toward her gently, and made my voice as small and kind as I could.

'It's okay, Po Po. I'm here. It's okay.'

She let me gently lead her back to her room. As I held her hand, it struck me just how cold it was. The thought came to my mind.

This is how a dead body might feel.

I fetched some antiseptic, tweezers and cotton wool. I remember how she lay on the bed, watching me with those large eyes that seemed to catch the last lonely slivers of light in the gloom. She didn't flinch when I pulled the shards of glass from her feet. I don't think she even felt it really. She watched me for a while. I remember feeling as though I were the adult and she the child. And then, just like that, I heard the low rumble of her snores. I finished removing the last splinters of glass from her feet as gently as I could, but my grandmother was a deep sleeper and, once asleep, difficult to rouse. I think people of that generation often were.

I crept back to the kitchen. My mother had cleaned up the mess but hadn't returned to her room. Instead she was just standing there, her face a severe outline in the shadow, her expression immobile and cold. She moved slightly when I reentered the room, the only acknowledgment she made of my presence. My voice arrived, tremulous and shaky.

'Why did she call you Chou Chou?'

There was silence. I thought at first my mother wasn't going to respond. But eventually she did.

'Chou Chou was what she used to call her own mother. My grandmother.'

I wanted to add something. To confirm that we needed to act somehow. But in the event, I didn't have to say a word. My mother spoke in that same dull voice.

'The doctor. Tomorrow I'll call the doctor.'

Nothing more was said. I returned to my room. I couldn't sleep. I went back to my desk. Pored over what I had written. I had managed some three thousand words, but all of it seemed worthless and trite. I thought about what the old man in the bookshop had said. To be human means to want to be remembered. But it is also about remembering. I thought about my grandmother. But what happens when you lose your memories? When you confuse them? When you forget?

And just like that I had my first couple of sentences.

Being human is about remembering. We are the sum of all our memories. And yet, everyone forgets. And anyone can become confused. But when we lose track of our memories, that is when we are at our most human. Because that is when we are at our most vulnerable ...

.   .   .

Some days later I was walking in a woodland area toward the outskirts of the city with Gen and my little brother. Qiao was walking up ahead. The slope we were climbing led to a parting of trees, revealing a clearing of dowdy brown grass and a single hut decorated in the classical Chinese fashion, with reds and greens and a curling tile roof. It was a peaceful place where the hazy ocher and green of autumn's last leaves flitted in a subdued breeze.

'Hey, Qiao!' Gen called out.

My brother, some way ahead, turned and frowned. He wandered back toward us.

'Hey, pal,' Gen said with a smile. 'Don't get too close to the hut.'

'Why?' my brother asked credulously.

Gen frowned.

'Well, I didn't want to have to go into this. But that place there, it used to be a place of worship for an evil cult long before the teachings of Buddha arrived on our land. They say the followers of that cult had the ability to coax wraiths from the darkness and shadows from the trees. They even had the ability to make the dead move again!'

Qiao looked at Gen with the exasperation of one who has seen much of the world and whose patience has long since worn thin.

'Gen, I am ten years old. I know there are no ghosts in that hut. I know that you are making it up because you are trying to scare me!'

Gen held up his hands and smiled in defeat.

'Well, I was just trying to warn you, that's all. But if you really don't believe me, why don't you go up to that hut yourself? Check it out?'

For the first time I saw a flicker of doubt cross my brother's expression. But then his voice hardened in certainty.

'Okay then, I will!'

I found myself smiling. I loved it when Gen was like this, when he was relaxed and playful, especially with Qiao. We followed my brother up the little hill. We watched as his small figure paused tentatively before the old hut, gathering courage before he darted inside. Some moments later he came rushing out with a big grin on his face.

'There was nothing there, there was nothing there!' he said laughing.

But Gen's face was stone-cold sober.

'Well, of course there wasn't. You didn't think that was the way the ghosts get you, did you?'

My brother blinked.

'Whaddya mean?'

'Well, that's not how it works.'

'How does it work?' my brother asked skeptically, but I could tell he was fascinated.

'Well, the closer you get to the hut, the more the spirits crowd around you. But they are invisible. Until suddenly one of them slips into someone you know. And then that person becomes possessed, that person starts to …'

Suddenly Gen crouched down, clutching at his face, shielding himself from view. Then slowly he began to rise and his voice came in a dull but eerie dirge.

'And then … that person starts to … have a hungering for human flesh whereby he …'

Gen took his hands away, his eyes wild, and promptly lunged at my brother with a zombie-like groan.

Qiao let out a little yelp before staggering back. He looked at Gen with a scandalized grin.

'I knew you were going to do that, I knew you were!' he chanted.

Still pulsing with excitement, Qiao ran back into the old hut. I took Gen's hand and gave it a squeeze.

'You are so good with him, you know? He is usually a little shy but you really bring him out of himself!'

Gen smiled.

'And I think he needs it now.'

Gen glanced at me quizzically.

'Recently, Grandmother has been getting so much worse. I think Qiao has noticed too. He hasn't said anything. But I am pretty sure he sees it. It's so much more obvious now. Sometimes she forgets what day it is, sometimes she forgets the time of day as well.'

I had noted my brother's feelings, and was genuinely worried for him. But once I had started speaking, I realized how much I needed to talk to someone about what was happening to my grandmother. I couldn't talk to my mother or father.

227

But a brief shadow passed across Gen's face.

I felt that speaking about my grandmother was difficult for him. So I tried to make what I was saying a little more light-hearted.

'I mean, it's really weird and everything. Sometimes she thinks we are about to have breakfast when we are settling down for dinner. And sometimes she forgets which toothbrush is hers and she takes my mother's, which causes an awful brouhaha!'

I snuck glances at him from the corner of my eye. His expression had returned to its typical equilibrium, a mild thoughtfulness.

'Families, eh? Can't live with them, can't live without them. I do love this place though. So peaceful.'

I realized that the conversation about my grandmother was at its end. Only then did he turn to look at me, his lips curled in the beginnings of a smile, intimate and inviting.

'I hope you won't mind me confiding something to you too.'

'No, of course not. Anything you want!'

'I wonder if next time we meet you might not bring your brother along.'

That same lurching, shuddering feeling in my belly. The feeling of being winded.

He touched the side of my cheek, and I turned into his touch, closing my eyes, willing away the tears that were forming.

His expression became ardent. He spoke softly.

'Please don't think for a moment that I am not happy to spend time with your brother. He is so much fun, so much larger than life. But ... perhaps ...'

He glanced into the middle distance.

'I was just hoping. Given that we spend so little time together. And given that we are, I think, quite serious about one another ...'

His voice faded. His eyes returned to me before moving away once more.

'... given that we are serious about one another, I was hoping our time together could just be you and me.'

I gripped his hand, squeezing it. I was grateful he wanted to spend time with me. But at the same time his comments about my brother had taken me aback. And I couldn't shake that sense of disturbance. Nevertheless, I arranged my features in a smile and said as brightly as I could:

'Of course. I had to bring him today but that was only because everyone was out and he had no one to look after him. I promise in the future it will only be us.'

From within the old hut my brother suddenly released a delighted whoop. He'd somehow managed to clamber to the top, and from his position as conqueror, he waved furiously out at us, elated by his achievement.

I waved back.

NINETEEN

VEN MY MOTHER, WHO WAS USED TO BUTTING HEADS
with my grandmother, played her cards close to her chest
when it came to the doctor's visit. She told my grandmother that
the doctor was coming to give her a checkup, something to which
my grandmother reacted spikily. She was fit as a fiddle, she said; she
did not need any medical attention, she had never spent a day in
hospital in her life. By that point, my grandmother seemed to move
in and out of focus: some days she was the stubborn squat presence
we had always known, as solid and strong as a workhorse; other days,
she seemed like the lingering memory of the person she once was,
forgetful, subdued, lost somehow.

But on the day of the doctor's visit, my grandmother was lucid. It
worried my mother because she was frightened the doctor might be
subjected to a tirade in my grandmother's spicier language, fretting
about how 'the young man comes from a good family' and 'we will
never live it down.' For my part, I was anxious that if my grandmother was too much like her old self, then the doctor might not be
able to recognize whatever it was that was changing her.

My father and brother had absented themselves from the apartment. My father – with a combination of discretion and cowardice – had recognized that the visit was about navigating the complex and inhospitable terrain of 'women's issues,' so for this reason he chose to discreetly slip out. My brother went with him as he had been promised a milkshake.

When we opened the door we were greeted by a young man of impeccable appearance with bright, kind eyes. He introduced himself as Yang Xiaosheng, which we already knew as his father was also a Yang and had been the doctor to our household before he retired. But my impression was that the younger man had a different attitude from his father. The older Yang had been a large portly man with a smoker's laugh and yellowing teeth, and had dressed in thick traditional clothing that gave off the sour scent of sweat from the body underneath. Yang Jr., on the other hand, smelled of almost nothing, except perhaps a vague and anodyne hint of antiseptic. Plus, he wore thin gray trousers, a white shirt and a sensible dark jacket. And he carried a neat black-leather bag that contained all his equipment.

We escorted him into my grandmother's room. Yang began by measuring my grandmother's pulse at her wrist. She complained through the whole procedure until finally he said:

'And that's just perfect. Seventy per minute. Excellent.'

My grandmother grumbled all the more – 'I know that, I told you I am as strong as a horse!' – but I could tell she was pleased.

The doctor asked her a series of questions: what day it was, what year it was. Sometimes she hesitated but was able to recover herself and answer correctly. At the same time, she got progressively more irritated. When the young man asked her who the leader of the country was, she looked momentarily baffled before she snapped, 'What does it matter? They are all as bad as each other. You learn that by the time you get to my age. Unfortunately, you are not yet out of your diapers!'

My mother at once chastised my grandmother and apologized profusely to the doctor, but the doctor simply brushed her worries away with a smile.

'It's okay,' he said, looking at my grandmother and winking. 'Being rebuked by such a formidable woman will surely be the highlight of my week!'

My grandmother scowled at him, but again I could see she was rather pleased.

He took her temperature with a thermometer, and touched the tips of her toes and fingers, asking her if she could feel his touch. This time she was more compliant.

'That's about it.'

He looked at my grandmother and grinned.

'Madam, I am happy to report you are physically very robust!'

He turned, returning his equipment to his neat leather satchel. And in that moment my grandmother's face changed. It was both subtle and vivid. Her irritability vanished. The sharpness of her self-awareness was gone and in its place was a bland expression of gentle bemusement. Her eyes found the young doctor again, blinking up at him as he stood over her. I realized she no longer knew who he was. I watched her eyes travel down his body to his midriff and then farther still. Her eyes focused there, in fascination and wonder. She reached out one hand and gently took hold of his private parts.

The young doctor gave a sudden, shocked gasp.

My mother gave an even louder gasp, before collapsing onto the bed.

At once my grandmother withdrew her hand. In that same moment, she turned to me and she had a child's expression, blinking and baffled, as though she knew she had done wrong but couldn't quite figure out how. Tears formed in her eyes. And my heart broke that little bit more.

I went over to her and kneeled by her feet, touching her hands before taking them in mine. I could feel her trembling. I'd never seen her shake like that. I murmured softly to her. The young Yang, to his eternal credit, had recovered himself quickly and was also providing words of polite consolation. My mother, who had recovered from her swoon, was ashen. Eventually my grandmother became calm and we crept from her room.

We saw the young doctor out into the hallway.

My mother began to apologize again, but he waved away her concerns. 'It really is all right,' he said.

He looked at us – our anxiety, our expectation – as he must have looked at so many.

'I am afraid it's not good news. She has a condition known as "dementia." It causes patients to become increasingly forgetful, to lose their sense of time and place. It also … ahem … causes a lack of inhibition. This cannot be helped and it is not the patient's fault. It's just part of the condition.'

'What can we do?' asked my mother.

'That's the thing. To be brutally honest we still know so little about this disease. There is no known cure. And your mother's stage – it is clearly quite advanced.'

'So she will …'

233

My mother's words trailed away.

'Yes, patients with this condition have a life expectancy of around five years, generally speaking, but, as I say … your mother's condition is considerably advanced. We may be talking about a year, perhaps less.

'I am so sorry I can't bring better news. I would, however, add a couple of things. She won't be in any great physical pain, it is a … *gentle* illness in that way. One of the things you need to do is make sure her extremities are kept warm. Dementia sufferers often experience sluggish circulation, so, as you may already have noticed, the hands and feet can get very cold. Thick socks, extra blankets, hot water bottles and so on. All these things are useful. But the care itself is important. In some ways it is helpful to think of dementia like a second childhood. Sufferers often have the same vulnerabilities, the same fears as young children. So making them feel safe and cared for is a wonderful thing to do.'

My mother and I nodded. The doctor buttoned up his jacket. He looked at us once more.

'I hope I have your permission to come back and check on the patient in the next couple of months.'

'Of course, Doctor,' my mother said, nodding her head.

The young man gave a wan smile and left. My mother and I stood in silence, watching him go.

.   .   .

We are, all of us, dying. Every single day of our lives. The thing is, however, some of us are doing it that much faster.

I had been living in fear for my grandmother for a while. But after the doctor's visit, that fear became real. From that moment on, there was a heaviness in the air; something you couldn't see, something you couldn't speak about, but it was there nonetheless. My mother and I felt the weight of our knowledge. And yet we couldn't confide in one another. We did not have that type of relationship.

So we adapted in our own specific ways. I noticed my mother did a little more for my grandmother now. Changing her sheets when she was out of her room. Giving her the better, softer cut of the pork, which hitherto she had reserved for my brother and father. And yet all this was done with a briskness, with a brittleness. She often spoke to my grandmother in clipped tones, with sighs of impatience, as though my grandmother were one more household difficulty to be managed with forthright practicality. Behind the tone of brusque irritation was something shapeless, fearful, something that couldn't be acknowledged. My mother's strategy was to brush it vigorously from her mind, in the same way someone might brush the floor of a particularly dusty room.

For my part, I came to relish leaving the house. Especially on the weekends when it felt as if I couldn't escape what was happening. We were well into winter and when I stepped out into the crisp cold air that Saturday, it felt like breathing again. In my bag was the essay I was about to submit, the one on what it means to be human. And I felt in my core that feeling I always had before I saw Gen. Anxiety mixed with longing. The need to say the right thing. The fear of saying the wrong one.

There was an air of tension in the class, a suppressed excitement. But Li Lei seemed strangely underwhelmed. She took out her essay and smoothed the paper down with her fingers. She was not humming with her usual anxious tension. Instead her expression seemed almost serene.

'What did you write about, Li Lei? How did you answer the question?'

She looked at me with a slight smile, secretive and mysterious.

'I wrote that I haven't been human that long, so I don't know all that much about it ...'

I smiled in turn. She had a strange way of phrasing things.

'... but even though I am only seventeen years of age, I have learned that an important part of being human is being happy. And that you don't always have to be the best, but just lead ... a kind life.'

She said that last part shyly, almost apologetically. I think if I heard someone say something like that now, I might consider it trite, the kind of thing self-help books are full of. But in that moment, I felt moved by what Li Lei had said, her simple unobtrusive need to lead that 'kind life.' I felt it was something that showed great wisdom.

After the class, I met Gen outside. We had met outside school on many occasions, and most of the time we went to his house. Even though I was a little disappointed at times, I understood why he never visited my home, especially after his initial experience of my family and the way my grandmother had treated him. When we were in his room, we would engage in heavy petting, and I would do that thing to him with my hand. But we also spent a lot of time talking and working on our respective projects. He had read my essay on memory and I had read the essay he had prepared, entitled 'World Culture and the Individual: What It Means to Be Human.'

I was satisfied with my own piece as I felt that in answer to the question what it means to be human, I had also managed to smuggle in a sense of what it meant *to be me*. Although I had not referred to her directly, my grandmother and her illness had informed a lot of what I had written. In its own oblique style, the essay had become the only way I could express my feelings about such things.

But Gen's essay was much better. It was so much smarter; he knew so much more. He quoted everyone from Buddha to Chen Duxiu. Whereas my essay was personal, tentative and hesitant, his sentences were sleek and confident and they seemed to encompass the history of the world. I wondered how he had come to know so much. But I didn't resent the fact that his work was more sophisticated. Instead it made me proud, because he was with me. Gen was my boyfriend.

After the class, he looked at me, threw up his hands, and smiled wearily.

'Well, we finally did it,' he said. 'We finally handed them in!'

'Yes, we did!'

He grinned.

'I guess what doesn't kill you makes you stronger, right?'

'What do you mean?' I asked, puzzled.

'Oh, it's just a phrase,' he said breezily. 'It comes from the nineteenth century philosopher Nietzsche, who was a gloomy German, and, believe me, in that country he had some competition.'

'Oh really?' I asked, intrigued.

'Yeah,' said Gen, warming to his theme. 'He was a truly modern thinker, a cynic and a joker, but the most beautiful writer I have ever come across. I really dig him. He speaks to me in a way in which none of our home-grown Chinese intellectuals do. Listen to this. He said that the Christian god was "a grim old graybeard of a god." And that when he proclaimed "thou shalt have no other gods but me," all the other gods died laughing! How great is that? The guy really had balls. Isn't that perfect?'

I nodded my head.

I didn't wholly get the quote, but I loved it when Gen talked like this. It felt as though he was opening up new worlds to me, and when he talked in this way there was a light in his eyes.

He kicked his feet, looking at the ground, embarrassed that he'd got so carried away. We walked for a bit in silence. I wanted to ask something intelligent about this gloomy German, about this Nietzsche, but I couldn't think of anything. It occurred to me that while Gen offered me so many new experiences, I provided very little in return. A sliver of dread crept into what had otherwise been a lovely few moments. I started to berate myself. I needed to show him something, anything, in order to provoke his interest.

All at once I hit upon it.

I looked at him.

'Would you come with me somewhere?'

'Sure, where are we going?'

'It's a secret,' I said mysteriously.

He looked at me quizzically, but went along with it with a smile.

I brought him to the old bookshop. On the way, I told him about how amazing it was, the books the old man had lent me and how interesting he was. How he was my friend. We pushed the door and the bell tinkled.

The old man was there, as always, and, as always, he looked up, smiling. His gaze fell on Gen and he smiled all the more. They bowed at one another.

'This is my ... friend ... Gen,' I said, feeling the blush rise high in my cheeks.

Gen perused the bookstore with a professional eye.

'This is some place you've got here!'

The old man grinned happily.

Gen wandered over to one of the shelves. He brushed his fingers across a row of books.

'Yes, very good,' he said thoughtfully. 'It's good that you have the Four Great Classic Novels, and while *Journey to the West* is still everywhere, you don't hear so much about *Water Margin* anymore.'

The bookseller nodded his agreement.

I felt a moment of deep happiness. Outside my own family, these two people were the ones dearest to me.

Gen looked at the old man shrewdly.

'One of my favorite poets, from the Song period. Su Shi. Do you have anything by him?'

'I do indeed, young man,' said the bookseller, still smiling. He shuffled to his feet, wheezing with the effort.

'I have several of his works just here.'

He motioned toward a shelf.

But Gen didn't go over to look. Instead, he launched another question.

'And what about the Warring States poet, Qu Yuan? I assume you stock him.'

The old man nodded gently, gesturing toward another shelf.

I saw something in Gen's eyes. A narrowing. Almost imperceptible.

'And what about Wang Wei? Do you have anything by the poet Wang Wei?'

The old man looked baffled. He frowned in concentration.

'I don't believe ... I am not sure if I remember ...'

'It's okay,' Gen said with a smile. 'You can't be expected to stock everything.'

I felt a sliver of discomfort wriggle inside. It seemed to me that Gen's questions to the old man weren't quite benign. But then Gen did something else.

He took the Su Shi book from its resting place on the shelf. He paid for it, bowing to the bookseller and complimenting the old man on his shop once more. He turned to me and whispered into my ear four single lines:

> *To what can our life on earth be likened?*
> *To a flock of geese,*
> *alighting on the snow.*
> *Sometimes leaving a trace of their passage.*

The poem was slight, and yet it was one of the most beautiful things I had ever heard. As Gen finished, I caught a glimpse of the tears in his eyes. He blinked them away. He coughed softly under his breath.

'I wanted to share that with you. Because … I knew you'd understand.'

He pressed the book into my hand.

He turned away. I was greatly moved. I clutched the book to myself. I clutched his hand to mine. We walked out of the store. Did I acknowledge Second Uncle? Did I even perform the most basic of respectful gestures, waving a hand to say goodbye? I really can't remember. I just remember how that happened with Gen. That he could say something to me, and, just like that, his presence alone swallowed everything else in my world. That throbbing feeling deep in my belly. That anxious joy.

I was certain I was in love.

When I got back that evening, I had barely stepped through the door before I heard the riotous commotion. My mother came storming out of my grandmother's room, meeting me in the hallway as though she had expected to find me there. There was no greeting, no 'hello.'

'I cannot deal with that old woman anymore. I will not be subject to her madness, her insanity!'

My mother was looking at me angrily, aghast at whatever it was my grandmother had put her through. She turned on her heel, slamming the door to her room behind her and causing the thin walls of our apartment to resonate and hum.

I made my way to my grandmother's room.

As I entered, my grandmother's head jerked up. She had always looked old to me, but in that moment her eyes were skeletal and her face seemed hollowed out in an expression of both anger and terror.

'What do you want?' she snapped.

I felt possessed of a surreal type of calm. I crept toward her slowly.

'I want to talk with you, Po Po. I want you to tell me what's wrong.'

As I got closer, my grandmother's expression relaxed in a semblance of recognition. She didn't say my name, but her voice was softer now.

'It's just that … I can't seem to …'

She held up one hand, in it a strip of leather. And then I realized.

For so much of her life she had worked leather into slippers and shoes. At first for her own beaten, destroyed feet, an act of rebellion of sorts. And then for others, for that final generation of women who'd had their feet smashed to pieces and remolded in order to better suit the male gaze. And when many of those grandmothers had passed on, my grandmother had continued to fashion slippers and shoes for their children, and their children's children.

The work that my grandmother did with her hands not only knitted material together, it also wove her into the fabric of our community. It had made her a prominent fixture in the life of our building, it gave her a role to play as the years went on and one generation became the next. Now, however, for the first time those timeless fingers had failed her. The need to work was still there, her sense of dignity was still strong, but the mysterious electrical impulses that connect brain to hands were slowly fizzling out. My grandmother was being consumed by her own helplessness.

I sat beside her. The tips of her fingers were pricked, a litany of little red dots. Back in the day, she had been so proud; she could go weeks without perforating the flesh. Not now, though. Now everything had changed. I took hold of one of her hands. She flinched ever so slightly, but she allowed me to continue. I took the leather strip in the other.

I had never been near to my grandmother's skill level when it came to sewing, but – because I was a girl – she had taught me a little over the years. Perhaps she felt that if everything else in life failed me, I could resort to sewing in the same way she had. And now I moved her hand with mine. The needle penetrated the flesh of the fabric and then began to thread. I sensed my grandmother's whole being calm, gradually but inevitably. The corners of her lips slacked. Her dark turtle-eyes shone with fascination and strange pleasure.

We couldn't have been there for more than a few minutes. By no means enough to make any real headway with the leather. But my grandmother was a little like herself again. She looked at me. She spoke softly.

'Thank you, Little One. But I am very tired now. I think I might go to bed.'

I got up without saying a word. I touched my lips to her forehead. The gesture came automatically, and she smiled before turning her face away. I left her room, closing the door softly behind me.

I wandered out into the living room. It was dark, but a single silver light swiveled and swung through the shadows. My mother had gone to her room. My father was in the little cramped space he called a 'study,' the place he always retreated to in the evening. That silvery light came from a flashlight that my brother was holding out as he played in the dark. A flashlight my father had bought for him some while before.

I crept closer and he swung the flashlight round, shining it in my face.

'I got you, I got you,' he said, but his voice sounded abstract somehow, as though his heart wasn't in this particular game.

Qiao often regarded me as a boring older sister, I think. Someone who told him off now and then, a necessary evil who sometimes impinged on his fun. I think if I had been an older brother our relationship would have been different, then he would have regarded me with a certain curiosity and excitement and perhaps even considered me a figure worthy of emulating. And yet, being the boring older sister also had certain advantages. When he was panicked or when he was sad, I think he found it easier to talk to me than he might a brother. And I had the feeling he was sad now.

'Are you okay?'

'Yeah,' he said, not meeting my eye, swiveling the beam from the flashlight all the more furiously.

I stood there watching him for a while, the pale light darting one way and the next.

Eventually he spoke again, his voice sullen and unresponsive.

'Mother and Po Po had a fight.'

'Yeah, I know. They always fight.'

'But ...' This time that same voice held all his child's anxiety. 'But ... it was different.'

'How so?'

'Just was.'

'How so?'

Another silence. And then:

'Because Po Po is different.'

'Yeah?'

'Yeah.'

I didn't know what to say. But as the boring older sister, I knew it was my responsibility to say something.

'Listen, Qiao. About Po Po. I think you should know ...'

'Do you know what?' Qiao burst out excitedly. 'Do you know what?'

'No, what?' I asked, somewhat flummoxed.

'I've got a friend and his name is Chuanli, and he has a television in his house, and the other day Papa said I could go round there after school, and I went there and watched the television, and we watched *Black Cat Detective* and it was about a black cat on a motorbike who has a gun and splats the bad guys, and you see it as he splats them, because you see their blood and stuff and it spurts everywhere!'

Even in the shadows, I could sense his roguish look.

'And do you wanna know something else?'

'What?'

His voice quietened to a level of secret secretiveness that only a small boy can manage.

'That cartoon is only for boys of thirteen or over, but we watched it anyway. Can you believe that?'

I told him that I could. And then my little brother's face fell in a fearful frown.

'You won't tell, will you?'

'I won't tell.'

He nodded in satisfaction.

He looked up at me and smiled.

'I wish we had a TV. And then I could watch cartoons whenever I wanted.'

His eyes shone at the infinite possibilities of such a dazzling scenario.

TWENTY

I T WAS JANUARY 29, THE DAY THE NEW YEAR FELL IN 1987. It marked the Year of the Rabbit. In the run-up to the day, my mother became manic. She cleaned our apartment, once, twice and then again. She polished until the furniture squeaked and her fingers gained a ruddy shine. In the years before, they would have cleaned together, she and my grandmother. As a third-generation female, I had been pulled into the performance too. It was a ritual of some significance for my grandmother, as she firmly believed a thorough clean in the run-up to the new year was an effective way of clearing the house of the bad luck that had accumulated the previous year. But by this point, however, my grandmother was barely aware of what day it was, let alone its broader significance.

My mother, of course, didn't put a great deal of stock in the superstitious aspect of the ritual. I think she did it because she and my grandmother had always done it, scrubbing together in a kind of stubborn silence and achieving an awkward solidarity along the way. And now my grandmother was no longer able to take part, my mother cleaned all the more, as though determined to do the job of two people instead of one.

By late afternoon, our corridor was abuzz with life. Neighbors were filtering into one another's apartments before Reunion Dinner, and children received presents in red packages, sometimes money, but more often than not homemade treats – cakey sweets consumed with sticky, busy fingers. My brother and the other children on our corridor dashing from one place to the next, high on a sugar rush and the excitement of celebration, buzzing around like flies in hot summer, fat and dizzy on the balmy currents of air.

I watched them with a gentle amusement; I remembered all the times I'd played exactly the same way. Of course, everything was different now. My grandmother did not get up at the crack of dawn as she once did. She did not head down to the cemetery to commune with her dead husband and place gifts on the graves of the ancestors as the first shards of light pierced the horizon. She stayed in her room, for the most part, and when a number of the neighbors demanded to greet her with cheery enthusiasm her expression remained faraway and only a few meager words fell from her lips.

Later, we gathered at the dinner table as we always did for Reunion Dinner. My mother and I had prepared a feast of dumplings, chicken and pork, and we had even managed to procure some fat choy, a delicacy otherwise known as 'hairy vegetable' that delighted my brother because of its grotesque appearance rather than its delicate flavor. My father, usually so self-controlled and inhibited, had a little more of the table wine than he might ordinarily have done.

'I just want to say … that I think …' my father began awkwardly, 'I think that this day is traditionally about remembering the ancestors but it is also … useful … to celebrate the living. Ahem. And I would like to celebrate everyone here at this table … my … ahem … my family.'

We all raised our glasses. My father looked both happy and embarrassed. My brother sipped his juice. I took a little more wine. Perhaps it was the warmth of the alcohol and the heat of the sizzling food, but I felt a moment of contentment as if I was a small child again and my whole world was secured by the four walls of our apartment building, and by the sounds of the neighbors' laughter in the halls.

A firework popped outside.

My grandmother's face slowly unraveled in an expression of utter bemusement.

'What?' she murmured, baffled and anxious. 'What is that? What is happening to us?'

I took her withered hand in my own.

'It's okay, Po Po. It's just the fireworks!'

'Why?'

'Don't you remember the story?'

'What story?'

'It's the new year. And they say the first new year started in a small village …'

It struck me, with the same thudding awareness, the same breathless impact, just how much my grandmother was like a child herself these days. She gazed at me, incredulous, before whispering in a small voice:

'I used to live in a small village.'

'Yes, yes, you did. But this small village was threatened by a monster. The monster was called the Nian, and it lived inside a mountain.

And sometimes it would come to the village. But the villagers realized the Nian was frightened by bright colors and loud noises. That's why the gifts Qiao and the other children have received are all wrapped in nice red paper, and why there are fireworks outside. This protects us from the Nian!'

I tried to tell the story with the same gentle amusement with which she had relayed it to me so many years before, but I felt my voice faltering. Her expression changed; a flash of searing self-awareness – a fleeting glimpse of my grandmother of old, the person she had been.

'Pfffff. A silly children's story. I lived in a village just like that as a child. And I tell you this much, Little One, red paper and a few loud noises couldn't ever protect children from monsters!'

The way she had said this, the coldness in her voice, the bitterness, was striking. The whole table lapsed into a kind of stunned silence. But in the next moment, that woman was gone. Her face had relaxed into the same vacant serenity. She blinked in wonder at the array of food. I felt my brother fidgeting beside me. My parents were aware of what was happening, but he couldn't quite understand; he experienced it secondhand, through the emotional waves we adults were projecting.

We adults! Was I now an adult? Was that the final unforeseen consequence of my grandmother's unrelenting deterioration? That it would sever me from my childhood once and for all?

We began to eat again. To chew and then to swallow. To take in the heat of the slippery hot dumplings. To be oblivious, to be as bodies that yearned for food and warmth, if only for a few moments – because the reality of what was happening to our family, of what was happening to my grandmother, was almost too much to bear. And

249

yet, behind the festivities and the laughter and all the other noise filtering in from our neighbors along the corridor, that reality was holding each member of our family in its cold and interminable grip.

Another firework popped and fizzed in the night. Again, my grandmother jerked into awareness in her chair. Again, she looked at me.

'What's happening? What are those noises? What's going on?'

My brother slapped his glass of juice from the table and onto the floor. It shattered instantly. He thrust his own chair back and stood up, pointing at my grandmother, his prepubescent body still a little chubby, his whole bearing arranged in an absurd and trembling gesture of accusation.

'Why are you doing this? Why do you keep asking the same thing over and over? Why are you making everyone feel so bad? I hate you. I hate you so much!'

My grandmother blinked at my little brother, her face baffled and hurt. My father stood up, and he too was trembling. His voice was soft as ever but there was an undercurrent of anger in it, one I had rarely heard.

'*You*, you will not ever talk to your grandmother that way! How dare you!'

My brother, who was already on the verge of breaking down, dissolved. Sobbing violently, he ran from the room.

Instinctively, I turned toward my grandmother. Her face was frozen, a single tear running down her cheek.

'Happy New Year,' my mother murmured under her breath.

Perhaps I should have gone after my brother to make sure he was okay. Perhaps I should have lingered in order to comfort my grandmother. But the weight of everything that had happened felt crushing, and I retreated to my room. Being nondescript, quiet and shy has its advantages. Slipping away was something I was always good at. I'd had a lifetime of practice.

Later that evening – when the fireworks had died down to solitary and distant pops and the activity on our corridor had diminished – I slipped out of the building to meet Gen in the same wooded area we had taken my brother to some months before. At this time of the evening, it was different. Whereas by day the trees had seemed rustic and colorful, hued by the haze of the sun, now that it was dusk, they appeared as spectral shapes, strange and indistinct, forking out of the dimness. As we climbed the hill we could see the lights from the city below winking in the murky purple and blue of the fading evening.

We stood for a while in silence, looking out across Beijing, and it felt as though we were the only people for miles around. Everything that had happened – all the anxiety I had accumulated – felt like a wedge in my body, something as real and corporeal as a cyst or a cancer.

'So my grandmother didn't even remember it was New Year's today. She can't really hold anything in her head anymore.'

I made my words soft, almost light, as if they were quirky observations that had just this minute occurred. Gen didn't look at me.

'I guess it's inevitable,' I said stoically, but inside my heart was pounding with panic. 'I guess this is just what happens when you get very old. It's just one of those things.'

Gen nodded slightly but remained quiet.

'It's Qiao I worry about,' I said, trying to sound grave and concerned. 'Because of his age, he doesn't really understand what is happening … I don't think.'

I allowed my voice to trail away.

Gen glanced at me. He coughed quietly.

'As you say, it's part of getting old, it's part of life. I am sure he will come to terms with it eventually. By the way, it's our last class on Saturday. It will be strange not going there anymore, won't it?'

'Yes, it will,' I said dully, but something inside me was cracking. I managed a wintry smile. 'Hey, do you remember when we were kids, and we used to play that game – Cat Catching Mice – and Fan always wanted to be the cat, but he could never get the game right, and he'd jump on you before he was supposed to, and it created such complete chaos with everyone rolling around on the ground …? Life seemed so much simpler back then, don't you think?'

'I don't know,' Gen said noncommittally. 'All that kind of stuff. It seems so long ago now.'

I turned my face away from him in the gray gloom so he couldn't see the tears in my eyes.

When I got home, I did what I have always done every time I've felt sad or hopeless. I opened a book. I can't say that I remember what I read that evening, I only know that I read. I turned the pages and took what literature provides. The feeling of escape if only for a short time. A distancing from your own life and the ability to participate in the experiences of others as an invisible presence somewhere on the outskirts of the page. I read in the way that other teenagers might sink into music, as an escape; reading had always been mine.

But it didn't last. The hour grew late. It must have been close to midnight when I heard that sound. Something human and yet strange. Childlike in its expression, and yet resonant with age. I knew at once the moan was coming from my grandmother's room. That it was coming from her. But I kept reading. At this time of night, I told myself, who knows what noises are what? Who can really tell?

She moaned again. I felt my fingers clench, not because my reading had been interrupted, but because there was no respite. I could no longer ignore that fearful moaning and its source. My grandmother was calling out the way a child might.

I felt angry. Thinking back, it was a selfish and unkind reaction to have and one that to this day leaves me ashamed. But up until that point, my grandmother's implacable presence had dominated my life. Stubborn, superstitious and determined, she was the most fearless human being I had ever known. And now I felt as though I had been cheated. Surely she didn't have *the right* to become this other person, this frightened little woman who could no longer remember our names. She didn't have *the right* to call out in the night like a small child.

But behind my resentment was fear. As much as I wanted to establish myself as an adult, there was still this place inside me where I would always be a little girl, her 'Little One' – a warm, wonderful and safe place where my grandmother remained large as life and nothing would ever change.

So I tried to ignore her calls. I wondered if one of my parents might go to her first. My mother, perhaps, because it was something my father was unlikely to do. Not because he lacked compassion, but because it would have been indecorous. My mother, however, was a heavy sleeper. And so it seemed that I was destined to inherit the problems that night spawned. I would usually be the one to go to my brother when he had a bad dream. And now I was the one who would go to my grandmother too.

I crept into her room with a sense of resentment and dread. I could hardly make her out in the darkness. I moved closer, inching my way to the side of her bed. I lit a candle. Her face was ragged and she seemed so terribly old. She had always been old to me, but now she looked fallible and decrepit too. Her eyes were haunted. She looked at me and I knew she wasn't sure who I was.

'Where is Hu Ren? Where is my husband?'

'Po Po. Grandfather passed, some time ago.'

'He is dead?'

'Yes.'

I wondered how she would react, but she took the news in a solemn way, nodding once, as though it was something she had suspected all along.

And then she looked at me with that ancient face, and those eyes – huge pools of darkness. Her lips trembled briefly. Finally, she asked in a childlike whisper:

'Am I dead too?'

All at once, the resentment I had felt toward her, the frustration I had held inside, melted away, and I was overcome by pity.

I reached out to her. I stroked her thick straggly hair. And I tried to stop myself from sobbing.

'No, you are not dead. You are my grandmother. And I love you very much!'

She looked at me with an expression of curiosity and wonder. Her lips trembled. And then, slowly, she reached out and touched my face.

'Little One,' she breathed.

I was sobbing now, but I fought to control it.

'That's right! I am here. You are okay. You are okay. You are with me,' I said.

Her turtle face crinkled in a vacant smile.

She sank back into her bed. She was no longer frightened. I had given her that, at least. It was, perhaps, the only thing I remember giving to my grandmother. Sometime later I recalled my words – 'You are okay. You are okay. You are with me' – and I realized she had murmured those same words to me, so many times, when I was a small child, recovering from a nightmare.

I sat at the side of her bed, watching her.

She had closed her eyes, but I reached out to her, and I felt her hand grip my own; a grip so soft, so fleeting, that in a moment it relaxed, and I heard the sound of her soft, whistling snores. I was so stunned by what had happened that the movement outside the door took me aback.

My mother was standing there in her nightgown. She was looking at me, as I held my grandmother's hand in my own, with something akin to hate in her eyes.

I glanced up at her.

My mother met my gaze, then turned and walked away.

TWENTY-ONE

HAVE YOU EVER SEEN ONE OF THOSE SPED-UP FILMS where people move in and out of the frame, whizzing one way and then the other? Only, you notice there is one person at the center of the picture who is motionless – a fixed, still point around which everything else rushes and blurs?

I felt a bit like that. My classmates were awash with activity and anticipation because we were to leave school that summer once and for all. Some talked about the universities they had applied for; others the lucrative jobs waiting for them in the state sector; others still had dreams of going abroad. But although I went through the motions organizing my own university applications and answering the odd question about my plans, it seemed I was separated from my classmates by a great distance; that their words were coming from far away, almost as if I was hearing them from under water. Everyone else was moving forward, time was continuing as it always had, but I remained stationary, locked into a sense of numbness, as I watched my grandmother gradually fade. In those last days she was never far from my mind.

All at once everyone was clapping!

I looked up from my desk. It was our final Saturday session with Liu Ping. Everyone was looking at me. Even Li Lei was beaming at me. Our teacher had just announced that my essay had scored very highly, not only in our school, but across Beijing: I had achieved one of the top ten grades. For a few seconds, it was difficult to process the information. Liu Ping handed me my essay along with a gift card worth 600 yuan. I had never held something of so much value in my life and it didn't seem real. Nothing did. Gen's essay had also scored highly; he won second place in our class. And Li Lei came third. They received gift cards of 100 yuan apiece.

Liu Ping told us how happy he was and that he thought we would all go on to do China proud. He seemed sincere, and even brought out a box of cakes and a jug of lemonade made by his wife. I was surprised to learn he was married, as he rarely spoke about his personal life, but on that last day, everything seemed a little looser and more relaxed. We didn't do any work. Liu Ping opened the window wide, and from outside came the scent of the spring air and the freshly cut grass.

While the others chattered away happily, I touched the smooth surface of the gift card and felt a spark of hope kindle inside me. It wasn't just about the money. Apart from books, there wasn't much I spent money on. But the idea that a piece I had written might merit such a reward was something in itself. That my thoughts put to page might be worth something seemed as wondrous as it was unexpected. For the first time, the idea of becoming a writer began to shimmer faintly on the horizon of my future.

The mood of the others was jovial and for a while I felt a door had been opened, letting in a little light. I noticed Gen leaning back in his chair, as solemn and as thoughtful as ever, gazing out at the spring sunshine, and I thought how much I wanted him to be part of my future too. And now I had won this award, I was certain he would be proud of me. I couldn't wait to talk to him.

At the end of the session, I wished Li Lei all the best, and very tentatively she hugged me. Her body was thin, slight. I felt a flux of quiet emotion. It surprised me. With the ardency of young people, we promised to keep in touch.

Of course, we never did.

After class, I walked with Gen. I had my gift card in my inside pocket. He was quiet, even by his standards. As always, when he fell into these swells of quiet, I overcompensated, chattering away, attempting to fend off the silence. Gen and I had both applied to Peking University. But although it was our plan to go to the same university, privately I was sure he would be accepted but I wasn't certain they would take me. A large institution attended by thousands of students, it had a massive campus near the heart of the city, and the most renowned scholars were invited to give lectures there. It was in the Haidian District – where Gen and I had seen that Italian film a year or so earlier. The university was a center of liberal culture, surrounded by bars, cafés and theaters, a place where artists, poets and bands from the farthest corners arrived to showcase their talents.

I looked at Gen.

'I think that, what with us both doing well in the essay competition, we have a good chance of getting into Peking University. Can you imagine that?'

He glanced at me and gave a brief smile. He lapsed into silence once more.

'What are you going to do with your prize?' I asked.

He looked me straight in the eye this time. He took out his own gift voucher. He examined it thoughtfully.

'This is always how it starts,' he said softly. 'They give you these little trinkets, these little incentives, these petty rewards. And that's how it happens. That's how you lose your critical voice, your ability to think. It's how they turn you into a little gray bureaucrat just like them.'

Deliberately and slowly, he tore it apart and scattered the paper on the street.

Perhaps he saw the way my face had fallen, for he at once assumed a kinder expression.

'Oh no, I don't mean that about you. I was speaking about my situation, not yours. Your essay was perfectly fine. I am sure you earned your prize. And I want you to enjoy it. I know that such affirmations are important to you.'

He leaned forward and brushed his lips against my forehead.

But his touch felt cold.

After he had gone, I thought about what he said. Was I the type of selfish individual who craved such petty affirmations? I thought he was probably right. The light and color of the delight I had taken in my achievement at once leached away. But it wasn't just about Gen. I thought about everything my family was going through. How could I take such pleasure in myself, permit myself such airs, while my grandmother was dying?

I thought about my little brother. Before I had left the apartment for class that morning, Qiao had taken my arm. He'd wanted to show me a picture he'd drawn, a picture of the 'black cat detective,' the main character in the cartoon he watched at a friend's house. It was rare these days for him to share something like that with me.

But behind the insistence that I take a look at his drawing, I knew he hadn't wanted me to leave. And I knew why. He didn't want to be left in a home weighed down by unspoken grief. What my grandmother's dementia taught me, taught all of us, was that it is possible to grieve for the living as well as for the dead. To miss someone while they are still alive. To experience their loss even though they are still breathing. My brother felt that too, I think. I remember his gaze – those large eyes, still the eyes of a child, but with that first speck of a more adult surliness and recrimination set into them. I remember him watching me, unsmiling, as I escaped the house while he remained. But I put his image to the back of my mind and got on with my day.

I held the gift voucher in my hand. It seemed negligible now. Worthless. Part of me wanted to do as Gen had done, to tear it into pieces and let the scraps of paper flutter away on the wind. At the same time, however, that voucher represented more money than I had ever seen.

I put it back in my pocket.

I took the bus to Chang'an Avenue. It was late afternoon. I headed west, away from the center and toward a concentration of much smaller electronic stores – stores to be discovered on the side streets that snaked away from the main thoroughfare. I had an idea of what I was looking for. After browsing a couple of shops I took a breath and committed to my decision. I bought a Jinlipu television, something that would remain my most expensive purchase for a good few years. My audacity both shocked and thrilled me. But what I hadn't counted on was the sheer weight of the set. I staggered out of the shop holding the boxed TV out in front of me, waddling in the way of a heavily pregnant woman.

Every now and then I had to bend down and rest the TV on the ground to gather my strength and rest my humming arms. Once I'd made it back to the main thoroughfare, I rested the TV again and took a breath. I looked up into the darkening sky. In the distance I could see the Monumental Entrance, the temple building you have to pass through in order to enter Tiananmen Square. As the shadows gathered, the great building was bathed in a solemn orange light that made it seem peaceful, almost holy, while all around the winking dots of cars zipped and flitted in a stream of movement. I felt a moment of well-being. Then I hoisted up my cargo and heaved it to the bus stop.

Sometime later I had got the TV back to the apartment, my whole body wracked with pain. I put it down before my brother who blinked at it suspiciously.

'Open it!' I said.

'Why?'

'Just do it!'

Another time he might have argued, but that day he applied himself to the box with weary acquiescence. As he peeled away the cardboard the expression on his face began to change: from mild curiosity, to surprise, to absolute wonder.

'Is it ... is it real?' he stuttered.

'Of course it's real, you ninny. Now you can watch all the cartoons you want!'

The excitement was too much – he began to whoop and shout, and it was good to see him be a kid again.

The commotion drew my mother and father.

I explained to them what had happened. I told them about the prize I had been awarded, and felt the blush rise on my face. I looked at the ground.

'Well done,' my father said softly, his voice warm.

'How on earth do you think we will get Qiao to do his homework now?' my mother asked in a tone of bitter disapproval.

And yet her gaze was riveted to the TV set and there was a gleam in her eye. I recognized the look. We were the first on our corridor to own one and my mother knew it would make us objects of envy and raise our standing. And that was something she craved just as much as my brother hungered for his cartoons. My father set up the TV. He turned it on. At first there was only static. He adjusted a dial. The image cohered. A large man appeared on the screen, and he was flipping pancakes. All of us watched, hypnotized. He wobbled as he cooked. He started to speak, but his voice was squeaky. It sounded like a woman's voice. The voice in no way matched the body from which it came.

'You must never ever cook your pancakes in ball batter syrup because ball batter syrup must only ever be used for battered balls!'

His admonishment was amplified by the TV's speakers into an almost cataclysmic shriek.

We jumped back.

And then we all burst out laughing.

.   .   .

My grandmother never got to watch that new television.

By that point she was too weak to move from her room. My mother and I took turns to change her bedpan. Before, she would bulldoze others with the sheer force of her personality, her frankness, her scathing remarks, her crude humor and those sudden flashes of compassion she would show to waifs and strays. Now, she would quiver violently the moment a shadow crept across the threshold of her door, or she would weep softly when she couldn't remember where she was.

Her full frizzy hair had retreated, and that robust old turtle's face of hers had collapsed into a sunken-cheeked ruin. Her life force had become depleted, such that it was a struggle for her to raise her head – the place where withered skin revealed the brittle outline of bone underneath. It was harder and harder to get her to eat. In the final awful stages of the disease the muscles of the throat refuse to contract – the body loses the ability to digest, as the last weak neurons in the brain fizzle out.

And yet, and yet. Something deep inside her responded to my voice. Mine and no other. I was sure of it. When she had her trembling fits, it was my voice that could calm her; and when she began to sob softly and fearfully, the tone of my words could, on occasion, stem her tears. It wasn't as though she any longer knew who I was. But when I spoke to her, there was something in her gaze. Her dim, tired eyes opened a little more. When I drew near, her gaze seemed to settle on me – vacant, yes, but gentle and warm too, huge eyes set into a withered ravaged skull; and just for a moment those eyes seemed to twinkle.

That final night, after we had called the doctor, she looked at me that way, and there was a sudden urgency in her gaze; her throat tightened, her lips were wobbling, and it seemed to me she was trying to generate one last sentence from that helpless mouth, that limp, slack neck. She looked into my eyes, her ancient head propped against the pillow, and in the same moment the childlike terror that had consumed her in those final months seemed to withdraw; she looked at me as though she had felt something wonderful and wanted to share what she was feeling. She struggled and stuttered, desperately trying to produce the sound.

I leaned in. The tears soaking my face, I leaned in.

For all my life she had called me her 'Little One,' and that phrase on her lips had become as everyday and ordinary to me as the blue of the sky or the feel of the pages of a book against my fingers. But at that moment, it suddenly became the most precious and rare of all things and everything in the world hinged on her calling me her 'Little One' one last time.

Her eyes lost focus, however, and glazed over. She never spoke again. Something final had settled upon her – a fug, a great sleepiness – and it was peaceful. For that, I will remain grateful until my own dying day. We gathered around her. My mother, myself and the doctor. And we braced ourselves.

My grandmother was no longer aware of our presence. Her last vestige of consciousness seemed to narrow to a single point. Gently, deliberately almost, she somehow found the strength to raise a hand. The same hand whose hard, brittle fingertips had been stubbed on so many occasions by multiple needles over the course of generations. The same hand that had helped stitch and sew so many slippers and shoes, bringing dignity to those like her who'd had their feet smashed by an ugly and stupid ritual.

She reached out from her bedclothes and raised her hand. She looked at it with an expression of wonder, almost as though she was seeing something miraculous, a thing separate from herself, possessed of its own independent life and power. It was as if there was nothing else in the universe left of her other than this mysterious entity, this hand. Her fingers lengthened and turned, until, gradually, her hand lowered and came to rest on her covers again.

And then she was gone.

Our doctor, Yang Xiaosheng, reached over to my grandmother's face, and very gently touched his fingers to her eyelids, closing them. That stayed in my mind, because I was in shock, and everything had frozen in that moment, yet at the same time his gesture seemed both tender and wise. And it occurred to me that Dr. Yang was so young, not much older than me, and my grandmother was so very old, and she was gone now and I would never be with her again. And the young doctor's movement, the way he had closed her eyes, caused something to catch in my throat, for it was fitting somehow.

I turned to my mother. Instinctively, automatically. She was standing over us, focused on my grandmother's body, and there was a look on her face that I had never seen before, a moment of utter bafflement crinkled with pain, and a tightening in the eyes – the expression of someone struggling for breath.

I moved toward her. She glanced at me. There was no cruelty or anger in her expression; rather it was as though she hadn't seen me at all, she simply looked straight through me.

Without ceremony, she turned and left the room.

I moved my own hand toward the hand of my grandmother. But I didn't dare touch it – that furrowed, wrinkled thing – and I didn't dare look into my grandmother's face either. I remember the room seemed suddenly, violently cold. I remember that I didn't cry, and yet the image of everything there seemed to darken and blur under a gaze filled with tears.

Yang Xiaosheng touched my shoulder gently. I looked up at him.

'My father used to say that your grandmother wasn't everyone's "cup of tea." But that she was a "hell of a woman" nevertheless. A force of nature. I'm so sorry for your loss.'

TWENTY-TWO

THE FUNERAL TOOK PLACE IN EARLY SUMMER. THE SKY WAS light blue, a breeze tickled the trees, and the afternoon sun was pricked by just a hint of cold. I remember I was wearing a blue dress that day. My grandmother was buried next to my grandfather. At the cemetery, we burned a selection of objects – flowers, bread and money – all of which had been fabricated from Joss paper. The tradition was that these things could be used in the afterlife. I think my grandmother would have been skeptical, however. Even though she was perhaps the most superstitious person I've ever known, for her the spirits resided alongside the living – in this world. What was the use of heaven if you couldn't tease your loved ones? And the thought of giving a little grief to her family in the here-and-now, reminding us that she was still around, would have tickled her. It would have brought one last smile to that old turtle face.

Of course, she hadn't been that same person, my real grand-mother, for a while. The dementia had taken one layer of her after another, sucking them into its void, until there was next to nothing left. Perhaps that's why I didn't cry on the day of her funeral. I had cried before. I had been grieving her for a while. What I felt instead was numbness.

Many years later, I was out with a couple of girlfriends. One had recently lost her beloved mother. The other laid her hand on the knee of our grief-stricken friend and said something I will never forget. She told her to 'enjoy' the funeral. Because it would be the one day in all her life when she could share stories about her departed mother with abandon – could talk to everyone and anyone about her without inhibition or worry. That it was important to take advantage of this, for she would feel the need to talk about her mother every day after. For as long as such days were given to her.

I wasn't able to take advantage of my grandmother's funeral in that way, despite how much I had loved her. Because something of me wasn't there at all. I just lingered in the background, at the corners of the room, that numbness filling every part of me. And yet the number of people who came to the gathering after the funeral was incredible. Hundreds filled our corridor, generations of women laughing and shedding tears, talking about my grandmother: her sharp-tongued humor, her cantankerousness, her fearlessness and the vein of kindness that had run through her like silver ore through hard, black rock. I didn't shed any tears of my own; I couldn't cry, so instead I watched, until it seemed as though I was little more than a faint presence at the periphery of my life.

I watched those large, rotund women giggle and commiserate, laugh and cry, and I watched their grandchildren wriggle impatiently around their legs, squalling, hot tears of tiredness and boredom filling their eyes. I watched my brother retreat into his own imaginary world while men ruffled his hair and women tenderly pinched his cheek. I hung back in the kitchen and watched my own mother as she played hostess, clasping hands and laughing and handing out small parcels of food. She was in her element, I thought. All the attention of the community was on her, and to my sense of numbness was added a sudden shock of hate.

She picked up on it, my mother. She came into the kitchen, closing the door against the warm heat produced by all those people and the chatter bodying out across the air. She caught my look, sullen and frowning, before I had the chance to look away. Her smile – still fixed – died on her face. She moved close to me, one arm arching on her hip. Her gaze was even but hard.

'You disapprove?'

I rubbed my mouth, mumbled something into the sleeve of my pretty blue dress.

Her gaze never left me, never lost its clarity, but her lips thinned. Her voice came in a hiss.

'You miss your grandmother! Always the two of you against the world, thick as thieves. You think you knew her so well, right? But did she ever tell you about the time she left me in the back garden for the night in the cold and the rain because I spoiled a chicken she wanted me to prepare? I was no more than eleven years old. She ever tell you about the time she threw a kitchen knife at me because I talked back to her? She ever tell you about that, your perfect, wonderful grandmother?'

My mother's voice became ragged. Tears welled in her eyes. She blinked them away.

'Oh, what the hell does it matter? What use is it anyway?'

She straightened herself up. She fixed that smile to her face once again. And then strode out of the room to cater to the guests.

A tightening against my chest. A feeling of not being able to breathe. Light shimmering across my field of vision. A faintness. Something I hadn't felt for some time.

I stumbled out of the apartment and through the corridor, which was thick with people. I heard some of them say my name, felt friendly hands on my shoulder, but I had to keep moving. I exited the building and I kept on moving.

By the time I arrived at Gen's house the weather had grown colder. Or perhaps that was just how I remember it. I remember that blue dress still clinging to me. I knocked on his door. His dad was away, his mother was shopping, I think. He took one look at me, and took me into his arms.

'You're shivering,' he said.

He made me some hot tea. We lay on his bed and he held me.

'Drink a little more, you're still cold!'

We stayed like that for a while. I was so relieved to be away. He touched my hair. But his voice, when it arrived, was awkward and pained – a whisper almost.

'I'm sorry I didn't come … today. I wanted to. But I thought it was … more a family occasion.'

'It's okay,' I murmured. My voice sounded soft and strange. That same numbness creeping in. 'Everything is fine.'

He held me to him, held me close, and for a moment I thought that numbness that had spread through me might abate. Then I felt his hand, tentative and gentle, finding my hand, guiding it down to his groin. It seemed so automatic I didn't even think about it. I just started to move my fingers up and down, gripping him. And I heard him emit that soft, guttural moan. I felt the splash of warm liquid against my skin.

And at some point I felt myself get up.

'I'd better get going.'

'You don't need to. You don't have to. You can stay longer if you want.'

'I should get going.'

As I left the house, his mother was coming up the garden path, carrying several bags of shopping. Even though she was much younger than Gen's father, and very pretty, to me she had always seemed pathetic somehow, forever projecting the kind of shrill, artificial brightness that edged toward hysteria. But when she raised her head and smiled, I caught in her soft dark eyes a look of genuine concern. She reached out as she said hello, but didn't quite touch my cheek with her hand. And then I realized it was she who pitied me.

I walked through the streets. I walked for a while longer. My body was numb. My mind was dull, like a thick murky soup, but one thought eventually came bubbling up. The thought of a book I had read all those years ago: Hemingway's *The Old Man and the Sea*. I recalled the triumph the old man had felt when he had hooked his great fish, but what my mind focused on was what happened next. The way the old fisherman had watched helplessly as the sharks circled his boat and feasted on his catch. The way the great marlin he had caught had been reduced to nothing by the gnawing of the sharks' teeth, the way his hope had been eroded in the process until there was nothing left of that either.

All that was left was the return to shore. The feeling of exhaustion. The cold. The numbness.

I got back to the apartment late. Everyone else had gone to bed. I moved through the living room in the gloom; it was littered with paper plates and other paraphernalia. I went into the kitchen, turned on the light, and its blue-white fluorescence hummed. Plates were piled high in the sink like towers. I thought about my grandmother. I felt numb.

Something caught my eye. The glint of the blade of a bread knife. I thought about my grandmother again, and I thought about what my mother had said about her, and I thought about Gen and his low guttural groan and the feeling of his emanation against my skin. I thought about these things, and they seemed to blur in the numbness, and the only thing that was real was the stark, sharp clarity of the blade.

I gripped the handle. The movement came naturally. That same sense of inevitability.

I pressed the cold steel against the soft flesh of my upturned arm. And suddenly everything that had happened forced itself against me with a sudden sharpening violence, and I took the blade and I jabbed myself with its point – not as hard as I might have, but hard enough to break the skin and draw blood. The sudden stab of pain was in some way relieving, for that carapace that had grown across me – that skein of numbness – was for the first time broken, and the feeling of my blood dribbling out of my body caused me to take in breath, violently. My heart was pounding.

And the rage – those feelings of loathing and disgust I had toward myself – had diminished now, as the warmth of that blood trickled and flowed. My breathing began to quiet too. The blood was soaked up by the thin, fine fabric of my pretty blue dress. And although, in the time to come, I would cut my arms on many more occasions, I would never wear that dress again.

.　　.　　.

Since my grandmother had passed away, my brother was quieter, less boisterous. It was to be expected, I suppose. I'd watch him sometimes when he was absorbed in some game. And sometimes I'd feel a sense of pity because even though he was on the cusp of adolescence, he still seemed so indelibly a child. He'd watch his cartoons with rapt attention. And sometimes I envied him his escape.

My mother did not mention my grandmother after the funeral. Instead, she stripped the sheets from her bed and gave away her clothes. But my grandmother's chair remained. It had, of course, belonged to my grandfather, all those years ago. When he'd died, my grandmother had commandeered it. Now it sat empty as the room itself gathered dust. I'd glimpse its outline through the gap of the door late at night as I went to get a drink of water from the kitchen. Sometimes I'd step into the room in the early morning, when the motes of dust flickered across sleek beams of sunlight, and I'd remember how she would sit there and sew. I'd remember the smell of her, and the huskiness of her voice, and those thickly veined hands and nimble fingers. I'd remember the full, unapologetic solidity of her – the strength of her broad back, but also the softness of the flesh around her belly. And I'd remember the rich darkness of her eyes, always somewhere between amused and defiant.

And that's when I'd feel the grief, hot and palpable against the edges of my skin, the back of my eyes. I'd look at the chair in that room, and the object itself seemed bereft, as though a great loneliness had settled on it during the night – and its old threadbare arms and the jutting outline of its legs would soften and blur through my tears. I had turned eighteen that summer but I'd never felt more like a child.

Fortunately I kept busy. I had started working. Both Gen and I had been accepted at Peking University. His family was wealthy, but mine was less well-to-do, and the government had abolished the old tax-funded system of education that had existed under Mao. Fortunately, as a result of scoring highly in the essay competition, I had obtained a scholarship, but that wouldn't cover the cost of books or rent. While Gen would stay on campus in the student dorms, I would remain living at home with my family, and that summer, before my first academic year, I worked in Mrs. Yang's corner shop, selling tobacco and lottery cards.

It was good to get out of the house. My relationship with my mother had devolved into a series of hostile silences. My father was as much of a recluse as ever. My little brother occupied the happy colors of his cartoon world. And even though I was not superstitious like my grandmother, her presence pervaded every inch of that apartment. Sometimes I could almost hear her clacking her false teeth in the mornings, or swearing colorfully as she pushed up from the toilet seat in the night-time cold, her arthritic legs creaking.

These thoughts I kept to myself. Around other people, I spoke less and less. I saw Gen often that summer. Other than the old men who came in to buy their lottery tickets – their strange chatter, their rosy breath, their smoky clothes – Gen was my one real contact with the outside world. Sometimes we went to the cinema, though I don't recall the films we saw. Sometimes we would spend time in his room, being intimate – always the same procedure, my hand on him. He was concerned for me in his way. Sometimes he would be holding forth on the latest existential writer who had tickled his fancy, or his father's callous behavior of late, and his voice would trail away when he realized my attention had slackened.

He wasn't nasty about it. I'd apologize profusely. I explained to him that it wasn't him. Only I didn't really know what it was. So I'd apologize some more. He'd smile in amusement. In a small voice I'd ask him to continue. Even if my mind had wandered. Even if I wasn't quite sure what he had been talking about. For it felt like Gen was my one remaining tether to the world. That without him, I would float away.

We were lying on his bed. Gen was talking excitedly – he would be studying politics and I literature and some of the modules we were offered by the university might overlap. He had already chosen the ones we should take outside the core curriculum and he was justifying his choices. Some part of me relaxed when he was like this, because he knew more about these things than me. But more important, when he was telling me about the book I should read or the course I needed to take, I felt he was concerned about me and invested in our future together.

'Hey, you know what we could do?' I asked quietly.

'What's that?'

'We could go to the bookseller not so far from my building. Do you remember I took you there once? That quiet old place. It always makes me feel so peaceful. And since I know the owner so well, I bet we could get some of our books for university from there a little cheaper!'

Gen didn't speak at once.

'Yes, that's a possibility,' he eventually said.

His tone had changed. And he said nothing after. Living with my mother and my grandmother, I was used to people thundering out their emotions in torrents. But Gen could go silent just like that, and his silence weighed on me until it became unbearable. Until I asked in a small voice:

'You think it's a bad idea? You don't want to go there?'

He turned my face toward his. Gently. Looked into my eyes.

'I didn't want to talk about this, especially not now,' he said softly, and it was as though he was a man burdened by great sadness.

'Talk about what?' I asked, feeling a sense of panic rise and clarify like fingers of ice.

'You know how intelligent I think you are, right? How sensitive. How kind. But I think, because of that fundamental kindness, you don't always see the world as it is. Rather you see it as you want it to be.'

'What do you mean?' I whispered.

'A man that age. Giving a young girl books for free. Almost as tokens, as presents. Having her over for cups of tea. The more cynical among us might imagine ...'

His voice trailed away in the gravity of the silence that followed.

I burst out laughing.

I hadn't meant to. It wasn't even funny. It was a kind of hysteria provoked by the sheer absurdity of the suggestion.

'You can't mean ... that's ridiculous. I've been going there for years, and he's never so much as looked at me in that way!'

He turned away and spoke in a clipped whisper.

'I'm sorry my concern for you is so amusing!'

'No, I didn't mean that. I really didn't. I just wanted to, I mean, I just think ...'

Again my words fell into the void of silence his seriousness had conjured up.

Neither of us said anything.

'I mean, I really appreciate it. I guess ... I don't really have to go there, if you don't want me to. If that's what you want.'

He looked at me ardently.

'It's not about what I want. It's about what's best for you. I ...'

His gaze flickered downward.

He seemed vulnerable then. I touched my hand to his thick shaggy hair. Even if everything in my apartment had collapsed, if it was hard to breathe at home through the fug of our grief – here at least, I had these moments with him. Where we were both in some way naked, vulnerable, but together.

'Okay. I can tell him. I'll go one more time, and ... tell him I won't be coming to visit him anymore.'

'Okay.'

I had been sincere in what I had said to Gen, about telling the old bookseller that I wouldn't be coming around anymore. And yet the promise had been abstract. I hadn't firmed up a particular day, and part of me hoped to put it off as long as possible. But Gen was quietly persistent, he kept reminding me, and encouraging me, and eventually, he even offered to come with me. I knew he wasn't going to forget. And besides, I felt tired. I just wanted to get it over with.

And that's why I found myself standing outside the bookshop one August evening. I had been going there for so many years; it was a sanctum of solace and learning, a place more than any other that embodied the magic of books for me. But Gen was watching me with a gentle gaze, reminding me of why we had come. The following week I would start university and my life would change. So perhaps it was necessary and inevitable that I break with the past. At least, that's what I told myself.

Gen waited outside. I walked through the doors one final time. With everything that had happened in the last few months, with my grandmother's deterioration, I hadn't been in for a while. As I entered the store, I felt the warmth and scent of musty books envelop me. The old man was sitting at the desk where he always was. This man had only ever shown me great kindness, but this felt like something I had to do.

He looked up at me, his eyes the color of the sea on a warm afternoon, soft and blue, infinite in their gentle haze. I felt my heart trip against my chest. I felt something inside me break, perhaps because I knew I wouldn't see him again. Perhaps it was about my grandmother too, the feeling that everything was being left behind. A door to an old tattered bookshop that I would never step through again.

He looked up at me. All at once the tears were streaming down my cheeks.

He raised himself up, that thin arthritic body, and in that moment a man who had only ever seemed old to me seemed older still, and yet he was reaching out to me, trying to provide me with support, and I could see the concern etched into his halting, painful movements. My tears flowed all the more. I hadn't cried on the day of my grandmother's funeral, and now it seemed as though I couldn't stop.

'Cup of tea?' he murmured, with a gentle, sad smile.

I shook my head. I couldn't get the words out.

He watched me for a few moments longer. He was distressed and baffled and he clearly didn't know what to say; how to calm this teenager who had appeared so suddenly distraught. He faltered, then managed:

'Would you care to take a book? You can take any one of them. Not just to borrow. But to keep. Free. No charge.'

Even at my young age, I realized this was his way of showing concern. He could no more ask me to explain why I was sad than I could ask him about the family he might once have had, or how he had ended up alone. I thought about that – he had never told me anything about his family, the people he had once known. I wondered about them. How many people does a person lose in the course of a life? How long is it before you lose yourself? I thought about my grandmother. I thought about her empty chair.

And then the words arrived, in a desperate, halting whisper.

'Do you have a book … to tell you what to do when someone is gone? Someone you've known … for as long as you remember. A book to stop it from … *hurting* so badly. Could you give me that one?'

He raised his eyes to me, and in his expression I thought I caught a hint of desperation. But his voice arrived as precise and soft as ever.

'I am afraid we don't have anything like that in stock. At least … not currently.'

The last part – that 'at least … not currently' – caused me a small involuntary smile.

I felt the tears drying on my cheeks.

I had the urge to reach out to him, to touch the thin white hair that remained, to stroke his face, to let him know how incredibly grateful I was for the kindness he had shown me all those years. For the love of books he had helped inspire in me, and which had so benefited the course of my life.

For a few moments, all those feelings whirled inside me, struggling for expression, and it occurred to me that in all our time together I hadn't ever asked his name. But Gen was waiting for me outside, and I knew it was time to go; that I had to go, and I could not return. I felt the tears burn my eyes once more.

So I did all that was remaining to me in that moment and mouthed the words:

Thank you.

Did he hear what I wanted to say without speaking? Was it ever important that he did?

Looking back on it, he may have shown the same kindness to many other waifs and strays. I am certain it was in his nature. He had played a massively important role in my life, which made it easy for me to assume I had played some kind of role in his. But was that true?

I don't know. I just hope he had some inkling of what he had meant to me.

I walked away and didn't look back. I heard the soft tinkle of the door as I exited the shop for the last time.

Gen was waiting for me outside. He kissed my mouth, a chaste but loving gesture.

'I know that wasn't easy for you. But I am very proud.'

I felt something in me light up. As he linked my arm in his, Gen had a spring in his step, and feeling his positive energy, I knew we were moving toward the future. He had been right, it was important to move on. He was proud of me. Whatever else, we had each other.

And that is how I was able to put the old bookseller to the back of my mind. Because it was necessary. Because I had to move on.

And when I got home later that evening, it was quiet in the apartment. Still. I could be alone in the kitchen. I could take the long clean blade of my favorite knife. And I could run it up and down the inseam of my arm. And when the image of the old man came to me again, along with my shame, I could stab the point of the knife into the skin. Over and over. Eventually I felt dizzy. I wrapped my arm in tissue paper and watched with a certain relish as the paper blushed red and my heart began to slow.

I got into bed. The gentle throbbing was the last thing I remember before I slipped into a peaceful sleep.

PART
III

TWENTY-THREE

THE FIRST DAY OF UNIVERSITY IS ALWAYS A RUSH. YOU reach the campus and move from place to place, signing your name to this or that class you have registered for. In addition, there is an overwhelming number of clubs and societies competing for the influx of new students: the university student union, the young communists' organization, the Buddhist collective, the theater group, the PKU weekly newspaper 'run by the students for the students,' and a host of other bodies.

Beyond all of this, what you feel most is the sheer energy and expectancy of the other students flowing into the buildings. Hundreds of young people just like you, only not like you at all, because they are dressed in such weird and wonderful ways. The well-to-do are in suits or demure skirts and have glittering Rolex watches, while others have leather clothes and spiked hair, and I even saw one girl with dark lipstick and a spider's web tattoo around her left eye.

It made me feel uncomfortable because it looked strange, and yet it was exciting too – not just because she was so different, but because she, and so many others, were different in the context of this place. The university, I felt very early on, was a place where all that difference and diversity could be housed together, allowed to breathe and flourish; a miniature city, of sorts, where vast numbers of young people were simply figuring out how to be themselves. Away from the irradiating gaze of the older generation – parents and grandparents, uncles and aunts.

At the same time, it is a little different when you are not living on campus. From the perspective of someone outside looking in, the university was its own magical citadel; but from the first moment, it was a place whose walls were raised high. This was something I would understand early on, too.

In that first flush of enthusiasm, I made my way to the office of the student paper. It was at the top of a slim winding metal staircase in one of the more run-down buildings on campus. I knocked on the door hesitantly and stepped into a squat room thick with body heat and cigarette smoke. The white paint on the walls was peeling. On one side, an image of Che Guevara, his stormy handsome features gazing toward some point you could not see, on the other one of Albert Camus, propped against a motorcycle, a cigarette dangling from his lips.

I had been around Gen long enough to recognize both these individuals, and I knew each had met with an early death. I guess at that point it didn't occur to me to question why there were no images of Chinese people in that space. The louche and raffish surroundings, along with the fog of smoke and the old football table standing grandly in one corner, made me feel I'd landed on Planet Cool.

The person who greeted me, however, was about as far from Che Guevara or Albert Camus as you could get. He was a lanky, stick-thin adolescent with a pudding-bowl haircut, and hard black glasses emphasized the violence in his crossed eyes – an effect mitigated when he began to speak, for then the shrillness of his voice seemed to steam up the lenses.

'Hi,' he said. 'How's it all hanging?'

'Hi. I wanted to drop in to make your acquaintance, and, you know, see if you ...'

My voice trailed away. I wondered if the phrase 'drop in' had ever sounded more lame. The tall young man had gotten up to meet me as I entered the room, but now I noticed several girls, my own age, sitting by typewriters, watching me with great interest. I attempted to raise my voice again.

'It's just that ... I was hoping I might get involved in a little writing. I've done some before.'

The goggle-eyed guy looked at me, and his glasses steamed over with fascination.

'You've done some before? May I ask what type of experience you have had?'

'I mean, nothing concrete. I just ... I write stuff cos I like to.'

'You write stuff cos you like to?'

He gave a goofy smile, but there was nothing friendly in it.

One of the girls smothered her laughter with her sleeve.

'Yeah, I mean ...'

The goggle-eyed boy became somber and professional.

'Well, this office might not look like much, but we try to do serious things here. Have you no experience beyond "cos I like to"?'

I felt a blush rise.

'Well, I mean, I managed to do well, I think, in a national competition, and that was the basis of my scholarship here to Peking University ...'

The goggly-eyed boy's sneer reached its zenith. His glasses were almost completely steamed over.

'I'm afraid that is not quite what we are looking for. We're looking for people who have experience of real writing, not those who have scored high in some elitist competition and think they are better than everyone else. Authenticity – that's our buzzword, that's what we are after!'

I wanted to respond. I wanted to argue my case. But the words died in my throat. Instead, I simply nodded, retreated and closed the door behind me.

After the pounding of my heart subsided, I calmed down. Much later it occurred to me that the young man with the glasses had one of the poshest Chinese accents I had ever heard. My own voice, on the other hand, identified me as someone from downtown Beijing, as someone with no money; and despite how much I tried to prettify what I had said, I'd been nervous and stuttered badly. He, on the other hand, had brayed his words in squealing, sarcastic delight.

It's amazing how a glancing look of contempt, or a throwaway phrase, can reduce someone to nothing. As stupid and as ridiculous-looking as he was, he could do that to me casually, and without a second thought. It occurred to me this was a power of a very real sort.

After that, I lost the impetus to sign up for clubs. I was going to try to find Gen's dorm, but changed my mind and left the campus – a small shuffling figure set against a backdrop of movement and life. I felt self-pity claim me – I knew I shouldn't have allowed the young man's words to affect me so negatively. He would have relished his moment of preening superiority and then it would be as if I had never existed. I shouldn't allow him to exist for me either. How is it possible to have your feelings so hurt by a stranger? I thought of my grandmother. I had thought of her every day since she'd been gone. She would have relished squashing someone like that. But I was not her. And she was no longer around.

I left the throng of students, crossed a wide road, and stepped into a quieter space, Haidian Park. The park had a long flat tarmacked path. On either side were neatly proportioned trees whose full green foliage was now speckled with flits of copper as summer melted away. I saw an elderly couple holding hands. They were struggling a little, walking awkwardly, but whereas others might have been frustrated and demoralized, they seemed amused by their infirmity – giggling ruefully at the difficulties of ungainly bodies and aching limbs. In my mind's eye, I imagined them as teenagers, traversing the same path many years before, moving easily and fluidly, the young man spinning the young woman, very much in love. I watched them hobble over to a bench, sit down and clutch each other's hand, and I thought they were very much in love still.

The sun had formed a molten glow over the skyline, and I felt a tickle of coolness as the afternoon faded into evening. When I looked back, the couple were no longer there. I don't know how long I had been standing there, but I felt calmer now. Calm enough to turn away from the trees, and the gentle rustle of their leaves, and make my way back toward the sound of traffic and the electric lights of civilization, winking purple and indigo in the gathering dusk. Once I'd found my way back to the main road, I took the bus, heaving with evening commuters.

Through the gaps in the bodies, I caught something of the out-side, the blurred motion of the buildings, and I glimpsed the outline of the Gate of Heavenly Peace, one of the entrances to Tiananmen Square. I saw its great shape looming for a moment, illuminated by layers of golden lanterns, their shine smooth against the streaks of blue and black of the evening sky. I saw it for a moment, and then it was snatched away, as the bus increased its speed along Chang'an Avenue. Having braved a bus journey at the peak of the rush hour, I arrived home far too late for dinner, but my mother had saved me a plate in the kitchen. I was ravenous, so didn't bother to heat it up, I just clawed the chicken balls and prawn toasts into my mouth. I looked up. My mother was leaning against the kitchen door watching me.

'So today was your first day?'

It wasn't really a question.

'Yes.'

She gave a look of distaste, she wrinkled her nose, and it occurred to me then that she was pretty in a way I would never be.

'Lots of rich kids, I would imagine,' she said, as though she were braving a bad smell.

I was not used to her taking that particular line. Wealth was something my mother had always coveted.

'I suppose.'

'And what must they have made of you?'

She regarded me thoughtfully. It felt as though she saw inside me, that the humiliating events of the day were playing out before her eyes. But, I thought darkly, my mother, wrapped up in her own world, is hardly that perceptive. I made my tone as upbeat and pleasant as possible.

'Oh, there were lots of interesting people. Friendly and curious, and it was a pleasure to meet them.'

'Friendly and curious,' my mother murmured, as though she were tasting the words.

We stood there for a few moments longer, regarding one another. She threw me a shallow smile, her eyes glinting shrewdly. I felt the blush rise to my face for the second time that day. I wondered if she was going to say more, but she turned on her heel and left the room.

My hand was trembling ever so slightly, and that cloying feeling of self-pity returned. Would just one word of encouragement have been too much to expect?

For as long as I could remember, my mother had been deeply unpredictable. At times unfathomable. I picked up another piece of prawn toast. Even though it was cold, it was still delicious.

She had left that out for me at least.

Later, when I was in my room, I looked out of my window and down to the forecourt. I could see the small figure of my mother under the stars. She stood with her hand on her hip, elbow pushed out in an unconscious gesture of disapproval. Of what? Of the world itself perhaps. I caught the glowing tip of her cigarette in the murky dark.

.   .   .

Later in the week I returned to university. As a literature student, I didn't have the same number of classes as those who studied the sciences or economics; they tended to have several seminars on the same day. I had just a couple each week, and a lecture here or there. So I only had to be in a few days a week. And that suited me just fine. The seminars were interesting enough, but most of the time I kept to myself. The lectures were the best though. In the darkness of an auditorium you could sit right at the back with no one scrutinizing you. Sometimes I'd make notes. Sometimes I'd allow my mind to drift. At the end of my first week, I had a lecture late on Friday afternoon.

I remember it because it was on the Russian writer Dostoyevsky. The title was 'Dostoyevsky and the Alienation of the Modern City.' In preparation, I had read the writer's signature work, *Crime and Punishment*. My only two literary influences had been the old bookseller and Gen, and curiously enough they had both concentrated on twentieth-century novels, the existentialists in Gen's case, while the old man had recommended writers such as Hemingway and Orwell. There had been the Chinese classics too. But nineteenth-century European literature was virtually unknown to me. I assumed that Russian literature would be dense and difficult to read, but forever fearful of arriving underprepared, I made the effort to read *Crime and Punishment* before the lecture. At first, it did seem a little fusty and archaic. But then the flow and the sweep of the novel pulled me in.

I thought about Rodion Romanovich Raskolnikov, the central character. He was very different from me. A little older, and male while I was female. He was intense and ungovernable whereas I was shy and nervous. He lived in a city that was cold and indifferent, whereas I'd spent all my life in one building, surrounded by family and community. At the center of all that had been my grandmother, and even now she was gone, the families who lived on our floor still constantly flitted in and out of each other's lives.

And yet, perhaps that's the miracle literature achieves. Despite the absolute difference in our lives, I found myself experiencing a real kinship with Raskolnikov as the story progressed. I think it was because we were both outsiders. At university, while other students gathered in their dormitories and talked together, I was conscious of my loneliness. I'd retreat from the life there, getting the same bus home each evening, slipping into my room.

But it was more than that. I didn't fit in at home either. The life on the corridor, our family and friends, the bawdy, easy way of the people I had grown up in the midst of – none of it came easily to me. It seemed as though I had been born a different species, was an interloper; as though there was something in my nature – stifled and introverted – that set me apart from those around me. As though I was destined to be different, watching everyone else from behind an invisible barrier.

When I read about the crime Raskolnikov committed, however, I felt nauseous. I had never encountered such a stark and graphic description of violence. Surely his world was completely alien from mine for that reason. Someone like me had never really known violence. And yet, after I put the book down, something in my mind was kindled. I heard the sound of my shoulder popping, I felt the resonance of my childhood screams as the policeman dragged me along the pavement all those years ago.

But those were memories I did not wish to scrutinize. And despite my distance from others, above all I still had Gen. Thoughts of Dostoyevsky were exploding in my mind, and I yearned to share my discovery with Gen – the sheer power of the writing – as though I were the first person in all of creation to have come across it. It was dark by the time I left the auditorium, and I made my way toward Gen's campus – the quaintly named Park Village – which was where the wealthier students stayed. Females weren't allowed into the male quarters and vice versa, so we had arranged to meet outside.

I was greatly looking forward to seeing him. Despite the cool autumn air, I felt a shiver of warm expectation. In the darkness,

I hugged my coat close. And then I saw him outside one of the dorm buildings, his face ruddy and happy under the glow of the warm orange light. He was with two other boys. I say boys, but they were tall and filled out, young adults really, and there was a coiled tension and excitement in the way they slapped at each other and laughed. I froze. I watched as the other two guys clasped Gen's hand, bumping fists in the way people did in the US. Gen performed the same gesture, easily and naturally, and yet it was unlike anything I'd ever seen him do before. Part of me felt a pang of regret – he had adapted to our strange new world so easily. Another part felt something like unease. The casualness of the gesture – it wasn't like him and I couldn't quite square it with the Gen I knew.

I was overthinking it, of course. Why did I always have to do that? The other two had ambled away, and that was when I took my opportunity. I stepped out toward him. And just for a second, I caught the dulling of his eyes. He readjusted his expression, however, and reached out, touching my arm, the gesture awkward but affectionate. But the laughter that had lit his face only moments before had been switched off just like that.

I am losing him, I thought.

I felt something close to panic. The feeling of being pulled toward an inevitable point with no control. I tried to make my tone light, and simpered:

'Are you having fun? They seem like cool guys!'

My voice was reedy and shrill. He blinked.

'It's an … experience,' he acknowledged, and I felt there was a wince of embarrassment in his voice.

'The thing is,' he said, calmly and studiously, 'I've been really looking forward to seeing you but I didn't expect you right now!'

Again that disorienting feeling: so much going on inside – a writhing, twisting panic – but on the outside frozen, unable to form coherent words.

I leaned into him. I had never played the coquette in my life, but I made an effort now. I stroked the side of his leg, close to his groin. My voice sounded syrupy and sticky and ridiculous, but I tried to purr the words out nevertheless.

'I just thought that … we haven't been alone for a while. And we are finally here. On our own, at university. So maybe we could spend a little time together.'

He made his voice inconsequential.

'Yeah, well, if you want to see my living quarters – but, I warn you, they are not up to much.'

'I'm not supposed to be there, though. With me being a girl and all.'

'There's no one on the front desk. And besides, everyone does it.'

Who was the 'everyone' he was talking about? And what exactly did they do?

I followed him through a shadowy lobby and into a corridor. He opened his door, and turned on the light. His room smelled of soap. As long as I had known Gen he had been devoted to cleanliness. His bed was unmade, however. I put my bag down. It contained the remnants of my lunch. I hoped it didn't smell, but one couldn't be certain. We stood facing each other, a little awkward.

'Would you like a drink?'

'Sure.'

He took out a bottle of whisky. It was a baroque black bottle latticed with gold threads. It looked beautiful and expensive, almost menacing in its grandeur. But Gen regarded it coldly.

'A gift!' he pronounced.

'From?'

He broke into a thin smile, but there was no warmth in his eyes.

'My father. He is a man for whom appearance means everything. He may not have spent much time in the house, with his family – with his son – but because I made it here, he feels the need to mark it with some grand, fatherly gesture. To make out that we have this bond. On the occasion of his son's entrance into adulthood. "Hey boy, you are a man now! Have some whisky on me!" Or something like that.'

His expression was bitter. Then it relaxed. He poured us both a thimble. I drank it. The liquid burned, but it was warming too.

'It's good whisky though,' he said, with that ironic smile of his I so loved.

He put on some music; he had a good-quality radio. Perhaps because of the whisky I felt a little light-headed. Awkwardly, clumsily, he wrapped his arm around my waist. Some European pop song was playing. He started to move to its rhythm, and I tried as well. We were both terrible. We'd never danced together; in fact I hadn't really danced at all, except as a little girl. We were both awkward, and we broke into laughter.

It was nice.

We lay down on the bed. I was a virgin. But I understood the logistics of sex, and in a world where I was frightened by many things, having sex wasn't one. At least, not with Gen. I had wondered if today would be the day I would lose my virginity. It was supposed to be an existential event in one's life, especially a girl's. If he had gone ahead then, I would have let him. It would have been okay with me, in fact it was something I wanted very much. But instead he drew my hand to him, and I moved it in the way he always enjoyed.

Once we had finished, we lay there. It seemed that the whisky and the intimate contact had only staved off the silence for so long; now it had returned and threatened to engulf us. I experienced that searing sense of panic, the feeling that I must say something – witty or coquettish, or clever or interesting – in order to weld him to me again. I tried to strike a breezy but worldly tone.

'So one of my lectures was on this guy Dostoyevsky. I'd heard of him, of course, but I always thought he was one of these old-fashioned, hoity-toity writers whose stories are about girls in frilly dresses and gentlemen riding in carriages. But once you start reading, it seems really modern ...'

I had found the guiding thread of my thoughts, and my feeling of self-consciousness disappeared.

'And there is something about his characters, the way he brings them together, so smoothly and yet so violently; all these weird and wonderful lives brought into collision ... The way he describes people ... it's almost ... painful!'

I was satisfied because these thoughts had been gestating inside me, but only now had they fully taken form. I had the sense that I'd said what I needed to say.

But when Gen spoke, his voice was toneless and abstract, as though he had heard the words but disregarded the meaning.

'Painful,' he murmured. 'Sounds more like a doctor than a writer.'

'Well ... I mean ... it's not exactly, I don't think ...'

He clutched my hand.

'Listen, I am really sorry, but I said – those guys you saw before. I promised I'd meet them. There is a little campus bar, it's called the East Slope, the guys hang out there and have a few beers.'

I snuggled into him. I touched my lips to his neck. Even though, only moments before, I'd had my hand on his penis, this was the type of intimacy we didn't usually share. I felt him tense. He didn't pull away. But I could tell he wanted to. Once he had finished, he nearly always became subdued and quiet, self-enclosed and remote.

The panic returned. I tried to come up with something else, something more interesting, but there was nothing left to me, and my voice came out desperate and whiny.

'Can't you stay a little longer? We've not really seen each other at all this week.'

The moment the words left my lips, I hated myself for them.

He looked at me gently.

'Listen, there will be plenty more time. Next week, when things have settled down a little.'

He was smiling, and he had spoken softly, but there was a finality to his words. I was being dismissed. I got up, adjusted my clothes, picked up my bag, turned to him and gave him a quick peck on the check.

'I'll look forward to it!' I said, making my voice as bright as possible – a last flourish of wretched artificial enthusiasm, even as he was gently leading me out.

He closed the door softly behind me.

I stood in the hallway for a few moments, gathering myself. And then I turned and walked away without making a sound. It occurred to me that I had always been a mouse. My whole life long. It was no wonder he wanted to join his friends.

TWENTY-FOUR

I STEPPED OUT OF THE DORMS, MY BAG SLUNG OVER MY shoulder. When I had entered the building, I'd felt nervous in case anyone saw. Now I simply didn't care. I walked for a while, a tightening feeling in my chest. I passed a gaggle of girls, laughing. The difficulty in catching my breath intensified. And with it came anger. I suddenly felt so fucking angry. I blinked away the film of water that had formed in my eyes. It felt white hot, like acid. I veered off the path and into a much bigger building. The door groaned when I pushed it open. It was gloomy inside. A little walkway led to a bigger space. The air was musty. In the corner there was an old grand piano.

I was fighting for breath now, but that anger was still white hot. And it wasn't at Gen, or my mother, or anyone else, but at myself.

The words ran through my head like scampering creatures.

'You are a mouse. That's all you are. A pathetic little mousey-mouse!'

I dropped my bag. I struggled to unzip it. My fingers fumbled about until I found the cold steel of the knife. I took it out as I pulled up my sleeve. The steel glinted dully. The edge was not sharp, but the point was sharp enough. I thrust the tip of it against my open wrist, nipping stabs that opened up the layer of scar tissue from previous contacts, and as the pain cut and sluiced its way through me like shards of glass, the pressure on my chest simultaneously began to relieve. My arm was burning, but I could breathe again and the hot trickle of blood felt calming. My eyes fluttered and I felt dizzy, but the sudden bout of rage was … exsanguinated.

'Greetings, Funny Bunny!'

I nearly jumped out of my skin. I spun around, the knife still in my hand. I must have looked quite maniacal, frizzy-haired with shock, the blood still dripping from the blade.

I hadn't even heard her approach. But watching me was a girl, around my own age. Whereas I was thin and petite, she was broad-shouldered. I noticed she had small breasts. Her body looked incongruous somehow, almost like a boy's. But her face was strikingly feline, sharp features slashed by green eyes whose curiosity was not quite wholesome. There was something inquisitive but also cruel in her gaze.

My mouth must have hung open. I stepped forward, wanting to say something, forgetting that I was still holding the knife.

She raised her hands.

'Hey, I'm all for stabbing people. I dig the direct approach. It's just that I wouldn't be so keen on stabbing myself!'

She smiled. Her smile was wayward yet beguiling, her eyes gleamed catlike in the gloom.

'I … this … I didn't even …'

My voice trailed away. I stuffed the knife back into my bag. I covered the nakedness of my wrist with my sleeve. I felt the cuts tingle. I felt the anger again. Perhaps it had never really left.

I looked her straight in the eye.

'What's it got to do with you?'

She raised her hands once more, that same gesture of supplication, but those eyes flashed with cruel amusement.

'Hey, I get it, Funny Bunny. You were blowing off steam. It's just your way. Why do you think I'm here?'

'Why are you here?'

'Same reason. Blow off a little steam. You a newbie? I'm starting my second year in this shithole! And sometimes when I get bored of the bars, and the boys that tell their stupid jokes and the girls that laugh their stupid laughs, I come here. Like I said. To blow off a little steam.'

I must have looked baffled. She nodded at me as she strode past. She sat by the piano, lifted the lid. And, just like that, she started to play.

The notes were soft and melodious, and even on that creaky old piano they came out in an intricate cascade, melancholy and luminous. She was playing classical music. Later I would learn that it was from Chopin's Ballade No. 1, but I didn't know that then. I only knew that the music she created infused the gloom of that room with its beauty. So infinite, so ethereal. My first impression of her had not been a good one. There was a streak of sarcasm, of sourness, that was off-putting, but now all I could do was watch as those fingers glided across those dusty keys.

She stopped. The sound of the piano dying away was a violence in itself: beauty so suddenly vanquished. She did not meet my eye. Her gaze remained on her stilled fingers.

'I'm sorry if you were expecting something a little more up to date.'

'No, it's … fine. That was … lovely!'

She did not raise her gaze.

'Classical is all I play these days,' she mumbled. 'When I was younger, when I was a teenager, I was more adventurous. I would write my own songs, play my own music – I would compose the soundtrack to my own life.'

I leaned in, intrigued.

'What happened?'

'My father was the director of the Central Philharmonic Orchestra of China. He had … high expectations for me. He wanted me to concentrate on Beethoven and Bach. Only I was little more than a child at that stage. And sometimes my mind wandered. He told me not to play my own stuff. But sometimes I just forgot.'

Her voice became halting, subdued.

'So … what happened?'

'Oh, it wasn't really his fault. When you are that highly strung, when you are so devoted to an art, it can become all-consuming.'

Her voice faded away. She still wouldn't look at me. I felt the hairs on the back of my neck prick. For I knew then that something awful had happened to her. Part of me didn't want to know, but the words slipped from my mouth anyway.

'So what happened?'

She gulped.

'One day, when I was supposed to have been working on Rachmaninov, I'd been fooling around with my own stuff instead … he just lost it. I mean, it really wasn't his fault. I guess he was just wired that way.'

'Lost it?'

'Yeah. He took a hammer to my right hand.'

She spoke in a muffled voice.

'I guess it was for the best in the end. I kept to the greats from that time on. Nowadays, even though I can't move my fingers quite as well, it's nice to come here. No pressure, simply to play for the sake of playing.'

She stifled a sob.

'Oh good grief. I'm ... so sorry. I had no idea. You play so well. I think it was some of the loveliest music I have ever heard, I mean ...'

She turned her gaze up to me hesitantly. Those green eyes shimmered, and her sharp, sculpted features seemed to contort. She is having a mental breakdown, I thought. My mind whirled. Should I scream for help? Should I call for an ambulance?

The contortions evened out in a slashing grin, wicked and amused. She looked at me like she couldn't quite believe I was real.

'I'm just fucking with you, Funny Bunny! Didn't you get that? Daddy Dearest could no more have directed the Chinese Philharmonic Orchestra than perform brain surgery or fly into space!'

I felt the weight of my exhaustion.

'Why would you say something so horrible? I've had a really, really bad day!'

For the first time her expression flickered.

'Okay, Funny Bunny. Point taken. I wasn't trying to upset you. I just ... say stuff sometimes.'

I didn't know how to respond to that.

I lowered my gaze and trudged past her.

'Yeah, well, it was real nice to meet you!' I muttered sullenly.

I felt her move after me.

'Don't be like that. Here, take this.'

I turned. She thrust a card into my hand. I took it on reflex and peered at it. It was the type of thing that Chinese businessmen carry to convey their position in the company. Only this one said: 'Madam Macaw's Marvelous Marauders.'

I looked at her.

'Madam Macaw?'

'At your service,' she said in a sultry voice, giving a theatrical bow.

'We meet every Wednesday, usually here, in order to work a little Marauder Mischief! But we go to other places too! You should come. You never know. It might even work for you!'

.   .   .

I didn't see her that Wednesday. Or the Wednesday after that. I buried her card deep in my pocket, until the memory of her became something surreal, an event glimpsed through a dream. It had been, by far and away, the most intriguing encounter I'd had at university, but I was still so focused on Gen and the terrible fear of losing him. I had always known he was smarter than me, better read, more self-assured, but in the context of our high school I thought I could keep up. Now that we were in an environment of precocious and confident young adults, I felt he was sure to leave me behind. That he would find a group of friends more interesting and more worldly – and yet, like a child stamping its feet, I raged against the possibility. More and more, I devised ways of impressing him, of saying something clever, of giving him the pleasure he desired in new and varied forms. But he hadn't asked me to his room since that first occasion.

I looked up his schedule; these were all posted publicly. I made myself available on campus, I made sure to pass him on the way to seminars. Sometimes we would have lunch together. But despite all my efforts, I could feel him retreating, day by day, hour by hour. And yet I couldn't stay the intensity of my feelings. We shared a childhood. We had similar intellectual interests. I'd touched him *down there* on so many occasions. I was qualified to love him. I'd worked for it. Surely he had to love me in return.

But it became even harder. Whenever I saw him, my heart would race, only it no longer resembled joy so much as fear. As we passed on campus, I would try making my voice breezy and humorous, but my comments barely elicited even a muffled reaction. He seemed to look straight through me, his eyes glassy and distant. His voice held that lack of emotion I was familiar with, only now there was a creeping coldness, too. I'd feel a dry heat in my mouth, my heart slamming, and the words I'd try to find would get clogged in my throat. The more desperately I tried to speak, the more what I wanted to say dried up. I became gripped by this silent but inevitable sense of panic, as if invisible fingers were gradually closing around my throat.

I thought about Gen all the time, and I dreamed about him too. Sometimes we were children again, and I was with Jian, Wang Fan and the others, who were just as they had always been. And when I saw Gen, he too was as he had been: a subdued, thoughtful boy with just a hint of cruelty, a boy whose strange mannerisms resembled those of someone older. A boy who never quite fitted in and yet it never seemed to bother him. But when I came to look on him in my dream, his features were obscured by shadow. I knew it was him, for his bearing and voice were familiar, only the more I tried to see his face, the more the darkness there terrified me.

Things eventually came to a head one evening. He was spending more and more time with his two friends, whose names I had learned were Aiguo and Sile. I had hung around campus all day, hoping to run into him and yet dreading it. I had to be careful with money, and while the other students spent a lot of time in the bars and cafeterias, I walked the campus in the sunshine, enjoying the grass and the feeling of warmth on my face. By that point, however, it had started to drizzle, and the day was already starting to fade into the evening's murky gray.

I made my way to the East Slope bar. I passed through the hard doors and into an atmosphere of cigarette smoke and pounding bass from the music of a band of sweaty and entangled figures performing under the bright light at the front. I saw him straight away, lounging with the other two at the back, a cigarette drooping from his mouth. I hadn't seen him smoke before. As I approached him, I felt the nervous anticipation one feels when approaching a stranger. When I reached him he nodded at me in greeting and smiled but the smile never reached his eyes.

His two friends nodded politely as well. For a while we just stood there watching the band. I noted that Gen was bobbing his head to the rhythm of the music while he smoked. It seemed to me that he was almost a different person, someone I would have to adapt myself to. But that was what I had always done. With Gen. With my mother. With my schoolteachers. The only person I had really felt I could be myself with was the one person who was no longer here.

I looked at Gen and cracked my coolest, most casual smile. I started to move in time with the music too. But the music seemed harsh and loud, the electric guitars scraping their way across my head. When my voice came, it was reedy and weak, a flailing shrillness, trying to make itself heard above the harsh metallic sounds crashing across the room and roaring in my ears.

'Hey, this is pretty rad. I really … I really dig this scene!'

Rad. Dig? Had I ever used those words before that night?

He moved his head a fraction of an inch. He didn't respond.

I tried to speak again. His smile thinned. He tapped his ears. He was indicating that he couldn't hear me, but I knew he could. I knew it and he knew I knew. It was in his expression, eyes lit with a hint of cruelty. I stood there gaping at him. One of the other boys cleared his throat. I turned on him in fury. I had expected that Aiguo and Sile would be smiling, that all three of them would be laughing at my wretchedness – the hysterical female to be ridiculed; a means to facilitate their male bonding.

But when I looked at the other two boys, what I saw in their eyes was pity.

I looked at Gen one last time, studied his face to see if there was any recognition of how I was being made to feel. I wanted to scream. I wanted to stay silent. I headed out of the bar and into the night. I walked for a while, hearing the music fade into an intermittent haze of sound until it was gone altogether. My legs were tired but I trudged on, making my way round the perimeter of the campus at night, a series of never-ending circles traipsed in the rain. Inside the campus buildings I could see groups of people, talking and laughing – a whole world playing out behind the doors of the residences, one that excluded me by virtue of some invisible barrier.

I thought of my grandmother. In my family, she had been the one who most supported my going to university, who was most vocal about it, even though she had never valued books or libraries or study. She had seen it as a means by which I might better myself, and she also believed it was my destiny to do great things, to go to places she and my parents had never seen. She believed in me. I wondered what she would think of me now, lingering in the shadows, the rain dripping from my lank hair, a morose combination of wetness and self-pity. She would have some choice words, of that I was sure.

I reached into my pocket simply to keep my hands warm. But my fingers found a weathered card: 'Madam Macaw's Marvelous Marauders.'

I had thought about her a few times since that surreal encounter, but with everything that had been happening with Gen, I had put her to the back of my mind. Now she emerged again, those feline eyes, that smile edged with cruelty. I had been feeling lonely and sorry for myself as the rain beaded my hair and dripped from my nose. Now, however, I realized that I hadn't been completely excluded from life on campus. She had invited me to whatever it was she did. She had asked me to come on Wednesday evening. And it was Wednesday evening now. Perhaps she had meant to mock me. She was difficult to read. But she had invited me to join her and the 'marauders' nevertheless. And, however strange or uncomfortable that might be, it wouldn't be worse than how I was feeling now.

I made my way back to the same building. I pushed through the heavy doors.

The great room had been dim and shadowy before; now it was bright and resplendent. There were nine or ten people in the room, but the center stage was occupied by two young men. One of them was wielding what looked like a club, the other was looking back at him with a ferocious stare.

'Don't you dare!' said the smaller individual in a high-pitched voice.

From behind them Madam Macaw screamed emphatically:

'Hit the bastard. It's fucking Shakespeare!'

I wasn't sure what was going on. At first glance, it appeared that the smaller individual – a rather well-groomed and effete young man – had, for some bizarre reason, been named Shakespeare. That Madam Macaw had developed an insane dislike of him and somehow arranged for him to be subjected to a ritual beating in front of me. And then I saw the props, the arrangements and the position of the others in the background. I realized I was watching a play. And yet there was a real intensity to what was taking place.

Madam Macaw shrieked again.

'Chiron wants to kill Bassianus. Because he wants to fuck Lavinia. Don't you want to fuck Lavinia, Chiron?'

The larger of the two individuals – a tubby-faced young man with a strangely placid demeanor – looked at Madam Macaw sheepishly.

'Yes?' he mumbled.

The smaller and tidier one went to say something, to point something out, but the other brought the club down and thwacked him over the head.

The club was a rubber one, of course, and yet the larger actor had brought it down hard; it wasn't as if he had put any menace into the gesture, but, given the sheer size of him, the impact had a certain effect.

The smaller man shrieked at his larger comrade. Then he turned and shrieked at Madam Macaw. The sound was impossibly high-pitched and indignant.

'Ow! That hurt.'

'This is theater, darling,' Madam Macaw drawled. 'It's about revealing one's inner pain. It's meant to hurt!'

The smaller young man peered at her balefully, looking to see if she was laughing at him. But Madam Macaw's features were unreadable. In the end he turned away from her stare.

The bigger guy tentatively reached out his arm, and then the two actors embraced. It was an awkward motion that at once became smooth; the smaller student seemed to relax in the bigger student's arms. And then the smaller guy kissed the bigger guy on the lips.

I'd never seen anything like it.

It wasn't the kind of kiss I might have given to my brother. It was instantaneous, it was over in a second, but there was in it the type of intensity with which I might once have kissed Gen.

It was romantic.

My mouth hung open.

At the same moment, Madam Macaw turned round. She saw me.

'Funny Bunny!' she exclaimed with delight. 'I didn't know if you would come or not. But I'm glad you are here!'

I realized it was the first time anyone in this entire place had seemed pleased to see me.

'Come hither, come hither, sweet, strange damsel!'

'What?' I blinked.

'I'm speaking Shakespearean. Get your butt over here!'

She snapped the words out but her eyes were smiling. I walked over.

'So this is Lan and this is Min.'

She gestured toward them.

Lan shuffled uncomfortably. He was big and sweating heavily, perhaps because of the lights and the heavy jumper he was wearing. He nodded at me, painfully almost, and then his soft, awkward eyes slid away.

Min, on the other hand, had lively eyes; dots of black darting everywhere. He leaned forward and kissed me on both cheeks.

'So lovely to meet you, darling. So sorry you have been co-opted into this satanic organization. There is, of course, no escape now!'

He looked at Madam Macaw defiantly.

'Oh, aren't you a cad?' she said. 'Let's call it a wrap! See you at Bar Wujiaoxing.'

'You and I are about to get drunk,' she said to me, taking my arm.

And when you are swept up in that kind of strange, magnetic energy, it is hard to resist.

TWENTY-FIVE

BAR WUJIAOXING WAS A PUB OFF CAMPUS. THE RAIN was coming down again but it wasn't too far away. When we arrived, the place was full of lonely old men who looked at us with hungry eyes. It made me self-conscious.

Suddenly, a hand pinched my ass.

I screeched.

I turned to Madam Macaw, who was grinning.

'You gotta be alert. I've gotta make you a *lert*!'

'A *lert*?'

'A lert. Lerts are the best type of creatures. Kind, good-hearted, but always vulnerable to a pinch on the bum!'

I thought about the two boys. The way Lan had kissed Min on the mouth, however briefly. I felt a shiver of disgust. I wondered if Madam Macaw wanted to kiss me like that. Was she some type of homosexual too? Or was she normal? Who on earth was she?

But then it occurred to me that no one wanted to kiss me that way. I'd had some kind of relationship with Gen but aside from that no boy had shown interest in me romantically. So it seemed unlikely that someone like her – so gregarious and full of color – would be interested in me that way. At once I relaxed.

'What are you having?'

I didn't know.

Madam Macaw smiled all the more.

'Barkeep,' she called, 'a couple of specials!'

The barman looked at her with a rueful grin.

'Coming up.'

'Something that will grow hairs on your chest!' she said with a wink.

The drinks were chocolate milkshakes infused with chili and a liquor I couldn't identify, a delicious hit to the taste buds.

I began to relax.

'So what's your story?' she asked.

I took another sip.

'I don't have much of one, I guess.'

She raised her glass, clinked it against mine.

'Nobody has a story. Then they drink and everyone has one.'

'Do you have one?'

Her expression assumed a flash of sadness.

'Yeah, I guess, but that's not for here and now.'

She spoke softly and with great seriousness. It didn't even occur to me to question her.

'But tell me, Funny Bunny, what's up with the old hack-and-slash?'

I blinked at her.

'The what?'

She peeled her sleeve up and began to stab theatrically at her wrist while humming the music from the Hitchcock film *Psycho*.

I had forgotten that she had seen me at my lowest ebb.

I wanted to speak, but my lips trembled and my eyes welled up. I was furious and helpless in the same moment. Was I close to walking out? I don't remember. But I remember she could do that to you. One minute you were having a casual conversation, the next minute her words were ripping out your innards.

'I don't know what you think you saw …' I mumbled.

She looked at me for a second or two. Then her arm shot out and she took my hand. Her grip was firm and warm.

'Hey,' she said, 'I'm not judging you. Your level of crazy is nothing compared with some of the things I've done. I'm a pro and you're an amateur when it comes to the insane stakes. But you got me curious all the same.'

'Curious about what?' I murmured reluctantly.

'You,' she said, with a smile that was almost kind.

My head felt heavy. The truth was I had never even considered why I did it. I sometimes noticed how the smooth caramel-colored skin of my left arm was overlaid by a faint lattice of white scar tissue. I knew what I did was odd. But at the same time it felt automatic and instinctive, like breaking the surface of water and taking a gulp of air.

I glanced at her, glanced away. Took another tentative sip of the rich cocktail. Eventually I found myself speaking.

'When I was younger, I'd get this feeling. This hateful feeling. Like I was a nothing. As if a great weight was pressing down on me, stopping my breath. Suffocating me. My heart would race. And I'd fight to breathe. And then one day something happened. And I took a knife. And did … *that*. And then, straight away, I could breathe again. Just like that.'

She watched me with her unnerving green eyes.

'And what was it?'

'What was what?'

'What was it that happened to you, Funny Bunny? What made you pick up the knife that first time?'

I gazed into her eyes, the alcohol melting into me, figures blending into the background; the old men in this dark, dusky bar, the softness of the shadows. I went to say something, but then:

'*Voilà*! We're here! Hold our seats while we get drinks!'

The two boys had arrived, Min wearing a small pink bruise on his forehead with a certain wounded pride. The much larger Lan was smiling shyly, his hefty body ungainly and out of place in this subdued, intimate space, a vulnerability in his bearing, like that of a lost child. He followed Min docilely to the bar, the contrast between them almost comic. The memory of their kiss was imprinted on my mind; a lingering stain of distaste. I thought about it some more. What if they did more than kiss? What if they did the type of thing Gen and I did?

I felt her studying me with amusement.

'You are picturing them having sex, aren't you?'

'No, of course not,' I blurted out indignantly. 'I would never ...'

She said nothing but smiled, a voluptuous cat's smile full of sly delight.

I looked at her for a few moments longer, feeling the tingle in my cheeks. I tried to keep the disapproval out of my voice.

'Why do they do it? Why do they do that kind of thing ... to each other?'

'Hooligans,' she murmured softly.

'Hooligans?'

'That's what the police call it. They call it "hooliganism." They say "hooliganism" is against the law. They are too disgusted to use the actual word: "homosexuality." When he was sixteen, Lan was sent to prison because he was caught with another boy his own age. They weren't doing much more than kissing and cuddling. Nevertheless, the repercussions were … cruel. He was locked in a cell for a few days. With men rather than other boys. Fortunately his father had some influence. Lan wasn't there for long. But I guess it was long enough. He doesn't talk about it. He doesn't talk about much. I imagine some things are too awful to talk about.'

An image flickered through my head, a memory from long ago. The bright lights of an official building. The shadows of men. Pain snarling in my shoulder and arm. And a fear so great it had left me trembling like a small animal.

'So why do they continue to take the risk?' I asked softly.

She looked at me, her eyes flashing and cruel. And then she spoke quietly, almost in a whisper.

'I imagine having to hide your true nature is the most awful feeling. A hateful feeling. As if a great weight is pressing down on you, stopping your breath, suffocating you …'

She'd thrown my words back at me. I felt a lump in my throat.

'That's not fair,' I said petulantly.

'No, it's not,' she agreed with a murmur.

But I knew she wasn't talking about me.

We were interrupted once again. The two young men took their seats. Lan glanced up at me nervously every once in a while. He smiled shyly, but didn't speak. Min, on the other hand, talked cheerfully and incessantly.

'So, have you ever done any acting? No, don't tell me, you are more of the directing type – quiet and thoughtful, I can see that. But maybe I'm wrong. I tend to prejudge people. You seem so normal! I don't mean that in a bad way, but we actors tend to be all over the place and, and … you don't seem as if you are all over the place. You seem normal. Did I say that already?'

Min spoke in a rapid babble. I found myself smiling.

He extended his hand tentatively.

'It's nice to meet you!'

His hand was warm and a little bit sweaty but his eyes were shining, as if he really was psyched to meet me. Perhaps it was the drink, but I began to relax. What these two guys did with one another didn't seem so important. Because they were both looking at me like I was a person who had something to offer.

And that's when Madam Macaw cracked a fart.

It was a volatile, violent sound that peeled across our conversation.

I was mortified. Women were supposed to be discreet about that sort of thing. To do it when nobody else was around. Anything to prevent the grim possibility of an eruption in public, anything to hide the fact that ours were bodies that farted. I had always been taught not to be a body at all – merely a metaphysical presence like my mother, a perfumed, coiffured creature who passed through life without ever emitting odors. That was what a woman was supposed to be. I looked at Madam Macaw and felt mortified on her behalf.

But there was no embarrassment in her expression. Instead she threw her arms back, releasing a long, luxurious 'ahhh' sound. She looked at us and winked.

'Better out than in, boys and girls!'

For the second time, I was shocked. But my feeling wasn't one of disgust but of amazed delight. The absurdity of the situation bubbled up within me, and I started to giggle.

It was hard to stop laughing.

Min looked at her.

'You dirty bitch!'

'Takes one to know one,' simpered Macaw.

But then her expression grew serious.

'This is definitely a warning. Defcon amber if you like. A clear sign of things to come. I'd better head to the little girls' room!'

I watched her go, astounded. In the weeks and months that followed, this pattern would be repeated. She'd say or do something scandalous, and I'd watch her, utterly astonished, secretly elated.

I looked back at the guys.

'Who the hell is she?' I asked in astonishment.

Min smiled as if he understood exactly why I was so baffled, why I was asking that question.

But it was Lan who started to speak. His bulk oozed into the chair, huge and belligerent, yet his voice was soft and slight.

'Well,' he said quietly, 'she is a real nice person. With her, you feel like you can always be yourself.'

I looked at him, surprised.

'No offense. But she has clearly got you dressing up and acting out scenes from some fifteenth-century play by a Western playwright. How is that possibly being yourself?'

Min interjected at this point.

'Sixteenth-century, actually. But that's beside the point. Let me ask you this. What do you think about Batman?'

I was flummoxed.

I searched for the criticism, for the trap. But Min simply sounded curious and interested. It wasn't like the way Gen looked to poke holes in what I was saying when I had the wrong opinion about a given poet or writer.

'Batman? I guess he is … pretty cool!'

I was in my 'pretty cool' phase back then, it was what everyone said.

It didn't seem to do the trick, though.

'But he was really Bruce Wayne, right? That was his secret,' I added, in desperate hope of scoring a point.

I thought they might be sarcastic and shoot me down. I knew next to nothing about Batman and had no idea why it might be important.

But Min's look was kind.

'He was really Bruce Wayne, wasn't he?'

'Well, I think,' Min pronounced with a flourish, 'that the real nature of Bruce Wayne was actually the man resembling the bat. That it's the Bruce Wayne persona itself that was a fake. And it was only when he was the Batman that he became who he really was. I think it is only by using a mask that some people can be true to themselves.'

I mulled it over. The idea was fascinating to me.

'But why would you need the mask in the first place?'

Min and Lan exchanged a look. My question must have sounded unbearably naïve. I understand that now.

Min looked at me.

'It's harder and harder to be yourself on campus these days,' he said seriously.

'Why is that?'

'Because things are changing. Did you know the administration has just introduced a "lights out" policy?'

'No, what is that?'

'Since the start of this month, Peking University has decided that you can't leave your lights on after 10 p.m. And that means people can't meet or talk to each other after that time. Of course, the university administration says it's all just a question of saving electricity. But it's more than that. It's about controlling our movements. And now, in the Triangle—

'The Triangle?' I asked.

'Yes,' nodded Min, 'the Triangle is the garden in the middle of the campus. Lovely, I should say.'

'Very lovely,' mumbled Lan in agreement.

'And it is the place where there are bulletin boards beneath the trees. You can find out about life on campus there, you can find out what is going on.'

I nodded.

'But much more stuff has been going up recently. Since the administration has decided to crack down on our movements, posters are appearing with the heading "No lights out!" Nobody knows who has made them or is distributing them, but they have proliferated in the Triangle. They argue for our rights, our freedoms. That grown men and women should decide for themselves what time they choose to go out at night, and what time they go to bed. That students shouldn't be blanketed in darkness like errant children.'

I knew nothing of this. But I felt myself swell with indignation. I thought about how my mother had controlled me. How she continued to do so. How powerless I felt a lot of the time. University, for me, had represented the possibility of an escape from that kind of thing.

'So what's going to happen?' I whispered.

'Well,' said Min, leaning forward, taking me into his confidence, 'it's all up in the air at the moment. But motions are being made. Steps are being taken.'

He looked around him, then slipped a single piece of sweaty paper into my hand. I brought it down to my lap. Glanced around at the old men in the bar, none of whom were paying the slightest attention to us. And yet, it all seemed so clandestine, so exciting.

It read: 'Our dorms are our collective home. As responsible adults, we can talk to each other, find solutions and live together as one. The school isn't our mommy, daddy or dictator. Autonomy is the foundation of democracy.'

The paper seemed to buzz in my hands. I looked at the two young men, their faces nervous but expectant, and I realized they had let me in on a great secret. But more than that, I felt thrilled. I thought about my long-lost friend, the old man in the bookshop, and I remembered my Orwell.

'Oh, for fuck's sake!'

Madam Macaw arrived, slamming a tray of drinks on the table.

'I'm gone five minutes, and you've already got her talking about this kind of shite!'

Min looked up at her and for the first time the glow of admiration had dimmed in his eyes.

'Don't you think this kind of stuff plays a part?'

She looked at him without missing a beat.

'Yeah. No. Maybe. Who knows? But do you think any of these student union assholes are gonna resolve the situation? Do you really think they are going to make life better? Let me tell you something now. They will issue their leaflets and their proclamations, and the same guys who issue those leaflets and proclamations will be the same guys who, sometime down the line, are the people on the university board demanding you stop issuing your leaflets and proclamations. And so the cycle of life goes on!'

She ended with a flourish of her arm.

Min looked as though he wanted to resist her with a stream of arguments, but in the end he only managed an aloof and detached throwaway comment.

'You're a cynical human being!'

Macaw's eyes flared with delight. It seemed the finest compliment she could have been given. She raised her glass.

'Here's to that!'

We all knocked back our drinks.

Min glanced at me, smiling. His resigned and warm-humored look implied that the personality of Madam Macaw was overpowering, and yet this was the way of things. I smiled back. Perhaps it was the alcohol again, but I felt a sense of camaraderie with him.

I glanced at Min and Lan. Min was still looking at me with awkward complicity. Lan was watching us both with an expression of gentle fascination. And although I was aware that these two boys were in some way 'unnatural,' I was grateful for their kindness. And it occurred to me that they went together well.

TWENTY-SIX

B Y THE END OF THAT EVENING, THE DRINKS HAD gone to my head, the alcohol leaving me flushed and dizzy. As I made my somewhat unsteady way toward the exit, I felt her grip on my arm. Madam Macaw gazed at me intently, her smoky breath stroking my face, her feline eyes glittering with amusement.

'Meet me here,' she said, thrusting a sliver of paper into my hands. She had scribbled an address on it.

'Four o'clock! A week from now, just you and me! Don't forget!'

Her expression lost its certainty. For a moment, she looked like a child.

'You will come, won't you?'

I nodded.

When I got back, my brother was still up. He was curled up on the living room floor, watching cartoons. Sometimes I marveled how at home he was in his own body. He still had a child's soft-limbed suppleness, his head lolling, his legs twisting and bent, his body rising out of them at a crooked angle. He was completely comfortable resting in that position, his eyes reflecting the glow of the TV screen. If, when I was younger, I had sat that way, my mother would have cuffed the back of my head and told me that my posture was 'unladylike.'

I sat down on the chair behind him – the alcohol leaving a gentle trail of mist across my mind – and I gazed at the back of his head for a while. I knew the time would come when my brother would no longer be a child, but at the same time I could never imagine him as a man; could not imagine his limbs stretching and hardening, his chin becoming more pronounced, his body solidifying and expanding, and hair sprouting from his face and arms. I knew the time would come, of course, and yet I also knew that in some way he'd forever be the quiet little boy curled up on the floor watching his cartoons from within the dark.

'Whaddya watching?' I asked tentatively.

He shrugged his shoulders without taking his eyes off the TV.

'I dunno. Something. They had *Rescue Man* on before and *Rescue Man* is great, but now it's just boring news.'

We sat there in silence for a few moments before my brother added:

'I was hoping they would play another cartoon … but they don't usually do that this late at night.'

'Where's Mother?'

'I dunno.'

Silence again.

I wanted to talk to him, but in that moment our worlds seemed so far away.

'Do you like Batman?' I said. 'I really like Batman.'

'Batman? *Batman*?' he asked incredulously, a note of contemptuous delight slipping into his voice. 'Batman is lame. Batman is one of the lamest of all! If not *the* lamest.'

'Why do you think that? I think he's kinda cool.'

He swiveled round to face me, his wide eyes weighed down by the responsibility of having to explain the most elementary and obvious things to a dense older sister.

'Batman is just a man. Superman can fly. Astro Boy can shoot lights from his eyes. But Batman doesn't have any superpowers. He just has … gadgets.'

He spat that last word – that 'gadgets' – out in a tone of disgust. I couldn't help smiling.

'I still think Batman is kinda cool though.'

'Why though?'

'Well, because …'

'Because?' my brother asked impatiently.

'Well,' I said, smiling to myself, 'he lives his life as Bruce Wayne, and everyone thinks that he is just this boring rich guy. But at night-time he becomes the Batman. He has this whole exciting hidden identity that no one knows about … I think it might be nice to have a secret like that!'

My brother looked at me drolly, as though it was impossible to fathom the extent of my ridiculousness.

'*That* doesn't make any sense whatsoever.'

He turned back to the TV. The image was a little out of kilter but I recognized the figure speaking. His name was Hu Yaobang and he was a member of the Politburo, the leading council of the Chinese Communist Party. But he wasn't like the other politicians. He had supported an anti-corruption program targeting some of the Party's fat cats. He argued for a less centralized political apparatus and it was even rumored he supported a move toward a more Western, democratic model of governance.

Perhaps for these reasons, he had been forced to resign as the Party's General Secretary a couple of years earlier, but he was clearly a popular figure, so it was thought the inner circle wanted to keep him on their side. That night he was talking about education reform. I remember almost nothing about the speech itself, only that he seemed to me, like most Chinese politicians, to be incredibly old. I remember he smiled a lot too – and that set him apart from the rest, who tended to be grim and dour.

I went to my room. Our building seemed strangely quiet that evening. A watery moon gleamed with silver through the night. I looked out west in the direction of Tiananmen Square and the Forbidden City. I thought about Gen, as I did such a lot then, and with that same stab of longing and shame. I remembered the pity on the faces of his two friends as they looked at me. Right now Gen was somewhere out there in the night, perhaps at one of the campus bars, perhaps in the dorm, meeting people and having new experiences, and I felt miserable, and so lonely. I gave a small sniff and consoled myself. It didn't matter how many new people he would come across or how exciting and sophisticated they were, there was one respect in which they could never compete with me.

For I was part of Gen's earliest memories, and he was part of mine; we knew each other as dirty-faced children scampering around the streets and the parks together – and in this context we forged the kind of imaginary world that only children know. That world was shattered one evening in summer at the hands of policemen in lonely cells, but Gen and I had entered that police building together. We had been together, in one way or another, ever since. It seemed to me, more than anything, that some cosmic force had been at work, intertwining our lives, from our earliest moments; and that whatever new experiences he was having and whoever he was meeting, they could never be to him what I was, for Gen and I had been woven together by fate into the fabric of each other's being.

I felt myself in the grip of something elemental; Gen's story and my own was as powerful and profound as anything the great sages and playwrights had ever described. I remembered what he had done for me that awful evening all those years before, how he had taken the blame, and I felt a feeling of love and pity for the child he had been and the man he now was – a feeling of melancholy taking hold at my core, melting into me. Nobody else could be to him what I was, just as no one could be to me what he was. Glowing with my feelings of love and certainty, I took a pen and paper and began to write. I wrote of our childhood, and I told him how I had been drawn to him even when we were fighting like cats and dogs. I wrote that I was, even then, able to see the person he was; that I had known he was different and special and courageous and bright. That I had watched him grow, had seen the man he was becoming, and that I knew he would march into the world, do great and incredible things. And that my most ardent desire was to be at his side.

These words of devotion spilled out of me in a deluge and I wept with happiness while I wrote. In the same moment I felt a great sense of pity for all the men and women who would never know the kind of love that I knew. I thought of my own mother, distant from my father, and I felt compassion, for it seemed to me the cause of her sharpness and pettiness was her unhappiness; in her whole life, she had never known the type of elemental connection that existed between Gen and me.

Without rereading it, I put the letter into an envelope. I stepped out of our building and walked to the postbox. It was autumn still, but the night air had grown colder. As I walked, I felt something brush against my face, not quite rain. In the lights of the bleary street lamps, a fine snow had begun to fall, so fine it was little more than dust. It almost never snowed in Beijing and I blinked in wonder. The streets were so quiet. For a moment I held my breath while the snow flickered and danced in an orange glow that was set against the dips and arcs of a much greater darkness. It occurred to me how beautiful the world was, and yet how solitary and strange. I posted my letter into the box, and made my way back home.

.   .   .

I spent the next few days in fevered anticipation. I didn't visit Gen at his dorm and continued attending my lectures and seminars as normal. But I could hardly concentrate, and even though winter was on its way, I felt as airy and breathless as one might on a humid summer's day. My professors talked about literature and society, about Chekhov and Cao Xueqin, but my mind was elsewhere. I was thinking about Gen, the way his face softened when he smiled, his critical verve, and his kindness. I played out scenarios where we met for drinks or a candlelit dinner; and in each of these creative enactments I became better than I was: more sophisticated, more knowledgeable and, most of all, totally at ease with myself. I would imagine how his eyes would light up – that slight shyness, the awkwardness that was part of his bearing, the streak of vulnerability that ran through him, visible to me and me alone. I would imagine how he would smile openly and in delight, charmed by my casual sophistication; how, in the act of reinventing myself, I would surprise him.

Sometimes my heart was in my mouth. I would stop in the middle of the campus and give a short gasp. Had I actually sent him that letter? I tried to recall exactly what I had written. Had it been too romantic, too full-on? Standing in the sunlight in the middle of the campus, I would feel a hysterical smile crease my face – a feeling of both horrified embarrassment and elated delight, for there was something exhilarating about putting all those feelings into words, packing them into a letter, then sending it out into the world. There was no turning back, and there was something liberating in that. Would he feel uncomfortable with what I had written? Or would it kindle in him something of the true nature of our connection that the novelty and excitement of the university lifestyle had allowed him to lose sight of?

I was drifting in and out of these very thoughts when I saw him emerging from one of the cafeterias on campus. When you are in love as a young adult you drink your beloved in; the image of him – every mannerism, every posture – becomes a form of mental Braille, a texture your mind can read almost physically. So I knew it was Gen, even before I saw his face.

In that moment, he turned and saw me. He gave an awkward smile, but his eyes were kind. He hesitated, so I walked toward him, the sun high in the sky behind him, his face cast in dappled shadow. I wanted to hold him, but when I reached him, I hesitated and he did too. We stood blinking at each other in the afternoon light.

'I wanted to talk to you. There are things I wanted to say.'

I felt my heart palpitate. 'The letter. It was … too much.'

He put his hand on mine to silence me. He spoke quietly, fervently, but his words made my heart dance.

'No, it was very nice, and appreciated. I read it several times. I want you to know that our relationship is precious to me too. Because I know that whatever happens in this world and wherever I go, you will always ground me. Because you understand my past. And you know who I truly am.'

He hugged me gently. I kissed his neck. My whole body shivered with pleasure. I felt tears well in my eyes. This was more than I could ever have hoped for. For a second I thought to pinch myself, in case it was a dream, but if it was, it was one I would never want to wake from.

He stepped back and looked at me.

'Can I show you something? Can I tell you about what I have been doing?'

I nodded.

'This way.'

He took me through several buildings and then along a path lined with trees.

'Where are we going?'

'To … *the Triangle*!' he said with a flourish.

I remembered Min telling me about the Triangle. The place where the students put up posters.

'That's where they are campaigning about the "no lights out" issue, right?'

Gen stopped in his tracks to look at me. I saw a flicker of disappointment pass across his face. Then he became buoyant again.

'So you have heard of it?'

'A bit.'

'Well, here we are.'

We stepped into a pretty little place. I had imagined something grittier, more urban – graffiti decorating the walls, or rap music from the US playing. Something with a more overt political feel. Instead it was rather genteel. In the middle of the Triangle there was a single circle formed by a green mesh fence. Within this grew two delicate and lovely pine trees emitting their sharp, sweet scent. On one side, a large flat poster board had been erected. Here a large number of students were gathered, peering at the information stuck to it.

As soon as they saw Gen, several of them raised their hands in greeting, and they parted a little way so that he could walk to the board itself. From there he began to address them.

'We all know about the university administration's lights out policy. Lights out – an interesting concept, no? When the lights go out, one cannot see, one cannot think – one is immersed in darkness, and therefore one cannot act!'

A ripple of appreciation ran across his audience. Gen was speaking softly, but with the same casual assurance that seemed to have been part of him as a child, that same instinctive certainty. Only now the others were picking up on it too.

'But perhaps, perhaps it is not just about Peking University. Perhaps this policy represents a broader malaise. That somewhere along the line, the lights went out, our political enthusiasm dimmed, and we ceased as a people to make progress in a mindful and enlightened fashion. But we are the new generation. And we are patriots. And that is why it falls to us … to turn the lights on again!'

The crowd of young people erupted, and I too clapped and shouted. I had always been aware that Gen was destined for great things, and now others were finding out. The thought of that made me want to hold him to me, for he belonged to me first, before any of them, and yet I was filled with a great swell of pride, and a happiness that others could see in him something of what I'd always known.

He looked over at me and flashed an embarrassed smile.

'And that is why I am going to stand as your representative on the Student Leadership Committee!'

Another cheer. But I felt a moment of trepidation. Some of what Gen had said sounded radical. I looked at the posters on the board, and at those faces – upturned, young and clear, gleaming hope. I thought about my father all those years ago and how he'd taken me to another wall, another place where people posted their thoughts. Only I remembered his sad and haggard expression; there was little hope in it, only a crushed, defeated sense of love. It was one of my most precious memories, but also one of my saddest. My father barely said a word to me these days, but then again, he barely spoke to anyone. He so often seemed lost in his thoughts. It seemed like sacrilege to even think it, but I would hate Gen to become down-trodden and defeated, to be rendered lesser than himself, in the way my father had been. From an early age I understood that, despite its show of benevolence in 'service' of the people, the Chinese state could prove a brutal handmaiden.

There was no place for such thoughts in this company, however. The enthusiasm of the students was everything. I noticed how Gen was flanked by Aiguo and Sile – the three of them had been thick as thieves since Gen had been on campus – and now a whole group of people gathered around Gen, sweeping him away from me in a bubbly rush of triumph. I followed them to one of the campus bars. I ordered a drink. Gen was surrounded by students, including,

I noticed, a couple of beautiful girls. I knew he wasn't the type to have his head turned, he simply wasn't built that way, but I felt smaller nevertheless. I tried to catch his eye, but I was invisible. After a couple of drinks, my feelings were a mix of inadequacy and determination, so I pushed through the crowd in order to be close to him.

For the first time, he looked a little uncomfortable; he was speaking smoothly, his face shining, but when I reached him he became awkward, and it was as though he had lost his thread.

'May I speak to you, Gen?' I asked softly.

'Of course.'

We walked out of the bar and into the cooler air.

'Are you okay?' he asked. But there was a tightness to his lips, a faint exasperation in his expression.

'I thought you were so wonderful,' I said. 'And I am so glad you are happy here, that you are finding your ... place, and that you ...'

My words trailed away. What I wanted to say hadn't cohered. I'd wandered into emptiness.

He looked uncomfortable.

I reached out, brushed the side of his cheek.

And that was when he winced.

That expression of pain on his face, the discomfort of it, burned into my mind in an instant.

'Look. I've told you how much you will always mean to me,' he said. 'But I brought you here today to show you about a different passion. Something I have found inside me. The necessity, the urgency of politics.'

His words were as eloquent as ever, but I had a feeling he was now speaking through me and to a crowd.

'You are so smart, so very bright. And this is going to …'

He gave an embarrassed schoolboy grin, and despite my trepidation, I found myself smiling too.

'This is going to sound so ridiculous to your pure heart, but what politics means to me now … it's become a higher calling! I realized somewhere along the line that something has built me for this. It's what I was always destined to do! I just never knew it before. Only … I am no longer sure I can give you what you need.'

I felt a coil of panic tighten inside me.

He looked at me wistfully.

'I am not sure we can be boyfriend and girlfriend in the traditional way anymore. As much as I would love to have that kind of life with you, because I have this calling, I suspect …'

His expression darkened in a frown.

'I suspect that in speaking out this way, things may not end well for me. In putting myself on the student body, I also place myself at risk.'

The thought of him being in danger brought tears to my eyes.

He touched his fingers to my cheeks.

'Please, please don't cry. The last thing I want is to be the source of your unhappiness. Because you know me better than anyone. Nothing can ever change that. You know I grew up with a pig of a father. You know he lied to my mother. He cheated on her. Which is why …'

His voice shuddered, he was overcome with emotion. I felt the power of his absolute sincerity.

'Which is why I always want to be totally honest with you!'

My voice came out in a single mewling sound.

'But why can't I be a part of what you are doing? Why won't you let me support you? I don't want you to do this alone, even if we can't be boyfriend and girlfriend!'

He looked at me solemnly for a few moments.

'I think you are the finest writer I have ever met, did you know that?'

I looked at him, giggled through my tears.

'Are you serious? Are you joking with me?'

But his face was serious, so very ardent.

'I knew it when you won that competition back in high school. I knew your essay was better than mine!'

'Really?'

'Really.'

His expression was grave.

'So why won't you let me be a part of this? Why won't you let me help you?' I asked.

He bowed his head.

'If you are absolutely sure. But if anything happens, I need you to be in the background, invisible. I'd never want to put you at risk.'

'What would you need me to do?' I asked solemnly.

'As such a gifted writer, perhaps … perhaps you could write down some of my speeches. As I move from place to place. Successful or not, at least in that way I'd leave an honest account of myself. For posterity.'

I nodded.

'Of course, Gen, whatever you need.'

He smiled at me, touched my cheek.

'I have to go back inside now,' he said. 'But I'm sure I'll see you soon.'

I watched him go back into the bar, at once surrounded by all those waiting to speak to him. I'd had my private time with him. I knew he had read my letter, that he appreciated me and that I would see him again soon; that he wanted me to help in his endeavors, that he needed me. A week ago, that would have raised my whole world.

So why did I feel so utterly desolate?

TWENTY-SEVEN

I WAS TO MEET MADAM MACAW IN THE LATE AFTER-
noon. I waited for her in a quiet neighborhood in the Shunyi
District. The sun was going down. The wide streets were bathed in
a honeyed light while the evening shadow crept from the trees and
the still air was interrupted only by the faint burr of a lawnmower. It
was not a poor neighborhood like mine, but neither was it a wealthy
area like the one Gen's parents lived in. It was a quaint, gentle kind
of place; the type of place I imagined children having water fights in
the heat of the day while grandparents puttered about in the gardens
as the last of the light drained away. Madam Macaw had wanted to
meet me here, but when I finally found the street, I realized that she
had not written down a house number.

So I waited. It was a warm evening and I had no place else to be.
I was glad to be away from the university for a while, and away from
home. I felt the last shafts of sunlight tickle my face, and a sense
of tranquility, for there was something calming about this place. It
would have been much the same ten years ago as it was now: the
same white, convenient houses with the same doors and windows,

every lawn smart and orderly. I heard none of the screaming rows that reverberated across the walls of my block, and living here you would never have to hear the groans and sighs of your neighbors making love, or catch the odor of their cooking seeping through the gaps in your door.

It was a spacious and clean area in which the life of every household was separate from every other, each as orderly and self-contained as one of those lawns. I found myself daydreaming; perhaps one day Gen and I would live in a place like this, perhaps our children would scamper across our own lawn and have water fights in the street. I took a deep breath – the momentum of my fantasy had taken me beyond myself, for I had never before thought about having children with someone. I suppose in one way I must have, though, because it was the type of thing we are encouraged to do as little girls – but such imaginings have the haziness of unreality that childhood dreams do. But now I felt a sudden prick of … fear, almost; a fear at the sheer magnitude of the revelation I was experiencing. I was someone who could one day give birth, who could usher new life into the world; I was someone who might well have a son of her own. Or a daughter!

Along with the fear was a secret excitement. I thought that Gen would make a good father; he was great at everything he put his mind to, and I was sure he would be great at that. But myself? Could I be a mother? The thought was bewildering and thrilling. I took another look at the sedate surroundings of this gentle neighborhood, and I thought how nice it would be to raise children in this place.

A place without fear or menace or crime.

The hand slammed across my mouth, stealing my scream before I had even managed to form it. I was dragged backwards with considerable force, my brain a surge of buzzing, electronic static, the white noise of instantaneous panic. Then I heard her whisper, as she breathed into my ear:

'Don't struggle, Funny Bunny! I needed to make sure it was you!'

Madam Macaw relinquished her grip. I staggered back, gasping.

'Well, who the hell did you think it was?' I spluttered.

Madam Macaw put a knowing finger to her lips.

'You never know.'

'You clearly did know. It was arranged in advance. There was clearly and absolutely no one going to be here besides me.'

She looked embarrassed for the first time.

'Well, yes, when you put it like that, I probably did know,' she said sheepishly.

Her thin lips formed in a sly smile.

'But you should have seen your face!'

I looked at her, smoldering. Finally, I asked:

'So, do you live around here?'

'Here? In this dump? Good grief, no.'

We stood there blinking at one another.

'So why are we here?' I asked with some exasperation. My heart was still racing.

Her eyebrow arched.

'We are about to conduct a top-secret military operation!'

'Are we?'

'Yes,' she said, 'yes, we are.'

'And who is this military operation to be conducted against?'

'My ex!'

'Your ex?'

'Yes, him, the bastard!'

I thought about this. I started to feel a little worried. I noticed she had a bag slung over her back, its greens and browns quite military in style.

'What are you going to do?'

'Don't you mean "What are *we* going to do?"'

'Yes. What are *we* going to do?'

'Do you mean, are we going to cripple, maim or kill him?'

'Yes,' I said nervously. 'That's something I would need to know!'

'No.' Macaw shook her head. 'We are going to do something much worse than that!' she said darkly.

'Worse?'

'Yes.' She leaned into me confidentially. 'We are going to balloon him!'

I must have looked baffled, for she ushered me forward in hushed and imperative tones.

'Move, move ... and if I say "duck" make sure you crouch down!'

We shuffled out of sight behind some cars, creeping down the street.

Into the cooling evening air slipped a clammy and rancid odor. I sniffed involuntarily.

'Eww! Can you smell that?'

'Yes,' Macaw said. 'It's coming from my bag.'

'It is? What on earth is it?'

'Oh, you know. Just the usual stuff. Offal, guts, the disemboweled contents of goat and cow.'

I went to say more, but my voice died as a result of sheer incomprehension.

'Go, go.'

Her hands pressing into my back, she herded me into a nearby bush.

'Stay down,' she whispered. 'We are close to where he lives. He'll be back any minute.'

I bit back my reservations. Sure enough, some minutes later, a car came gliding into the driveway of the house we were observing.

A man got out. He was dressed in the suit of a professional. He was not ugly exactly, but he must have been around my father's age: he had the sagging belly of a middle-aged man, he was balding although his eyebrows were thick, his face was lined, and there were small pouches of flesh under his eyes. He was as far away from the reality of my own life as I could imagine: someone old and nondescript and wholly asexual.

As he got out of the car, the door to the house opened. The sky above had darkened, and the light from the open door flowed outward into the dimness, revealing the faces of a family. A middle-aged mother who looked as portly and plain as the father and two fat-faced children jumping up and down at her feet. He walked into the house and closed the door behind him.

I gawped at Madam Macaw.

'That's your ex?'

'Yeah, what of it?' she muttered sullenly. And then: 'Stay focused, this operation requires crackerjack timing!'

She reached down into the foliage before producing some kind of rubber fabric. She opened it up and tipped in the contents of her rucksack. As the sudden profusion of slimy viscera slithered inside, I was hit by a wave of nausea. Macaw pinched the material shut, leaving a slight funnel, before turning to me almost indignantly.

'Well, start blowing then!'

'What? What the heck?'

'Blow on it like it's Hou Dejian's cock!!!'

Hou Dejian was a famous pop singer, but with his tidy hair, soft features and glasses, I really wasn't sure he was my type. Nevertheless, there was something exhilarating in what she had said, for I had never heard a young woman speak that way.

The stench was appalling.

I held my nose and began to blow. I put everything I could into it, without being quite sure why. My face must have turned red, for at some point she took over. And now the fabric was expanding. It grew. Until it was about the size of a small person. And then she blew harder, and it expanded all the more.

At which point Madam Macaw tied the end. And then she pulled the large inflatable along with her, waddling as she crossed the street, trying to balance. She reached the man's car and tied the balloon to its roof. It was not far off the size of the car itself, billowing and bouncing on top.

Panting, she returned to me. Fixing me with an intense stare.

'Okay, so now go do it.'

'Do what?'

'Do you know that game kids play? Teng-Teng the Tomato?'

'Yeah.'

'That's all you have to do. Just knock on his door, and run away!'

'Why me?'

'If I do it, there is a chance he will see me fleeing. But with you, even if he does see you, it won't matter. Because he doesn't know you!'

'I don't know,' I muttered.

She looked at me.

'Two things. I know I am asking you to do something for me, and you don't know me that well. But … he is a real asshole.'

'And the second?'

'Second is that you don't think you are brave. But I know you are.'

She looked so serious at that moment.

I crept out toward the house, my heart pounding. The last time I had done anything like this was when I was a kid, but everything had changed once I had been taken into custody that evening all those years ago, and now the thought of breaking the rules put sick anxiety into my belly. But I had committed to this, committed to *her* – so I moved forward, and soon I was crouching behind the car. I looked at the balloon we had blown up. Across it in bold black strokes was a single message:

'Professor Yu Zhanwei likes to fuck his students!'

I bridled. I realized this man was one of the teachers at the university, and I felt an icy chill of fear creep across the nape of my neck. My scholarship was precarious, and those who were in my economic category had to be especially well behaved. But everything had already been set in motion. So I rapped on the door hard, and ran as fast as I could. At first I made a beeline down the street, but then in panic I ran backwards and flung myself into the bush where Madam Macaw was crouched.

'He's a teacher? He's a dammed teacher?' I exclaimed.

'Hush,' Macaw said. 'Look, there is movement.'

I followed her gaze.

The man had come out of the house. The light was dimming, but the inscription on the balloon must have been visible, for when he gazed up at it, his mouth opened in an expression of slack-jawed horror. Behind him, timidly, came the rest of the brood: the placid-faced wife, the waddling kids. They too were looking up at the balloon floating above the car. For a few moments, the man had a shit-eating grin on his face, and I could see that he was trying to tell them how the situation was just one of those things, that it was some kind of random event. But their faces had changed too, as they made out the words on the balloon, at which point his own expression was crossed with a type of desperation. He took out the car key from his pocket, and started to jump up and down like a mad man, lunging at the offending balloon, as if – in bursting it – he might somehow erase the stain of those words from the consciousness of his family.

I heard Madam Macaw whisper fervently:

'Just a little bit more, try a little harder, you can do it!'

His belly was wobbling, his whole face had reddened, but then, with a gasp of satisfaction, he finally made it.

He connected with the balloon.

It burst.

And he was deluged with the animal viscera from inside it.

He blinked. This small, rotund, middle-aged professor slick with blood and goop while his family blinked back at him with an expression of baffled astonishment. All at once it was too much.

He dashed into the street.

'You bitch! You FUCKING CUNT!'

He was waving his hands.

He ran one way and the next, his middle-aged frame and sagging belly wobbling with the sheer effort of his fury.

At one point, he was almost within touching distance of us.

For the second time, Madam Macaw touched her hand to my lips. We were huddled together under the bush. Although I look back on it now without fear or trepidation, for this man was clearly absurd, at the time I felt myself shaking with the weight of my fear. And even though it was she who had put me in this situation, when her words came to me – a whisper in my ear – I was calmed.

'It's okay. You are with me!'

Eventually he went back inside, the door closed behind him, and a light went on in the living room. Crouching under that bush we heard raised voices, which after a time quietened. Tentatively, Madam Macaw and I crawled out from our hiding place and made our way briskly down the street, before repairing to a local bar. As we stepped into its smoky darkness, I could still feel my heart pounding. When I had first met Madam Macaw, her strange charisma and the overwhelming force of her personality captivated me. I'd wanted to please her, to impress. But now, exhausted, bereft of energy, I felt a sense of resentment, anger even. I realized how close we had come to being caught. In China, once you are thrown out of an institution, you are blacklisted. If you have money, if your parents are well connected, then it's possible to begin again somewhere else. But neither of those things applied to me. My time at university – everything I had worked for – could have ended right then and there. And it would have been in pursuit of some craziness unleashed by a young woman I barely knew.

Madam Macaw brought us a couple of drinks. She slid one over to me across the table. I couldn't look at it. I was upset now, but, as always, I could not give voice to my emotions. I couldn't say what I needed to.

'Oh come on, Funny Bunny! Don't sulk. You gotta admit that was all rather exciting!'

I looked at her.

'You know that's not my name, right? My name is not "Funny Bunny." And I … don't like it when you call me that.'

She looked surprised. It gave me a small sense of satisfaction to think that I could unsettle her.

'Hey, relax!' she said. 'Don't take things so seriously. It was just a touch of Marauder Mischief, the world needs a little of that now and again.'

I felt so many different emotions. Macaw's indifference, my isolation from Gen, from everyone, and most of all the pain of missing my grandmother, the only person who seemed to truly hear my voice.

'Hey, it was just a joke!'

I looked at the young woman on the other side of the table. I felt tears of anger and anguish burn in my eyes. I said huskily:

'People always say that. They say you shouldn't take yourself so seriously. They ask why you can't take a joke. They make you feel like a stick-in-the-mud even as they do something that can hurt. That man was a professor. If he'd seen me, he could have got me kicked out. University … here … now … For me, it's my only chance.'

My voice faltered. Although I had skipped seminars, so preoccupied was I with Gen … At that moment I realized how important it was I stay the distance at university. My mother had been skeptical, but my grandmother had always wanted me to go. She had realized university would be my passport to another place. She'd always wanted a different type of life for me.

Madam Macaw looked at me more softly.

'Your only chance?'

'Yes,' I said in a whisper.

She thought for a few minutes and then nodded her head just once. She glanced away.

'I think I understand what you mean,' she said quietly.

It may have been the closest she ever came to saying 'sorry' in all the time I knew her. But she didn't apologize. Instead she just slid the drink toward me again. This time I took it. I was grateful to have something to do with my hands. All the emotion that had suddenly welled up in me had taken me aback, and now I felt embarrassed.

We sipped our drinks, glancing guardedly at each other. But the tension had gone. And along with it, my anger. Suddenly it all felt like a bit too much to carry. And she, opposite me, looked wistful, almost sad.

'Why him?' I murmured.

Perhaps she had been swimming with her own thoughts, for now she glanced up at me in surprise.

'He deserved it. He's a shit.'

I thought about the middle-aged man I had seen, his bald patch, his pot belly, the jowls of his cheeks – even in the twilight he had looked flabby and tired and ordinary. I couldn't imagine Madam Macaw with someone like that.

I looked at her.

'No ... I mean ... how come you were with him in the first place? I mean, he is so much older and he looks ... I mean he looks ...'

She flinched then, and bit her bottom lip gently, involuntarily.

'When I first started at Peking University, I was doing the same as you, a literature course, right? Later I moved to drama, but at first I was doing that. He was one of my teachers. He taught me poetry ...'

She trailed off. Took another sip of her drink.

'He took an interest in my work. Said it had potential. And ... he seemed nice!'

She took a gulp of her drink and expelled air hard; her expression sharpened, it became cruel and sardonic once more.

'I didn't really give a shit about him. I had way more things going on at that time. But it was fun stringing him along nevertheless. And every now and again, I like to have a little fun at his expense. I like to remind him who's boss, the flabby piece of shit!'

She chuckled, a cold, mirthless sound. Then something in her expression softened. She looked at me coquettishly, but those glittering green eyes were unnerving, peering, as they always seemed to, into one's very soul.

'Do you really hate it when I call you "Funny Bunny"?'

'I don't know. It's not so bad, I guess. When I was a little girl, one boy used to call me "smelly bum" – so this nickname is definitely an improvement on that one!'

She chuckled and I found myself laughing too.

She looked at me, the smile still warming her face.

'I never asked you your real name. What's your real name?'

It felt strange and intimate on my lips. But when I spoke it, I experienced a great relief, as though all those emotions that had been building up inside me simply unclenched, just like that.

'My name is … Lai! And you?'

'My name is Anna. And I'm pleased to meet you, Lai!'

She blinked at me, smiling. And in that moment, it was as if she actually saw me. The first person in that place ever to have done so.

TWENTY-EIGHT

I DON'T REMEMBER MUCH ABOUT THAT EVENING. NOT that we drank a huge amount. We got to the point where we giggled about that middle-aged professor, his belly wobbling, shrieking vengeance into the night. But more than that, I think it was the first time at university that I felt I had made a friend. The journey home was tedious, the bus trundled its way through the city center and toward the outskirts, and when I finally returned it was late and our apartment was quiet. Without my grandmother, it was not just less crowded, it was as though the shadows had grown longer, the late-evening stillness absolute. My grandmother's death had created this echoing emptiness that lived with us all of the time, even when we weren't aware of it. And none of us knew how to fill it. As I passed through the hallway, the door of my brother's room creaked open. I glimpsed his form wrapped up in his bedcovers, his closed eyes – even larger in sleep – set into a countenance that was youthful and unblemished, and in that moment seemed to speak of absolute peace. He was not snoring exactly, he was still too young for that; however, the air flittered through his nose, making the faintest whistling sound. It moved something inside me, for he was perfect and untouched and yet the world awaited him cynical and corrupt, relentless and unending. At the core of myself I felt a swell of emotion: the need to hold back the tide, to protect him come what may, so that he could always sleep this way – a child's way, peaceful and untroubled. And yet, despite the strength of my emotion, I was aware of its absurdity. Its futility perhaps.

I closed his door quietly, the gap narrowing to nothing.

I crept down the hall.

There was a small light coming from the kitchen. I glimpsed her silhouette by the open window, the tip of her cigarette glowing in the gloom. My mother was leaning against the sink, a glass of wine next to her. She turned a fraction, and although I was unable to see her expression, I knew she was aware of me.

'You get back later and later, it seems,' she said, her voice soft and sardonic. 'It must be an exciting life you live at that place of yours.'

She never said the word 'university.' As though naming it was somehow distasteful. As though this stage in my life was beneath her contempt. And yet I also knew that she bragged to the neighbors about my entry into Peking University.

I stepped into the kitchen.

'Where's Papa?'

'In his study, where else?'

She blew out smoke in a soft whispery plume. The kitchen was still warm from that day's cooking, but a streak of stealthy cold had slipped through the open window. Outside, I could see the fading colors of the neighbors' washing; reds, greens and blues, subdued by the night such that they were melted into gentle shadow. My mother tapped her cigarette, shedding particles of ash that fluttered out of the window into the gathering darkness below. Her eyes flitted across me, casual, indifferent, with just the slightest hint of disdain. I shifted from one foot to the other, seeking to extricate myself from her, and yet, seeing her there like that – cigarette in hand, wine by her side – it seemed to me she had a certain mysterious elegance.

She was my same mother, of course. And yet, once upon a time she would have been my age, and perhaps her thoughts might not have been so dissimilar to mine. Her hopes. I looked at her. She had always seemed old to me, but I realized then that she must have been stunning as a young woman. I knew I was ordinary-looking; on a good day, if I was lucky, someone might describe me as pretty. But she … I saw it with such clarity. Even the tiredness and disappointment that come from experience – such things had not eliminated her beauty but in some way emphasized it in hard, bitter outline.

She watched me with mirthless eyes.

'What are you looking at?'

I stuttered. Made to withdraw.

'Don't be such a wet blanket. Have a drink with me.'

I glanced at her glass. The bottle stood nearby.

'You mean the wine?'

She smiled. It was the closest her expression had come to gentleness.

'Yes, I do. It's not like you don't drink when you are at that place of yours! I know you are used to it.'

There was an accusation there, but it came with none of her usual hand-wringing melodrama. Just a shrewd acceptance. She seemed different then, more real somehow.

I nodded.

She took a glass down from the cupboard and trickled some wine into it. Handed it to me and smiled, a watery smile fissured with regret.

'You know what day this is?'

'No.'

'It's your father's and my anniversary. Twenty years together!'

'Congratulations, Mother!'

'Thank you, daughter.'

Her voice was toneless, but she raised her glass. Sipped. Delicately as she always did. For the first time I realized she was probably quite drunk. She rarely took alcohol.

'It is actually an achievement. Your grandmother, who you worshipped so much, was absolutely against it. She thought your father was a good-for-nothing bookworm. If she'd had her way, you and your brother wouldn't even exist.'

My mother gave a strange smile.

I winced.

'So why did you disobey her? Why did you marry father?'

She seemed to relax. She pulled on the last of the cigarette, before pressing the butt into the sink. She took a luxurious sip of the wine and her eyes fluttered.

'Oh, that's good, oh, that's so nice.'

I waited. She focused again but she wasn't looking at me. She was gathering her thoughts. When her voice came it was precise and careful, not slurred by drink.

'Your father seemed to be part of a world that was amazing to me. He had ideas. Big ideas. I never went to university, but there was a time when I wasn't so different from you. You might not believe it. But it's true.'

She looked at me and in her eyes there was a strange sense of appeal that I'd never seen before.

Her focus shifted. Her voice softened.

'He wasn't the best-looking of men. He wasn't even all that charming. But there was … there was something kind about him. Which I liked. Because that meant something. Especially given how cruel men can sometimes be.'

A shadow crossed her face.

She brightened.

'So I fought for him. At the time it was all I could do, I guess.'

She stared out over the rim of the glass, looking back to a time in the past that I could only dimly perceive.

She smiled. She looked guileless, beautiful.

'You know, every year on our anniversary, he used to buy me a posy of cherry blossom and he would enclose a short poem. The poem was always bad, clunky – even I could see that. But it was sincere.'

I found myself smiling too.

'Do you know what he got me this year?'

'No, what?'

'Nothing.'

She turned away, took another sip of her wine.

'I know not everything is his fault. God knows what happened to him in that place. During the Cultural Revolution. But if he had just been a little more … if he could just have fitted in a little better …'

Her words trailed away wistfully.

I looked at her. I felt a surge of compassion. I concentrated, trying to get what I wanted to say just right. My voice came soft and low, but with conviction, I believe.

'I think what you and Father have achieved is very significant. I don't think love is just about romance and poetry. It's about holding yourselves together, even through terrible times. I hope that Gen and I enjoy something of what you and Father have shared.'

She looked at me for a few seconds, almost thoughtfully. And when she spoke, I heard the words, but didn't take them in at first.

'You stupid, stupid little girl,' she said softly. 'What do you know about anything?'

I heard a wheezing sound then. And I realized the noise was coming from my own throat. I blinked at my mother. But her image had blurred. I turned away and stepped out of the room.

And then I stopped. I wiped my eyes. And I took a couple of deep breaths.

I walked back into the kitchen.

She was pouring the last drops of the wine into her glass. She turned to me again, her expression still sharp with contempt, but tired too.

'If you are going to have some kind of tantrum, now is not the best time. Your brother has already done that once today and I am exhausted.'

I walked toward her. My hands were shaking. I was looking her in the eye. I hardly ever looked people in the eye. She looked away, then glanced at me again.

'You … you must have … surely there must have been some time when you did. When you actually did.'

'When I did what?' she said, sighing quietly in exhausted exasperation.

I looked at my feet as I finally said the words.

'There must have been a time when you … loved me. When I was very small perhaps …'

My mother's expression seemed to ossify, the irritation frozen faintly on her lips. She looked at me for a few moments longer, and blinked as though confused. She glanced back at me again, and something rose up in her, and I saw the tears fill her eyes. Then she turned away and walked past me. I turned on the tap, rinsed the sink. From somewhere outside I heard the noise of a couple, two people, arguing or perhaps just talking, their indistinct voices wafting up through the darkness. I closed the window. Turned off the light. Left the kitchen and went to bed.

.   .   .

It was early December when I next heard Gen speak. The weather was colder now, but that made the gathering in the Triangle that much cozier; students huddled together, sharing thermoses of whisky and mulled wine, and the atmosphere, as ever, was jovial. And yet, a mood of greater seriousness had begun to intrude. The 'lights out' policy – which Gen had made a name for himself by protesting – was due to kick in on the tenth of that month. The ability of the students to make a difference to our own living situation was being tested for real, and in a few days we would know if any of our speeches or protests had succeeded in repealing the hated initiative. But, for the time being, there was a sense of optimism and anticipation, and when Gen stepped onto our clumsy makeshift podium, his smooth austere features were ruddy in the dark. He was applauded. He nodded his head bashfully a couple of times and then raised his hand in a brief, elegant gesture. At once the smattering of people was subdued. He seemed so much more confident now.

'Our university is not just a place for education. After classes some of us may take in a film, or have a stroll in the park of an evening. Some of you – dare I say – may even repair to one of the local bars to partake in some less "wholesome" entertainments!'

His face was knowing and at the same time kind, an ironic smile playing on his lips, and a ripple of laughter at once ran across the small crowd. I felt myself laughing too. Before, Gen's speaking had been forceful and effortlessly logical, but now he was using humor to create a light-heartedness that hadn't been there before. At which point the casual playfulness of his words sharpened into something more serious.

'And yet, wherever we go – cinema, park, bar – we all come back to this place. The university. We go back to our dorms, if only to lay down our heads. And that's the point. The university is not just a place for education. For us, it is also a home. The university is not a parent or a politician, and still less a dictator. It is our communal home. A place where we live together as one. And every man should have autonomy in his own home. That is the most simple and honest of all human rights. And that is what we demand, nothing more, nothing less!'

The students broke into applause. I was busy scribbling down an approximation of what Gen had said. Fortunately he was not a verbose speaker – and at the end of his delivery, he walked off the stage in the same way he might have strolled in the park, absent-minded almost, as though oblivious to the applause. And I felt that same wave of longing. He was everything I was not and yet longed to be. He walked through the world with a nonchalance, as though he fully belonged, with an insouciance, unconscious and automatic. Gen had a breezy ability not to register the judgment and disapproval of others. He had got even taller since we had been at university – his frame even more gangly and awkward – and yet he had a charisma that was somehow weightless. I wondered if he himself was even aware of it.

The next speaker had nothing vaguely resembling charisma. She was a mousy little thing, even smaller than me. She wore huge black-framed glasses that sat on her face like a great contraption. Her squeaky voice halted and stuttered as she summoned up the strength in her tiny body necessary to maintain it, to project it outwards. But as absurd as she appeared, the other students regarded her kindly, for there was a feeling of solidarity that day.

'I would … I mean I hope to … I mean I just wanted to regale you with some lines from a favorite poem of mine. It is from a great poet whom I am sure many of you already know: Sándor Petőfi. The lines read:

Life is dear, love is dearer,
Both can be given up for freedom.

She blinked out at her audience, and even in the evening gloom I could see her eyes were glossy with tears. I felt embarrassed for her, aware of her ridiculousness. The university bureaucracy might have acted in a haphazard and authoritarian manner in trying to impose conditions on the students, curtail their activities, have them all in bed by ten. It was, of course, outrageous and paternalistic. And yet the appeal to life and love and the sacrifice of both in response? That was surely absurd.

The young woman adjusted those heavy-set glasses on a face that seemed oppressed by them. She started to speak again in that same high-pitched stutter.

'I … very much appreciated the comments the last speaker made …'

She nodded in Gen's direction. He was standing a few feet from me, and he smiled, a small benevolent smile.

'And yet, I think … I mean I would suggest … there was more he might have said. He used the word "autonomy." And I … of course I agree wholeheartedly. But "autonomy" on its own is an abstraction. Yes, we would all like this thing, but we must be much more concrete.'

Her voice had grown shriller, but at the same time more confident.

'We can only achieve "autonomy" if we have a political and social system that might facilitate it! In practice, autonomy means democracy. A working, functioning political democracy! That is what we lack. That is what we must fight for, as a genuine, concrete demand.'

Some of the students looked a little uncomfortable. But the slight young woman dug her heels in, becoming even more animated. She came down the steps rather awkwardly before ripping a poster from the wall.

'Look at this,' she said, stabbing her finger furiously. 'This is a poster that the university administration has posted, here in our Triangle. It reads: "Too many cooks spoil the broth! In a country as populous as China we need a strong patriotic government, and we need you, the people, to preserve the peace!"'

Some of the students murmured to one another.

'Don't you see what it's saying?' the young woman squeaked indignantly. 'It is nothing short of an advertisement for dictatorship. Communist parties all over the world say the same thing, as if they have been programmed in advance. Individualism must be destroyed in order to achieve unthinking consensus, and anything else – anything against the government line – is contrary to the nation!'

Now the other students were shifting and murmuring. Many looked uncomfortable. I felt their discomfort, for this kind of talk was extremely radical, extremist almost. But she was so far gone that she didn't seem to pick up on the mood of the crowd.

'The last speaker spoke of "autonomy." But he provides no blueprint by which such a thing might be realized. The only way we can do this is to create a system that will give us autonomy, here in the university but also in the country as a whole. We need to fight for a national democracy where every voice can be heard!'

Some of the students were listening attentively, others had begun to talk among themselves, and a few had turned away, pretending she wasn't even visible to them.

The speaker started to panic. She began to stutter her words again, in desperation this time.

'I am just ... I ... just ... needed to ... listen, all I am arguing is ... please, I won't take up too much ... time ... just that ...'

The discomfort of some of the students morphed into something else. As her voice rose, the more shrill and desperate it became. The first giggles rippled across the crowd. Then sniggers. She looked out at us for a few moments longer. She looked as though she had been slapped. I felt some sympathy, because at that moment she seemed entirely alone despite the fact that she was surrounded by people. And yet she had brought it upon herself with such desperate and extreme polemic. She turned and ran from the stage.

I looked to the side to find Gen.

His lips were curled in a strange smile. I don't imagine he thought anyone was watching him. And as beautiful as I found his features, in that moment there was something grotesque about them.

Someone hit the button on a radio, and music started to play. The mousy young woman was at once forgotten as some of the students began to dance. The tension had evaporated. The politics were out of the way. Now the drinking could begin.

We made our way to the East Slope bar. Again, Gen was surrounded by celebrants. I felt my head spin. I clutched the paper in my pocket. I thought I had documented what he had said almost perfectly, and even though he was swarmed by admirers, I felt myself light up inside, because I was the one whom he had trusted to record his words. And I was certain his speeches should be recorded for posterity.

I was lost in my thoughts when I felt a brief touch on my hair. Gen was looking at me.

'Do you wanna get out of here?' he asked, his eyes tired but smiling. 'It's been a long day!'

I think there was no cocktail, no drug, no experience that could have given me more pleasure, more delight, than seeing him in front of me, touching me gently, asking for my acquiescence. The joy was so great all I could do was nod.

I followed him back to the dorm, where we sneaked into his room once again. He poured us a couple of whiskeys. Outside it had started to rain.

I took out my paper.

'I think I managed to get everything,' I said softly. 'It really was … I mean, what you said … it was genuinely very …'

I chuckled in embarrassment. He smiled too. I felt as close to Gen as I had for months.

'I'm sorry,' I said, 'I'm speaking like an idiot. But I want you to know what you said today really meant something. Not just to me … but also to the people out there!'

I placed my record of his speech tentatively on his desk.

He smiled in embarrassment, but he seemed relaxed and content. I could feel everything about him, even without touching him, and this too gave me a pleasure that was beyond erotic. It made me feel more than myself.

He glanced at me, then glanced away.

'You are, as always, too, too kind. I ... don't think what I said was all that great. I think I just said what everyone else was thinking ...'

His voice trailed away.

'Perhaps the ability to do that is a gift in itself,' I piped up brightly.

'I don't know about that.'

He gave a sudden adolescent giggle.

'But whatever else, at least I wasn't as bad as that ... that stupid bitch who followed me!'

This crude utterance was so out of keeping with the tone of the speech he had made on the podium and the delicacy with which he had spoken to me when he invited me back. Perhaps I couldn't keep the shock from my face, for it was one of the few times he retreated.

'No, I am sorry. That was a hideous thing for me to say. But you have to understand ...'

He looked at me as though everything in the world depended on my judgment. And he spoke with great conviction.

'You have to understand. That someone ... like that ... with those kinds of far-left views ... Maybe they mean well. But when they talk about radical democracy – well, you must see how that turns out! It's the key to undermining our own political system, to letting the West in through the back door, for us to end up being dominated and controlled by the United States. I always wonder with people like that. If they hate China so much ... why don't they just go and live in the US?'

'No, no, I agree. I don't know what she was thinking. She was so weird, right?'

He nodded his head and grinned.

'She was ... *so friggin' weird.*'

We looked at each other for a few moments, smiling.

'Are we being unkind?' Gen asked, still grinning.

'I don't think we are,' I said with a giggle.

In that same moment, the door to his room burst open. A pretty girl stood there, laughing vivaciously as she saw Gen. 'Hey, I just wondered if you wanted ...'

Her face fell as she saw me. The tone she had used with him, so intimate, so soft and playful, at once became polite and cautious.

'Ah ... I'll come back later. It's ... not important.'

I remember her eyes. They were beautiful, eloquent in a way my own unremarkable eyes could never be.

Gen's face was turned upward, frozen for a few moments.

I knew that they were together. I knew in that second, seeing her face, and then his – I knew it with absolute certainty. And yet I fought the knowledge down.

'A friend of yours?' I tried to make my voice light.

He didn't say anything. It was as though he didn't want to admit any connection, but didn't want to deny it either.

Tears filled my eyes. I didn't want them to, but they did.

He looked at me.

'Hey, look ...'

I didn't want to let him finish that sentence. I felt a rush of desperation. It didn't matter about her. The only thing that mattered was him and me. For once I would be the bold one. I moved close to him, I put my hand on his crotch, I told him that it was okay, that I was 'cool' with 'it,' that I understood him – or words to that effect. I don't remember now. I only remember that it was like something was dying inside me. And I felt the desperation of loss.

He pulled my hand away. Without looking at me, he hissed sharply:

'You know that you mean a lot to me. But you can't keep doing this.'

My cheeks were wet with tears. I couldn't help it. But I held down my sobs.

His voice became softer.

'We need to live our own lives. It's not normal for people of our age to be so intense!'

I got up. I couldn't look at him. I shuffled out of the room. He didn't try to stop me.

It was odd in a way. When the worst thing happens, there is sometimes a little relief. As devastating as it is, it can provide a type of clarity. I knew now that Gen was with someone else. I wondered if he'd had full sex with her, or whether he just had her touch him with her hands down there in the way I always had.

I suspected they had had proper sex. It was something I couldn't quite imagine, and yet I couldn't stop picturing it. The girl I had seen at his door was so much more beautiful than me, and clearly so comfortable with him.

TWENTY-NINE

I SAW MADAM MACAW A WEEK OR SO LATER. I WAS NUMB AT that point. Before, I had always been able to rationalize Gen's behavior. I could tell myself that he was naturally aloof, arrogant even – that he lived his life according to the beat of his own drum, and yet, despite his callousness and his defensiveness, there was a part inside him that was protective of me; that was aware of the deep and abiding connection we had shared since childhood. Or to put it more simply, despite everything, I would always be special to him. But he hadn't even tried to deny the nature of his relationship with that absurdly perky and pretty girl. He hadn't even bothered to reassure me. He was moving away from me once and for all.

I had, at that time, some quite ridiculous premonitions that make me wince looking back, but which seemed so real – so absolute – to me as I was then. I imagined Gen making great speeches, drawing more and more people with his words. I envisaged the success he would have, how he would inaugurate a more liberal set of reforms, harnessing the power of the students and others in order to change the status quo. I imagined his rise to political stardom with his pretty bimbo by his side. And by that point, I would be nothing more than a distant footnote, the vague memory of a humbler beginning that must be discarded in order to step into the future. To seize and shape the destiny that was his by rights.

I stopped trying to bump into Gen on campus. I no longer sought him out at his dorm. I didn't write him any more letters. I stayed away. But it was abject misery. I found myself drinking more. After lectures and seminars, as the winter sun was diminishing in the gray Beijing sky, I would repair to a bar off campus for a couple of beers or a baijiu, because I couldn't bear the thought of returning home.

And it was on one such evening that I was scheduled to meet Madam Macaw. I was in something of a funk, and wasn't in the mood to socialize. And yet, in her weird, reckless way, Anna had been nice, showing an interest in me at a time when I was baffled as to why anyone would. So I made my way to the place we had arranged to meet. She had given me an address, on campus: Hu Shih Building, Block Four.

It was a Friday night, so most of the students had moved off the main campus, and as I walked through the central sections of the buildings, my footsteps echoed. I found the Hu Shih building, but oddly there was no Block Four. In fact, the campus map I stopped to check showed only three buildings. I thought at first Madam Macaw must have been mistaken. But when I arrived at Block Three I saw a little glass door at the end. I pushed it and stepped out into a grassy courtyard.

It was dark and shadowy. And then I heard a low male voice.

'Hey, baby, you've got a really nice ass!'

I felt someone grab my bottom, and I pulled away in shock. At the same moment, lights came on. I spun around to confront the person who had groped me; as shy as I was, I felt a sense of fury, my heart pounding with anger and shock.

A young man stood before me. Through my anger, I noticed he was good-looking in a strange sort of way. His hair had been cropped short, slicked back and parted to the side. He had a thin, elegant mustache. His features were sharp, and he was grinning at his own audacity.

Everything flared in a white-hot rage. I moved forward, raising my hand, on the edge of striking him, something inconceivable to my normal timid and frightened persona. And yet, from within the white-hot electricity of my rage, I glimpsed something about him that gave me pause. Those magnetic, emerald-green eyes, shining with amusement and just a touch of cruelty. And that ridiculous mustache – I saw now it wasn't real, rather its swirls had been elongated by a rich dash of black pigment.

The image cohered. And I realized I was looking at Madam Macaw. It seemed obvious now, but the expression she had assumed, the way she had moved, even the guttural sound of the voice she had put on – all captured a genuine masculinity. For a few moments, I had truly believed she was a man.

I stood there gawking at her in indignation. The only words that came from my mouth were:

'There is no Hu Shih Building, Block Four, is there?'

For the first time, Madam Macaw looked sheepish.

'No, no, not exactly. But remember what the Western Bible says: Wherever his followers gather there is the church!'

I looked at her.

'What ... the ... fuck?'

At that moment, several other people came bursting out of another door and onto the square of grass.

Lan came lumbering over to me, his big body wobbling with delight, and he clutched me in his arms. He felt warm, and his smell was not that of other men, but rather the smell of warm milk like a baby's. Even though I was not a tactile person, I found myself smiling. I looked over his shoulder and saw Min, who at once snapped his hand to his head, in a friendly soldier's salute.

Alongside them were four other people, two boys, two girls.

The boys were Jin Feng and Li Xin. They looked like brothers, both small and stocky with thick eyebrows. But Jin Feng spoke in a cocky and boisterous voice, while Li Xin was more thoughtful. His partner Ai Xiu would sometimes nudge and encourage him, pushing him forward, tweaking his nose playfully, causing him to blush. Her friend Pan Mei was a very large young woman, and I worried about getting distracted by her size, for it was easy to become fascinated by the massiveness of her bulk, those undulating layers that would at times ripple with a fluidity that was almost hypnotic.

But if I did gawk at her, she never expressed any resentment. Looking back it occurs to me that she was used to it, for she must have known it all her life. She was shy and kind, but she was also a natural comic; she could reel off these incredible impressions of famous Chinese actors and singers. Very quickly, her size became invisible; I stopped thinking about it because she was such good company – funny, but in a quiet way that carried none of Madam Macaw's sharpness or cruelty. When she laughed, you found yourself laughing too.

I looked at Macaw again.

'Why do you keep grabbing my ass? And why on earth are you dressed like that?'

She looked even more sheepish and turned her face away. Then those glittering green eyes were raised to me once more, fixing me with their magnetic, overarching intensity.

'Because … you have a nice butt. You don't know anything about Shakespeare though. In his day, all the girls had to be played by boys. Women couldn't perform on the stage. So now, this girl is the one who performs. Only she has chosen to be a boy!'

'Oh God, stop with the melodrama,' Min said with a sarcastic smile. 'Always giving yourself these high-minded reasons. Why don't you just admit that you like dressing up in drag?'

'Fuck you. I hate it when you're right!' Madam Macaw said.

'Is it Shakespeare again then?' I asked.

By way of an answer, Macaw simply looked at me, and then called out to the others:

'Players, please take your positions.'

Then and there they came together to perform a scene from Shakespeare's *The Tempest*. I was still fragile, shocked by Macaw, and now thrust into contact with this new set of people, both weird and wonderful. I came to realize these young people were, in their own ways, different in the way I was different, struggling with life in the same way I was. And yet, under the direction of Macaw – with her strange and ironic charisma – their weirdness and inadequacy pulled into something else, something that brought them together. Something that brought us all together.

I watched as they took on the roles she had assigned them. Of all the writers I had read at that point, Shakespeare was not one I favored. And yet, under the soft light of the evening, these individuals put aside their doubts and fears, coming together seamlessly, faces lit by the emotions of the characters they had become, eyes shining with the joy and terror from another time. And through it all, Macaw stood back, directing her players in the way a conductor might an orchestra in the grandest of auditoriums. Only we were outside, on the soft, wet ground, in the gap between buildings, and despite these modest circumstances, I don't think I have ever been so moved by a performance.

Afterward, Madam Macaw invited me to a bar. By this point she had changed: unraveled her hair, removed the white shirt and black trousers, applied normal lipstick and makeup – in short, becoming a beautiful and elegant young woman once more. All the manliness of her costume, of her performance, had been erased. And she was happy. Jin Feng and Li Xin and Pan Mei and Ai Xiu were also happy, breathing hard, laughing with the release of post-performance joy. It had started to drizzle and the low rumble of thunder could be heard reverberating in the surrounding dark. Lan and Min stood to one side, Min gesticulating, his small neat features eloquent with joy, and Lan, his massive frame locked into helpless laughter, giggling with the abandon of a toddler. All the actors had turned their faces upward, gleefully, using the rainwater to wipe the makeup from their faces, cleansing themselves of the people they had been, and returning themselves to the people they were.

And though the rain was clammy on my hair, I felt a sense of well-being, and a sense too of gratitude that Macaw had invited me to this place. Or, more specifically, that she had invited me to these people.

I looked up at her with concern.

'Aren't the others coming with us?'

She looked at them and grinned wickedly. She made a circle with the thumb and finger of one hand, and began to vigorously prod the index finger from her other hand in and out of it.

'I think they may have better things to do!'

We went to a different bar this time. It was in a hotel and like nothing I had experienced. The hotel was on the corner of Chang'an Avenue to the east; later I discovered it had several different annexes. We were in Block D – a rather spartan name for a place of such untrammeled luxury: a huge building that rose up into the night sky, eclipsing even the towers and turrets of the Forbidden City in its size. I had seen it, of course, on my bus trips to the university. But I had never properly looked at it before. Now it loomed above me and I shrank back, in awe of its smooth ivory glow. We entered the building through sleek black doors opened by a gaggle of porters, and Macaw ushered me across the marble floors toward a discreet lounge and bar. The bar was illuminated by low humming neon, the carpet was velvet, and the prices of the cocktails made me catch my breath.

I looked at Macaw hesitantly.

'Anna, I really don't think I can afford these prices.'

'Don't worry, Funny Bunny! I know a fella or two here. This evening is on me.'

She glided toward the bar, sleek and feline, and I watched as the men in the shadows turned their gaze to her. It was astonishing to me, for only minutes before, with her voice lowered, her bearing bombastic, she had so easily passed as a man, completely at home in the world, the type of person who could casually grab another person's ass with a cocksure grin and an absence of shame, because that is what it so often means to be male.

Now I saw a different person. She smoldered with a strange and ineffable beauty, and it was as though everyone in that bar felt it. The majority were affluent Europeans or Americans, though there were some wealthy Chinese, and a scattering of Japanese. But all were captivated, all followed her with their eyes as though they had been commanded.

She returned to our table holding two huge, rich, coffee cocktails, and a plate of crisps. Even the crisps tasted like heaven.

'So, did you enjoy my performance?' she asked.

She did not say 'our performance'; she had not acknowledged any of the others who had helped bring the play to life.

I sipped my cocktail. It felt like taking warmth and sweetness into myself. I shuddered briefly.

'Yes. It was … very good.'

'Is that all you have to say, Funny Bunny?'

I felt dazed. And then spoke softly.

'I thought it one of the most marvelous things I have ever seen. Outside books!'

Her eyes glowed with satisfaction, and then just a hint of irony.

'But is it possible to see books?'

'Oh yes. Those I can see more than anything. I haven't been reading so much lately. But I knew a guy who owned a bookstore, and he would lend me all these books and he always knew the best ones … or at least the ones that were best for me, if that makes any sense?'

'This guy, this bookshop owner, were you fucking him?'

I gasped.

'Eww. No. Why would you say that? He must have been, like, eighty or something!'

'Must have been? Did he die?'

'No, no, he is not dead. At least, not that I know.'

'So why don't you see him anymore?'

I pondered the question.

'Well, a friend of mine, my boyfriend actually … he didn't feel too good about this guy. He thought I was spending too much time in his shop, and …'

'And?' Macaw prompted.

I giggled nervously.

'I don't know. I guess he just wanted to make sure I spent more time with people my own age. I mean, this guy, he really was old, and he was lovely and everything, but I've always spent a lot of time in my own company, or maybe only talked to a couple of people. I think Gen just wanted to make sure that I would get out there a little more, especially because we were about to go to university … and stuff.'

'And this Gen? Is he at the university too?'

'Yeah, for sure. He is amazing, he is prominent in the "no lights out" campaign, and he is so cool, and so kind …'

'So he is your boyfriend now, right?'

'Well … not quite. I mean, we have known each other forever, we have this connection, we first met when we were six or seven years old …'

My voice trailed away.

'So … he is not your boyfriend?'

I took another sip of that delicious caramel liquid. I couldn't meet her eyes.

'No, not right now. I mean, Gen is so busy campaigning … and I want to support him … in that … I don't want to tie him down.

He needs to be able to breathe, I think he is going to do amazing things, and he—'

She raised one hand, gently.

'This Gen, Lai. He sounds like a little bit of a cunt.'

The shocking word, the word that nobody should say, arrived in an almost matter-of-fact fashion from her lips.

And it was a revelation. I began to protest, in fact I felt angry.

'What right do you have to say that about him?' I stuttered. 'Gen is an incredible person. I am certain he is going to do the most amazing things, politically speaking. He could rise high in China, he could change so much ...'

She was watching me, but her expression was softer this time.

'He still sounds like a cunt!'

I blinked at her. I wanted to lash out, but she had spoken so calmly. She was not being confrontational, and I realized she was not trying to put me down.

And for the first time, it occurred to me: maybe Gen really was the way she saw him. Maybe he was different from how I thought of him.

Two men approached our table. They were both clean-shaven. And they were both good-looking. One was smiling, cocksure, his dark eyes gleaming in the soft light. The other stood a little back, looking at us with a hint of regret, as if to apologize in advance for his friend.

'Excuse me, ladies,' said the first, 'but is heaven missing a couple of angels? Because it seems as though you two have fallen to earth!'

I felt myself flush. I didn't know where to look. Macaw, on the other hand, didn't blink.

'Is that really all you have got? I'm Chinese, just like you. Most of us are Buddhists in terms of religious inclination. There is no heaven for us. Just a great wheel that, at some point, we all need to jump off. May I make the suggestion that you jump off it now?'

Macaw was sharp with her irony, but her eyes were dancing.

The first guy smiled all the more.

'A good point. But what most people don't know about the original Buddha is that, as well as surviving on a grain of rice a day, his other principle was never to refuse a drink!'

Despite herself Macaw laughed.

'So what will you have?'

We ordered the same again.

They sauntered off toward the bar.

I looked at Madam Macaw.

'What's going to happen? I mean, we don't even know them!'

'Go with the flow, Funny Bunny. Go with the flow.'

When they returned, my vision was already a little hazy; the cocktails were strong. The first guy introduced himself as Wei Bao and he cocked an eyebrow as he did so. The other guy mumbled his own name: Li Jie.

Wei Bao set down our cocktails and proposed a toast.

'Here's to drunken Buddhism!'

'You are very full of yourself, aren't you?' Macaw responded, amused.

Li Jie was looking at me gently. Whereas Wei Bao had sharp cheekbones and elegant eyebrows, Li Jie had softer features, leaving him unguarded somehow, and yet when he spoke his voice held a quiet assurance.

'I apologize for my friend.'

He nodded at Wei Bao, who was deep in conversation with Madam Macaw.

'He is a lovely guy. But he can be … a bit too much!'

I glanced over at Macaw. And I burst into laughter.

'Tell me about it!'

We smiled at each other, awkward, tentative, but with understanding, for we knew what it was to have wayward friends, and as those friends jabbered away, we remained encased in gentle calm. And I thought to myself, this guy, this man, is very beautiful. He wasn't wearing glasses, but I could see the vague imprint they had left on his face. He had thick, beautiful hair, a perfect nose and full, pronounced cheeks. I blurted out:

'How old are you?'

'Me?' he asked as though surprised by the question. 'I am twenty-four.'

'You don't look like twenty-four. You look younger!'

I wasn't being flirtatious; it was a genuine observation.

'I feel like twenty-four, though. Whatever twenty-four feels like.'

I nodded.

There was a moment of silence between us. He was twenty-four years old. I felt an illicit thrill. I was in a luxury bar, drinking cocktails with a twenty-four-year-old, and he seemed interested in me.

'Do you have a girlfriend?' I asked.

Again the question just leapt out.

'No, not at the moment. I was engaged for a while though. For three years in fact. But it didn't work out. What about you?'

I shook my head. I felt a sense of affinity with him. I might not have been engaged to Gen officially, but I had thought us committed to each other.

'I was with someone for a while,' I said.

'And now?'

'It didn't work out.'

He nodded again, as a burst of laughter came from Macaw and Wei Bao. I kept thinking to myself how handsome Li Jie was. Despite his quietness, I sensed a certain strength.

We drank our cocktails. The boys got up to get some more.

Madam Macaw pinched my arm.

'This place is ridiculously expensive. So they have invited us up to their room for drinks.'

'Should we go?' I breathed out. 'I mean, we don't even really know them.'

'I think they are okay,' Macaw said.

I finished my cocktail. And I thought, why not?

We got into the elevator together. My mind was a little fuzzy – it didn't take much to get me drunk. We entered their hotel suite. There was a jukebox in there that reminded me of an American film I had seen with Gen.

Wei Bao activated it, and a sixties song started to play: 'Blue Velvet,' by Bobby Vinton.

Wei Bao stood up and began to sway, crooning the words in pidgin English, his voice husky and painfully raw. We were in hysterics.

Macaw placed her hand on mine.

'Are you having fun, Funny Bunny?'

'Yes,' I said warmly. 'I always do with you.'

She smiled then. Everything was hazy but I had a feeling of warm well-being. I remember seeing her take Wei Bao by the hand, walking him into a bedroom, and I wanted to call after her, for she was my friend and there was so much I wanted to tell her, but I couldn't put my feelings in words.

And then Li Jie was leaning into me, and I could feel his lips on mine, and I remember how hot I thought he was. The image of Gen flashed across my mind, and I gently pushed Li Jie away.

We sat on the sofa in the main suite. He – Li Jie – was breathing heavily, but once I pulled back he immediately stopped, even though I could tell he was turned on. He was excited by me. This twenty-four-year-old guy, who had been in a serious relationship, who had experienced the world – I could feel how much he wanted me. And everything that had happened with Gen seemed to fade away. I reached down and stroked his crotch.

He looked astonished at first, and then almost dizzied by my touch.

'Are you sure?' he whispered.

'Yeah,' I breathed.

In the background we could hear them, Macaw and Wei Bao, their moans passing through the walls of their room, sounds both strange and compelling. Now Lie Jie had hitched my dress up and he was fumbling with my underwear. I knew I was about to lose my virginity. I had committed to that. But what I didn't expect was his mouth between my legs. I shuddered.

'Please ...'

It was a plea that worked both ways, both to continue and to stop. I had never properly examined myself down there in ... that place. To have someone else see me like that ... The feeling of being so open, so exposed, was embarrassing. But he was kissing me right there, looking up at me while he did it, like there was no one else in the world.

375

'Can I?' he murmured.

His penis was so hard, so perfect, and a thrill ran through my body; it was I who had provoked this, for he found me beautiful, and I him.

I nodded briefly.

He moved in between my legs. I felt him inside me. I contracted a little, there was a moment of discomfort rather than pain; I looked at his face moving above me – he was looking at me too. All at once the discomfort gave way, and sudden ripples of warm shuddered through my body, my vision blurred, and in the soft light I could no longer see his face, only his outline, and the feeling of his body, so warm, so close, encasing me. I let out a desperate sigh. Then he was clear to me again, I saw his expression ossify in a pleasure that verged on pain. He pulled his penis out and I felt a spattering of ejaculate on my belly.

'Oh,' he gasped. 'Oh, I'm so sorry.'

I didn't understand what he was apologizing for. I felt that warmth float across my body in a gentle ebb and, instinctively, I held him to me. He put his arms around me. We lay there for a while, too lazy to move.

'Wow,' he said.

'Wow.'

We burst into muffled laughter, and held each other some more.

A little later I was using the shower, and like everything else in the suite, it was luxurious. The floor was a jet-black tile, smooth and yet not slippery. At a touch of a button the water came in warm caressing streams. I lathered myself with soap, my body present in a way I had never known, full and palpable, the liquid warm streaming across it. I stepped out and got dressed. I slipped out of the suite, closing the door quietly. When I exited the hotel, it was still night, but the first fissures of deep sapphire light glowed softly against the dark. When I finally made it back home, the early morning light had broken through and I could hear birdsong all around. I crept into my bedroom and lay down on my bed, utterly exhausted, and yet sleep would not come, for my mind was alive and whirring.

I got up, splashed water on my face and headed out again. It was still early morning, no later than seven, and people were beginning the day, queuing for buses, voices intermingling with the noise of the road. I crossed the wide street, and walked down a slope; the sounds of the people and traffic grew faint and indistinct as I entered the cemetery. Then came the low sweet song of a nightingale, smooth and melancholy, and in the background the hysterical, high-pitched twittering of sparrows. As I stepped out onto the soft grass, the rows of graves were wreathed in a fine morning mist made bright and translucent by the sun.

I found my grandmother's grave.

It always made me catch my breath. For even then, I still had moments when I would forget, when I would be wandering around the house absent-mindedly and expect to hear the click-clack of her knitting and stitching, or her low strong voice muttering indignantly about something said on the radio. Even when she nodded off in her chair, there seemed to me something solid and durable about the way her presence filled the room; as I watched her though my child's eyes, it never occurred to me that she might not always be with me. I think some part of me was a child still, for I couldn't reconcile the small tidy gravestone in this serene, sad place with the memory of her sheer presence, the size of her personality, her bellicose, bombastic nature and the soft certainty of her kindness. I felt the quick lightness of grief, the way it could softly steal your breath, before I was able to reorient myself. I tidied the flowers at her graveside and began to speak.

'I am sorry I haven't come by recently, Po Po. But there has been a lot happening. I have been working hard at university ...'

I tried to say more, but it was difficult. I spoke in a softer voice.

'Things have been so terrible with Gen. I don't think we will ever be together again, but that would have pleased you. But I was with another boy last night. And I know that wouldn't have pleased you. Please don't judge me too harshly. He was ... really nice. And he was ... kind. Everything is changing so much and so quickly. Sometimes I wish I could just hold it all back, keep things how they were. I really wish that. And I wish you were here. Say hi to grandpa for me.'

I touched my finger to the cool rock of her tombstone. Pigeons cooed delicately and I could hear the traffic in the distance. I don't think I really believed my grandmother could hear me, and yet, at the same time, speaking to her lightened something inside, and I felt a tension – a sadness – lift as tears pricked my eyes; tears of happiness for what had been and trepidation at the immensity of the future I was gazing into. I got up and started to walk back, through that quiet solemn place, and I thought about the night just gone and Li Jie and his gentle intensity. Only yesterday I had been a virgin, now I was no longer one. Life's impossible transitions, impossible but somehow inevitable too. One day my grandmother had been there, the next she wasn't.

I touched my hand to my belly and it occurred to me that the body that was my own could bear children, create new life. There was something wondrous and daunting in the thought, and I felt a moment of warmth, of pride. For I felt as though I had, in a very real way, grown up.

PART
IV

THIRTY

IT WAS NEW YEAR'S EVE, 1989. FEBRUARY 5. THE YEAR OF the Snake. And the first year we had spent without my grandmother. It was evening time. The festivities on our floor, in full swing, were as fun, raffish and colorful as ever – the children buzzing around, hyped up on sweets and presents, the adults chatting warmly or leaning back with amusement, surveying the scene and sipping wine. None of us mentioned my grandmother, but she was in our thoughts, I think.

I caught a glimpse of my mother in the kitchen, a pot of rice on the boil. She was lost in her thoughts and wore an expression of gentle bemusement at odds with her sad, exhausted eyes. It struck me then that she had the aspect of a little girl, but the steam from the pan had strafed her hair, and I could see the developing streaks of gray, and the lines around her eyes, and the thinness of aging skin. She seemed so much older now, and quite alone. I slipped away, back into the throng of people drifting in and out of our apartment.

I glimpsed my brother and his friends playing with their new packs of Garbage Pail Kids cards, each cartoon kid exhibiting grotesque and colorful deformities. I thought the cards horrid, but my brother and his friends were obsessed by them.

At the far end of the hall, I saw a figure I didn't recognize. She was around my age, but dressed formally in demure blacks and grays, with elegant high-heeled boots. I knew right away she wasn't someone who lived in the building. She looked a little uncomfortable; there was a tension in her bearing, as though she was late for a meeting. She was young and professional-looking, and I was curious to know how she had found herself in the traditional environs of our old and out-of-the-way apartment block. I moved closer. She had dark eyes and a small pretty nose that wrinkled involuntarily every so often, like a deer sniffing danger in the air. And then I felt a glimmer of recognition. She glanced up and saw me. At that moment I realized. I went to her.

'Al Lam?' I asked hesitantly. 'Is it really you?'

She smiled slightly and her face lit up with relief.

'Lai! I didn't know if you would still be here! It's been such a long time.'

I looked at her in wonder. A couple of kids screeched past.

'It's so noisy here, do you want to go somewhere quiet?' I said.

She nodded.

We went to a nearby bar, pushing our way through the queues. The place was predictably packed and there was nowhere to sit, so we took our drinks and stood outside. The warm, fetid atmosphere of the bar gave way to currents of icy air and the forlorn blackness of the night above. Al Lam shivered, set down her wine, and opened an elegant cigarette case. She took out a cigarette, lit up and exhaled, breathing out a fine plume of smoke. She seemed so delicate and refined. I was impressed.

'I can't believe it's you. The years have really passed. How long has it been?'

'I'm not sure. It seems like forever.'

'It really does,' I said.

She retrieved her wine and sipped at it tentatively.

'Time is funny like that.'

I frowned, concentrating.

'The last time we saw each other … I remember, they were sending you away. To Hong Kong. You weren't very happy. None of us were. But what was it like?'

She smiled.

'At first I hated it. I missed you all terribly. I told myself I would never talk to my mother or father again. But that lasted all of a week. I really did miss my life back here and my friends. When you are a child, those things, the familiarity of them, are your whole world and you cling to them fiercely – it is painful to be torn away. But at the same time, things change so quickly. Within a few weeks you are immersed in your new existence. The school I went to was a good one. There were Chinese like us, but also English and French children, and the atmosphere was liberal and open. We put on theater performances, listened to music on our Walkmans and sometimes we watched cartoons, especially *Transformers*!'

She giggled as though this were the height of wickedness, and I felt a sense of recognition – I saw in her the child she had been, both serious and kind. I felt a rush of fondness.

I spoke quietly with a touch of regret.

'We had always planned to go to Hong Kong to rescue you. We swore an oath, do you remember? But we didn't even manage to stay in touch!'

She laughed now, openly and spontaneously.

'We were just kids! Kids say stuff like that.'

The laughter died. She grew thoughtful.

'And … that last summer. It was kinda weird, don't you think? More than just me leaving. Like something was coming to a close. Remember the curfew? For Brzezinski and his entourage? And how we broke it and got chased by the police?'

My skin tingled in the cold air.

'Yes.'

Her expression lightened once again.

'I'm hogging the conversation, Lai. What about you? What are you doing these days?'

'Well,' I said evenly, 'I'm studying Literature at Peking University.'

She nodded as though I had confirmed something she had always known.

'You always were smart and imaginative.'

'I don't know about that. But I find it interesting for sure,' I demurred. I was not used to compliments. And while I loved books, I had never considered myself particularly imaginative.

'What about you?' I asked.

'Well, as I say, the school I went to was liberal. Lots of music and performance. For a while I wanted to be a musician, I studied the flute. But I realized I didn't have the talent.'

She spoke matter-of-factly, without any sense of disappointment.

'Even though I have quite a logical mind, I was still very much into the music scene. So I shifted my focus from the practical side to the organizational one. That's one of the reasons why I am back here in Beijing. I am studying event planning and music culture at the National Academy of Theatre Arts.'

'Wow,' I said, genuinely impressed. 'That sounds very cool.'

She smiled.

'And what about the old gang? Are you still in touch with any of them?'

I took a long sip of my wine. In the cold air it made me feel momentarily dizzy.

'Not really. After that summer, it wasn't just you. We all kind of lost contact. Became teenagers. Went to different schools. Except for Gen. We ended up at the same high school. Became close. He's at my university now. I still see him from time to time.'

I looked away.

'Gen,' she said thoughtfully. 'I do remember him … but not as clearly as the others. He always seemed distant and … a little unkind, to me.'

She must have seen something in my face, for she at once held up her hands in supplication.

'Hey, I am sure he is not like that really. As I said, I don't remember him that well at all.'

I smiled wanly. Even though my relationship to Gen was painful, hearing him criticized still made me flinch, almost as if I was the one being attacked.

Delicately, diplomatically, Al Lam changed the subject.

We lingered for a while outside, sipping the last of our wine in the cold. We laughed about the times we had shared, the local haunts we had frequented. A childhood neatly folded into a few lines of conversation, for the memories were dimmer now, as dim as the outline of clouds in the darkness above. Soon our wineglasses were empty. We stood facing each other, smiling awkwardly, for we had come to a point where there was nothing left to say. Gently Al

Lam extracted herself. We clasped hands with genuine affection, we swapped numbers and we promised to meet up in the near future in order to touch base – both of us, I think, knowing such a meeting would never come to pass. Her cheek felt slight against mine in the coldness of the night, and it was suddenly clear to me how much I had missed her without ever fully realizing. I watched her walk away, a small, elegant figure bobbing into the middle distance, before melting into the darkness beyond.

.   .   .

It was quite poetic really. Everyone in Beijing called them 'winter haze days.' The bucolic beauty of the phrase belied a somewhat more prosaic and depressing reality, however. The 'haze' in question would settle on the city for days on end. It wasn't the product of some sea-struck mist rolling in from the ocean to the east, but rather the result of the landlocked Beijing traffic belching out steam and smoke, and the air from the thermals above sealing in the smoke so that it felt as though one was moving through a thick pea soup. It was beautiful at times, though. The afternoon sun appeared as a burnished blemish of gold high in the sky, a faraway patch of bright with mist swirling around it, while at the level of the city the buildings seemed to materialize out of nothing, vast, elegant shadows taking shape from within the miasma of pale fog. Such beauty was deceptive; if you were outside for too long breathing in the fog, by the time late evening came your throat would be raw and your nose streaming – so those in the streets often wore masks, or sometimes simply pulled their shirts or jumpers up over their mouths and noses, all of which added to the sense of an apocalyptic landscape frequented by shadows, a population of people without faces.

When I reached the campus and entered the main cafeteria where I was to meet Madam Macaw, the place was buzzing with expectant energy. Plates clattered, students laughed and shrieked, people at tables huddled and pressed together – the warmth of body heat contrasting with the cold mist clawing at the windows. It felt a bit like being at school on a day of a great storm, when the teachers would summon you inside during the lunch hour to watch a film while the rain pounded on the roof and windows, and you felt an excitement that came from the strange interruption to your routine, and a sense that great events were at hand. I felt the same that day in the canteen, and it reminded me that, as much as we tried to deny it, we students were at times still close to the excitable and credulous children we had been.

Even before I saw her, I felt her gaze on me. I turned. Macaw had her hair pulled back, cropped. She was wearing the same black trousers and white shirt. In her hands she had a couple of bags, and by this point I knew they held the ingredients that enabled her transformation into a man. They contained the makeup she used to shade her skin, making her jawline seem firmer; the gel that allowed her to lacquer her hair into a short, masculine crop; the liner that emphasized her eyebrows, making them appear fuller and less feminine. But these tricks would hardly have paid off were it not for her bearing, her expression. There was no doubt it was her – I could see her looking out at me – and yet it was from within the guise of a well-kempt, baby-faced young man. To see her like that was not uncomfortable exactly. But it was discombobulating, like when you look at one of those pictures where there is just the one image but you can interpret it in two different ways – see it this way and it's a duck, see it another and it's a rabbit.

If you looked closely, of course, you could see the components of the illusion that she had crafted; if you were in the know you would see the mechanics behind the deception. But when she asked a guy on the table next to us to pass the sugar for her coffee, he barely gave her a second look, saying, 'Here you go, pal!' and Macaw responded in her lower, more gravelly voice, 'Thanks, fella!' She turned back to me and gave a very male wink – knowing, confident and lascivious. I looked at her in astonishment; I leaned in close and breathed one word:

'Why?'

I really didn't understand why she had chosen to dress up like that, on that day. As far as I knew, Madam Macaw's Marvelous Marauders – her rather odd and wonderful theater troupe – were not due to stage any performances. But more than that, it was beyond me how she could act like this. In a normal situation in front of other people. What if someone realized? Wouldn't she die of embarrassment?

She looked at me and those eyes changed again, softening and shimmering, becoming vulnerable.

'I've got an interview. It's related to performance art. I'm a little nervous. I was hoping you might come with me!'

To tell the truth, I felt proud and excited – touched, even. She was so confident and charismatic, and yet clearly there was another side to her, this aspect of doubt or hesitation, and I took it as a token of our closeness. I touched her hand.

'Of course.'

She 'became' the young man again, her voice gruff, her movements heavier and more deliberate. We left the cafeteria and walked to one of the university's central buildings, before taking an elevator to a higher floor. We got out and walked to the door of an office whose sign read 'Vice Chancellor.'

I looked at Macaw the moment before she knocked.

'Why,' I whispered, 'would a vice chancellor of the university be interested in performance art? Why would he want to interview you about this?'

Macaw looked at me seriously.

'Vice chancellors are strange creatures, you never know what one is going to think or feel!'

I went to say something, but she pushed through the door and I followed her in. From behind a desk, a bald-headed, elderly man with a white mustache directed us to sit.

We sat down.

He glanced at us. I remember being awed by a computer terminal sitting at his desk, for so few people had computers in those days.

'You are here for the 5.15. And you have something urgent to tell me?'

Macaw looked him straight in the eye.

'Correct. Your information is correct.'

I looked at her in astonishment. In bewilderment.

Her eyes never left his face.

'My name is Yu Yulong. And this ...' She motioned toward me, 'is my girlfriend. We are due to be married in April!'

My jaw dropped. The capacity for speech had left me.

The vice chancellor looked at her impassively.

'I offer you my congratulations, Mr. Yu, but that doesn't explain why you have requested this meeting.'

Macaw's expression was inscrutable. With the same gravelly, masculine voice, she said:

'For the past year I have been attending the seminars and lectures of Professor Yu Zhanwei. He was very inspiring to me. Unfortunately, he began to ask me to stay behind after class. And what happened there, I have come to believe, was completely inappropriate.'

'What are you saying?'

'I am saying he behaved in a sexual way that was unwarranted.'

'You are saying he touched you?'

Macaw looked at the vice chancellor, then down at her feet. She spoke in a choked whisper, full of emotion.

'No, not exactly.'

The vice chancellor's voice was soft, but held a hint of impatience.

'So what are you saying?'

'I am saying he made me blow up balloons!'

'Balloons?'

'Yes, the very same.'

'What … I mean, I'm sorry, but you are not making much sense.'

Macaw looked at the vice chancellor. She looked him dead in the eye.

'For men like you and me, it doesn't make any sense whatsoever. At the time, it seemed ridiculous to me. But after everyone else had gone, he would make me blow up balloons and then pop them!'

'But that's absurd!'

'I don't disagree. But he has been doing this kind of thing for a while. I've got a list of other students he has abused in this fashion …'

'With the blowing up of balloons?'

'Indeed. It is a fetish. I have spoken to the authorities. The technical name for this type of behavior is "loonerism," and the individual who partakes in it is called a "looner." Sometimes, when he would make me blow a balloon, I would see him …'

Macaw's voice grew faint and horrified; she couldn't go on.

'You would see him what?' gasped the vice chancellor.

'I would see him … fiddling about with himself! Down there. And when the balloon popped – I mean, you are a man of the world, I am sure you can imagine!'

The vice chancellor of my university had a look on his face of utter astonishment, and I realized it was mirrored by my own.

Macaw regarded the elderly man seriously.

'I've escaped Yu Zhanwei's balloon depravity. But there is a whole generation of students who may not. You need to act now. Because this guy is a desperate, sick balloon pervert!'

Having said her piece, Macaw then leapt out of her seat, striding from the room. For a few moments, I sat face to face with the vice chancellor, one of the most powerful figures in our whole university.

I blinked at him a couple of times. And then stuttered:

'I am so sorry …'

I had to try and put into words what it was I was sorry for.

'I am just so very, very sorry!'

I bolted from his office.

I slipped through the doors of the elevator just as they were closing.

She stood watching me, lips twitching in the beginnings of a smile.

'Him again, Anna? The same teacher? I get that this Yu Zhanwei must have really hurt you, but is it worth risking your position here for? Is it worth risking mine?'

Her face fell, her features narrowed, that feline sharpness both cold and cruel.

'Let's get one thing straight: he never hurt me. He doesn't have that power.'

I went to say something more, but something in her tone cut me off. But I still felt annoyed. I stood there smoldering, as the elevator descended. Finally she broke the silence.

'Hey, look, nothing bad will come of it. You didn't give your name. And I gave a fake one. The smarmy bastard won't even lose his job!'

'So why do it?' I asked, throwing my hands up in a gesture of helplessness.

She smiled an impish smile.

'To add a touch of Marauder Mischief, of course.'

I blinked at her.

'Can you imagine? The good professor won't get fired, because I used a fake name, so, ultimately, nothing will come of the complaint. But the vice chancellor will still have to talk to him. Will still have to ask him about the student I was claiming to be. And that means he will have to talk about the nature of the complaint. I would love to be a fly on the wall when that happens. That bastard Yu Zhanwei will be mortified. When his boss asks him if he gets off to the feel of rubber and popping balloons? Can you imagine his face?'

I kept my own as straight as I could but there was indeed something humorous about it. Macaw asked in a quieter voice:

'Are we still on for Friday?'

'Sure,' I said.

We were outside by this point.

She gave a dazzling smile, and turned away. I watched her go, and despite everything I found myself smiling. I didn't know this Professor Yu Zhanwei, but he sounded pompous and, despite her protestations to the contrary, I did believe my friend had been hurt by him. As she walked away, I noticed something fall from her side. I ran after her and bent down to pick up a wallet. When I stood up, her figure had already disappeared through the heavy curtain of mist.

I was in something of a bind. Nowadays, of course, it wouldn't be a problem. You'd just message the person on your mobile phone to come get their wallet. But in those days, I had never even met someone who owned a mobile phone, and although they did exist, you couldn't send a text on one. As for Macaw and me – I don't think I even had her home phone number. We would make arrangements for future meetings when we were together, that was the way our friendship worked. Later it occurred to me that she was abnormally protective of her privacy and personal details, but at the time it seemed perfectly normal.

I wandered back into the main building. I opened the wallet; despite myself I was intrigued and prepared to snoop. She had a little cash, a few of those cards reading 'Madam Macaw's Marvelous Marauders,' and a snippet of a quotation that read:

A woman drew her long black hair out tight, And fiddled whisper music on those strings, And bats with baby faces in the violet light Whistled, and beat their wings.

Last but not least, she had a student card. On the front was printed her name (Tang Anna) and department (Arts and Drama) and on the back in smaller writing was printed her home address: No. 4 Jiamenwai Avenue, Binhe Sub-district, Pinggu District 700003. I glanced at my watch. The Pinggu District was some distance away in south Beijing, but it was still early afternoon. I felt responsible for returning Macaw's wallet as soon as I could, but in truth my motives weren't completely high-minded. Everything about her intrigued me and I wanted to see where she lived.

THIRTY-ONE

I TOOK A BUS THAT TRUNDLED THROUGH THE MIST, pulling up hard every so often, the bleary lights of the cars glowing like the eyes of animals in the fog. Every now and then there would be a cacophony of horns before the vehicle lurched forward once more, and eventually the looming shadows of high-rise buildings gave way to more modest abodes. Above these, the late afternoon sun had cast the drifting vapors of mist in a strange, sallow haze. I got out and had to ask a few stall owners for directions before finding the road I was looking for. It was less of a road, more of a gravel alleyway, thin and uneven, with dwellings on either side. The houses here were single-story shacks with thin concrete walls unadorned by paint. Some had bars on the windows. The roofs were made from strips of corrugated iron, and scattered across the narrow walkway was a series of old scooters and bicycles, propped up like drunks against the guttering.

At first I thought I had got it wrong. Macaw couldn't live somewhere like this. And it wasn't just the squalid poverty of the place, though the area clearly had no small share of that. It was the drabness, the mud-smeared gravel, the tawny walls and the dull grays of the roofs. It was hard to imagine Anna – someone whose personality was so full of color – languishing here. I had the urge to turn back, to get the next bus out of there, for it was as though I was seeing something I shouldn't. But there are times when rational thought gives way to deeper impulses and currents, and I found myself raising my hand and knocking on the hard wooden door nevertheless.

She opened it. Even without makeup she still looked beautiful, only tired, her skin a little more faded, her hair pulled back haphazardly, and she wore a frayed kimono with a faded image of a dragon. She regarded me coldly.

'What are you doing here?'

'I … I … you dropped this. And I thought it might be important to you.'

I handed her the wallet.

She took it without saying a word.

'I like your kimono. Very snazzy!'

I caught the ghost of an amused smile.

'I guess this is the point where I invite you in,' she said, and for the first time there was a dullness in the luminescent depths of her eyes.

I followed her inside.

There was not a great deal of space. A small hallway. A poky kitchen that opened into a living room at the back. It was disorderly but not dirty, and the appliances looked old-fashioned but well kept, although, in the fading light of the afternoon, the cupboards and surfaces were lightly covered in a grainy dust. The air had a smokiness to it.

'So what do you think?' Macaw asked, regarding me with cold amusement.

'It's … very nice. It's … quaint.'

At once I regretted those platitudes.

'Yeah, it's the perfect dream home,' she said sarcastically.

'You know, Anna, I'm hardly from money myself.'

She nodded her head a fraction.

'I should introduce you to my father. It's his house. It's only right.'

In the living room there was a large moth-eaten chair and the diminutive frame of a man sunk into it, so small that I hadn't noticed him at first. He was watching TV, a miniature black-and-white device with a fuzzy picture that buzzed and crackled. Around the chair was a collection of empty beer cans. Perched on one of its arms was an ashtray, with a cigar stub cold and moldy against a carpet of ash. As I got closer I could see his face. He had large eyes, and thin salt-and-pepper hair that straggled down the sides of his head. There was a little of Macaw in him – the same straight, sloping nose, the same fine jaw – but his expression was softer, almost flabby, in terms of its gentle unrecognition. He blinked and smiled spontaneously, the way a baby might.

'Father, this is my friend Lai. Lai, this is my father, Tang Daiwei.'

There was a large window behind him. The mist had thinned. In the small porch outside stood the skeleton of a barbecue that looked as though it hadn't been used for years.

He reached out and cupped his hand in my own.

'I am very pleased to meet you. I don't meet many of Anna's friends.'

I smiled at Anna's father.

'It is an honor to meet you, sir!'

His hand felt like a little bird in mine.

'I would offer to make you some tea and serve you some cookies, but unfortunately a migraine has kicked in.'

'That's quite okay, sir. I completely understand.'

We retreated to Anna's room.

It was different again. Whereas the small area outside had allowed in some light, her room was softly shadowed, the walls shrouded with dark silk sheets. She hit a switch and the darkness was interrupted by a series of blue and emerald lights, threading through the dark silks in winking, glittering gleams. Photos had been pinned to the material, and I couldn't disguise my fascination. There were pictures of Macaw as a child, pressed into a tight gaggle of girls in a photo booth, all smiling out. But the majority of the pictures were of Macaw as a young adolescent, tucked into an oversized and tattered black gown with golden moons and stars emblazoned on it. She was nearly always standing on some makeshift stage or mini-podium, but her head was only a little higher than the audience. Sometimes she was standing before a table, sometimes pointing a long silver feathery wand, but in all these pictures she was smiling at the camera without artifice or care.

I looked at her.

'I never knew you did magic.'

She smiled ruefully.

'That was a long time ago.'

'Show me a trick.'

She looked at me poker-faced.

'Oh come on, I am sure you were great!' I cajoled gently.

'Well, since you ask ...'

She reached into a basket underneath her bed and produced a stout, wide-bottomed bottle of peach liquor.

'I am going to show you ... *how to make this disappear!*' she declared with a theatrical flourish.

She popped the top off, took a swig and handed the bottle to me. I was always quite finicky about drinking from other people's vessels; my grandmother would sometimes tease me for being a prude. But that day, in the velvet darkness of her room, and with tendrils of mist swirling outside, I took a swig and it felt as if we were teenagers once again making some kind of girlhood pact – drinking illicitly – and we started to giggle. The drink was sweet and warm, forming a glow at my core, but as I looked at her the smile on her face faded. She seemed almost hesitant.

'You haven't asked me about my father. Why he is as he is.'

'I didn't ... I mean, I didn't think it my place to ask ...' I stuttered.

'It's okay,' she said softly. 'Some part of me would like to talk about him. As you can tell, he is old before his time. But he wasn't always that way. Before ... it was different. Then everything changed.'

'What happened?'

'It was years ago now. When my father was still a veterinarian. He loved animals, loved tending to them. As a small girl, I sometimes fretted that he loved animals more than he loved me! He would often work late, see. And that's when it happened.'

'When what happened?'

Macaw tensed up visibly. She gestured for the bottle. I handed it over. She took a longer drink this time. Coughed slightly. Pushed her way forward through the words.

'Sometimes they would tend to more … exotic animals. Zoo animals. Nothing too dangerous or too large, like tigers or bears. But smaller creatures, lizards, snakes and the like. At that point, they had been looking after a Komodo dragon. Have you ever seen one of those?'

I nodded mutely.

'My father was thrilled. It was a real win for his business, to be asked to nurse such a rare specimen back to health. It had a damaged limb or something, I don't remember too well now. What I do know is that one of the staff must have left its cage open …'

I edged closer on the bed. She took a full, mournful breath.

'Anyway, you can imagine what happened. My father, always working late. He didn't notice the giant lizard until it was on him. Komodos are big and strong by lizard standards, and they have a poisonous bite. He managed to pull it off him, get out of his office, close the door, trapping the beast inside. But by that point he was in a bad way. If the lizard had been at full capacity, well …'

She shuddered, as though someone had walked over her grave. She handed me the bottle. I drank – this time without even thinking, so focused was I on the gravity and horror of her account.

'His arm had been torn. He was bleeding. He tried to walk along a dirt road to a nearby hospital. But unfortunately … he didn't get there!'

'Why not?' I whispered.

She looked me in the eye, her expression cold.

'His clinic was on the outskirts, where the edge of the city meets the land. They often had problems with wild dogs. Pests and vermin, they wouldn't normally attack human beings. But it was late evening.

And my father was wounded. Perhaps they smelled the blood. In any event, a group of them started trailing him.'

I was dumbstruck.

'They came closer and closer, until suddenly they were on him. With his good arm he picked up a rock, pushed it in their faces, somehow he managed to make it to the door of a nearby house. The dogs were chased away. And the owners called an ambulance.'

'Thank god,' I murmured, 'the poor man.'

Macaw looked at me again. She reached over and took the bottle, her movement slow and weary. She took another sip.

'Think again. I sometimes think that fate does not favor the meek or the kind.'

I looked at her in astonishment.

'What do you mean?'

'The elderly couple in the house were good people. They chased the dogs off with a stick, and once they had set my father down in the living room, they went to call the ambulance. Unfortunately ...'

'Unfortunately?'

'Unfortunately, they were collectors of cats!'

'Cats?'

'The very same. Perhaps because my father was lacquered with dog drool, the cats in the house at once sensed in him their natural and eternal enemy. As he was lying there, all seven of them ... they ... set on him tooth and claw and they ...'

At this point her voice broke with the weight of her emotion, and she cupped her hand to her mouth, turning her head away. She was trembling violently. I was shocked and astonished, and I reached out to her.

And then I realized she was laughing.

'You bastard!' I exclaimed.

'I can't believe you bought into that, Funny Bunny. You really are the last of life's innocents!'

I snatched the bottle back from her.

'I had a feeling it wasn't true. When the cats attacked him as well, I knew you were pulling my leg!'

She laughed with savage delight.

I found myself smiling too. She was like that. One of those people who had an edge of cruelty, but could somehow tease a smile from you all the same.

We drank some more. The small beads of the threaded lights glinted and gleamed in the soft shadow. She spoke in a quieter voice now, with a kind of thoughtful resignation.

'No, Funny Bunny. The truth is much duller. My father was never a vet. And for the last few years he has spent his days wasting away in front of the TV because my mother left him. Some time back, he had a mild stroke that took away some of the movement in his left leg. It wasn't too bad – and he was encouraged to exercise, to get better. But he just gave up. People choose to do that sometimes … to abandon the rest of the world in favor of a single room and a television!'

Her eyes narrowed.

'Especially if they know someone else has been left behind and can look after them,' she added, the bitterness in her voice palpable.

I handed her the bottle once more.

'Do you ever see your mom, Anna?'

'No, she left when I was eleven. Not seen her since.'

'Do you want to?'

'I guess I probably should. But I don't care all that much now.'

She took another swig. And then she broke into a smile.

'They were funny though, the two of them. My mother was more like me, dramatic. She wrote poetry in her spare time. She did some performance art too. Maybe that's where I get it from. My father was a wet sock, even back in those days. As you can tell, the walls in this house are thin. I'd hear them arguing in the night sometimes, after I had gone to bed. Well, it was more her screaming, and him desperately trying to calm her down. Afterward I'd hear them make love as well. It kinda grossed me out at the time, every kid hates to think of their parents in that way. But it was nice too.'

'Howdya mean?'

'Well, just that they were both there. Present. At that age, your parents are very much your world. And even if you are angry with them, when you go to bed at night and you hear their voices, raised or lowered, you feel secure somehow. Life seems as it should be!'

She took another drink. I was feeling the effects of the alcohol now.

'I don't blame her, though,' Anna continued philosophically. 'See, what you have to understand is that man out there. Sometimes it feels like he can drain any hope from the room just by his presence. He stays there staring at that TV, and sitting with him in those long silences feels like drowning. He saps your energy. All of it. He knows there is always someone there. To cook. To clean. And he just … accepts that. He takes it for granted. As though the world is obliged to provide someone to cater to his needs. That's the most incredible thing of all. So I get why my mother left me to it. Sometimes I think I *actually* hate him!'

She said this last part almost to herself, as though she were mildly surprised by the realization.

'How do you manage if he doesn't work?' I asked softly.

She smiled wryly and took another drink from the bottle. One of the things about her was her strong masculine streak. I don't mean in appearance. She appeared strikingly feminine. But there was something in her behavior, the way she related to the world – a certain hungry confidence, a voraciousness almost. She would drink from the bottle without giving it a second thought, and she could drink a great deal; rarely did alcohol overwhelm or subdue her. When she liked a guy she would approach him in the same way a cat might stalk a mouse. And she seldom failed to secure her prey. She was competitive too – she loved to play games and win; the world to her was something whose vitality was to be sucked and savored like a luscious piece of fruit. It was something she could impose herself on.

Perhaps that is why she could play-act being a man so effectively, slip into his clothes so easily, into his guise – because a masculine sense of confidence was immanent in all that she did, the way she moved through the world, the way she was. Perhaps, too, that is why her relationship with her father was so galling to her: it was the only aspect of her life where the size of her personality and the sheer force of her will had no impact on her powerlessness, her inability to change the situation.

'You know those quilts that old women make? The patchwork ones where they weave lots of different squares into the one blanket?'

I blinked.

'Of course.'

'Well, it's a bit like that. I get by doing that. Threading together little squares. Since my father had his stroke, the government pays him a small stipend. That's one square. I do some shifts at the local grocery shop. Another square. And then there's the Marvelous Marauders. Sometimes we do performances at bars, and we receive a little in tips. Another square. And so on. And so I get by. I think that's how most people get by. And ... and I manage to continue my studies. There's a small victory in that, I think!'

She smiled, and for the first time there was a trace of uncertainty in her expression.

'There really is,' I told her sincerely.

That peach alcohol was perfuming across my brain now, leaving a fuzzy haze in its wake.

'I think I should get going. Before I pass out.'

'I'll see you out. And ... thanks for coming.'

I stood waiting by the door as she gathered a couple of things. I looked back through the small, squat dwelling. She was standing in front of her father, and he was looking up at her, listening to what she was saying. Anna's face was shadowed, indistinct, but I could see she was frowning. The man in the chair seemed diminutive and shrunken as he looked up at her.

And then, just like that, she passed her hand across the side of his face, stroking his cheek, the gesture tender and impossibly brief.

When I stepped out, the brightness of the late-afternoon sky met the grogginess of my alcohol-clouded mind. The mist had all but abated, some lingering strands outlined momentarily in the cool of the air. I felt the warmth of the sun on my face; the winter giving way before the first signs of spring. I walked through the neighborhood, retracing my steps toward the main road. I thought of Macaw and her balloons, and I found myself grinning involuntarily, and then I thought of Anna and her father, and of my own father and a whole generation of men who had retreated into the quiet of their studies or their living rooms; then I thought of the latest outbreak of student protests in the university, and a new generation – my own – and while the sunlight tingled against my cheek, inside me bloomed a sense of hope.

THIRTY-TWO

I HAD BEEN WORKING ON SOMETHING FOR MONTHS, BUT it was not a seminar project, nor was it something I shared with anyone, not even Macaw. I kept it completely to myself. At first the notion was hazy, I don't believe I really intended to follow through. Nevertheless, one day I was in the students' office and came across a prospectus for an exchange program that offered a year's study in various universities around the world.

At night, when I couldn't sleep, I would flick through it, gazing through the pages into worlds I could scarcely imagine. One in particular caught my imagination. It was Toronto University, in Canada. It was not as distinguished as some of the bigger universities in the US, UK or France. But the picture in the pamphlet showed a silvery-gray building with ancient doorways, high vaulted arches and turrets, and a looming tower of gray stone at the main entrance. It looked more like some great medieval church. But whereas the latter might have been forbidding, this building was festooned with the pluming green of cheerful trees and well-kept bushes. Leading to it was a vast plain of flat grass, rippled with a hue of gold where it had been struck by the clean, clear sunlight. The sun was high, set in a blue sky without a cloud. There were groups of students lazily picnicking on the grass. In the darkness of my room, by candlelight, the idyllic glow that seemed to emanate from the picture helped offset my loneliness.

For it gave me the feeling that beyond the pall of black outside my window and the shadowy cityscape, there was a gentle, undescribed world that maybe one day I could settle into, leaving my troubles behind. It was a simple, almost childlike fantasy – but nevertheless, in the months following, I found myself filling out the lengthy application form, a bit here, a little more there, whenever I had a spare moment. And then one day it was complete. I addressed the envelope and took it with me to university. I sat in the cafeteria nursing a cup of coffee for a couple of hours, the envelope snug in my pocket. The lunchtime crowds gradually melted away, until it was simply me and a few odd bodies left, lingering as the afternoon light faded and the objects of the cafeteria were softened by the creeping shadows of the coming evening. Finally, I slipped out and went to the students' office, where, after taking a deep breath, I posted the application form.

It was early April, some weeks after I had visited Anna's house, and the evening air was unusually sweet and balmy, glowing with the fragrance of spring. Students were milling about, ready for the night ahead, and there was a sense of expectation in the air. I didn't feel like returning home right away, so I walked to one of the bars on campus and had a large glass of white wine.

I watched the people around me as the bar became busier, and the enormity of what I had done began to sink in. I felt nervous but exhilarated and somehow proud. Some months before, I had lost my virginity, and beyond the pleasure and excitement of the experience lay a more abiding feeling: I had reached some kind of invisible milestone, and my path into adulthood and independence was that much more complete. I felt something similar now. I had applied to go to a country on the other side of the world, not just to visit, but to live there! I thought it was unlikely I would be accepted for the program, but the very fact of applying not only made me dizzy with possibility: it gave me the sense I could shape my destiny according to my own requirements in a way I never had before.

Were I to be accepted, though, I couldn't even begin to frame the conversation where I would inform my parents and my brother of my decision to leave. I had applied on a whim, on an impulse that wasn't wholly serious, but the more I filled out that application, the more I realized I didn't want to stay in Beijing. I wanted what my grandmother had wanted for me. To do something no one in our family had done before: to travel the world, to encounter new horizons.

When I got back to the apartment, I could tell something was different. There was a soft light coming from the living room, my mother was there, at the table, and she was talking, but her voice was raised slightly in a shrill, overly enthused way, striking a note of artificiality. I assumed one of the more well-to-do neighbors had come round for a visit, for she would often use this tone in company. But when I stepped into the room, I saw her sitting with Gen.

Gen glanced up at me and smiled, that small smile of his, ironic, tinged with a little melancholy.

'Hello, Lai, it's been a while,' he said quietly.

I stood there lost for words. Although it had been only a few months, he looked thinner, taller, more adult somehow. My pulse began to race, but with it I felt something sickly.

'Hello. I didn't ... erm ... I didn't realize you were coming. We hadn't arranged to meet!'

'Ha, my daughter! As if a dear childhood friend requires some kind of formal invitation. Gen knows he is welcome here anytime. And he has been telling me about his activities on campus. His campaigning to make the university a better place. You,' she said, looking at me accusingly, 'could do with some of his ambition!'

Her expression softened as she turned to Gen in amusement. 'I've known this lazy one to sleep until ten on a Sunday morning!'

I felt something clench inside me. Gen being here with my mother in our home seemed wrong, and made me feel helpless somehow.

I glanced coldly at my mother.

'You always said student activism is about pampered brats with more money than sense, Mother. You said they know nothing about the real world, that they're silly sods who don't know they're born. Do you remember that?'

'Of course I do,' she snapped.

Her voice lightened again.

'But Gen isn't like that. Gen isn't always going on marches and screaming at people. He is working his way up in the hierarchy, patiently and diligently, so that he can make some sensible and moderate changes that will benefit everyone. Politics should be a discussion, not a fight!'

For a split second, a wincing discomfort passed across Gen's face before he regained his equanimity. Even so, when he spoke again, I could hear a tension underlying the words.

'Well, it is a good deal more complicated than that. Sometimes you have to show the authorities your determination, your conviction, your strength, so they know you mean business.'

He hadn't raised his voice, but I realized that my mother – even though she was trying to compliment him – had actually irked him. He gave a brief glance at his surroundings, and for a second he looked as though he had tasted something sour. Again, it was only for a moment, but I saw it now.

My mother gave a vague, mirthless laugh.

'Well, I don't know about any of that, I am sure. I'll leave you kids to it. So nice to see you after all this time, Gen!'

She bustled out of the room, and the silence settled upon us.

'Would you care to take a walk?' I asked.

He nodded. We left the apartment. The evening air was mild now. As we stepped out, Gen touched my arm.

'Follow me?' he asked.

He said it softly, tentatively, and just like that his confidence and aloofness seemed to drain away, and there remained the figure of an uncertain small boy. I was pulled back to those times spent in his vast empty house studying, the times he had told me about his father's infidelities, his anger and, behind that, the hurt. The hurt that a child feels. I felt my heart rise in my mouth. I nodded.

We walked in silence. I had no idea where he was taking me, in my own neighborhood. But perhaps I should have known. We walked uphill. It wasn't too far. As the sun was descending, we arrived at a patch of gravel, an abandoned square of land, punctuated by patches of grass and spiky weeds. In the corner was an old gnarled tree, a shadow against the brightness of the sunset. Beyond, I could see on the horizon the shape and form of the buildings of the business district and, past them, the Forbidden City and the Great Gate leading to Tiananmen Square.

'Do you remember this place?' Gen asked softly.

'We played here when we were younger!' I said. 'I could never forget,' I added softly.

Gen smiled slightly, and reached into his pocket. He produced a tattered piece of paper, which he smoothed down and began to fold into sections. He shaped it into the semblance of a paper plane. He took a step forward and floated the plane upward into the sky. It soared for a few moments before making a nose dive and clumsily meeting the ground.

I laughed.

He looked at me with a small smile, gently amused, but with a touch of regret.

'Do you remember how Zhen would make them? So well, and they would fly so high you'd have to crane your neck to look at them. I was so, so jealous of him for that at the time. I never said anything, of course. But I wanted more than anything to be able to make paper planes like he did.'

'Times change, I guess. You have a new set of friends now,' I said softly.

I thought about the pretty girl who had surprised us while we were talking in Gen's campus accommodation. I experienced a sudden rush of bitterness, and turned away. Tears sprung to my eyes, and I felt both ridiculous and exposed.

He put his hand on my shoulder. Turned his face toward me.

'I didn't behave well, I know that now. I nearly lost you ...' His voice trailed away. He gazed into the horizon, toward the outline of the Forbidden City and Tiananmen.

'But I'd also like to think that we could never lose each other. Not truly. For better or for worse we have kept step together, your life with mine, mine with yours, for as long as I can remember. Nothing can change that.'

His voice was soft and husky.

'The situation on campus is getting worse. The radicals and the conservatives are constantly at each other's throats, and it seems to me they would prefer to squabble amongst one another than to see any kind of genuine change. But like it or not … I feel that I have been tasked with making that change happen!'

He looked exhausted then, and unbearably sad. My bitterness was at once vanquished.

'But Lai, I don't have the strength to do it on my own. I need you to be with me. I need your wisdom, and above all your compassion, to make me strong. I feel I can't do what I have to do if you are not with me. I don't have the strength.'

He turned to me, his eyes wistful and pensive, and then he kissed my cheek almost as a plea. His lips found mine, and for a few moments we kissed – a lingering, passionate kiss in this place where we once had played as small children. I had always loved kissing; for me it was in some ways more rewarding than the sexual act itself, the intimacy of your mouth against someone else's was so close, so searching and yet so delicate.

But although we had never spoken of it, I was aware that Gen was a self-conscious kisser. He never fully gave himself to the experience, his contact was often brief and perfunctory as though he was holding something of himself back. I think that is the only day I remember where he kissed me properly, where – for a few moments – he abandoned himself to the experience.

He withdrew, still holding me gently, and looked me in the eye.

'So you will come? You will return to the Triangle? We can ... work together again.'

'Yes, Gen, of course I will,' I said softly, my heart still fluttering with the surprise of the kiss.

Just a few months before, I would have paid a devil's ransom to have him hold me like that, to hear him speak such words. And part of me *was* happy. Yet that feeling no longer went all the way, it no longer reached my fingertips. I was happy to be with him in that moment, but the emotion did not possess me in the way it once had, for there was now something in me that was abstract, separate and perhaps even cold.

A Scottish poet once wrote: 'The best laid schemes of mice and men go oft awry.' Gen and I did not link up in the way he had intended, for events overtook our plans. I arrived at the campus one day in late April, and straight away I knew something was different. It was early evening. I'd come for a lecture, but when I got to the auditorium it was almost empty. I rarely, if ever, missed lectures, but on this occasion I slipped out and made for the center of the campus. All around students were gathered in groups, muttering furiously. As I walked by, I was met with quick, furtive glances. I plucked up the courage to ask a passing girl what was happening.

'Haven't you heard?' – her whisper a combination of awe and shock. 'Hu Yaobang is dead.'

I stopped in the middle of the path as she hurried by. This was indeed momentous news. By politicians' standards, Hu Yaobang had been much admired and respected, because he had not toed the line. A couple of years before, he had been the General Secretary of the Chinese Communist Party, a position of incredible power and prestige. But as a result of his outspokenness – his suggestion that the Chinese political bureaucracy should reform in favor of a more democratic model – Deng had demoted him.

For the students, then, he appeared to be someone who put moral values above self-interest, and at that time – against the backdrop of the ambitious and ruthless apparatchiks that populated the Politburo – he was seen as an almost romantic figure. Both the liberals and the radicals in the student section admired him. But, as I looked around, I realized what was happening was much more than that. This had gone beyond the somewhat closeted and introverted world of the student union and its internal politics. There were vast numbers of people now, forming in crowds, at a time in the evening when the campus would normally have been quiet. And the emotion I read on every face was a kaleidoscope of grief, sorrow, disbelief and anger. One group of students had already raised a poster with the provocative slogan:

> *Those who should die do not, and those*
> *who live have gone – forever Yaobang*

I shuddered, not necessarily because I disagreed with the sentiment, but because the wording was so extreme, and I knew it could very well get those students indicted. I think that was the first time the level of bravery of the students was brought home to me; they were so very brave.

I made my way to the Triangle, along with so many others, a stream of people filtering through. When I arrived I couldn't see Gen anywhere, such were the numbers. A young man was making a speech.

'Why can't we choose our own jobs?'

'Why must we let the Party assign us to a workplace?'

'Why does the Party keep a personal file on each of us, and why don't we have the right to see it?'

They were simple questions, and ones we had all asked ourselves over the course of our lives; yet to hear them uttered in such a plain yet anguished tone was moving. It was as though, over the years, certain questions had been exiled to the silent shadowlands of one's inner thoughts, one's private moments, and you were never sure if others thought the same. Because you didn't feel you could ever ask. A strange kind of loneliness that you weren't even fully aware of, but one that was with you all the time.

Reading the ardent, angry expressions of all the people who had gathered in the Triangle, I felt a deep sense of solidarity. I don't remember the name of the speaker, but his simple, plaintive questions brought us together as if we were of one mind, as though the invisible walls that separated one person from another – walls of loneliness, self-consciousness, fear – had now been collapsed by our presence here together. It was a heady feeling, almost frightening because of its intensity, because it would carry us along in its wake like a great wave, but it was also a most wonderful thing.

And just like that, suddenly the collective emotion was too great, and the students spilled from the Triangle, back into the main grounds of the campus, and onward, gathering more and more to their numbers. I had been due to meet Macaw after my lecture, and now it was almost time. I found her in the grounds, outside the cafeteria where we often met, though it was closed for the weekend. Macaw was watching the crowds roll by with real fascination; spectacle and drama were at her core, I think.

417

'Hey, Lai! Get your ass moving! Let's see where they are going!' she said.

We joined the crowds of people as they rolled out of the university grounds, spilling onto Chang'an Avenue, chanting and roaring and clapping, and soon we found ourselves before the Gate of Heavenly Peace, the entrance to Tiananmen Square. At this time of night, any access to the square would have been restricted by security, but as we flowed through I caught the expressions on the faces of a couple of security personnel: astonished, frightened even, before the flood of people that had been unleashed.

But that was just the beginning. When we swept into the square, something else was going on, something quite remarkable. From the southern entrance, from the Xinhua Gate, there was a great commotion, another flood of people spilling through. We didn't realize at the time, but students from all the major universities in Beijing, including Beijing Normal University, Tsinghua, People's University and many others, were converging on the square in their thousands.

I remembered all the occasions my mother had dismissed the students as wealthy good-for-nothings with too much time on their hands. Even though I hadn't liked what she said, part of me had seen the students I encountered through my mother's gaze. But now something had changed, in the protesters perhaps, but in myself for sure. It was dangerous to be here, and yet almost everyone had come out. The fear I felt virtually every day was overcome by this rushing sense of solidarity and compassion, for these were young people with little power, prepared to risk everything.

The crowd ebbed and flowed toward the Xinhua Gate where the other students were arriving. This gate also guarded the compound called Zhongnanhai, where the headquarters of the Communist

Party were located. Soldiers marched in, rifles in hand, gazing at the students with blank fatal gazes, and yet the students kept coming.

I was trying not to cry, but I had never in my life seen anything more noble, more beautiful.

At my side, Macaw giggled. 'This is completely bonkers! I can't wait to see what happens next!'

I looked at her, shocked. I realized that for all I was feeling – all these emotions swelling up inside me – for her this was simply another performance, a theater of a kind that was exciting and surreal but meant little more. That was what she took from everything that was happening.

I realized by that point, I had come to love my friend. But that was one of the few occasions when I came close to hating her as well.

Perhaps she registered my expression, perhaps she said something. It's hard to be sure. All I remember was that the mood of solidarity on the part of the crowd had graduated into one of building fury and now they were chanting with thundering resolve.

'Come out, Li Peng. Li Peng, come out!'

Li Peng was the premier; in fact he had reached that position at the expense of the late Hu Yaobang when Hu had been compelled to resign. It was well known that Li Peng was an engineer with zero political qualifications. But he had connections in the upper echelons of the Communist Party and held deeply conservative views, and this was why he had been selected. For months, he ignored the polite letters sent by the student lobby conveying their protest of the 'lights out' regulations the government had enforced the year before. But it was as though we would no longer be denied. We had occupied the square, we had taken control. We had only ever been the children of those who shaped and molded the world; now, for the first time, we were shaping it in our own image.

There was a sudden, shrieking scream.

'The police are coming!'

I looked back toward Chang'an Avenue. A large number of people were streaming in, but it was different now. They were no longer moving with the ebb and flow of the great feeling that had passed through us. Instead, they were running for their lives, staggering and falling. Behind them, uniformed men, police, were going to work, hitting them furiously with batons. I remember the expressions on the faces of those police. They weren't professional or dispassionate; rather, they were etched with sadistic rage, flushed with an obscene hunger as they struck the heads of the students in their midst over and over.

I was rooted to the spot. The chants of solidarity that the students had raised had been transformed into a cacophony of shrieking anger and fear. I tried to look around, to get my bearings, but suddenly it was difficult to breathe.

I sank to my knees. It was more than panic, though. Sensations flashed across my mind like lightning; memories from years ago – the feeling of the softness of my body and then the sharpness of the pain … my arm wrenched from its socket.

In the midst of those crowds on Tiananmen Square, I was as a child again. I was on my knees. I couldn't breathe. I was struggling for breath.

The crowds were rushing forward, the people running past, their movement a violence that buffeted us one way and the next. I think Macaw took an elbow in her side, she screamed out, 'Fuck!' and then I felt her hands on me, pulling me up. I was gasping for breath.

She took my face in her hands.

'Look at me.'

I did. All the movement, all the violence, seemed to diminish and slow, until I heard only the softness of her voice.

'It's okay. You don't think so, but you are going to be okay!'

She was holding me, cupping my face. The police were still going to work – she must have been panicking herself. But she was so calm. And she calmed me. She gently led me out of that place, out of Tiananmen Square, even as other students were being beaten down all around us. I never imagined the authorities would hurt us that way. But they did.

THIRTY-THREE

AFTER A BUS RIDE OF WHAT FELT LIKE HOURS, I finally arrived at the apartment, shaken and exhausted. My brother was in the living room with his back to me, sitting cross-legged in front of the TV, his profile cast into shadow by the flickering glow of the screen. He still slouched like a child, but within the last year he had shot up several inches, and was almost as tall as me. When before we would often snap at one another or mock each other playfully, now a certain distance had crept into our relationship; when he stood before me, his eyes nearly level with mine, he looked away as though embarrassed, and his voice was quieter and more serious as if weighing unspoken considerations. When once I would have ruffled his hair almost without thinking about it, now an invisible barrier had formed between us, such that touching him in the way I had done, casually and affectionately, was no longer possible. It would almost have felt inappropriate, like touching a stranger. A phrase came to my mind, unbidden. I had seen it scrawled on a poster, just before the police mounted their awful attack.

The warm one has died, the cold one has buried him.

I stood before my brother almost shyly.

'You watching your cartoons?'

His eyes remained fixed on the screen.

'I don't watch them so much anymore. I'm watching a mini-series now.'

I sat beside him. I felt his bearing change. Almost imperceptibly, but there was a tension in his body, an awareness. I looked at the screen. A beautiful young girl was onscreen, she seemed frail, almost melancholy.

'Why is she sad?' I asked.

'Her mother died. And now she lives in her grandmother's house, and the family don't really like her.'

I felt a glimmer of recognition.

'What's this called?'

'*Dream of the Red Chamber.*'

'Ah, I see. Did you know it's based on a classic novel? And that novel was written more than two hundred years ago!'

'No.'

'Of course,' I added slyly, 'the novel is much better than the mini-series, they always are.'

My brother turned to me with a scandalized grin. And for a moment, things between us were as they had been.

'No way. No way are novels better than TV.'

I raised an eyebrow.

'Way! And what's more, novels are much much better.'

My brother went to say something else, no doubt defiant, but all at once he grew thoughtful.

'I don't see how you can think that,' he said finally. 'When you are reading, that's all there is, just words in black and white. But when you see things on TV, you actually see the people. It's so much more real and colorful, and you can hear the sounds of their voices and everything.'

'Maybe that's true. But, do you know what an old friend once told me? He said films and series are monologues but novels are dialogues.'

'What do you mean?'

'Well, in the film or the TV series, they show you everything, and that makes you passive. You don't need to do anything. But in the book, because you can't see the characters directly, you have to imagine them. You help decide how they look and sound in your own head. So, in effect, you help create the characters yourself. That is why a book is interactive – a dialogue between the author and the reader! Quite amazing, don't you think?'

He thought about it for a while and then a grin crinkled across his smooth, unblemished face. He looked at me wickedly.

'I still think books are boring!'

I grinned back at him. Then he turned back to the television, instantly absorbed by its fictional and exotic landscapes. His body grew slack, at which point I knew my presence was redundant. Nevertheless, as I got up to go, I touched my hand to his shoulder, ever so briefly, the smile still lingering on my face.

I went to my room. I lay on my bed gazing at the ceiling, alone with my thoughts. The evening was turning into night, and the gloom had settled like murky water. I could still hear the sounds from the television, but they seemed distant now, as though they belonged to another time. I felt myself to be an outline of a person, faint, diminished, the only substantial part of my being the pounding of a heart driven by guilt and powerlessness. I couldn't rid my head of the images: the policemen, some no older than myself – their youthful masculine faces snarled in hate, eyes bright with rage – bringing their truncheons down on shrieking, desperate people. What right did they have? My heart throbbed all the more. I felt so angry. Surely they must understand that human beings were not supposed to behave this way toward one another? But behind that anger was the fear and helplessness that had been with me for as long as I could remember. The feeling of constriction in my chest, the building panic around the edges, the sense that soon I wouldn't be able to breathe.

I caught a movement from the corner of my eye. Turning, I saw a silhouette at my door. At first I thought it was my brother, but as the figure cautiously passed the threshold of my room, I saw my father's gentle, pensive features arranged tidily in the shadows. My father rarely came to my room. I thought perhaps there was something wrong – my mother had had another migraine, had been taken ill, something along those lines.

'Is everything okay?' I asked.

'Oh yes, everything is fine, of course.'

We stood there blinking at one another. My father stretched awkwardly, and then his expression eased and he smiled shyly.

'I just got to thinking. Do you remember how, a few years back, your grandmother and that boy down the corridor used to play tricks on one another? What was his name again? He was a mischievous boy. Everyone else was a little … frightened of her, I think. But not him. They got into an argument about something or other. And after that, he got his hands on some eggs, painted them purple and orange, put them in with her hens and told her his father had said they were radioactive because of the Chernobyl disaster. She was completely shocked. She came and talked to me about it, and I told her there was no such danger, that the child had been pulling her leg, and she used some pretty colorful language about him, I don't mind telling you. And then later …'

My father chuckled at this point, to him this was clearly the height of wickedness.

'Your grandmother was very cunning. She baked him some chocolate cookies as a peace offering. But instead of chocolate chips, she put raw black beans in the dough. We could hear him retching from all the way down the corridor!'

I nodded and smiled.

'But the thing is,' he said, 'even though it was a ridiculous, absurd feud, I think, when I look back on it, I think she liked that boy. She liked warring with him. She was quite a character, wasn't she?'

'Yes, she was,' I said softly.

My father smiled then, as though he had needed this affirmation from me, as though this was what was required for the memory to make sense. He bowed his head slightly, a half-smile still playing on his face, and he made to leave, but at the last minute he hesitated. The smile disappeared.

'And you. You are okay, aren't you?'

The images of that day came rushing up again, the violence and the powerlessness, and that churning feeling of dread, always a part of me.

I smiled kindly.

'I am doing just fine, Father. Thank you.'

.   .   .

I awoke from strange dreams. Dreams breed paradoxes. Before the morning sunlight stroked my eyes, I had been in a place that was simultaneously familiar and strange. A place I recognized, and yet somewhere I had never laid eyes on before. It was early afternoon and the sun was high in the sky. There was a great building, its entrance adorned by high Doric columns; I caught a glimpse of it momentarily, but the light was so bright. I was aware that I was entirely alone, exposed, like an insect before the sun. I was standing on a great expanse of concrete, the sun beating down. And something was moving toward me; a dark brooding thing, a terrible thing, a monster perhaps – only it was completely lifeless – and still it moved. I could hear the low machine-like rumble that emanated from it. In my dream I was terrified, but at the same time I was driven by some compulsion alien to me to draw nearer to this thing that held in itself the power to obliterate me. Despite my fear, something was driving me toward it. I got closer and closer, its noise grew louder and louder, and from within me formed a silent scream.

I woke up. I was struggling to breathe, my heart throbbing, the acute fear a white-hot heat behind my eyes. I drank in my surroundings hungrily: the desk where I wrote, the soft billowing quilt that my grandmother had made for me years before, the arc of the low ceiling, the winking morning light. I felt a delicious rush of gratitude, for the awareness that it was only a dream, that I was safe in the room where I had slept all my life, and I heard my mother's voice from across the hall chastising my little brother. That sense of recognition was like a warm and protective border across which I would never again seek to stray. I clung to the covers, enjoying the feeling of safety, of warmth rippling over me, and the awareness of my slackening body. It had been a while since I'd had a nightmare of that intensity. That level of dread.

By the time I headed out to the campus some hours later, I felt more secure, in spite of what had happened with the protest and police the previous day. The uniformed young men who had behaved in such an irresponsible and fiery fashion would no doubt be reined in by their superiors. It had been shocking and violent, but ultimately it had passed.

And that's when I saw the newspaper.

I'd stepped off the bus at Chang'an Avenue. A small news stand, with the papers piled up. I caught the headline.

SUBVERSIVES TAKE ADVANTAGE OF STUDENTS' GRIEF!

I bought a copy. And stood in the middle of the busy pavement, reading, my breath caught in my throat.

ENEMIES OF THE STATE

Following the memorial meeting commemorating the death of Hu Yaobang, a small number with a hidden agenda continued to take advantage of the young students' grief for Comrade Hu Yaobang in order to spread rumors to poison and confuse the people's minds ...

... This is a planned conspiracy. Fortunately the prompt and professional actions of the police force were able to deter this criminal element who are trying to negate the leadership of the CCP and

the socialist system. But we must learn from this and be vigilant
in the future. If citizens are tolerant of such subversion and allow
it to go unchecked ... a China with bright prospects will become a
chaotic and unstable China without any future.

It wasn't exactly anger, the feeling I had then. It was more a creeping
feeling of absolute cold. The sense that everything in a warm body
was gradually being turned to ice. I had to rescan, reread the paper.
I wasn't completely naïve. Most people understood that the press
had limits in terms of what they could and could not say. And yet,
those few dozen words printed in black and white had shocked
me to my core. The image of the students – of all of us – being
driven forward by sick subversives, wanting to overthrow the state,
desperate to sow violence and anarchy – was completely at odds
with what had actually transpired. We wanted reform, yes, but the
majority of us were patriots too – we weren't seeking to destroy
China, but to see a China where the younger generation had some
kind of voice. I trembled with the anger and disbelief of the young
person who finds their elders have lied to them, blatantly, without justification or qualification. As I made my way through the
campus, gripping the newspaper, it felt as though others had the
same sense of things. The police had brutally put down the gathering
in Tiananmen Square only days before, and the grounds were no
longer swamped with students, but there was a palpable change
in the air. As I passed by, I saw no warmth, no lively expression
on any face, only solemnity and grimness. My mother had always
derided student protest as nothing more than a tantrum enacted
by rich children still tethered to their parents' coattails. And even

as I'd argued against her, part of me had believed that perhaps we were all still children play-acting as adults. But that wasn't something I believed anymore. I believed instead that something greatly important rested on our shoulders.

When I met Anna in the cafeteria, later that day, all these thoughts were jostling in my head.

'Can you believe what they did? Those bastards. The way they went at us like that!'

Macaw shrugged her shoulders casually.

'Meh!'

I looked at her. Waiting for her to say something more. But she just returned to her plate of food and continued eating.

'I mean, it's not going to end there,' I said indignantly. 'We can't take being treated like that. Something has to change!'

She glanced up at me again.

'Bleah!'

Another exclamation of indecipherable noise as though she couldn't be bothered to form a sentence on the subject. She had rescued me from significant danger during the protest. But now I found myself enraged by her casualness, which suddenly struck me as an appalling expression of apathy.

'What's wrong with you? Why are you being like this? Hu Yaobang meant something. Progress, hope, I don't know. But he meant something. They just wanted to let people know. *We* just wanted to let people know. Do you think we deserved to get clobbered for that?'

Macaw stopped her chewing. She turned her face up to me, fixing me with her stare, curious, appraising, but with an edge.

'Let me ask you something,' she said. 'Name me one of his policies.'

'Whose policies?'

'Hu Yaobang. Name me one thing he introduced. One policy he achieved in his time in the Politburo.'

I blinked. She had put me on the spot. Like many students, I thought Hu Yaobang an admirable figure, but I realized I didn't have much of a sense of what his policy contributions had been.

'You see,' she said sardonically. 'The majority of those people protesting were just like you. Pulled along on a tide. Not knowing the details of who or what they were protesting.'

She seemed so self-satisfied. It made me angry.

'So what if I don't know every policy Hu Yaobang enacted? So what if some of the others don't either? The point is ... he represented something.'

'Maybe. Maybe he became the focal point for something vague, nebulous. A call to protest, the hunger for some abstract sense of justice. But most of those students protesting are able to do that because they can afford to. They are not like us. It doesn't matter whether they are right or not. They have the luxury to indulge their whims. But I don't.'

I blinked at her in disbelief.

'Don't you realize? Don't you realize there is something so very wrong? With all of it?'

She sniggered. She actually sniggered. I felt myself bridle.

'And what's so wrong that you can't live with it?' she said. 'They can have their spontaneous outbreaks of self-righteousness and their struggle! But people like us, we just have to try to get along.'

I was on my feet, standing over her.

'Have a look at this!'

I threw the paper down.

'Read it!' I muttered.

I watched as she scanned the gist of it: the awful propaganda, the rationalization of the beatings, the dismissal of the students as merely the dupes of some sinister anti-Chinese conspiracy. I saw her lips tighten.

She looked up at me; she was going to say something else, but I preempted her. The words came in a whisper.

'You ask me "What's so wrong that I can't live with it?" Well, I'll tell you ...'

I felt a hoarse, rasping sob rise in my throat, but I fought it back. I was not going to break down over this. Until that moment, I thought I would never speak about it to anyone. But now that I had decided to, I would get the words out. I was determined about that.

'When I was a lot younger a policeman ... hurt me. And, and I lived with it ... just as you say I should. I never protested. I never spoke out. But what I never fully realized, until recently, was just how frightened I have always been. Ever since that moment. I've been so ... fucking ... afraid.'

The emotion formed a lump in my throat.

'And when you are always frightened, you feel like something can happen to you at any time. You feel like a victim. I was so, so frightened when the police charged. So frightened I couldn't breathe. Do you understand what that's like?'

She was looking at me and her eyes had changed.

I felt my emotions stabilize. My vision cleared.

'But just before that ... the moment before the police charged.

432

When we were all together. I felt … I felt secure. I didn't know anyone there apart from you. And yet, I felt loved. And strong. For just a few moments, as stupid as that sounds. That has to mean something, doesn't it?'

She had turned away from me. When I look back on the scene from so many years later, I think she turned because she had tears in her eyes. Perhaps it was the only time I had ever moved her. I would very much like to believe that. But when she turned to me again, her gaze was sphinxlike, inscrutable.

'You may be right in what you say,' she said softly. 'But the fact is … the students are going to lose.'

THIRTY-FOUR

ESPITE HER SKEPTICISM, MACAW AGREED TO ACCOMpany me on the day of Hu Yaobang's funeral. The funeral was held in the Great Hall of the People, but only dignitaries and officials were allowed to attend. In response, the students once again flocked in their numbers to Tiananmen Square. Despite the ferocity of the attack leveled against them by police only a few days before, some fifty thousand students came out from all over Beijing. And this time we held the square. It was April 22. The students covered the plinth of the Monument to the People's Heroes with pictures and flowers and wreaths, so the austere white block was now aflame with color. The students were more organized now, their demands more coherent. They were chanting:

'Dialogue, Dialogue,' and 'Brutality is shameful. We want free speech!'

I felt the hairs on the back of my neck stand up. Even Macaw was taken aback. Standing next to her, I just managed to catch her words against the great rumble of that mass of people.

'This is certainly something!' she said.

Only days before, such a scene would have been unthinkable. Some of the uniformed police watched from the sidelines, pushed to the edges as that vast human sea lashed and curled. Some of the students had prepared a letter of grievance for Premier Li Peng, and, finally breaking through the lines of police, they were able to deliver it, though I doubt the mirthless little man ever bothered to read it. But it didn't matter. That day we had asserted ourselves, and in our strength of numbers we had shown not only were we able to brave attack, but that our strength of purpose was enough to force the state to take a step back. I had needed to be there. I had been terrified at first. But as we left the square, chanting in celebration, I had never in my life felt so bold.

We returned to the Triangle. It was night now and the mood of the students was jubilant. People were drinking and dancing, speeches were being improvised, various groups were holding impromptu debates. Even Macaw seemed to be taken by the mood, watching the proceedings with a good degree of fascination. In the center, someone was about to address the crowds, and for a few moments the students quieted. A mature student began to speak. She couldn't have been much more than in her mid-twenties. But she seemed older to me at the time.

'Comrades. Brothers and sisters. Friends. Today has been a wonderful day. We have stolen a march today, and we have shown our commitment to the type of China we hope to see.'

A loud cheer erupted.

She smiled ironically.

'But ... and there is always a "but"! *But* ... as an engineering student, I understand something very simple. Energy, steam, motion ... they need to be directed or else they dissipate into the air. The same

435

is true with us here and now. We have occupied the square, but ultimately they can wait us out, wait for us to get tired, wait for us to … dissipate. So we need to do more. We need to be proactive.

'Some of the other comrades have argued for a strategy I wish to support. They suggest we boycott classes until the government acknowledges our petitions and our voices. I think this is a fine idea, an essential one in fact. People say of students that we are not serious. But having been here with you and shared these incredible times with you, I know that's simply not true. We are deeply serious. We came to university to study. Nobody wants to lose classes. But if we disrupt the university, if we threaten the salaries of the university administration with collective action, we can hit them where it hurts. And they will have no choice but to hear us!'

Another roar.

The next speaker mounted the makeshift podium. That voice – soft, measured, with a little irony, eloquent yet always precise. It was one I would recognize anywhere.

'I applaud the last speaker's conviction and feeling. I think we all share it,' said Gen. 'But I wouldn't be doing my job as a representative of the students' union if I didn't make clear what a disastrous strategy she's proposing.'

There was a low murmur of perturbation, resentment almost, on the part of the crowd.

'I would ask comrades to remember. Remember what happened during the Cultural Revolution. It destroyed knowledge. It made academics figures of suspicion. Are we sure we want to head down that same path? The path of radical extremism? Do we really want to revisit those dark days?'

436

He was met by a series of boos. And even though I was far away, I caught the expression on his face. It was one of surprise. I think – given his eloquence and his sense of reason – Gen was sure he would talk people over to his side in the end. And yet even I could tell he had misread the feelings of the people there. Perhaps because he hadn't understood what it meant to us, collectively. The sense of being disregarded and ignored and even brutalized. And now the sense of our own building power.

'Is it not better to negotiate, rather than threaten?' he asked, his tone higher-pitched, a hint of panic creeping into an otherwise poised delivery.

'Difficult to negotiate when you are getting kicked in the face by police!' someone shouted.

Gen looked anguished.

'Not all police are brutal. And not all the people in the university administration and the government are bad. They are not all right-wing conservatives. Some are sympathetic to our plight. It is these people we need to target. If we do anything brash, if we don't act reasonably ... we are in danger of alienating those who might come to our aid. We have to be sensible and rational above all things, we have to be balanced rather than—'

He was drowned out by a litany of boos and jeers. At my side I caught Madam Macaw shaking her head.

'What a dick,' she said.

She didn't know that the speaker was Gen – 'my' Gen. Only a few months before, if she had made that same comment, something inside me would have bridled with irritation, or anger even. I would have wanted to tell her how little she knew about him, how brilliant and persuasive he was, how his star was in the ascendant, how he was destined for great things. But seeing him there, baffled, blinking in desperation, I was aware something had shifted.

Throughout our relationship, Gen had been the one with the answers. When we went to restaurants or bars, he always knew how to attract the waiter's attention with an ease and a snap of the fingers that seemed ingrained and so adult. He was always able to retrieve a fitting quote from his well-stocked brain, from a philosopher or historical figure, in response to a dilemma or uncertainty I had. But for the first time I knew, without a doubt, the significance of these events had left him behind. I watched him on that platform trying to marshal his words, and he simply looked lost. I no longer felt anger or admiration toward him. Only a sense of pity.

Later, we were in the student bar, Anna and me. We met Lan and Min, and Jin Feng and Li Xin, and Pan Mei and Ai Xiu. Lan grasped me as he always did, his huge arms gathering me up with the excitement of a child. Pan Mei smiled at me shyly but fondly, I thought. The same air of jubilance, of expectation, had infused them. Even Min, the most sarcastic of us, seemed encouraged and excited, and he winked at me knowingly. When Lan sat down, I saw him glancing at his smaller, slighter boyfriend tentatively; Min, for his part, took his partner's large hand in his own and clutched it briefly. Looking at them all I realized, though I had never done any acting, I was now one of their number. And I felt a rush of affection for them.

Min looked slyly at Madam Macaw.

'So, Anna,' he said. 'We've all been thinking.'

Her eyes flashed at him with amusement.

'Uh-oh!' she said.

'Now don't be like that. Cynicism doesn't suit your radiant visage and your splendid character. Hear me out. We were thinking. With everything that has happened, we Marauders might play a small walk-on part. When great events call …'

'Oh god, here we go!' She threw her hands up in exasperation. 'We are a theater troupe; we are performers, not politicians.'

'That's true,' Min said, reaching out his hands in a gesture of placation. 'You are totally right. But sometimes the artistic gesture can be political. It shakes people up. Forces them to think. Creates chaos and turmoil in the emotions. Marks a break with the traditional and the ordinary and the dull.'

Macaw regarded him suspiciously.

'What did you have in mind?'

'Well,' Min said, 'it's not so much what I had in mind. Actually, Pan Mei was the one who came up with the idea.'

Pan Mei blinked, her small kind eyes set into that large, flabby face – a single ripple of trembling fear driven through the great bulk of her body as people's gazes were diverted to her. Pan Mei was a kind soul, bright and thoughtful. She absolutely adored Madam Macaw, who had taken her under her wing in much the same way she had me. But at the same time, Pan Mei was a little terrified by her, I think.

'Well?' Macaw asked, looking at Pan Mei in a not unfriendly way.

'Well, there is this play called *Mother Courage and Her Children*. It was written by Bertolt Brecht, who was European. It's set centuries ago, but it speaks to us today because it provides an allegory for fascism and extreme nationalism.'

'I've read that,' I said, looking at Pan Mei. 'It's absolutely brilliant.'

She looked at me and smiled, a big beaming smile of pleasure.

439

'And it's apposite too,' I continued. 'The government is cultivating a mood of ultra-nationalism. That's how they justify their repressions in the press. They are saying we are *disloyal* to the country.'

'Brecht!' Macaw winced. 'Really? Seriously? We might as well just sing the Internationale for three hours. It will send everyone to sleep.'

'It's actually a very compelling play,' said Min, his eyes twinkling. 'It's all about this stubborn, glorious and completely crazy woman who leads this ragtag outfit of misfits around the land singing and performing as they go. Oh, and did I mention her name is Anna?'

Despite herself, Macaw grinned.

Min grew serious for a moment.

'There are already rumors of another big demonstration. It's set for May 4. They reckon it's going to be bigger than anything we've seen. We could put on a performance. Think of it: a ready-made audience of thousands. There are worse ways of getting publicity.'

Macaw nodded, then frowned.

'But that's not much more than a week away. I doubt we will be performance-ready in that time.'

'It's an ask,' Min admitted. 'But it can be done. It's a short play, relatively speaking. Also, we can trim it down.'

He turned to look at me.

'I am reliably informed that you are the best writer among us, Lai! And you are clearly familiar with the play. Do you think you could strip it down to something that can be performed by seven actors on a wing and a prayer?'

They were all looking at me. I wasn't sure how to answer the question. But the fact that he'd said 'among us' gave me a sense of belonging and solidarity that I wasn't about to refuse. I was frightened that I might fail them. I was frightened about so many things.

But I realized such fear was negligible compared to what so many students had already faced.

I found myself smiling.

'I can but try!'

The Marauders let out a roar.

.   .   .

The work went well. Min had given me his own battered, dog-eared copy of the play. The characters took shape in my head rather quickly. Of course, Anna herself was to play Mother Courage, that much was a given. And the other characters fell into place behind her. I clipped and cut here and there. I learned quickly – I had to – even though it was a form of writing I had never done before. And it brought me into contact with the play itself, which was deeply moving. At that point, the atmosphere on campus was fraught, but there was a sense of excitement and joy despite the looming dangers. The play, set centuries earlier, during a decades-long war, seemed far away from the tempo and rhythm of the events I was immersed in. And yet, uncannily, it seemed to rhyme with them somehow too.

For a while now I had thought that the student movement was beginning to chime with the rebel in Macaw. Nevertheless, she didn't believe the students could win. She thought the situation hopeless. Courage's pilgrimage across the darkest parts of a war-torn Europe, dragging her cart, bringing her family along with her, was a journey that would ultimately yield the most terrible loss and defeat. And yet her actions spoke to something vital, something human. The movement that had erupted all around left me full of fear and anxiety because I was expecting the forms and structures of the world – those that seemed so iron-clad and permanent – to crush us at any moment. But the creativity that had been unleashed, the debates we'd had, the sense of solidarity we'd experienced – all of it felt as though we ourselves were making a great pilgrimage together even if it was doomed. That, whatever happened, what we were doing was worthwhile. That was what I took from the play. That is why it spoke to me, and why, despite its distance, it seemed so contemporary.

It has taken some years for me to parse everything that took place, to comprehend it intellectually, and from a distance this is now easier to do. I am not claiming I understood the play back then in the terms I have outlined previously, but that doesn't matter; what is important is I felt the truth of it. The more I worked on *Mother Courage*, the more I felt its bearing on my own reality, the more I despaired and the more I hoped – in one single moment. I worked feverishly and somehow managed to finish. It was the night of May 1. I had redrafted the script several times, but now it had achieved a form that was pleasing to me. The disadvantage was that the players would only have two intensive days to learn their lines. It couldn't be helped. All that was left was to turn the work over to them.

That night, my eyes sore with scouring concentration, I reached the end. I had copied out the final speech of Mother Courage, which is also a song. It happens after her daughter sacrifices herself, beating a drum in order to arouse the townsfolk and warn them of an imminent attack. Kattrin, the daughter, is then shot. The last scene takes place early in the morning, when Courage sings a lullaby, lamenting the loss of her child.

When I had written the last line, I put my pen down, brought my fingers to my red-rimmed eyes and rubbed them, and yet, despite my exhaustion, the power of the play coursed through me like the throbbing of blood. I had managed to do what was needed. I'd thought I would never get through those few days, and, if I did, all I would yearn for was sleep. But now it was finished, sleep would not come. Quietly I crept out of my room and our apartment.

At that point, there was no curfew, but the news of the students' protests and the police violence had created a trepidation that hung across the silent streets. I left the building at around 11 p.m. or perhaps later, but the streets were empty, it was a ghost town. I made my way, a short walk, until I found the place. In the darkness, a few candles burned, illuminating the shapes and contours of the monuments and graves. I found my grandmother's easily. I had been there on many occasions. At first out of a sense of duty – I hadn't wanted to confront my grief but I felt she deserved my efforts – eventually, however, it became almost cathartic.

At that time of night there was a chill in the air even though it was late spring. But being there I felt as though I could breathe. It was so quiet I had to whisper.

'I wish you were here, Po Po. I don't know what you'd make of it all. You'd probably moan about the protests. But I think they would have cheered you up too!'

I awoke early in the morning of May 4 with a squirming feeling of anxiety and expectation deep within my belly, a feeling as elusive as light.

The demonstration had started as a rumor, something whispered about in student bars and gatherings, more legend than fact. But the students had been out on the streets, they had braved police violence, they had resisted the authorities and they were getting better at it. I wasn't aware at the time, but at the beginning of May a new body had been called into being: the Beijing Students' Autonomous Federation. It circumvented the official student associations, bringing together student leaders from some eighteen schools and universities. The traditional student union leadership had been left behind, and the new affiliation had the ability to coordinate protests, to organize and unite them on a scale never before seen. The first thing they did was to legitimize the boycott of classes. I was at the university in that period when the lecture halls were ghostly and quiet. Hardly anybody defied the boycott, such was its popularity. Some sixty thousand students from forty-eight colleges and universities in Beijing refused to go to class.

The second thing the Autonomous Federation did was to coordinate the protest for May 4. On that day, we, the Marauders, entered the campus to encounter a mood of almost holiday-like jubilation. Seventy years before, students protesting the First World War had sparked a revolution, and their protests had been dubbed 'The May Fourth Movement.' We were more modest, I think. We wanted only to get the attention of the government, to create some level of mild reform in a system that until then had demanded total submission. But that legacy was a potent reminder that fundamental change didn't always have to be a utopian or naïve aspiration. And so the protests on my campus were concentrated in a large sports field on the eastern side of the university that quickly became dubbed 'The May Fourth Field.'

It was incredible. It was both serious and fun, both festival and protest. Students had set up stalls, roasting meats on barbecues on the grass; there were places for cold drinks and beers, there were performers, even clowns. At the same time, there were debates, political speeches and tables where people could cast votes for representatives.

It was like nothing I had imagined. Even Macaw – historically suspicious of the student mobilization – was clearly impressed. We unpacked our meager equipment; as accustomed to performing as the Marauders were, I think they were more trepidatious that day. Everyone sensed this demonstration was of great significance. Alongside the outbreaks of frivolity and joy, there were more serious moments. One of the speakers was interrupted when a young man in the audience accused him of being a spy, and a scuffle broke out. At the start of the performance we were all nervous, though my job as writer had been done, so I had the luxury of watching the play as a spectator.

But we needn't have worried. We soon amassed a respectable crowd, and the audience responded to the play with enthusiasm. The props were makeshift and minimal, the special effects virtually nonexistent. Macaw played Courage with her unique brand of fierce, frightening charisma, and the other players gathered around as if energized by her performance. We did not receive any financial compensation; it wasn't that type of gig. But we were rewarded afterward with barbecue chicken and as much beer as we could drink. And although it was generic and cheap, I don't think beer has ever tasted so good to me – either before or since. The numbers in the field grew and grew, and when we passed each other we made the V for Victory sign with our fingers as a form of greeting. It became one of the symbols of the protests. As the afternoon faded into evening, we made our way out from the field – roaming numbers of students gradually filtering out of the university toward Tiananmen Square and the burnished sunset that illuminated our lives in its rich copper flame.

Masses and masses of people flowed through the tributaries, toward the main square, but it was clear the government had been informed of our project. There were scores of military police blocking the edges of the square, determined to keep us out. But the numbers kept on growing. The soldiers looked tense and urgent – these were numbers they simply couldn't have imagined. I felt the tight pull on my breathing, but decided I wasn't going to run away, whatever happened. Not this time. I looked to my side. Macaw had a frown on her face – that stubborn determination of hers, that will. The soldiers had offended her with their presence.

She looked at us, green eyes glowing, and a wicked smile flashed across her face.

'Let's do it again. Let's do it here. Now!'

And that is how we came to put on a second performance of *Mother Courage and Her Children*, on the outskirts of Tiananmen Square, with battalions of police and soldiers facing us down, amidst the single largest protest of the government ever held. To this day, I don't know how we managed to carve out the space, how the sheer level of noise from the crowds didn't render the actors inaudible, or how the Marauders managed to hold it together to give such an incredible performance. What will never leave my mind, until my dying day, is the final monologue Macaw delivered. As Courage, she cradled the corpse of her dead daughter, the innocent who had banged the drum in order to warn the townsfolk – a gesture that had sealed her fate. Courage held her dead daughter and said the words that brought tears to my eyes: 'I think she's going to sleep.'

Macaw went into a lullaby and her voice broke with tenderness, the tenderness of someone so much older, someone who had lost something – someone – unbearably precious, and whose world would never see color again. And yet, because there was love, there was hope too. Moving, unbearable, wonderful human hope. I saw tears on the faces of the protesters watching, I felt the tears hot on my own. Anna stepped forward to utter the final words of the song:

The new year's come. The watchmen shout.
The thaw sets in. The dead remain.
Whatever life has not died out
It staggers to its feet again.

I see her there in my mind's eye, so many years on, Anna's face shining its beauty and its defiance, while behind her the police and military begin to move toward us in a flowing wave of black. I hear too the screams of the students all around, as the awareness of what is happening settles on us.

And then something else happens. Something no one expected. The thousands of Beijing residents who had gathered on the sidelines – road workers, waiters, couples, cleaners, bystanders of every type – stepped out, forming a barrier between the students and the police and military. The latter were halted in their charge, baffled by what was happening. The numbers of Beijing residents pouring out just grew and grew. They brought us bread, water bottles and ice cream. As we reached Chang'an Avenue once more, there was a sea of people before me, young and old, men and women, flooding the eight lanes of the great boulevard from every direction and from every part.

And for the second time that day, I wept.

THIRTY-FIVE

WHEN I GOT BACK LATE THAT EVENING, I WAS exhausted but elated. As I walked in the stillness toward my building, I turned to look out over a cityscape spread across the darkness, a swathe of lights glittering against the black, and it seemed to me that each of those lights burned with possibility. Every one of them represented an existence determined to forge itself in the dark and I felt a moment of great hope, and a sense of power too. We, all of us, were shaping the horizons of the future and creating the types of possibilities our parents' generation could scarcely have imagined.

I was insignificant, I felt my own smallness every day of my life – and yet I contained within myself whole worlds that were unfolding, for I was part of this wonderful and terrifying uplift that went beyond the classroom and my family and the narrow confines of my life, drawing me into the great and interminable movement of thousands upon thousands of souls stirred to their very depths. Macaw was skeptical of the students, but the image that burned itself into my mind that day was of her – eyes gleaming, face upturned, luminous in the darkness – delivering those final lines to the crowds, while behind her the lines and lines of police began to move.

Many years later, I saw Delacroix's painting *Liberty Leading the People*. I was hardly an art aficionado and, although the context was so very different, seeing the figure of Liberty bearing her flag in the midst of the people manning the barricades, defending the streets, at once took me back to the image of Anna on that day, strident and so fiercely beautiful, delivering those words in the smoky dark. I was with my husband and my two small children, but I had to turn away from them – for the force with which the past had risen up to claim me had so easily unraveled my emotions. I found myself coughing into my hands, making my excuses and heading for the toilets, trying somehow to stifle the violence of my crying. It was unexpected, and yet inevitable, perhaps, too.

Looking back on the night of the performance, everything still seemed possible. In childhood things often seem wondrous, in adult life less so. But that night was imbued with wonder and surprise. I returned to the apartment, my head buzzing. I was exhausted, yes, but I was seized by the momentum of the occasion and I wanted to write down what had happened, to record the extraordinary happenings of the day. But as I entered the apartment, I caught the flickering glow of the TV. At first, I imagined my brother was watching his cartoons, but it was eleven at night, far too late for him to be up. And my father, despite his rational and scientific mindset, was distrustful of anything broadcast on television. So I went into the living room to investigate, that sense of euphoria still kindling inside me.

My mother was there. She had a glass of wine. It occurred to me that I saw her more often with a glass of wine these days. Not all the time by any means. But more so. It didn't bother me greatly.

As little more than a teenager, my own reality offered scant room for that of my parents. And besides, my mother was too brittle, too self-controlled to slip into alcoholism. Still, it was a little incongruous seeing her there, at that time of night. Did I have a sense of her loneliness? Perhaps. But when great events are in the air, the smaller details are that much easier to forsake.

'What are you watching?' I asked, for want of anything else to say.

She turned to me. She smiled but her eyes were closing a little.

'Have you never seen this?' she murmured. 'It's *Farewell My Concubine.*' She turned away. 'What is the point in a university education if it doesn't teach you about something like this? Something that is so important to our patriotic spirit. Something that informs who we are!'

I felt that familiar ball of tension, a small dot inside my being. I glanced at the TV. I wasn't unfamiliar with the opera, but it had always struck me as being turgid and clichéd, perpetual war coupled with garment-rending, operatic warbling and the customary suicide in conclusion. More than this, I suspected that deep down my mother was not all that keen on the performance herself. But the fact that she hadn't been to university like my father rankled her. The opera was considered highbrow and elite, and her 'appreciation' of it allowed her to balm her feelings of insecurity with an elevated sense of superiority. She looked at me slyly.

'But there it is. So much money we spend on your education, yet instead of learning the classics, you spend your time in the streets shouting and drinking!'

'I am on a scholarship. You don't pay the majority. And it seems you like a drink too!'

The words had tripped from my lips, almost involuntarily. My mother got to her feet, shaking, already furious. And I kicked myself because I realized that this was exactly what she had wanted. Some part of her required this confrontation.

'I am sorry, Mother. I should never have said that. I appreciate all you and Father do for me. It's late and I'm tired.'

She looked at me hard.

'I am not surprised. It's been on the TV, you know? What *you* have been doing!'

I knew she was referring to the protests, but she encompassed them under the one pronoun 'you,' as though I was collectively responsible for the movement and action of hundreds of thousands of people. It was so ridiculous that I couldn't avoid a slight smile.

And that enraged her all the more.

'*You* and your *student* friends' – she sneered the word 'student' as though it were a dirty, contemptuous word – '*you* and your *student* friends are so busy marching and shouting because you can! Because you have never had to struggle in your lives, because you have been given everything and you don't know you're born. What do you think actual real people make of your tantrums? What do you think they care about how loud you and your friends shout?'

I felt myself bridle for a moment, but with her I'd spent a lifetime controlling my anger. I saw her – the glass of wine raised in her hand, her red-rimmed eyes, the spittle flying from her lips – and I felt a great distance, a sense of pity even. I wanted her to know what we were fighting for; it felt like if she could come to terms with that, she might somehow come to terms with me.

'Mother. It's no longer just the students ...'

I found my voice growing hoarse with emotion.

LAI WEN

'Mother, if you had been there, you would have felt it too. The students were there first, yes. But we were joined by others. So many people. The workers of Beijing were cheering us from their balconies. They came to give us food and drink. Almost everyone in the city is behind us now.'

I stopped speaking. I had never spoken to her so frankly but I was imploring her to understand. Hoping she might.

She smiled slightly and for a second I thought there was sympathy there. Understanding. Just for a second. And then she spoke in a silky, cloying voice, thick as treacle, a parody of kindness.

'I understand that you are not the prettiest of girls. And since Gen has obviously abandoned you, it is clear that you are searching for some kind of meaning. And maybe these protests provide you with that ...'

Her voice trailed away but she was still smiling that small, slight smile.

I felt the knot of tension in my belly harden like rock.

'These protests provide me with something,' I said softly. 'They help me determine my own future. And that way, I might not end up a housewife who is angry and bitter and trapped, and has never in all her life left Beijing!'

My mother blinked. And then she slapped me.

She put everything into that slap. The suddenness of it reverberated through my head. For a few moments, we just looked at one another, blinking. I felt the flush of angry red climb up one cheek.

She looked at me. Her eyes were moist. And then she walked out.

I stood there in utter shock. Although she had hit me before, it hadn't happened for some years. The sound of the opera was still

452

cascading gently in the background, the images still casting their flickering blue light. I went over to the TV and hit the switch. At once everything was dark. My heart was pounding. I made my way to my room, undressed and slipped into bed.

I lay there, furious. I felt so angry. I rejected her assessment of the students as dilettantes – as spoiled brats with too much time on their hands. But by allowing her to provoke me, to make me lose control, I had let my mother win. I'd returned to the apartment buoyed up by a sense of optimism for the future and my own possibilities as an adult, but she had reduced me to a bickering, desperate child again. I lay there hating her with a passion and at the same moment hating myself. Lying in bed, fists clenched with rage, I felt as though I was seven years old again.

.   .   .

In the days that followed, a few things happened. The students and their new representatives had been trying to press their demands. I say demands, but these were, for the most part, simple and patriotic appeals for free speech and a more democratic structure. The watchword of the protests had been 'dialogue,' after all. We were, in the majority, reformists at that point – people looking to shape and change the tone of the government. Not to overthrow it. But the state remained deaf to our petitions and protests. However, given our surging numbers and the increasing support from the citizenry for the students, the government finally issued a direct proclamation. Representatives of Li Peng, the hard-line premier, appeared on television to say that they didn't recognize the Beijing Students' Autonomous Federation and refused to negotiate with a 'dissenting group' that had used the protests to usurp the 'democratic' power of the 'legitimate' students' union.

In other words, they weren't prepared to give an inch.

Everyone knew, of course, that the students' union had long since been co-opted by the interests of the government, that it was morally bankrupt; the very nature of the protests had thrown its impotence into relief. But even as hundreds of thousands flooded the streets, day in, day out, the government and the media continued to insist it was just a handful of subversives who were intent on violating the will of the people.

It would have been comical had the stakes not been life and death.

The protests continued. I returned to the Triangle some days later. I knew more people now, not by name, but so many faces were familiar to me, and we would nod at each other and smile. I can't tell you how wonderful it was, that feeling of solidarity and friendship even among strangers. That evening, the speeches were in full flow, and whereas before the mood had been careful and trepidatious, with the government continuing to ignore all our requests and demands, we were now growing more militant. The speeches were still couched in patriotic language, but there was a growing sense of betrayal, and a much more vivid opposition had emerged.

The university authorities sensed this. At 9:30 that evening, the power was cut to the Triangle, and to the campus more broadly. Deprived of electricity, the loudspeakers ceased to function, the lights went out, and the whole area was plunged into darkness. But we were not deterred. Using flashlights and cigarette lighters we streamed from the campus, making our way toward the square once more, chanting and singing in the darkness. I was in a crowd, a mass of people making their way toward Tiananmen, when someone grabbed me. The shock of it stunned me, but when I regained my bearings, I found myself face to face with Gen. His face was distorted, panicked; I had never seen him like that. He looked drained, pale, as if in the grip of a fever. He didn't greet me. He seemed to stare right through me.

'You know this is insane, right?'

Taken aback, I stuttered:

'What? What's insane?'

'This whole thing. The madness of crowds. The mob mentality. These people. They are teetering on the edge of a cliff.'

He had forcibly grabbed me, pulling me to the side. I was still shocked. I managed to find some words.

'Maybe they feel there's no other choice. When you are desperate for recognition, when everyone around you makes you feel invisible and unheard, perhaps all that remains is to shout at the top of your lungs!'

His expression calmed then, and that ironic smile that I knew so well tripped across his lips. Only now it seemed ghastly, the rictus grimace of a stroke victim.

'I would have thought you of all people might know better. That you were smarter than this. That you wouldn't get caught up in all the emotion and propaganda. My father once said that hasty climbers have sudden falls. You really can't see it, can you? How all this is going to end.'

Sheer rage overcame me. It wasn't just that he'd manhandled me. It wasn't just the cavalier way he'd treated me over the years, expecting me to always be on tap for him. It was about the protests more broadly – and that group of men in the Politburo, so entitled that they could brush off the feelings and privations of hundreds of thousands like dust from their shoulders.

'Your father?' I said with barely repressed fury. 'You are quoting him, now? Of all people? No wonder!'

He blinked at me, taken aback by the strength of my feeling.

'No wonder what?'

My words evened out. I spoke calmly.

'You are more like him than I ever realized. I can't believe I didn't see it before. But I do now. I really do.'

He flinched. His right arm jerked and I genuinely believe at that moment he had to stop himself from striking me. But he regained some semblance of composure.

He looked at me, blinking, as though he were seeing me for the first time. And then he spoke, as if to himself.

'I can't believe it. I didn't think I'd have to deal with this. I thought being with a girl like you … I wouldn't have to deal with all this crap.'

I looked at him.

'A girl like me?' I queried softly.

'It doesn't matter,' he muttered.

But it did matter.

I knew exactly what he had meant. I felt it instinctively. It was what my mother had said before. I wasn't beautiful like the girl I'd seen in his dorm that day. I wasn't charismatic like Anna. I was plain. And that is what he had meant. I knew this with absolute certainty. That a girl like me should have continued in her subservience to him. It was suddenly so clear, and yet it felt like a body blow. The tears welled up, and I was so angry I couldn't avoid it.

I turned away from him. I walked toward a nearby restaurant. I heard the last words he ever spoke to me.

'Hey, I didn't mean that,' he said. 'Why do you have to be so emotional?'

But he didn't come after me. I felt that same constricting pressure on my chest. I made it to the restaurant toilets. My stomach lurched but nothing came out. I washed my face. And I looked at myself in the mirror. I saw a young woman with dark eyes, a nose too small to be pretty, lips too thin to be considered sensual. There was something in my appearance that was dowdy, almost mothlike. I looked at my reflection in the mirror in that restroom and felt a deep hatred for myself. The scars across my arms tingled. If I'd had access to a knife, I would have started cutting myself again.

And that was when I saw her.

She was standing behind me. She wasn't moving, she stood so still. Her ancient toad's face was creased with a smile of great warmth. My grandmother was there, looking at me with kindness and compassion and an expression of such great love. I saw in the mirror her image, faint but indelible, and although I knew she was not really there at all, for a few moments it felt like she was. And now the tears came flowing down my cheeks. And I had to wash my face again.

I stepped out of the restaurant. I watched the masses of people flowing toward Tiananmen Square, their lights blinking in the darkness; a series of winking, glittering flames set against the black. I was no longer angry at Gen. And perhaps I was no longer angry at myself either.

THIRTY-SIX

THINGS WERE COMING TO A HEAD. DESPITE EVERY-thing the students had gone through, all they had laid on the line, the government remained intransigent. In fact, the repression was intensifying. The *World Economic Herald*, a Shanghai publication, had run an article commemorating Hu Yaobang that resulted in the firing of the editor and the closing down of the publication by the local Party boss. Their journalists joined us on the square holding up posters that read: 'Don't force us to lie anymore!'

It is difficult to explain just how unprecedented this was. Under communist rule in China, papers were tightly censored; the fact that there were now dissenting voices in the media suggested just how widespread the movement had become. It was now much more than a student protest. It was becoming a revolution.

And yet the revolution had been met by implacability on the part of the state. The boycott of classes, it seemed, had done very little. Now the Beijing Students' Autonomous Federation pushed for more drastic action. They called for a hunger strike.

We were sitting in a bar. All of the Marauders: Lan and Min, and Jin Feng and Li Xin, and Pan Mei and Ai Xiu. And Anna and myself. Anna was holding forth.

'You know how stupid this is, right? You know it's insane, don't you?'

'Extreme times require extreme actions!' said Jin Feng, laughing in his cocksure way.

Macaw turned scornful green eyes on him.

'Extreme times require extreme actions?'

He grinned lopsidedly.

'Well, yeah.'

'And starving yourself, that's what is needed? 'Cause that's really going to hit the powers that be where it hurts!'

Pan Mei spoke up. She was tentative, her largeness wobbling with the strength of what it clearly cost her to raise her voice, to dissent from Anna, whom she clearly loved. But she spoke up anyway.

'Look at me, Anna.'

She said this with such calmness.

'The thing about being overweight ... the thing about being a very fat woman is that everyone sees your size. Everyone feels it's okay to make nasty comments about you, even total strangers. But while they see how you look physically, they don't see who you are at all. The person that you are. Does that make sense to you?'

'Yes,' acknowledged Macaw, 'but I don't see what that has to do with—'

Pan Mei cut across her.

'You don't see, and that's okay. But that's the point about these protests. It's our chance to achieve genuine recognition. Did you know that Mikhail Gorbachev is due to visit the country in the next few days? The leader of the Soviet Union is due here in Beijing. The hunger strike makes sense. We do that, and we make ourselves visible. We can embarrass them. We do that, and no one can turn their faces from us!'

'Fuck yeah!' muttered Jin Feng.

I think it was the only time I had ever seen Anna driven into a corner.

'You are being fucking idiots. And you are crazy. Don't expect me to join you in this.'

She got up and walked out. We were in shock. Macaw was our lynchpin. And yet, in the moments after she left, although we didn't talk all that much, I think our resolution deepened. It seemed there was little else left to do. Years before, Brzezinski, a Polish-American politician, had come on a diplomatic visit. And on that day – that evening – my childhood had been unraveled by my terrifying awareness of the force and brutality of adults, of the security forces. They had hurt me badly. I suspected my timorous and gentle father – in his own time – had been hurt by such people too.

But there was fear now, on their part. However strong the government was, it was afraid of protest. Years before, we were just a few kids having an adventure, an adventure that became a nightmare. But it was different now. There were thousands of us, hundreds of thousands, and not just students. Working people too. And journalists and pensioners and shop owners, and everyone you might imagine. Mikhail Gorbachev's visit was drawing close. The government might remain impervious to our protests, but they would be forced to heed us under the weight of a national embarrassment. The visit had come at the opportune moment. It was this that would make the hunger strike effective.

I didn't see Macaw for some days. Perhaps she felt as though the Marauders were developing a will and direction independent of her. She had always been the center of the organization, and it must have felt like things were spiraling out of control. And yet, when I saw her next, she didn't seem greatly perturbed. I had left my building, planning to head to the university, and there she was outside. I'd never given her my address. She was dressed in a leather jacket and dark sunglasses, and she was perched atop a motorcycle. I remember thinking how cool she looked, as though she had stepped out of a movie. With that same lazy charisma, she gave a single command.

'Get on!' she said.

I found myself doing just that.

I had never been on a motorbike. As the wind blew through my hair, I felt elated. The bike screamed through the city and beyond, onto the lonely, windy roads heading to the north.

'I had no idea you could ride one of these. I didn't even know you owned a motorcycle,' I gasped.

Her voice floated back to me as the wind whipped my hair.

'Well,' she said, 'it depends on your definition of the word "owned."'

I felt a familiar sense of anxiety. Despite my increasing activity and commitment to the protests, the thought of breaking the law was still abhorrent to me.

'You mean you stole it?'

'Well,' she said sheepishly, 'I guess it depends on your definition of "stole." "Borrowed" would be more fitting!'

She twisted the throttle and the bike roared forward, the sound of my laughter lost to the wind. We rode out past fields and flatlands, along a smooth open road, and the bike hummed as the clouds above peeled away. We rode for a long time – it was surely the furthest I had ever been from the city – and yet that journey seemed to pass in the blink of an eye.

Eventually the smooth road became a dusty trail, and Anna had to reduce speed as the bike rattled and jerked its way across the ground. We disappeared into a thicket of trees with thin, tall trunks that shot upward only to plume in light yellows and greens, soft and feathery like the decoration of birds. As we slipped under the canopy, we were cast into gentle shadow. The sun was high in the sky, and the light winked from within the trees. I flinched, for we were still moving rapidly across the jerky terrain, and the trees had gathered in from every side, branches and leaves whipping our faces, but it seemed as if Anna knew the route well. A few moments later, the bike shot out onto the hard gray sand that had formed a small incline around the rim of a great lake.

The water was smooth and unblemished in the early afternoon, a turquoise glow that expanded outward as far as the eye could see, and beyond, the tawny ridges of ocher mountains were flushed at their foothills with dark streaks of wild grass and moss. I felt dizzy as I got off the bike, not simply because I had stood up so suddenly, but because of the great dome of deep blue sky and the vastness of the open space, the crisp, clear beauty of the lake and the outline of the mountains. For much of my life I had read about beautiful landscapes of every variety, but all from the confines of my bedroom. The air here – sweet with the fragrance of flower and leaf, yet cold with the kiss of the water and the breath of the wind – was reviving and disorienting in the same moment. I felt a flush of joy. I looked at Anna, exhilarated.

'What is this place?'

She shrugged nonchalantly.

'The original name is in the Mongolian language, but a much older form of it. Spoken at the time of Genghis Khan. Nobody knows what it actually means. So everyone just calls this place No Name Lake.'

'It's wonderful,' I gushed.

'Yeah, I suppose,' she said, though I think she was pleased by my admiration.

'What are we doing here?'

'Just thought we would eat, drink and hang out.'

She unhitched her bag from the bike. She took out a pack of beer. And she tossed me a package wrapped in foil.

I caught it automatically. Opened it up. It was tuna sandwiches.

I looked at her, astonished.

She squinted in the sunlight.

'What? I can't come prepared?'

'The beer isn't much of a surprise. But I can't really see you in the kitchen making sandwiches,' I said, grinning.

I thought she would laugh then too. But instead she smiled softly, as though embarrassed.

'Well, you know. I do a lot of that sort of thing for my father. The lazy sod rarely does much for himself these days!'

I felt as though I had been unfair to her. I started to mumble my apologies, but she curtailed them with a laugh.

'Take a bite!'

I did. Perhaps it was the setting itself, that sweet crisp air, but the flavor of the sandwich was deep and smooth, the soft paste of the fish fresh in my mouth.

'It's delicious. It really is!'

'It's only a sandwich.'

She smiled again, softly, secretively.

All at once she seemed different; and I different for being with her. I felt shy, as though we were strangers sharing a meal.

She leaned the bike on its side and motioned me to a place on the sand. We lay back, popped open the beers, and ate the sandwiches.

I lay for a while, listening to the sound of her breathing – and to the sound and rhythms of my own body under that great expanse of blue, and the gentle lapping of the waves, not far from our feet. She gave a chuckle.

I looked at her.

'What?'

She shook her head. But she chuckled even more. She was laughing now.

I found myself laughing too.

'Seriously, what?'

'You remember those two guys from the hotel?'

'Yeah.'

'My one. When he was … getting close. He made these …'

By this point she had dissolved into tears. I had never seen her laugh so hard. I was shaking with laughter myself.

'Go on, go on!'

'He made these … Oh fuck, I can't even say it …'

'He made these … these … hooting sounds. Like an owl. Just as he was … you know! Hoooo … hooooo.'

I was crying with laughter.

'I did hear … some really strange things … that night … I have to admit,' I spluttered through my tears.

'Haha. Hahahahahaha,' she laughed.

Eventually we managed to pull ourselves together.

'It's good though!'

I looked at her. I felt myself blush.

'You mean the sex?'

'Well, that was perfectly fine. Plus the two of them – your one as well – they were both nice guys. And not all of them are. But I wasn't talking about that so much.'

'What were you talking about?'

She took a long drink of her beer, put the bottle down. Turned toward me. Her laughter faded into a simple smile.

'I mean everything happens so fast, sometimes. To me, it seems like only the other day I was a child. My father was still working. My mother was still around. And then I blinked, and everything changed. I am at university with you. My father is … as he is now. Perhaps when I blink again, I will be in my thirties, or forties even. I think life happens that way, especially when you look back on it. Everything before fades, it's gone in the blink of an eye. But …'

'But?' I asked.

'But, if you have formed certain memories – even those that involve some guy making like an owl when he … you know. Even strange and weird ones like that. Especially the strange and weird ones like that – they remind you …'

'Remind you of what?' I smiled.

'They remind you …'

She turned those beautiful green eyes toward the mountains.

'They remind you that you were around, you know? That you lived.'

We popped open another couple of beers. We sipped them for a while in amiable silence.

Across the lake appeared a boat carrying fishermen. Although they were some distance away, I could just about make out the old wood of their barque, the crusty nets that were draped over one side. One of the men caught sight of us. He began to wave. And both of us – Anna and I – started to wave back, gently at first, then furiously. We got to our feet, waving, calling out. Soon more of the men had gathered, and they were waving too. We waved at one another until the boat had faded into the middle distance, until our arms were tired.

And I remembered when I was very young and my grandmother would take me out to the park. There was a railway line nearby with a bridge across it, and we would wave at the trains as they passed underneath. Waving at the boat, I felt that same sense of childhood exhilaration. Often it was a risk for young women to wave at men they didn't know, but on that day, it wasn't like that at all. It was about people taking simple joy in human contact.

As the boat disappeared from sight, something in Anna's mood changed, her face shadowed by a frown. At first she didn't say anything. And then:

'You really believe this hunger strike to be a good idea?'

I considered the question. I took a little more of the beer.

'I don't know. But I don't see what else we can do.'

She thought about this for a while and nodded fractionally. She didn't say anything more.

She popped open another beer, drank most of it in a swift elegant motion.

The blue of the sky had paled into a deeper color now.

The air grew colder, filtering through the mountains and across that great lake, bringing with it a touch of ice from the Mongolian north, pricking my skin.

Macaw took another swig of beer.

'Are you going to be okay to drive us back, Anna?' I asked.

She looked at me, her eyes bereft of any emotion, her voice flat.

'I don't know. But I don't see what else I can do.'

THIRTY-SEVEN

THE HUNGER STRIKE BEGAN ON MAY 13. I WASN'T SURE whether I would commit to it until the very last moment. Chang'an Avenue was already packed with students. As I walked toward Tiananmen Square, strangers greeted me with the V for Victory sign that had become the defining gesture of the protests. Although they were about to take an action that could have the gravest of consequences, the mood among the students was both jubilant and defiant. As the evening began to melt into night, we saw a glittering streak of silver trail across the darkening sky – a comet hurtling through the cosmos. On catching sight of it, the crowds let out a spontaneous cheer. It is difficult to describe the optimism and hope we felt – even as our tactics were becoming more perilous.

In the square, we settled down to food and drink, some of which had been cooked by the students themselves using makeshift barbecues, the rest provided by the civilian population who were supporting the students and were anxious about our plight. It was to be the last meal before the hunger strike.

I caught sight of the Marauders – all of whom had chosen to heed the call by wearing the white headbands that would, over the coming days, become an instantly recognizable emblem of the hunger strike. In that huge gathering, vast numbers of people were wearing those headbands. The symbolism of our protest was clear and simple, and it went straight to the heart of our culture. In Beijing, after all, another way of asking how someone was doing was to inquire, 'Have you eaten?' What better way to show our resolve and determination than to stage a hunger strike?

When I reached the Marauders, they seemed animated by another purpose. Jin Feng, perhaps the cockiest of our bunch, approached me with something like shyness.

'I am really glad you made it, Lai. You are just in time!'

I smiled at him, bemused.

'In time for what?'

He hesitantly took my arm as we gathered. Pan Mei was wearing an old-fashioned orange-and-white robe that strained over her massive frame. In any other context, it might have seemed ridiculous. But her face was peaceful, beatific almost. I watched as Lan and Min walked slowly forward, their hands clasped, and came to stand in front of her. I was baffled until I realized the significance of what was happening. Both Lan and Min were clothed in white with golden streaks rippling across their shirts, the traditional dress of those who are about to be married in the Buddhist tradition. A religious tradition but also a secular one. No hope for an afterlife, only hope for the future of this one.

Pan Mei was usually so shy when she wasn't acting, and rather stuttery and inept in her speech. Now, however, she spoke softly, but with great certainty. Lan and Min glanced at one another briefly.

469

Lan, so large, so strong, yet almost unable to look Min in the eye, overwhelmed by emotion like a child. Min reached out his much slighter arm, gently moving the face of his partner toward his own, so that they had no other option and no greater joy than to gaze at one other, to behold each other, in a place where – despite the chaos, uncertainty and danger all around – they could, for a few moments, be completely and utterly themselves.

I remembered my first impression of them. The sense I had of their relationship being in some way unnatural. It seemed as if a chasm of time had passed between then and now. I felt as though I was a different person. And I felt the tears, warm on my cheeks. The wedding would have no legal validity, it wasn't backed by law or by the state. But those two young men fitted together, theirs was a love to take joy in.

I tried to quiet the sobs that were convulsing me. I turned to Jin Feng and managed a couple of words.

'And Anna?'

His smile faded.

'You know she has been against these demonstrations from the start. You know how she feels about politics!'

I nodded, a momentary sadness swallowed up in the cheers and jubilation that followed Lan and Min cementing their vows and kissing one another passionately. All those nearby, who had no idea who the couple were, shouted and clapped in celebration all the same. I return to that moment in my mind sometimes. I think that was when our power, our sense of affirmation, and our love for one another were at their height. People talk about revolutions in clinical and prosaic terms – the need to change a given social system. To fight oppression. But they often forget the incredible uplift to individual relationships the power of a revolutionary awakening provides.

I regretted that Macaw wasn't with us; it saddened me to think she had missed out on something so precious. But although I would have followed her into hell itself, I knew she had misread the situation with the students.

After that glorious makeshift wedding, we partook in drinks and food until eventually the celebrations died down and the time for the hunger strike began. It's strange, these arbitrary borders we draw – when to eat or when not to eat, for example. Our bellies were full, and yet as soon as the hour was declared, there was a seriousness, a tension in the air, a gravity to our actions even though we were far from suffering the pangs of hunger. Those would come later.

I spent the first night with them in Tiananmen Square. We talked about many things and we laughed that night. Many years later, my daughter got a splinter in her finger, and a cruel boy in her class told her it was going to go septic and she was certain to die. For days, she carried that knowledge around with her before finally she broke down and came to me in tears. As I held her, as I laughed to reassure her of the ridiculousness of her fear, my eyes were nevertheless wet with tears. As I told her that she was in no danger, that she had so much more life to live, I have never felt closer to a human being. But that night among the students in Tiananmen Square came a close second.

As the night deepened, some of us slept, some of us talked, some of us performed. The adrenaline was whirling within me and I couldn't sleep, at least not yet. As time wound its way into the early hours, I remember a waif-like woman standing to make a speech. She looked almost like a child, a small silvery outline against the black. She spoke the following words in a voice that was soft and sad, inexorable and timeless:

'During the glorious days of our youth, we have no choice but to abandon the beauty of life. And yet how reluctant, how unwilling we are … Who will shout if not us, who will act if not us … Though our shoulders may be frail, though we are too young to die, we must lead, we have no choice. History demands this of us … democracy is not the concern of only a few.'

I looked at the Marauders; they were all nestled in sleep. Beyond, there were students awake and listening, their faces streaked with tears just as mine was. It was at that point I knew I had no other option. Slowly, gently, I took out the spool of white fabric and carefully wrapped it around my head. I wasn't courageous, I knew that too. But I was going to commit to this. Because life would simply have no meaning if I didn't. That was the power of those days.

I drifted in and out of sleep. I woke; it must have been four in the morning, or thereabouts. The stars were still sparkling in the darkness of the sky. I felt the tip of a foot pressing into my side. Someone was kicking me!

I looked up to see Anna, her expression verging on fury. She proceeded to give each of the Marauders a similar sharp kick. We woke up, blinking at her.

'So you are all going through with this madness!' she hissed.

We were so shell-shocked that none of us could muster a reply.

She glared at me.

'You are supposed to be the smart one and you are advocating this?'

She looked at Jin Feng.

'And you, you always have something to say. Are you just going to go along with everyone else?'

While she was belittling him, he had next to him a single piece of paper that he fingered nervously. Her anger reached its zenith.

'What the fuck is that?' she barked.

Jin Feng looked at her.

'Nothing really,' he said mildly.

'Come on, don't bullshit me. You've got a big mouth. Why so quiet now? Just ... tell me what is going on?'

He turned away, almost embarrassed. But he spoke anyway.

'Just in case. Just in case this doesn't go the way we hoped. We have all of us left ...'

'Left what?'

'Left a ... series of directives. For our families.'

I saw it. I saw the moment Macaw's face changed, when she realized what exactly it was she was being told. I looked around, seeing what I hadn't noticed before. The rest of the Marauders, and many other students, had by their sides the same white envelopes. Those papers: each student had written a last will and testament addressed to their families, because they understood they might die.

Anna's expression broke. Her whole body shuddered.

'You idiots,' she said. 'You stupid bloody idiots.'

She turned on her heel and strode away. For a second I wondered if she had ever been there at all. By the time the sun rose, the whole episode seemed like a dream.

It wasn't until the next day that the hunger started to bite. I returned home that afternoon.

Even though it had been less than twenty-four hours, the thought of food had already begun to plague me. The images of young men and women – donning their white headbands, keeping close the scraps of paper outlining their wishes in the event of their deaths – swirled in my head. I had watched death come to my grandmother, but although she was the greatest loss of my life, she was old and she was suffering, and when she finally passed, there was something of necessity in that passing. Through my pain and grief, I felt her time had come. I had never really considered my own mortality – except as we all do, at the most abstract level. Now, however, my being in the world felt that little bit fainter, my grip on reality that little bit more precarious. How far would things go? I felt a subdued sense of panic. The protests had, until this point, assumed an air of unreality. Now, though, I was terribly frightened.

I came across my mother in the hallway. I will never forget her face. She was both angry and haunted. She looked at me as though I was deliberately trying to hurt her. I wanted to say something, but I was exhausted. She brushed past me. Her body felt thin, fragile. But her anger, as ever, was palpable.

I went into the living room. My father was at the table reading a paper. I attempted levity.

'I think Mother is angry with me. I don't know why. I am just trying to do what's right.'

He raised his eyes to me. He too seemed exhausted and small. But when he spoke it was with more emotion than I had ever heard from him.

'You can't know why. You …'

His voice broke. I'd never seen my father cry before. But he was close to it. He gave a small, quiet cough, a brief rasping sound. And then he continued.

'You can't know why until you have children yourself. Then you will know why.'

I looked at him.

'I thought you of all people would understand why we are doing this. Why it is important to fight.'

It was the closest I ever came to speaking about his past. Years later, I realized how much of a shadow it had cast across our family life, what had happened to him during the Cultural Revolution. My father was perhaps the most mild-mannered man I have ever known, but the darkness that trailed him was ever present.

His expression was forlorn, his face haggard, and he too seemed so terribly old. Then he stood. Picking up the paper, he folded it neatly before walking from the room.

I slept a little. The hunger pangs were kicking in, so sleep was intermittent. Even though I was exhausted, I made my way back to the square and, despite the hunger and the fatigue, the mood of the students revived me. The crowds were buoyant, for intellectuals from across the city had come out in favor of the protests. A large poster sporting the words 'We Can No Longer Remain Silent' was held aloft – it had been reproduced on all the campuses. A letter was read out in Tiananmen Square from the teachers expressing their solidarity with the student movement. That day, too, twelve of the most famous scholars in China – including the great writer Su Xiaokang – came to the square to converse with the students. It is true that they were hoping to turn our course, to persuade us to stand down. Nevertheless, their words were warm and kind, and I was thrilled by the presence of Su Xiaokang in the square, for it did much to cement the importance of our cause.

That same day, we started to see the first casualties. Students fainting. Though it was shocking at first, we soon became familiar with the toneless wail of the ambulances. Some students had also refused water. These were the first to collapse. There was the ominous feeling that it wouldn't be long before the first person lost his or her life. But we were also reaching a great turning point. The square was now inhabited by a body of foreign journalists as well, and the movement was able to claim its international resonance. The citizens of Beijing came out en masse to show their support for the students. In their eyes, we were showing we were willing to make the ultimate sacrifice for the people. We were the 'people's children.' Even some national media, at great risk to themselves, reported on the hunger strike – not only acknowledging it was happening but also recognizing the bravery of the students.

Most important of all, however, the hunger strike succeeded in its ends. Gorbachev, the president of the USSR, was due to meet Deng in a glorious national event, culminating in a great parade at Tiananmen Square. But that wasn't to be. The fact was that the highways and roads into the center of Beijing were crowded with students and the large number of civilians who had come out to support us. The students had remained in control of the square and had proved to be immovable.

Gorbachev's visit should have brought the Russian president deep into the capital city, where he would have received every honor and dignity. Instead, he was greeted by Deng and other officials at Beijing Airport. He never even left the runway. Deng's humiliation was complete. The government offered to negotiate with the students – finally recognizing our presence. Across Tiananmen Square there erupted a great cheer. We thought we had won, and the hunger strike was called off. But we had no real understanding of just how vicious those ancient waxwork bureaucrats – accustomed to absolute power – could be when that power was threatened.

Behind the scenes, Zhao Ziyang, one of the more 'radical' ministers, was blamed for everything that had happened. Ostensibly, the premier, Li Peng, agreed to meet with our representatives in the days following. But Deng had no intention of allowing his humiliation to go unchallenged.

Instead the government delayed and prevaricated, hoping we would tire. Their gambit met with some success. As the occupation continued, the promises made by the state melted away in the hard light of day, and gradually the momentum achieved by the hunger strike started to fade. The leadership of the student movement began to lose cohesion. The stench of rubbish on the square was palpable, alongside the odor from overflowing portable toilets. And everyone was so incredibly tired. The state had billions at their disposal. All we had was our belief.

And then a small group of art students carried out a shocking but inspirational action. The numbers in the square had dwindled, just as the government had intended. But a rumor began to circulate. That was the thing about the student movement. Despite the violence of state censorship, a whisper moved faster than any police baton. And sometimes it could prove even more effective. Rumors abounded in the square. Something was about to be unleashed.

On May 30, in the dead of night, amidst those dwindling numbers, a structure was wheeled out into the center of Tiananmen Square. It was more than thirty feet tall, draped in a great sheet. The following day, the rumors and whispers were rife. People began to return to the square again in their droves. The security forces on the outskirts, ever present, were taken aback. More and more people arrived. And then, on that beautiful bright day, the structure that had been smuggled in was unveiled.

I was there to witness the unveiling. The brightness of the sky made everything seem misty, almost white, as summer heat can sometimes do, and when the statue was unveiled, it too was sculpted from finest powdered white. It was both effervescent and awesome in its proportions: a vast towering woman – 'the goddess of democracy' – holding aloft a torch, striding forth, facing in the direction of Tiananmen Gate where she stared down a giant mural of the old dead dictator Mao Zedong. And, as she shimmered in the pale white heat of the late morning, he, for his part, looked shriveled and wizened and blank, much as he had on that day all those years before when I caught a glimpse of his real-life cadaver in the mausoleum.

Of course, the unveiling of the statue was a clear provocation to the authorities, but it was about more than simple defiance. It was about a rupture in historical time: it gave visible form to the new era staring down the old. I caught the expressions on the faces of those around me, many of whom were openly weeping. Perhaps the security forces could have acted quickly, slipped in, dragged the structure down, broken it into pieces, but it was too late now, for more and more students were flooding the square.

And perhaps it was this that forced the government into action. Finally, they made good on their offer to meet our representatives. The meeting was a sham, of course. The student representatives spoke passionately, angrily; the government officials gazed at them with barely suppressed loathing, unable to mask their outrage at finding themselves in the same room with these types of people – the sense of absurdity experienced by any elite group of bureaucrats compelled to engage in face-to-face conversation with the people they are supposed to represent. It was a scam, a ploy. Some thirty years later, leaked records demonstrate that the government had already decided to declare martial law. I imagine Deng and his cronies, so accustomed to power, had been sent into a fit of apoplectic rage by this point, and perhaps, behind it, lurked a genuine sense of fear.

The students were not completely naïve, however. Rumors of retaliation began to circulate. It was no longer a question of local police. We were told that soldiers from other districts were being amassed in the south of the city. On June 2 the government made it official. They declared martial law. It would take effect from 10 a.m. And that's when the students raised the barricades.

I wanted to get back to Tiananmen. But martial law also brought with it a curfew. Radios crackled out on our landing, warning all citizens to stay indoors. For the first time, both my mother and father were glued to the TV. Neighbors came in to watch too. It was all propaganda, of course, the usual lies – dissenters seeking to undermine and destroy China, counter-revolutionaries wishing to dismantle the communist system. Perhaps it was reading Orwell all those years ago, but for me the slogans 'dissenters,' 'anti-communists,' 'counter-revolutionaries' seemed to have lost all their charge, despite the rabid tone with which they were uttered. My father watched the images on television with quiet regret and a hint of sadness. My mother glowered mournfully at me each time I passed her on the corridor, but said nothing. We heard a gunshot. The shattering of a window. My mother, quietly frantic, pulled out the darkest sheets from the cupboard and draped them across our windows. She wasn't alone; many of our neighbors would do the same. From downstairs we heard the police beating against a door, and the sound of some-one being dragged away.

I lay on my bed staring at the ceiling through the darkness. I knew I should make my way to the square. But the fear was as a sickness in my belly. I was a coward. I am one still. I desperately wanted to act, for I understood that I owed the students and my friends a great obligation. They were out there, protesting for something I too had argued for and felt in the depths of my soul – even if I wasn't quite sure how to describe it. 'Freedom,' perhaps. Freedom from. Freedom to. An overused word. In Canada today, a liberal epitaph bandied about casually and automatically, in conversations, in commercials. But the yearning for freedom that we had in China in 1989 felt at times almost visceral. It brought us together. Nothing was more important than that.

And yet I stayed where I was, in my bed, gazing at the ceiling. I was so frightened. I didn't want to put myself at risk. My father frustrated me, I loathed my mother at times, and I felt the distance between myself and my brother widening with each year. But the idea of never seeing them again was the same feeling you have when you step close to the edge of a cliff: that dizzying sense of vertigo. The protests would continue without me. Nothing I could do would make any fundamental contribution. After all, I was not one of the leaders. I was not even one of the most active figures. Whatever would happen … would happen. I settled deeper into my bed. It wouldn't be wise to go out during the curfew.

But that same strange twisting feeling was at work in my belly. It wasn't just fear. It was the sense that I was part of something, had committed myself to it. How could I stay here in the warm and comfort? I thought about the Marauders. Every one of them except Anna had committed to the protests. We had been in it together.

To hell with it.

I sneaked out of the front door.

At once I felt that sense of panic that had once affected me so frequently. The sense of my chest contracting. My lungs being squeezed. The fight for breath. Instinctively, automatically, I made for the roof of our building, pushed through the rickety old door and stepped out into the cold night air simply in order to take a breath.

I hadn't been here for a while. My grandmother would bring me here when we would wash clothes together; there were large slabs of stone you placed the clothes upon before working in the soap and water, rinsing them, then hanging the garments on one of the lines that crisscrossed the roof.

It was quiet up here. I looked across the city and saw a plume of smoke rising from a nearby neighborhood. The wail of a siren broke out and then stopped. Everything fell quiet.

'Hey!'

I jumped, my heart pounding violently.

Turning, gasping, I saw my little brother.

'You little shit,' I exclaimed, 'you almost killed me.'

He smiled.

'Well, I am not so little. In fact, I am almost as tall as you … Also, you don't usually say *that*! You don't use that word.'

'I don't usually have a heart attack. You frightened me. What on earth are you doing up here?'

He shrugged.

'I didn't mean to frighten you. I just come up here sometimes.'

'Why?'

He was older now, more guarded, but sometimes he responded simply and instantaneously, making me realize he had not fully shed his childhood.

'Po Po liked it up here. So I like it too.'

I felt moved. I missed my grandmother because she had centered me. She had been a great rock across which every ebb and flow in my being moved. But I sometimes forgot that she had been an important presence in my brother's life too.

'Yeah, she did,' I said.

We slipped into silence.

'Are you going to die?' he asked in a much smaller voice.

'I don't think so. I hope not.'

'Mother says that if you keep carrying on the way you are, if you keep putting yourself in the ... protests, you will be in danger and you could die because of that!'

'She told you that?'

He turned his head away from me. He did not want me to glimpse his emotion.

'No, she said it to Father. But I heard her say it. I hear more than people think.'

Again, he seemed so childlike.

I reached out to him, but stopped. I thought about what it was I wanted to say. I made my voice soft but as firm as I could.

'Listen to me. I don't think Mother is right. But ...'

'But ...?' He gazed at me with those full, wide eyes.

'I hope I'll be here for a very long time. But all people die eventually. It happened with Po Po. But she lived for a very long time. I will too. And I think you will live even longer!'

'But why will I live longer than you?'

'Well, you must do. Because you are younger than me. That means you are going to have the longest life of all.'

He thought about this for a few moments.

And then he grinned wickedly.

'Do you know what I think?'

'What do you think?'

'I think I am never going to die at all.'

I blinked, lost for words.

'Well ... that's ...'

He fixed me with a gimlet gaze, secretive and knowing.

'Me and my friend at school, Fenhua – me and him, we are going to make a lot of money. We are going to be rich!'

Slightly baffled, I couldn't help but ask:

'But how will that—'

My brother interrupted me with the violence of his enthusiasm.

'Once we are rich we will have our bodies frozen before we die. And then, centuries later, they will have the technology to revive us. And that way we can live forever!'

I blinked at him. I stuttered.

'Well ... certainly ... that's a plan.'

He didn't interpret my hesitation as any kind of skepticism toward his scheme, however. Rather, he understood my response in a different way. His face fell, and he became concerned.

'Don't worry,' he said ardently. 'I will make sure we freeze you too.'

'That's ... very gracious of you!'

He nodded gravely. He had said what he needed to say. He moved away toward the roof's exit. Then he turned and fixed me with another wicked grin.

'You'll have to be nice to me, though. From here on in.'

I looked at him, an involuntary smile rippling across my face.

'I will try!'

He nodded and disappeared down the stairs. I stood there for a few moments. It was colder now at this time. I was about to go back, when I heard a roar. At first I thought the police had returned, to drag someone else from our building. I walked to the edge of the roof and looked down. There was Macaw on her bike, revving her engine.

.   .   .

I stepped out into the night. We looked at each other. She remained stubbornly silent, the hint of a smile playing on her lips. I went to ask her what she was doing here, but as soon as I opened my mouth, she revved the engine, and my words were swallowed by the noise. I blinked in astonishment, went to say something else, but she revved again, drowning me out. She grinned wickedly.

I couldn't help but laugh.

'You are such a bloody child sometimes, do you know that? You'd give my little brother a run for his money!'

She shrugged.

'Seriously, though,' I said. 'You shouldn't be riding around on that thing. It's stolen. The police. They were just here.'

She looked at me with genuine consternation.

'You don't think much of your friend, do you? Do you really believe I am stupid enough to bring *that* stolen bike around here?' she said, aghast.

I gazed at her perplexed. I motioned to the bike.

'So what's that you are sitting on then?'

She looked at me as though having to explain things to a child.

'That is a completely *different* stolen bike. I stole this one about an hour ago!'

My mouth dropped open. I was at a loss for words.

She smiled, sphinxlike.

The smile faded.

'I saw them, you know?'

'Who?' I asked.

'The police. Before you came out. I hung back. They shot into a window. Dragged someone out. One of your neighbors. Poor sod. Maybe it's better you don't head out to the square tonight.'

Despite my earlier fear, I felt defiant.

'I am going! And besides, you've clearly been riding around the place.'

She looked at me.

'But I'm different!'

I laughed.

'Maybe you are,' I said.

I thought about it for a moment or two.

'Maybe I am different as well!'

She raised one eyebrow but didn't say anything. She just sat watching me. When Anna looked at you, you felt like you were the only person in the world. You wanted to talk, you wanted to let her into your head, to tell her the kind of things you would tell no one else. There was always something dangerous about her, and yet you couldn't help trusting her.

'I've felt different all my life,' I found myself saying. 'My family … they are not much like me. My father has a scientific mindset. But I can't even change a light bulb. My mother … well, where do I begin? She has always been pretty and flamboyant and the center of any room. Sometimes she looks at me like she can't quite believe I'm her daughter. My brother doesn't speak much to me these days, he's becoming a teenager. And my grandmother. I loved her very much. Because she was strong. But that's hardly me either.'

I chuckled ruefully.

'I guess I am trying to say I feel different too. But … joining these protests, I haven't felt that difference so much. In fact, I've felt …' I struggled to find the words, '*the same*. And it's been kind of wonderful.'

I smiled shyly.

She looked at me, her expression a strange combination of contempt and kindness.

'Funny Bunny,' she murmured, 'you really are the last of life's innocents. How will you ever get along in this life without me?'

The way she had said it. She spoke so softly, as though she were voicing her inner thoughts aloud, as though she wasn't addressing me at all. The oddness of her diction stayed with me, but only seconds later her expression changed and her voice became more definitive.

'I get that you want to head out. I'm not trying to stop you. But maybe it would be better to go in the early morning, outside the curfew. You're more likely to reach the square intact!'

'Maybe you're right,' I said in a reluctant voice, but inside I felt a glow of reprieve. I had been terrified about heading out. At least now it could wait until morning.

'And what about you? Will you be coming to the protests?'

She shrugged her shoulders. Revved the engine. And sped off into the dark.

THIRTY-EIGHT

I DIDN'T SLEEP WELL THAT NIGHT. I SLEPT SOME, BUT the trippy nervousness of my anxiety meant that my dreams were close to the waking world, yet when I woke, it was as if I was still dreaming. I hovered between one state and the next until the first tendrils of sunlight thinned and lengthened through the window. Always nervous, always afraid, but my fear was of a different texture now – sharper and sadder.

Rubbing my eyes, I washed. The thick fug of hunger and exhaustion still weighing on my brain, I staggered out into the early morning. The odd lone figure was wandering through the streets, head bowed; the only other people about were the late-night taxis still hoping for one final fare before dawn. I took a taxi toward Tiananmen Square, but the driver was nervous and would not take me all the way to Chang'an Avenue. He told me that he was old enough to be my father. That I should be back home. That it was dangerous for a 'miss' like me. His eyes were tired and kind. When I tried to pay him, he refused the fare. And perhaps because I was so tired myself, I felt my eyes well with tears.

'I can still take you back, miss.'

'That's okay,' I said. 'I'm going to be absolutely fine.'

As I watched the taxi drive away, I felt a sense of yearning, a desperate craving to be back in the warm car, heading home to curl up in my bed, the bed I had slept in all my life. I envied the driver his escape, but I was almost there now, and it was important to head on. I made my way along one of the side streets that led up to Chang'an Avenue, and from behind there came a violent roar. I felt greatly afraid, for I was a child again, and I was certain the police had come for me.

Instead, it was a young man on a bike. I knew he was a student just by looking at him. I felt a burst of relief and gratitude. He raised a gloved hand to me and made the V for Victory sign. At once, I responded in kind.

'You can't go down Chang'an. The police are there in droves. The military is amassing from the south. Use the side streets. Enter the square from the east,' he said.

I must have seemed confused; it was that early in the morning.

'Get on!' he said with a wink and a smile.

I straddled the motorbike, put my arms around him, and we whizzed away. The state may have had the police and the army. But we students had developed a force too. This young man was a member of what had become known as 'the flying tigers,' students on motorbikes who zipped around the city, passing on messages, relaying the activities of police and military, helping to coordinate our protests. We arrived at the square through a side alley and, despite the massive police presence, we were not accosted. As I dismounted, he gave me another wink. He was a goofy guy, and he'd actually got a 'flying tiger' flag wrapped around his bike, not the most discreet or sensible of measures given the circumstances. He didn't look like a hero.

But he definitely was one.

The atmosphere in the square had changed. I sensed it as soon as I entered. For the last couple of weeks we had all been living under martial law. But martial law hadn't achieved what the government wanted; it hadn't managed to clear the square. Two hundred thousand soldiers had been deployed to seize control of the seven central Beijing districts that surround Tiananmen Square in order to constrict and then crush the student movement. But things hadn't worked out as expected.

As schoolchildren we had sung songs with lines such as 'the army loves the people.' The army itself was called the People's Liberation Army because it had been formed in the fight against fascism and dictatorship. The students and the citizenry more broadly were often suspicious of police because of their contempt and casual brutality. But we tended to have sympathy for the army because of the historical link between the military and the population.

So when those two hundred thousand troops marched on the city, the students and members of the public at large greeted them with flowers, questioned them, talked to them and fraternized with them. Large numbers of soldiers were infected by the joyous atmosphere of the protests, and for this reason, the potential for violence was negated. I remember being on the square when the announcement came through that the army had been halted in their advance by 'the great citizenry of Beijing.' We all cheered. Years later we discovered that the army had been riven with divisions and mutinies at every level. The commander of the 38th Army – the Beijing division – had point-blank refused to carry out orders.

At the same time, the protests intensified. Every day, trains packed with students arrived from the provinces to replenish the numbers in Tiananmen Square. In Hong Kong, a protest in support of our movement saw six hundred thousand people take to the streets. Similar protests occurred in Shanghai, Wuhan, Chongqing and in many other regions and cities. In Beijing itself, more than one million workers had gone on strike in support of the students. On May 23 detachments of workers arrived at the square to show their support for us, making it clear they were prepared to lay down their lives, having dubbed themselves the Citizens Dare to Die Brigades. It was unbearably moving. Our resolve was strengthened. And within all this human drama was a moment of light comedy. Posters appeared across the city put up by members of the criminal underclass. Beijing's thieves, the posters informed us, were putting on hold their thievery in order to show their solidarity with us students!

But as this explosion of popular power was unfolding, behind the scenes something more opaque and disturbing was playing out. The divisions and mutinies in the army, along with the wave of protests engulfing the country, meant the government was reaching its breaking point. In Deng's own words, spoken at a clandestine meeting with the eight elders in the Forbidden City, 'Party and state are facing a life-and-death crisis.' The government itself was fracturing, with more and more ministers seeing the wisdom of delivering a program of liberalization in order to meet some of the students' demands.

But the old dictator had no intention of allowing any type of compromise. Wizened, arrogant and bloated from years of power and privilege, Deng curled his ancient, rotting lips in a sneer of contempt set against the millions of people our protests had set in motion. Clandestinely, he brought in some of the most powerful

Party hard-liners, and then, against every constitutional caveat, he began to crack down, singling out the reformists in the government, putting under police surveillance those whom he suspected, preventing them from leaving their homes. In this fashion, he was able to perform a coup d'état, to create what was, in effect, a dictatorship within a dictatorship.

And once he had returned absolute power to himself, he began to plan a more ruthless and lethal form of mass oppression. It was true that the whole country was engulfed in a revolutionary situation, but the epicenter of our revolution had always been Beijing, specifically Tiananmen Square. In his final gambit, Deng would concentrate all his forces here. The army had split, the Beijing section refusing to brutalize the students. Deng now recruited troops from the outermost provinces. These troops were housed in great camps on the outskirts of Beijing, completely isolated from the local population. While there, they were systematically and ideologically groomed to crush the uprising once and for all. They were told that the students were rioters, that they had been killing soldiers and that there were plans afoot to kidnap major Party officials. Such poisonous lies spoke to the tenor and tone of Deng's 'patriotism' and his 'regard' for the population to whom he so often proclaimed his loyalty.

When I entered Tiananmen Square on June 3, none of this was known to me, or to any of us. These details would gradually leak out of closed files over the decades to come. But while we had no idea what was taking place behind the scenes in government, we intuited very swiftly that a new and terrifying repression was coming. The rumors of the troops amassing on the periphery had reached us. The atmosphere in the square had changed. It was serious and fearful; where once we would greet each other with the V for Victory sign, boldly and playfully, now that had been replaced with the grim gesture of a hard, clenched fist. The sense of the division between the state and the people, us and them, had never been so pronounced, never seemed so insuperable. We all contained a flicker of fearfulness at our core, the sense of a fatality set in motion, of events finally reaching their crescendo.

I was tired. I hadn't slept well the night before – how could I have? I felt a moment of exhilaration when I stepped into the square, but that soon died. There were vast numbers of students, all of them solemn. In the morning light, before the Gate of Heavenly Peace, in front of the square, the national flag was raised. From the loudspeakers that were everywhere came the sound of the Chinese national anthem. Everyone in the square stopped, stood straight and saluted. Police and civilians on the outskirts, and the students in the square – those of us who had been branded traitors to the country – we too saluted, and with genuine feeling, though there was no longer any joy, only a sense of solemn respect. It was a brief and precious moment of unity. But it was soon to come to an end.

A faint mist tinted the summer-morning air. There were so many people. I made my way to the People's Monument, but saw no one I recognized. In previous days, it wouldn't have mattered that you were alone. Groups of students from other universities would have embraced you, would have invited you to share food and drink. But there was little of that spirit left. I wandered for a while, until the thin seam of mist abated. I thought for a moment about Gen. Would I run into him? Would he be here? I was almost certain he wouldn't be. He had long since abandoned the movement, if indeed he had ever been part of it. Before I had pitied him for never having felt the solidarity and wonder of the protests. But at that moment, as a cold sliver of apprehension uncurled in my belly, I envied him. I envied all those who remained at home, warm and safe.

When I eventually stumbled across the Marauders, I felt a sense of relief. But it didn't last long. On each face, I saw my own anxiety reflected back at me. Even though it was a mild summer's day, an element of cold pervaded the square. Pan Mei had dark shadows under her eyes, while Jin Feng, usually so fresh-faced and cheeky, looked as though, behind his youthful features, there was a hesitant old man peeking out. All of them seemed significantly older. Perhaps it was anxiety and lack of sleep, but some part of me can't help feeling it was a premonition of what was to come. The danger we all sensed, but none of us could imagine.

Only Lan was still smiling in the way he always did, his huge frame irrepressible, his face beaming with some spontaneous and happy thought. At one point he started giggling, I can't remember at what, and his husband told him he was a 'silly sausage' – but Min said this with light and laughter in his eyes.

The previous day, the pop singer Hou Dejian had come to the square and performed his song 'Heirs of the Dragon,' a song that referenced the Boxer Rebellion that had begun in Beijing in 1900. The students had cheered and sung along with the lyrics. Now a lesser-known band was performing to a more subdued audience. There was something different about June 3.

It started with the bus. A group of students had found an abandoned bus on the edge of the square packed with ammunition, AK47s and machine guns. At once people began to panic. Was this a sign of the approaching military? Had they hidden their supplies here in order to unleash live ammunition from the epicenter of the protests? Some of the student leaders urged caution. Appealed for calm. This was almost certainly a provocation, they argued. The state had been monitoring these protests for weeks, months, refining their tactics. They would not be so sloppy as to leave an unattended bus full of munitions right in the heart of our forces. The guns had been left on purpose, in order to sow fear and create panic. They were hoping to incite us into rash and impulsive action.

But if that was true, it could mean only one thing. Without question, the state had committed to out-and-out repression.

The atmosphere in the square hardened. People began to argue furiously. Paranoia crept over each of us like a second skin. An eagle-eyed individual had managed to discover army infiltrators in our midst, undercover soldiers who identified themselves to one another by their clothing. They were all wearing white shirts and khakis. The students at once responded, jostling and isolating the agents provo-cateurs, deriding them and sending them into a panic.

Day became evening, and evening quickened into night. The darkness spread itself across the sky like blackened blood. The arteries that led into Tiananmen Square had already started to bleed, great plumes of smoke arising from the barricades that had been erected only half a mile away. We heard the distant rumbles and saw the smoke climbing into the sky. But no one knew at that point what was happening. We had a vague sense the military were on the move. We know now that the news of the military crackdown had spread. During the weeks and weeks of protests, the citizens in the surrounding areas had come to love the stu-dents. They'd shared in our tribulations. And, knowing what was in the air, these same people – workers, nurses, shopkeepers, street sweepers, cleaners, taxi drivers and many more – had once again come out, filling the entry points into the square, seeking to block the legions of soldiers and the tanks that were rolling toward the student occupation.

And it was these men and women who were the first to find out that the ammunition the military was using was live. They were shot down in their dozens. They fought back, of course. Throwing bottles and stones. They had come to believe in us entirely. I don't imagine they wanted to leave their families, their children, in order to come out onto the streets. But they couldn't bear the thought of what was going to happen. So they did.

In Tiananmen Square we saw the smoke rising from the barricades but we were unaware that the death toll had begun. We were both terrified and defiant. At eleven o'clock on the night of June 3 all the students in the square once again held their hands aloft in a V for Victory, the sign that had come to embody the very best of our movement, the lofty hopes we had.

Some minutes later, the student broadcasting station at the corner of the square began to relay the news. The army was advancing. There were already casualties. In the distance I heard the sound of an ambulance siren. A feeling of absolute fear came over me, such that for a few moments I felt paralyzed. We looked at each other. The Marauders were dumbstruck, none of us capable of mouthing a word. One of the student leaders was speaking into a microphone, the sound crackly and desperate: 'There is still time before the troops get here. I urge you to remain in the square, but when the army comes, don't resist.'

From the flickering lights of the square, the city beyond was an ocean of darkness.

That's when the first tank arrived, the sound of it a growl from within the black. It came powering into our midst. Its visceral, rumbling presence seemed to break the tension, its appearance shattering the fearful anticipation and uncorking a blinding rage. While our leaders tried to urge caution, students armed with Molotov cocktails hurled them at the tank until it was illuminated in blazing flames against the backdrop of the night.

And that's when things reached a flashpoint. Having broken through the barricades and the ranks of civilians, the army now entered the square. There was no preamble, no hesitation; they started shooting in the dark, and from every angle. The popping sounds seemed unreal, but the balmy air was swiftly tinted with the scent of hard, hot metal. I saw people stumble and fall. And although I knew the military was upon us, nevertheless my first thought was that these people had simply tripped and fallen by accident. I was a good way back. Those students who had created their own battalion – the student security service – had formed a line between us and the oncoming soldiers. They were the bravest and physically strongest amongst us, but they could do little before a military machine surging forward, and they simply flopped and folded like rag dolls. Again, it didn't seem real. Because, despite their bravado and courage, they were only students like me. And we were all so young.

Mercifully, after that first rally, after that first set of bodies hit the ground, the military stopped. Our chants and protest songs had died out, each of us shocked to the core by what had happened, but the expectation was that we had endured the worst and now the situation would calm.

A group of ten People's Liberation Army soldiers formed a line, and began to march forward methodically. I remember there was no anger in their movements, no emotion. It seemed as well coordinated as military operations should be. With a single precise motion, they stopped dead. The rifles held aloft at their shoulders were lowered. And, surreally, they were then pointed at us.

Even then, I think we expected some kind of demand. Some form of negotiation or threat. 'If you don't do ... we will ...'

But those pops rang out once more. Again, more flopping, collapsing bodies. And all around, screams of anguish, screams of rage.

Suddenly, the lights in the square were cut. We were blanketed in darkness. And now large numbers of soldiers rushed forward, killing indiscriminately. I found myself rooted to the spot, watching. Despite everything, it didn't seem real. I knew it was, but my mind hadn't quite caught up. As though there was a lag between the noises and the flashes of light and the agony of the faces all around – the insulation inside my head forming a barrier between imagination and reality. None of it seemed real.

The soldiers came crashing in. Many were already shot. Now they got to work at close quarters. I heard Min scream as a soldier charged into his small, thin frame, and in the same moment I heard Lan shriek with rage, an unnatural sound coming from such an amiable and soft-spoken young man. He charged over to his husband. I don't think Lan ever knew violence, or what to do with it; his fists were clenched, I am sure, but he had never in his life swung them. He simply did not know how to hurt another human being, and yet the sheer power and bulk of his body charging in a frenzy of fear and love hoisted the soldier off the ground, sending him flying. Another shot rang out, and Lan staggered for a moment, like a tottering child, before falling to one knee.

I turned away. I should have gone to them, I know that. But I turned away. It wasn't a conscious decision. The terror was like an electrical charge driven into my body, sending me scurrying through the darkness. People were screaming, over and over. I ran as fast as I could. I ran toward the Great Hall of the People. Still bathed in light, it seemed the only sanctuary from the dark, and the popping sounds and the screams. I felt that light might somehow herald safety.

I was wrong. A new set of soldiers poured out from the base of the building. They were shooting. I heard the bullets, like insects whizzing by. I recognized a young woman beside me, from another university in Beijing – the briefest glimpse of her features, and then another sound, and her face a flash of red from the corner of my eye. All at once, the struggle to move was too much, and I sank to one knee. The Marauders had vanished long ago, or perhaps it had only been minutes, but it no longer mattered. I was alone. In all this violence, I was alone.

I cowered on the floor, the fear overwhelming. Eventually I tried to stand, but people were rushing past me so quickly, and I caught a blow to my stomach, from a soldier or panicked student – I don't know which. I wriggled on the ground, fighting for breath, but the shock of the impact had also revived me, for now the sounds and screams from the night came sweeping back into my consciousness and I felt the warmth of the tears on my face. I realized more than anything I was desperate to live. For an hour, for a day, for a week. I just wanted to live. I had to live.

I picked myself up once more, careened through the darkness, only now as I moved, the earth itself seemed to crack and rip – a single roar peeling across the ground, shuddering through my body and shattering my ears. I heard a voice in the dark, desperate and indignant and forlorn:

'The tanks are crushing people, the tanks have crushed people!'

It was uttered in a tone of revelation as though, on hearing these words, someone might take heed, and the horror of what was unfolding might be put to an end. I never saw him. I heard his voice as the thunder of the tank opened up behind me, and it was the loudest sound. It seemed to split open the world. I couldn't help looking back. The tank was moving some feet away, veering off in another direction, and as it disappeared into the darkness, the echo of its roar reverberating, I glimpsed just the briefest slip of a blue dress caught beneath its treads.

I was swaying forward, my lungs screaming for air. I was terrified as never before, but at the same time, the need to lie down, to slip into the dark, was there with me. I felt the violence of my breathing, but I managed to keep moving through the expanse of dark. I glimpsed another brief outline of light, and I staggered toward it. I was crying.

.   .   .

By that point, I had arrived at the northern section of the square. A small tent had been set up. It was a medical emergency tent manned by students from the Beijing United Medical College. I don't know what kind of salvation I hoped for. Perhaps we all believe, in times of crisis, that there will be people who know exactly what to do. People who are calm and methodical, who are used to working in a desperate situation, and can help persuade you that you are sure to survive the chaos, that you are going to be okay.

The young man who was one of the people manning the tent was of this mold. I was shaking violently.

'How are you doing?' he asked softly.

'I am okay.'

He looked me over. He briefly touched his fingers to my forehead.

'Yes, you are okay. Are you good to stay here for a bit?'

'Oh yes,' I gasped in relief.

'Would you sit with my friend here?'

For a moment, the question baffled me. I nodded dumbly.

He guided me to a bed toward the back, where a young man lay wrapped in white, the wounds he had sustained seeping through the bandages. He'd been shot in the side of his head.

I looked at the student doctor who had ushered me in. I went to say something, but I had no words.

He registered my look. He spoke softly to me.

'We can't do anything, we don't have plasma, drugs,' he said almost apologetically. 'Would you just stay with him for a while?'

I nodded again.

I was not a carer. I had looked after my grandmother, of course, after she became ill. And years before, when I was much younger, my mother had made me change my brother's diapers on the odd occasion. But I had never felt as though I knew what I was doing. It wasn't something in my nature. But I didn't want to leave, to go back out to face what was happening on the square. So I stayed. I looked at him, prostrate on the bed. Half his face was covered with a bandage, one eye flickering in and out of consciousness. He didn't appear completely human.

'Please,' he said in a rasping whisper, thick with blood.

I wanted to feel compassion, but all I could feel was panic. I regretted everything – coming here, all the protests. I should have stayed at home. I was so tired.

'Please!'

'Please what?' I whispered.

'Will you bring my mother?' That gargled whisper again.

My instinct was to tell him there wasn't time, she wasn't here, but something stopped me.

'Yes,' I said.

His shivering frame relaxed somewhat.

And in the next moment, a single question:

'Mother, are you here?'

He was bleeding so badly. For a few moments I was taken aback. And then it happened almost automatically, it was something I never intended. My voice arrived softly, a whisper almost.

'Yes, I am here.'

'I'm sorry, Mom. I am so sorry. I love you.'

I fought as hard as I could to keep my words soft and under control, to fight back my sobs.

'It's okay. You have done very well, my son. And I love you very much.'

I put my hand on his. It was, by that point, so very cold. I don't think he even felt my touch. But his eyes changed. He was between consciousness and unconsciousness. Then his closed eyes seemed to relax a little, and a slight smile lingered on his face just as he died. In those last moments, his expression seemed almost warm and at peace. I really do believe that what I said had given him that.

I have to believe that.

It was early in the morning. The lights came on again at around 4:30. I wasn't witness to what happened, but two students – in defiance of their lives – approached the military lines. Their bravery, in coming forward, stayed the guns of the soldiers and they were able to beg for a truce. Records note that the officer in command spoke the following words: 'You have limited time, but if you can do this you deserve merit.'

Thus, a fragile balance was established. The military made the following demand: 'Leave quickly. If you do not leave we will have to implement the cleansing order and there may be bloodshed.'

Ironic, that last touch, 'there may be bloodshed,' when the square was strewn with the bodies of our dead.

The students, given everything that we had gone through, everything we had learned, made one final decision. We put it to the vote. It was the last democratic mandate we would ever use. Because of the large numbers of wounded and dead, we finally decided to vacate the square.

The government had won.

But as the early-morning light seeped in, I was relieved to be alive. I thought about little more than that. In the blue-white light, the devastation of the square was laid bare, people hobbling away, supporting one another.

As we were let out, I flinched when my face was bathed in a sudden brightness. A foreign film crew had been waiting. The US reporter asked me:

'How do you feel right now?'

'Like ... I can't breathe.'

'Do you think anybody was killed?'

I looked at her in disbelief. As shattered as I was, I knew answering this question would be dangerous to my future. But I was beyond caring. I felt a sudden swell rise up within me. I was still alive, and so very angry.

'Of course. Many students were killed. I saw it with my own eyes.'

I turned from her. And hobbled away.

THIRTY-NINE

I SOMEHOW MADE IT HOME. MY FACE WAS CAKED WITH dust and dirt. On the side of my left hand there was a rash of blood, from the student in the hospital bed – dried to a rusty brown. I went to the bathroom and scrubbed it until my flesh was pink and raw, but it wasn't enough. I showered with my eyes closed, but the sensation of the water on my body seemed vague and distant, as though my skin had formed an outer barrier of rigid dead material, like a shell. From within the darkness of my own head came a shuddering throb – a rhythmic pain that stabbed at me. The water ran over my face, pooling in my eyes. At some point I got out. And it was cold. That was the first real sensation from the outside. I hugged myself. Put on some clothes.

My mother and father were up by then, my brother still asleep. I met my father in the hall. He looked absolutely haggard. But he didn't reprimand me. Instead he moved close to me and put his arms around me so gently, barely touching me. I tried to smile, to give some kind of reassurance. But it was as though the bones in my face had hardened and immobilized, as though I had been turned to stone. He held me so gently, the way he had when I was a child. But I felt nothing. Only numbness.

I found my mother in the kitchen. She looked at me in a way I had never seen before. Her pinched pretty face, the lines around the corners of her mouth, her eyes filled with a strange muted light, somewhere between fury and delirium. As my father had done, she too moved close to me, only I felt sure she was about to strike me. Instead her hand reached toward my face, but she didn't touch me. She was looking at me as though I had said something strange, a look of puzzlement twisted into pain. But I had not spoken. Her eyes grew vague, and she turned her gaze to the ground. She hesitated, trying to find what she wanted to say; but when the words arrived they were no more than a whisper.

'I've … there is some chicken left for you in the oven.'

She turned away. And that was the point when tears finally welled in my eyes.

I retreated to my room and took off my clothes. The curtains were almost closed, a thin seam of light running between them, but it was enough for me to see the bruises in the soft shadow. There were bruises on my arms and shoulders. There were scores of cuts on my knees and legs. And a purple and black welt spread across my belly. My small dangling breasts. The hard arches of my pelvis pushing up, visible through the skin. I had always been thin, but now I was almost skeletal. As if what I was had been stripped away, and what was left of me was withered and negligible, fading in the shadows. I got into bed. When I opened my eyes again, the light in the room had changed, thinning in the late afternoon. As I got out of bed, I winced, feeling the violence of my bruises and aching joints. I bit my lip to stifle a cry. I got dressed and slipped out of the house.

The Marauders had arranged to meet that afternoon. But, given everything that had happened, I wasn't sure whether they would be there. I needed to go, nevertheless. It felt like one final obligation. We were to meet on campus, and thankfully that meant I could bypass the square and the military presence. I avoided the Triangle too. We were due to meet in the old hall where I had first met Anna.

They were there already. Those who had made it. Min, Jin Feng and Pan Mei. Anna was there too. When I arrived they were talking quietly. They greeted me, and Pan Mei touched her hand to my shoulder. That was the moment when I felt I might break down. For I remembered what had happened to Lan. How he had just folded and fallen. The unnaturalness of it: a split second in time, a human being turned off like a light. In the struggle to survive, I had forced it from my mind. I glanced at Min. Much of his face was bruised and damaged, a craterous shadow emphasizing one large wild eye at the expense of the smaller one. And yet, even though his features were swollen and unrecognizable, his voice was still very much his own. He was speaking quietly to Anna. But there was something in his tone, a plaintiveness almost like a child. He kept repeating the same thing.

'So we got him to the ambulance. But it didn't matter. Because the military stopped them. They stopped the ambulances leaving the square. They blocked them. I don't understand why they would do that. But they stopped the ambulances leaving the square. And so it didn't matter. By the time they finally got him out, to the hospital, it didn't matter.'

His words drifted into me, almost gently, the way he kept repeating himself as though he couldn't quite understand it, and then I blinked, and the breath caught in my throat, because the meaning of the words had begun to clarify. I realized what he was saying, and yet at the same time it was incomprehensible.

'Lan didn't make it?' Anna asked him softly.

Min went to say something else, but the cost of the word was too great, so he just shook his head.

And then he started to cry.

She put her arms around him.

I don't remember much else of what was said. Jin Feng spoke about the next few weeks, suggested we all lie low because the government would very likely continue the repression and mass arrests were sure to follow. The advice would prove to be prescient, though we were too shell-shocked to take it in.

Eventually we went our own separate ways, until it was just me and Anna. We looked at each other and a coldness crept through me. It felt as though she didn't have the right to share our grief, for she had not been there when the massacre had happened. It felt as though she had not been with us for a while. Perhaps my coldness was evident, for she seemed uncomfortable, and I had rarely seen her like that. She went over to the piano, and ran her fingers across it, playing delicate arpeggios that faded in the gloom.

'We met here.'

'Yes.'

I could barely manage the word. I felt a sudden intense anger.

'Seems like long ago,' she murmured.

'Does it matter?'

She didn't answer. She turned away.

'So I guess you were right,' I continued, abandoning myself to my bitterness. 'The students were destined to lose all along. You called it accurately. You must feel very ... satisfied!'

She flinched. It was one of the few times I saw her hurt. And although something inside me told me to stop, I couldn't restrain the emotion that was pulling me in its wake.

'There was no point in any of it. So kind of you to let us know.'

She looked at me, and her expression was naked. I saw how tired she was, the shadows under her eyes, the lack of makeup, and that vulnerability – an anomaly in itself – touched something in me. But I was too angry to acknowledge it. Angry at her. Angry at the world.

She gave a weak smile.

'Maybe I was right and I was wrong at the same time,' she said quietly.

I looked at her coldly.

'Maybe the fight was worthwhile. Maybe sometimes it is more important to kick back whatever the cost, because if you don't …'

'If you don't?'

'You will always be afraid,' she murmured.

She smiled a little more brightly, her eyes shining, but the sadness fissured through her expression.

She looked at me and there was a kindness in her aspect.

'Perhaps it's not all over yet. Who knows? Maybe there is time for one last piece of Marauder Mischief!'

My lips tightened.

'Yeah, whatever you say,' I muttered.

I turned and walked away. I'd only gone a few steps when she spoke again.

'Lai,' she called out.

I turned to her one last time.

She took a step toward me and raised her hand. With a slight smile, she made the V for Victory sign.

I looked at her. She seemed, in that moment, different, vulnerable. Some part of me wanted to acknowledge her gesture. But the anger and helplessness inside me had twisted itself into a knot and, for the only time, I felt contempt for her.

I turned and walked away. I didn't look back.

.   .   .

It was early evening, June 4. Beijing was as I had never seen it. Burned-out barricades forming ridges across the streets like prehistoric monsters. The skeletons of vehicles that had been set ablaze, sinking into the concrete. The shattered windows of buildings and the heaps of debris, which, in the early evening gloom, took on the shadowy aspect of funeral pyres. Only a few lonely souls crept through the side streets, and it seemed this was how a once vibrant city would look after having been abandoned for many hundreds of years. Every now and then, a police car or military vehicle would come speeding by, its lights cutting a bleary glow through the murky gray air, the rumble of its engine trailing away like some primitive creature rolling onward through the undergrowth. The sense of the city as a city of ruins and half-life reflected the devastation of my own tattered and shell-shocked mind.

I made it home and crawled into bed. I lay there and I thought about Lan. I couldn't stop thinking about him. I wondered if some mistake had been made, at the hospital; that his death might have been confused with someone else's. I needed him to be alive because he had been so huge and yet so kind and gentle, and his great body had only ever emanated warmth. I couldn't conceive of him as being dead, as a lifeless corpse in some faraway room, distant and strange, and separate from the person I knew.

I couldn't grasp that I would never hear his voice again. That he wouldn't be there with the others. And yet I understood he was gone. I thought about his last moments. Did someone hold his hand? Was he at peace? Or did he feel lonely and terrified, fear screaming through him, not knowing why any of this was happening?

I lay there, tears cooling in my eyes, everything draining from me except one coherent thought. No matter what happens, no matter how long I live, I am never going to escape this.

In the morning, just before I opened my eyes, I thought about Anna; how she had been the day before, the fragility of her. But more than that, I was struck by what she had said – 'Maybe there is time for one last piece of Marauder Mischief!' – the expression on her face strange, alien almost, somewhere between hope and madness. I felt myself wither inwardly; I knew I had been unfair to her, but sometimes you have to hold on to your anger, because once you let it go, all that remains is pain. I knew she had been in hell too, that she grieved for Lan as much as I did, or more, for she knew him better.

But it was that final look she had given me. The words she had uttered – 'one last piece of Marauder Mischief' – spoken in strange, soft defiance. The more I thought about it, the more it seemed out of sync with her usual behavior. My sense of this wasn't coherent or clear; it remained in the background of my thoughts, like something in the corner of my vision that I couldn't quite glimpse.

I lay in bed. I could not face leaving my room and interacting with my family. But alongside the horror of everything that had happened, the thought of Anna – the way she had been – began to intrude more and more. She had been speaking to me, though it seemed she was only addressing herself. 'Maybe there is time for one last piece of Marauder Mischief!' Was she deluded? Had the shock of everything that had happened unbalanced her? Or, given her nature, was there something else?

I shut down these thoughts. I had turned away from her, it was true, but then again, she had turned away from us long before that. I had nothing to feel guilty about. Whatever was going on with her would be okay; we would get through it when we next spoke. Wounds would be repaired by words, and somehow – even though I couldn't conceive of it yet – life would return to normal.

It was a little past noon when I finally emerged from my room. The household was remarkably quiet. I made my way to the living room, where my mother, father, and brother all sat watching TV. They were watching the state channel, the image of tanks rolling down Chang'an Avenue in grainy flickering footage. For all my mother's diatribes against the students, she was watching in forlorn silence. Nobody could condone what had happened, other than the reporter who was declaiming in excited tones just how the Chinese Communist Party had managed to save the country from terrorist subversives.

My mouth felt hollowed out and dry. I went to the kitchen and poured myself a glass of water. I heard the voice of my father.

'Oh God,' he said. 'Oh God.'

Only that.

Something inside me sank.

I went back into the living room, a sense of dread rolling in the background – but I was calm, because I was okay. I was back at home. And yet, my father didn't speak like that. He never spoke like that.

I felt a momentary sense of relief. For they were all still gathered there, my family. Comfortable, safe, as they had always been. And yet my father's exclamation had interrupted whatever security remained to us.

I turned to the television.

And that's when I saw him.

A young man, he must have been a student, I thought. As the tanks were rolling down Chang'an Avenue, a diminutive figure had darted out across the wide boulevard. The cameras of the state propaganda machine zoomed in, unable to turn away, just like us. I moved closer with a terrible fascination. That single lone figure in front of the massiveness of those tanks; it was incongruous, like seeing an iceberg float across the warm waters of Hawaii. For a moment, my mind couldn't organize the scene into anything that resembled sense. Facing the convoy of tanks, he seemed ridiculously tiny. And yet he was making himself known; the first tank that reached him attempted to swerve around, but he danced toward it, blocking its path.

As I watched, hypnotized almost, something inside me altered. A muted sensation, the recognition of something as yet unformed, the tingle you feel just before something awful occurs. My fear came before the realization. The way this young man moved was familiar to me. I felt a glimmer of recognition. The two bags he held at his side. The way he whipped one of them over his shoulder and behind his back in a dramatic flourish. The theatrics of his movements.

It was then I realized.

I was not looking at 'him' at all. I was looking at ... *her*.

She was dressed in the billowing white shirt and the simple black trousers she always wore when she wanted to inhabit the life of a man.

The tank moved again. And she danced into its space once more. I saw this through the flickering image of the television. And I blinked, because the realization was not yet real; it was a mental sensation that had not sunk itself into the heart of my being; for those few seconds I could pretend to myself that what I was seeing was in some way a projection or a trick of the eye.

But *she* was there. Anna ... was there.

She had brought a whole line of tanks to a halt. I thought to myself, you can still get away. Please, run away now. Please do this for me, I am begging you.

But she had no intention of running. This I knew. She climbed up onto the foremost tank as quick as a whip, still gripping the bags that had contained her male costume. She got on top of that first tank and seemed to squat there for a few moments like she was taking a shit. Anna was the most brilliant, wonderful human being I have ever met. But she was crude at times, and she delighted in it. Perhaps it tickled her that her last recorded moments on earth might be recorded in such a fashion.

She got down again. I am told that there was the sound of gunfire at this point, though our TV did not pick it up. Perhaps that gunfire was a last-ditch attempt to intimidate her. To make her flee.

It didn't work. The tank rolled forward once more, and she blocked it again.

She had reduced the whole convoy to a standstill. Madam Macaw had stepped forward to halt the mighty power of the People's Liberation Army. Of course, no single individual could have achieved such a thing.

Except Anna. For that is precisely what she did.

By this point, men had been mobilized, as they always are, several of them stepping into Chang'an Avenue so as to snatch her away.

She would never be seen again.

At that point, I was on my knees, my face in my hands, screaming at her to run. I was crying so hard that the violence of my sobs threatened to break me apart, and yet I longed for that – I longed for it, more than anything.

It is possible my family thought I had lost my mind. They couldn't imagine what the images on our TV had meant to me, no one could. My family came together with me, nevertheless. Touching me, in the brief tentative way one touches the disturbed – they were obviously taken aback by the force of my reaction. I am told that, just before I collapsed, I staggered toward the TV, with my arms reaching out.

My mother gave me this information. But, for once, she was kind about it.

The days that followed are a blur. Despite my brief history of cutting my arms with knives as a way to deal with the pressures I felt as a teenager, I don't think I'd ever wanted to end my life. However, in those few weeks after Anna's 'disappearance' I came close to doing something along those lines. For a short while I was teetering on the edge.

But then something else happened.

I received a letter telling me I had been awarded the scholarship for the program in Canada I had applied for. My mother – perhaps persuaded by my father – agreed to shell out the cash for my plane ticket. She imposed her reluctance upon me, of course, but I think everything that had happened to me had frightened her, and she was, in her way, relieved to give me this gift.

She hugged me tightly at the airport.

Getting on the plane was a surreal experience. Especially for someone who had never left Beijing – except for the occasion when Anna had transported me to that lake with no name. And sometimes I wondered whether that memory had even been real.

Once the plane had climbed high, away from the brightness of the afternoon, enveloped by the oncoming darkness of the night, I turned to look at my reflection in the small porthole window, and in its pearly blackness, I saw Anna looking back at me. I saw Macaw, her eyebrow raised, inciting me to Marauder Mischief with that amused look of hers, and I felt the tears warm on my cheeks, for I was still alive and she was gone, and I had let her down, and I had loved her, so very much.

EPILOGUE

THE YEARS THAT FOLLOWED, THE YEARS THAT HAVE led to me writing this, have been uneventful, at least from the purview of my own existence. I am writing this over thirty years later. I've led a quiet life. I teach literature. I am the mother of two beautiful, wonderful children, the youngest almost thirteen, the oldest now twenty.

It strikes me, often, that my eldest – whose name is Anna – is much the same age Madam Macaw was when I first met her in that university room with the grand piano. But my own child seems so much younger than Anna ever was. Perhaps that's because Anna herself has become frozen in my mind: an eternal emblem of someone youthful and fearless, brilliant and charismatic, perfect such that she has become some kind of impossible idol. Isn't it always the case that slain saints enter into our minds in terms of a perfection that could never be achieved in reality?

And yet, not a day goes by that I don't think of her. Sometimes I am wandering down a Toronto street and I see a Chinese woman, and for a second I imagine it is Anna, grown as old and flabby as me, a couple of kids dangling from her arms. On the one hand, Anna wasn't the maternal type: the thought of being responsible for the lives of small, vulnerable, needy human beings would have repelled her; on the other, she would have made the best mother in the world. Imagine the stories she would have told, how easily she would have enraptured childhood with a single one of her creative fingers.

Sometimes I allow myself to fantasize that she made it out, because sometimes the pain of what happened that day is just too great. But I know she is gone. She was in my life for less than a year, and although I didn't realize it at the time, I know she saved me. Sometimes I go back to our last conversation. I don't want to, but I can't help it. The wan smile she gave me, the V for Victory gesture she made. By that point, she had already decided on her fate. She refused to live life on anyone else's terms, whether that meant a cruel lover, a best friend, or even the Chinese state itself. In the moment she made that final gesture, I am certain she knew she was going to die. She wanted, perhaps, some moment of kindness from me. And it is the single, biggest regret of my life that I turned away. Sometimes, in my dreams, I see her again, and she is happy. We both are.

But I am happy most of the time. My job satisfies me, my children inspire me. Originally, my move to Canada was supposed to be only temporary. But I ended up falling in love, in a gentle, nondescript way, with a gentle, nondescript partner. Underneath it all, however, has always been the fear. I have never really stopped being frightened. But I return to Beijing every so often. For the funeral of my father who died in the way he had lived, quietly and with little fuss. For the marriage of my brother, which took place on a wonderful bright winter's day.

When I visit Beijing, I do it alone. Without children and without husband, because I have had to cordon off that aspect of my life, partly because of the pain, partly because of my shame. When I took that plane out of Beijing at nineteen years of age, I was fleeing. And I have never since stopped running away.

I remain tied to that world, however. My mother is still alive. My brother has brought into existence my three wonderful nephews. On Facebook's Chinese equivalent, I am in touch with some of the people I once knew. On there, I even have a 'mutual friend' with Gen. She tells me that he has achieved a 'respectable' position in the state bureaucracy. He is married with two children. And it is common knowledge that he regularly cheats on his wife.

As I get older I watch the world. Tiananmen Square fades into the past, but new protests arise. In Hong Kong, as I write, there is a new generation of protesters challenging the authoritarian central state. Deng may have died, blessedly, but his cruel, rigid, waxwork replacements are always waiting in the wings. And yet the bravery of the protesters – this too is replenished as the generations roll forward, and I am certain there are a good few Madam Macaws in their number. I have watched protests erupt across the world: the Black Lives Matter movement and #MeToo. The young people who put their hearts and souls into those fights inspire me; my eldest throws herself into those struggles with a bravery and fierceness her mother is incapable of. I fear for her. I am in awe of her.

Her name is Anna, and I have never told her the story of the person she was named after. But I will. For my daughter deserves to know. And the story of Macaw deserves to be told. I have been so very frightened, for so many years, but I have at last decided to put pen to paper – which, in my own way, is the greatest bravery

I can offer up. It is small and negligible in the scheme of things, but it is something at least. Although I have spent my life living in fear, I know what courage is. For I am there with Anna as she steps out into the great stretch of Chang'an Avenue as it was that day with the sun glittering brutally in the sky. I am there with her as she obstructs that first tank, and I see her beautiful green eyes, sardonic and mocking, as she brings them to a halt, with all the casualness of someone playing a game, only it is anything but a game. Those flashing green eyes, a last-ditch dramatic performance, the fatal creativity and charisma of a single person who forces one of the mightiest armies on earth to a standstill while the whole world watches.

Could she possibly have known? Could she have realized that, in stepping out onto Chang'an Avenue that day, she was also stepping out into history? That her image stepping out in defiance of those tanks would come to represent millions of people struggling for freedom the world over? That her figure would become a symbol of resistance and hope that would echo down the generations, symbolizing human courage and human sacrifice? For perhaps as long as there is time itself. Only Anna could have done something like that, because her light burned brighter than that of anyone I've ever known. And I feel, every day of my life, that the world is so much poorer without it.

I wish I could have been braver, stronger. I wish I might have been there for Anna in those last days. But although I have not been a protagonist in great historical events, I have, nevertheless, been a witness to them. And that is why I am writing to you now, having held all this inside for so very long. It is the only lasting thing I can give you. As women across the world explode in protest, in the MeToo movement, in the fight to attain abortion rights, in the struggle against rape and murder, I want to tell you, all of you, that I knew Anna and I loved her so very dearly.

I knew who she was and what she did.

I knew that 'Tank Man' was in fact … *Tank Woman*.

And now you know that too.

ACKNOWLEDGMENTS

My thanks to Mark Richards for the delicate improvements he made to this book, for his faith in it, and the consideration and kindness he has shown an unknown author. My thanks also to Robina Pelham Burn for a wonderful and meticulous edit that really uplifted the story.

READING GROUP GUIDE

1. Many accounts of the 1989 Tiananmen Square massacre center on the political conflict of the demonstrations and the brutal, hard-line response of the Chinese state. Yet Lai Wen's novel, for the most part, follows the coming-of-age story of its protagonist in the years preceding the demonstrations. The protests only occur toward the end of the book, and Lai, the protagonist, is a committed supporter rather than a vocal leader of the movement. In what ways does Lai Wen's distinctive telling of the massacre differ from other stories you have read or heard about it? Discuss how this novel earns its title as a story about Tiananmen Square.

2. Lai's parents have contrasting, almost binary personalities: her father is a "distant presence" throughout her childhood, while her mother is "hands-on, seeking to police every aspect and inflection of her family's life." We learn that they are both marked by the Cultural Revolution. How did this fact shape your understanding of their relationship to each other and to their children? What are some other examples of how different

characters in fiction (or people in your own life) respond differently to a shared experience and historic or current events?

3. Within her family, Lai is closest with her grandmother, an outspoken, colorful individualist. Which of the interactions between Lai and her grandmother most moved you? These types of multigenerational households are customary throughout Asia and many non-Western countries, with children, parents, and grandparents all living together under one roof. How does this compare with a conventional nuclear American household? What are some of the cultural customs or family dynamics in the book that resonated with—or differed from—your own upbringing?

4. After a shocking run-in with the police as a young girl, Lai returns home and receives an unexpected display of tenderness from her mother, who gently bathes her wounds. This is a stark counterpoint to her mother's behavior elsewhere in the novel, where she appears temperamental, jealous, or resentful of Lai. What is your understanding of Lai's mother's motivations? What is the source of her resentment? Why do you think Lai and her mother's relationship is, and increasingly becomes, so complex and fractured—and how does that affect Lai and the choices she makes in her own life?

5. In her early adolescence, Lai chances upon a mysterious bookseller, who introduces her to literary classics such as *1984* by George Orwell, *The Stranger* by Albert Camus, and *The Old Man and the Sea* by Ernest Hemingway. Lai's reading and discussions with the bookseller widen her understanding of the world. What books have you read that changed the way you perceived the world? Are there people in your childhood who

influenced your literary tastes in the same way the old book-seller did for Lai?

6. Lai's school visit to Chairman Mao's mausoleum excites her mother and her neighbors, all of whom deeply revere Chairman Mao's legacy. Soon after, though, her father brings her to the "memory wall," with accounts, stories, and letters from the Cultural Revolution, including a poem he had written. Why do you think Lai's father brought her to the "memory wall" at this point in her life? As a man of few words, what do you think he wanted to express to Lai in this moment? Did this change your understanding of him?

7. Gen and Lai do not initially get along as children and seem like an unlikely pairing as teenagers. Where Lai is sensitive and empathetic, Gen is more reserved, righteous, and sardonic; Gen comes from a well-to-do, aristocratic background, while Lai and her family live in a working-class neighborhood. What did you make of their relationship? What draws them together? What are some other romantic pairings in fiction or film that you might compare them to?

8. In the essay that eventually wins her a scholarship to Peking University, Lai writes: "Being human is about remembering. We are the sum of all our memories. And yet, everyone forgets. And anyone can become confused. But when we lose track of our memories, that is when we are at our most human." Do you agree? Reflect on this statement in the broader context of this novel—and of your own life.

9. After Gen and Lai enter Peking University, their lives diverge even further. Gen attempts to forge his own path as a student leader, and Lai soon falls in with a group of outsiders, Madam

Macaw's Marvelous Marauders, including the rebellious Anna and a queer couple, Lan and Min. How did your own identity and friendships change from adolescence to adulthood? Were there friends from that period that helped define you and changed the trajectory of your life?

10. The Tank Man refers to an enduring image of the Tiananmen Square massacre: the Chinese protestor who fearlessly stood in front of a row of tanks, who remains unidentified to this day. Lai reveals at the end of the novel that Tank Man is actually a woman—Anna, her close friend with an affinity for cross-dressing. How does Lai's revelation change your perception of Anna? What does it mean to connect Anna's story, character, and gender, to Tank Man's legacy?

11. Today, any mention, reference, or allusion to the 1989 Tiananmen Square protests is censored in China by the Chinese Communist Party. At the same time, the practice of banning books with "controversial" subjects is on the rise across America. What are the implications of censoring or banning books such as this one? Discuss the ways censorship and book banning affects culture and education. Are there instances in which you believe this practice is justified?

12. The author, Lai Wen, has said that her novel is drawn from autobiographical experience and that she took inspiration from Elena Ferrante in writing under a pseudonym. In Wen's case, her anonymity protects her from reprisal over the novel's subject matter. How much of your reading experience of this story depends on it being true, especially as it is based on a historical event? Think of other novels written under pseudonyms.

Does an author's anonymity—not knowing their real name or identity—affect your response to the work?

13. The novel comes to a sudden close with Anna's disappearance and Lai's departure to Canada. The epilogue finds Lai thirty years later in Toronto, a literature teacher and a mother of two. There are small glimpses of how the lives of the other characters—Gen, Lai's mother, and Qiao—have unfolded. What do you imagine happened for Lai and the other characters in the immediate aftermath of Tiananmen Square? What do you think happened to those we don't know about, such as Anna or the old bookseller? What else might you want to know about Lai's life?

ABOUT THE AUTHOR

LAI WEN is a pseudonym.